# A SOUTH SIDE STORY

Quillan Kelly-Dunn

# DEDICATION

This book is dedicated to John Hughes, whose genius work completely saved me and many others, probably for many years to come. His stories are legendary, and I quote them daily. His movies taught me how to have a conversation and provided me with the dialogue I needed to understand life. Every movie he wrote I absolutely adore. In this book, I've referenced his movies *The Breakfast Club*, *Ferris Bueller's Day Off*, *Pretty in Pink*, *Mr. Mom*, *Home Alone*, *Uncle Buck* and *Some Kind of Wonderful*.

To the cowriters Jean Shepherd and Leigh Brown and the director Bob Clark, whose hilarious and candid realness taught me to laugh at my parents' "human-ness" and my childhood mistakes. Clark taught me how to laugh at my family's idiosyncrasies and embrace them by watching his. His brilliance has made a legend for Christmas and a childhood for the world to enjoy. To Peter Billingsley who I think is the most amazing childhood actor of all time, his facial expressions, delivery and impeccable acting skills is part of what makes this movie so hilarious, real and relatable.

Referenced: *A Christmas Story*.

To Nora Ephron, whose knowledge, brilliance, and humor regarding relationships inspired friendships that shouldn't have happened, but everyone lot smarter. Also to Rob Reiner for directing this kick-ass movie.

Referenced: *When Harry Met Sally.*

To Lowell Ganz, Babaloo Mandel, and Ron Howard, whose comedic masterpiece changed parenting and marriage for everyone. Watching *Parenthood* as a kid allowed me to learn what's normal and what isn't. Watching it as an adult and a parent…it's an entirely different movie that keeps on giving.

Referenced: *Parenthood.*

To William Goldman, who wrote this forever-quotable screenplay; I still laugh at and quote its subtle humor and sarcasm to this day. Also to Rob Reiner, who directed yet another amazing work of art.

Referenced: *The Princess Bride.*

To Graham Chapman, John Cleese, Eric Idle, Terry Gilliam, Terry Jones, and Michael Palin, who pretty much kept my family together and provided us with cohesiveness and togetherness that made us off the wall and silly.

Referenced: *Monty Python and the Holy Grail.*

To Cameron Crowe, who wrote and directed a beauty that provided women a visual for a sweet, funny, and chivalrous *guy* (a.k.a. a man).

Referenced: *Say Anything…*

This movie got my family through some really tough times (we even watch it in July), and I live my life every day striving to be George and Mary Bailey. Screenplay cowritten by Frances Goodrich, Albert Hackett, Jo Swerling, and Frank Capra.

Referenced: *It's a Wonderful Life.*

To Bernard Malamud, Roger Towne, and Phil Dusenberry, whose collaboration of greatness still inspires me and gives me the chills every time I watch it.

Referenced: *The Natural.*

To Sylvester Stallone, whose true story and imaginary friend Rocky Balboa always ignite motivation and fire.

Referenced: *Rocky.*

To Nicholas Pileggi and Directed by Martin Scorsese—I mean, they made the masterpeice *Goodfellas*. Need I say more?

To David Mahmet who wrote "Sexual Perversity in Chicago" and screenplay writer Tim Kazurinsky, together made up the under-rated movie "About Last Night". This movie I can be watched repeatedly and is so true what can happen in relationships.

# 1

"You. Are. A. Cunt," he said while driving and looking straight ahead.

My mother always told me that this was the worst name a man could call a woman. She said it's the most disrespectful name there is. She described being called this word as stinging like a slap in the face. I waited for the pain. I didn't feel anything. I actually felt like laughing. I had more of an urge to laugh, because it seemed so stupid. I didn't see what the big deal was. It's just a *word*.

He called me this because I wore a fitted yellow tank top under my jean overalls. Apparently I'm not allowed to look cute, because if I do, he gets jealous and pissed off that someone will look at me. When I left the house, I thought I looked pretty good. I'd expected a compliment from him. "Cunt" wasn't the response I'd hoped for. We'd just finished going through the Burger King drive-through, and when I reached for the drink tray, he glanced at my chest, and I saw him grit his teeth. He glared at me with obvious and intense contempt.

"I'm sorry. I'll remember to wear a garbage bag next time," I replied sarcastically. I smirked at him, attempting to dismiss his behavior and not allow him to think he'd gotten to me.

"You fucking cunt," he angrily whispered, which was more eerie than shouting it; he also looked me right in the eyes as he said it. His eyes were vacant and dark.

A lump emerged in my throat as I got choked up. Ah, I got it now. The hissing whisper was a dead giveaway. When I didn't know how to react, my brain naturally went to movies as my frame of reference. My brain sped through movie files in my brain, searching for some familiar content—something I could relate to. I did recall seeing some old movie once where a woman was drinking a martini and holding a cigarette at the bar when a man approached her and obviously said something offensive. She casually tossed the drink into the man's face. The woman in the movie did this without blinking an eye, turned around, and went back to her conversation with her girlfriend at the bar. I was really thirsty, so I didn't really want to throw my drink. Instead, I lifted the hamburger bun out of habit to make sure they'd given me extra pickles, which then gave me an idea— so I impulsively acted on it. I picked up the hot burger and flung it right at his face. The burger was like a Frisbee, and the ketchup and mustard were like glue, and that burger just stuck to the side of his face. The pickles flicked off the burger and onto the windshield and the driver's side window. I laughed when I saw the ketchup, mustard, and cheese streaking down his cheek as the burger slid slowly to his shoulder. He gritted his teeth, and his face flared with blazing anger and humiliation. "God, you're a fucking whore!"

I fumed inside. I suddenly remembered Rizzo tossing her strawberry milkshake at Kenickie in Grease. I curled my lips under my teeth attempting to camouflage my smirk and I impulsively whipped my Coke at him. It spilled all over the car, his lap, his food, and his pride. He swerved in the street; luckily there wasn't much traffic on the side street we were on.

When he slowed down at the stop sign, I quickly opened the car door and jumped out. He demanded that I get back in the car. Then he shouted through a clenched jaw to "get the fuck back in the car!"

I looked over at him as he was slowly driving next to the curb, eyes blazing and face beet red. He looked so ridiculous that I couldn't resist the urge to laugh out loud. His usual hazel eyes were now green and flaring, and his cheeks flushed with streaks of ketchup and mustard. The pickles were still sliding down his window. It probably wasn't really funny, but my response to emotions has always been distorted. My psycho boyfriend's reddened face, darting eyes, and seething anger probably should have frightened me; instead I found it all hilarious.

The psycho was still driving slowly next to me, and I continued to ignore him. I turned my attention to the women gardening and men sitting on their porches reading the paper. He blared on the horn, which infuriated me. I walked to the passenger-side window as if I was getting back in the car, and a satisfied grin emerged on his face. I leaned down and glared at him as coldly as I could and said, "Get away from me. It. Is. Over!"

He made a "pfft" sound to give me the impression that he didn't care. I resisted my impulse to spit at him, turned around, and quickly cut across a yard and into the alley. I heard a screech, and he sped away. Relief washed over me as I walked briskly through different alleys to get home.

It was an early May evening in Chicago's South Side in 1992, and many people were outside on their front lawns and porches. I saw a woman talking on the phone, sitting on her porch next to a man drinking a Miller High Life. Kids were running around in the street playing football and kick the can. I caught myself smiling as I looked at the kids. Kids were everywhere, and in the spring/summer it became evident just how many children lived in this neighborhood. It seemed like everyone I knew had at least four or five siblings. I was one of five kids, which was the norm around these parts.

I always sensed I was missing something or was behind, as if all the other kids knew what was going on and I didn't. I suspected that somehow the more siblings you had, the more of a chance there was for you to get lost in the shuffle. I considered myself lost in that shuffle. When I'd get into trouble and my parents would scold me for what I'd done, I understood the "what" I'd done wrong part, but I suffered utter confusion about the "why" part. *Why* was that wrong? Was I not supposed to tell my grandmother I didn't like her hair? What should I have done differently? My parents skipped the part about conveying to me *why* what I said or did was wrong; they just told me I was wrong and punished me. What would be the right thing to do? I wasn't sure. The result was that, most of the time, I walked around assuming everything I said and did was wrong. I was clueless during most of my childhood and adolescence.

My parents, quite frankly, didn't have time for me. I didn't take it personally. They didn't have time for any of us, and I assumed other parents in the neighborhood didn't have time for their kids, either. We also didn't expect their time; we played outside from the moment we woke up until the streetlights came on. Obviously, kids learned social skills from one another—the South Side version of *Lord of the Flies*—and I did OK for a while when I was able to be around other kids.

Then I began to get into trouble, as most kids do. I didn't do anything that crazy or out of the ordinary—just normal kid stuff. But my parents overreacted, and the more I got into trouble, the more I was grounded and isolated. The more I was isolated, the more I'd feel lost and confused. I craved answers and guidance. I needed to know what was expected of me, other than "shut the fuck up" or the idea that "children are to be seen and not heard." Silence exacerbated the clueless sensation, and eventually I became depressed. I would have nothing to look forward to if I had to stay in the house all the time. How do you learn if you're not allowed to be around other kids? This is where my perpetual social problems originated.

I suppose I was just one of those kids who learned by getting into trouble; I needed to know the limits. If my parents told me not to do something, what do you think I did? Of course I did whatever it was, because I wanted to know what would happen. I believe my parents weren't sure what to do because they were kids themselves when they'd had us. It truly wasn't their fault, and I knew that. I did struggle with feeling resentful at times, because they're supposed to know what they're doing; after all, they're the grown-ups. When I'd eventually be allowed to see daylight again and to go out with friends or be around other kids, I wasn't sure how to act or what to say in social situations. My typical go-to affect would be a deer-in-the-headlights expression. People would speak to me, and my mind would go blank. I walked around in a daze most of the time, not really present. It seemed like I was in a perpetual state of detachment, like my head wasn't attached to my body. I'd physically be there, but not really *there*.

My parents and extended family were huge movie fans, so that's one thing we did together. Movies provided me some kind of guidance or frame of reference that I craved. The only time I didn't feel clueless was when we were quoting movies. I felt like a genius, actually, because I could remember lines; my brain was like a sponge for movie quotes. My family and I would spend hours quoting *Monty Python and the Holy Grail* and would laugh hysterically. It appeared to be the only time when my family was cohesive and I felt somewhat normal. Wouldn't life be easier if it had a script?

I presume it was my defense mechanism and my escape. I was safe watching movies—no risk on my part. I could quite simply watch and learn. Since I couldn't model my friends' behavior because I was isolated from them so often, I modeled Ralphie Parker, John Bender, or Ferris Bueller. I could become any cool, funny, or likeable character I wanted to. Eventually that deer-in-the-headlights affect with a vacant stare and blank mind was replaced with every John Hughes movie script ever made, along with a few random favorites. If I was at a loss for conversation with someone, then discussing a movie would be an icebreaker. I was now prepared for what to say because I had a script. Therefore, my brain always goes to movies, no matter what situation I'm in.

Anyways, I strolled down alleys and cut across yards feeling like Ferris Bueller when he races to beat his parents home. If I was Ferris Bueller in this scenario, then the psycho was Ed Rooney. Trying to control someone who can't be controlled is a pointless battle. The scenes with Ed Rooney and his secretary, Grace, popped into my mind. I smiled to myself as I walked down the street, and I probably looked like a lunatic. I hopped another fence and unlatched the gate to my yard, unnoticed.

When I arrived home, I put in my VHS copy of *Ferris Bueller's Day Off* into the VCR and lay on the couch. The psycho knew better than to come to my house after the stunt he'd just pulled. I was surprised that I wasn't upset or hurt. I guessed I was getting immune to his verbal abuse. In my gut I knew that what had happened between us was his problem, not mine. I knew I hadn't done anything wrong for him to talk to me like that. His shit was getting old.

Soon my mom came home, looking worn out. She looked at me, sighed, and went into the kitchen. I'd done my laundry and the kitchen was clean, so I didn't know what she was sighing about. I paused the VCR and went into the kitchen to see what was bothering her.

"What's wrong?" I asked her.

My mom was sitting at the table, still in her lab coat from the pharmacy and with bags under her eyes, but she still looked pretty. She's only twenty years older than me, so she looks more like my sister than my mom. She was looking at coupons and writing a list. She looked up at me, her slate-blue eyes looking lost.

"Nothing, just tired. How many times are you going to watch that movie?" she said bitterly. Deep down, I knew she would love to lie around and watch a movie, too.

"It makes me laugh. I don't know—until I find something else I like better," I replied. *What does she care?* I thought.

The almost-summer breeze whipped into the window, and we both closed our eyes and smiled. It did smell good. It also felt good on my moist brow after sitting in a house with no air conditioning. The breeze smelled sweetly of flowers, humidity, and clean, fresh laundry. It was dusk, and the clouds were an orangey-pink color from the setting sun. The streetlights were about to come on; a time I disliked most of my childhood because it was a signal that meant we had to come home.

"One of the great reasons we don't have air conditioning," my mom proudly stated. We couldn't afford air conditioning, but she always claimed she hated it.

"Yeah, I agree, but it does suck at night. I sweat my ass off in the summer," I said reluctantly, and I knew I was going to regret it. My mom sighed again. She didn't seem to have the energy to go into a lecture. *Phew.* I walked into the living room, pushed "play" on the VCR, and lay back on the couch. I had a pang of something in my stomach as my mind drifted to the earlier events of the night. Was it guilt, sadness, hurt? I had no idea. I started to punch my stomach to make it go away.

It did suck, because I could think of a lot of really great things about my boyfriend—ex-boyfriend—whatever he was. He was funny, really funny, and he could be sweet and cute. But his temper, jealousy, and possessiveness were exhausting and draining. As I looked at the 1976 Chevy Malibu out front that his parents had given me, I did feel guilty. Is it possible to stay with someone because of his family? Sometimes I wondered if that was what I was doing. I liked his family better than him most of the time. I loved how his mom could be so decisive, assertive, and confident. I loved how his dad was nothing like mine, for one, and had this amazing ability to make you smile even when he was giving you shit. He could be yelling at me, and I still felt loved and protected.

I thought about this as I went to my room. Even though it was 1992, I primarily listened to records. I only had a record player with a cassette player. I could listen to the radio, but I had no patience for commercials. I put on the Rolling Stones and lay in my bed. "Paint It Black" skipped a bit from overplaying, but I let it go. My parents had shelves of records. Any song I could think of prior to the '80s could be found in my basement. My mom said she'd played Fleetwood Mac's *Rumours* one too many times when I was in utero. I think she was surprised that I chose to listen to this music instead of what was playing on the local radio stations. I knew I was a weirdo; I couldn't help that I didn't like something unless it was old. I had recently began enjoying 80's music because it had aged a decade and also because I could buy 80's cassette tapes cheap. I often made mixtapes with records; you could hear the clicking of the records in the background.

After I couldn't take the skipping of the Stones anymore, I put on Van Morrison's *Moondance* album. The song "Into the Mystic" always soothes me; it makes me feel hopeful that there's some kind of passion out there and that there's a soul mate out there for everyone. This song has some sort of calming effect on me; it soothes me immediately. I thought about this and decided to make a pact with myself: if I make out with someone and that song comes on, I'll marry him. With any luck, I thought, the guy will have the same effect on me as this song does. Pure contentment and true happiness seemed impossible right now.

Sometimes I regretted having my own phone line installed with my own answering machine because I struggled with leaving it off the hook to avoid calls. As I was thinking this, I was startled at the eeriness that my phone rang, and reluctantly picked it up after four rings. Assuming it was "the dickhead," I didn't want him to leave a message. I didn't want to hear any more of his excuses.

"Hey. What's up?" Joy said. It was my best friend since we were babies. She lived across the street.

"Hi!"

"I'll be on your porch in a minute, OK?" Joy said.

"Good idea."

I grabbed my pack of Newport cigarettes from my dresser drawer and headed downstairs. She was sitting on the front porch already, looking tan and pretty as usual. She licked her lips and smiled, holding out a lighter and waiting for me to hand her a smoke.

"So funny, isn't it?" she said.

"What is?"

"That my parents couldn't give a rat's ass what I do, where I go, who I'm with, but they won't let me smoke."

"I know, right? It's funny that my parents hold me hostage in the house my whole life and don't let me go anywhere, but I'm allowed to smoke."

"It's fucked up, if you ask me," Joy said with a laugh. Her teeth looked perfect and exceptionally white against her brown skin.

"I agree."

It was fucked up. Joy had been able to ride her bike anywhere she wanted to since like age five. I had to be escorted everywhere by an adult. My grandma would walk me to tap and ballet when I was six, and Joy would pull up on her bike and ride with us, even across the busy street. They rarely even called her home for dinner or even when the streetlights came on. Joy still would go home when the streetlights went out because the rest of the block did, too, even though her parents didn't care. It goes to show that you can still turn out all right even if your parents don't actually practice "parenting." Joy truly was a good kid and a great person; she had a good heart. It was as if, because she was allowed to do whatever she wanted to, she didn't. My parents restricted everything I did, which just made me want to do it more. But her parents would go ballistic if they knew she smoked. They were already asleep by now.

"Remember how my dad thought I wouldn't go anywhere if I smoked at home?" I asked her and laughed. She nodded. My dad would even buy me and *my friends* cigarettes. I'd look like such a liar when I'd tell my friends how much of an asshole my dad was. To them, he was awesome; what parent buys fifteen-year-old kids cigarettes? He even bought me a Zippo lighter for Christmas one year. After I lost it in less than a week, I was actually grounded for losing my lighter. How's that for distorted parenting? I eventually found it. It was a useful gift with a lifetime guarantee.

Joy and I smoked and talked about our day. She was going away to college in the fall. I wouldn't be joining her. My grades weren't good enough to get accepted anywhere; even if I had, we couldn't have afforded it, so it would be community college for me. I couldn't even talk about it with her; my eyes welled up a little with envy, sadness, and fear. What would I do without her? I closed my eyes to make the tears stay inside. I took a big drag and held it in until it burned. I began to cough so that I could let the tears come out a little. She'd just think I was crying from choking.

"Why do you even smoke, man? You can't handle it!" Joy said jokingly.

"What would you do if I didn't?" I joked back.

"True," she said. "I guess hang out with Carly." We both laughed. Carly was our neighbor, who was like ten years older than us but still lived at home. We used to have to beg her to swim in her pool as kids; she cherished it, I think. She treasured making us beg to go in the pool, even though her mom would always say yes right away. Most of us on the block didn't have air conditioning, so if you had a pool, it made you quite popular in the summer. Also, Carly had caught on when we stopped calling her completely from fall until spring. Making us beg was her way of getting revenge.

"She'll be useful this summer going on beer runs for us," I said.

"Yeah, really. I can't wait."

"I heard a lot of people have been drinking in the cemetery."

"Hmmm, that sounds interesting, yet kinda creepy," Joy said sarcastically. She rolled her brown eyes and took another long drag, as if she'd been suffering nicotine withdrawal all day. I liked the menthol, minty taste of the cigarettes, but I didn't think I even liked smoking. It didn't agree with me. I bet that if my parents hadn't let me smoke, I probably would have been much more into it. If they'd said, "Don't smoke," then I probably would have loved smoking.

"It's not near any kind of graves or anything like that; they're hanging out toward the back end that hasn't been used yet. The cemetery has a lot of trees and stuff, so I think it camouflages people pretty well." I was becoming excited with the romance of risk that teenagers love.

My mom came out the front door just then and scared the shit out of us. She was very quiet on purpose, and I was sure she'd been eavesdropping. Underage drinking wouldn't fly with her. She looked irritated, but luckily it wasn't at me—I saw her eyes look at the street. My brother and his friends pulled up in this tiny hatchback, and like ten of them got out, like from a clown car; my brother was having his band over to play in the garage again.

"*He*...is now calling my phone looking for you," my mom said with a sigh. My mom stood there waiting for me make a decision about coming to the phone or not. I sat there paralyzed, wondering what

I should do. I stared off into the distance and let the cigarette burn down to the filter. The heat began to radiate to my fingers, which shook me out of my frozen state.

"Uh, jackass? Your mom's waiting for you," Joy said, clearly puzzled.

"Oh, sorry, guys," I said to my mom nonchalantly so she wouldn't worry. "I checked out for a minute there. Mom, Joy and I are going to get some ice cream. Tell Gerry I went out, but you don't know where. If he starts getting demanding or rude to you, please hang up and leave it off the hook."

My mom sighed, probably exhausted from the drama: the Gerry and Mary Kate saga.

"Ice cream? OK, then. Be careful." My mom dismissed us.

Joy smiled a mischievous grin. Her eyes lit up like a firefly. She bent over and turned her head upside down to fluff her hair. After she flipped it up, she took a final drag of her smoke, twisted it on the sidewalk to extinguish it, and flicked it inside the neighbor's ginormous evergreen tree, where we always put all our butts. There must have been seventeen hundred cigarette butts under that tree. He was an asshole, so we didn't care.

I loved that Joy knew exactly where we were going without even discussing it. It was comforting to have a friend who could read your mind, go right along with your parental lies, and smoothly follow your lead. We started walking toward the cemetery. Neither of us had really drunk alcohol all that much before, but we'd decided recently that we should take up drinking as a new pastime. I wasn't allowed to drink, and neither was Joy, so of course we both wanted to badly.

The main entrance of the cemetery was padlocked, and I'd heard of a broken fence on the other side that everyone had been entering. Just the *thought* of doing something illegal was exhilarating, let alone actually doing it. I felt like I was heading up on a roller coaster; the jumping butterfly feeling in my stomach was in overdrive. Joy seemed to be feeling the same way, her mouth in a smirk but her eyes wide open, like she was scared shitless. The inner juxtaposition of good and bad was making me feel dizzy.

# 2

As we approached the back entrance of the cemetery, I could hear faint voices of boys talking and laughing. I could see in the distance tiny dots of light—I assumed cigarettes or lighters. We walked to the gate, and when no cars were approaching, we slipped under the curled-up fence. The farther we walked into the cemetery, the darker and darker it became due to lack of streetlights and the fact that the sun had finally set at 9:00 p.m. I felt on edge, like I was watching a scary movie and someone was going to jump out at us. I looked at Joy's face, and she looked petrified, with face flat and eyes bulging. I could almost hear her swallowing hard with a big gulp in her throat. Her fists were clenched, and as she looked at me, a huge grin slowly emerged on her face. She looked suddenly gorgeous and alive with enthusiasm.

"This is so fucking fun! I love you!" Joy said. She put her arm around me. I felt warmth growing inside my chest as if my heart was a completely engulfed log in a fire. I put my arm around her, too, and we walked toward the crowd, enamored with each other. We were drunk with adrenaline, excitement, and fear, and I was abuzz with affection for my best friend—my soul sister who would be leaving me in three months. I gulped back the pain and shook that thought off my mind as we approached the...*boys*. That's right—all boys, with not one girl to be seen. The entire high school football team appeared

A SOUTH SIDE STORY

to be there. They all looked at us greedily as we walked toward them. This was a social cue to Joy and me, so we slowly let our arms drop from each other and put our game faces on. Two guys I didn't recognize stared me up and down with a hungry appetite and lustful expression. Fear washed over me when I realized that Joy and I were walking into a very dangerous situation. I was kind of surprised at my fear because of my usual clueless, naive, and innocent way of thinking. I was also impressed with myself for thinking clearly for once. I made note of this as I realized it was too late to turn back now without suffering serious social annihilation as word spread throughout the neighborhood that Joy and I had run away like two little freaks for no reason. "We thought they were going to gang-rape us!" I could hear myself saying while everyone laughed hysterically and told us to get over ourselves.

I looked at Joy, and, as always, she seemed to be able to read my eyes and caught wind of my thoughts. We had an unspoken understanding of what we were doing and what might happen. Under my breath, I began to tell her a plan I had quickly come up with as my fight-or-flight response kicked in. I always went with my gut, and I didn't have a bad feeling about this. My judgment could have been clouded by my anger (or lack thereof) from earlier. I considered that maybe a part of me was getting back at Gerry for trying to hurt me—a little revenge. It was too late now.

"So, if either one of us feels uncomfortable, threatened, or cornered, we take off. We're not leaving each other's sides, OK?" I whispered this to her urgently. She nodded in complete agreement, as if she'd thought the exact same thing at the exact same time.

"Wassup, guys?" Joy said calmly and coolly. Her tight white T-shirt against her golden tan skin seemed to glow in the darkness as if a black light was nearby.

My snow-white skin that usually blinds people in the daylight gives me a supernatural appearance in the moonlight, and the full moon was out. I'm sure I looked undead, with my pale white skin, jet-black hair, and yellow eyes. Too bad I didn't have some plastic glow-in-the-dark fangs or black lipstick; I could have scared off any sexual predator in seconds. Actually, maybe not—vampires can be kinda sexy.

"Wassup, hotties?" Rich, one of our friends, said. Relief settled over me that we did know someone loyal who would definitely be on our defense in case of a gang rape. Rich was crazy about Joy and always had been. Joy currently had a college-age boyfriend she felt loyal to, even though he was probably cheating on her left and right. Tonight, Joy had that lustful look in her eye from not seeing her boyfriend for weeks, since he was staying away at college for summer school. I'd attempted to persuade Joy to break up with him to open the door for other suitors, but she declined, saying, "I have nothing else going on with my love life, so why end it?" I sensed that this was about to change today, with the way Rich and Joy were looking at each other, completely mesmerized.

I smiled excitedly inside and casually glanced through the crowd for any familiar faces, and I relaxed when I saw no sign of Gerry. I sensed a pair of familiar yet piercing eyes gazing at me, and when our eyes locked, I felt oddly entranced. He turned to his friends, mumbled something, and walked over to me. As he strolled over, my recognition became clearer. He had tranquil blue-green eyes, sandy-brown hair, and porcelain skin. I couldn't remember his name, but I knew him from somewhere. When he reached us, I couldn't resist becoming mesmerized by his eyes, which seemed to pop against his flawless, marble-like complexion. His eyes were lustrous against the bizarrely bright moon. Suddenly I remembered who he was. It was Marty. He was the cute cook at the Greasy Spoon.

*Whoa! Where did his braces go?*

"Hey, Mary Kate." He said this shyly, his full lips turned up as he talked—a habit that made him look like he was always joking. His regular expression looked to be on the cusp of laughter. He gave me a big smile, and my insides jumped. His teeth were gorgeous, and his smile was glorious!

"Oh, hey, Marty. Did you just get your braces off?" I asked him casually, noticing how exceptionally *more* good looking he was without the braces. He looked much older—and hotter.

"Yes, thank gawd, had those things on for four years. I've been eating corn on the cob every day this summer!" He chuckled as he said this. His teeth had that same glowing appearance as my skin and Joy's T-shirt-under-the-full-moon-black-light appearance. There was something cool and eerie about the moon, and as I was staring at it, I caught Marty staring at me from the corner of my eye.

"That's a weird looking moon, eh?" he asked, eyes wide, the whites of his eyes glowing as if under the black light. He had a goatee whose reddish hue was different from his sandy blondish-brown hair. The hair on his head looked baby-fine soft, but his goatee hair looked strong and prickly, like porcupine quills. He resembled a werewolf in this light, and I looked like a vampire. It seemed as if we had all entered a horror movie, walking into this cemetery at night with a full, iridescent moon.

"Yeah, weird," I said tensely, on edge that some monster was going to jump out of the bushes. "I've never seen anything like it. It would probably be really cool outside of the cemetery, but in here, it's giving me the creeps."

"Your entire body looks as if you're glowing, like there's a black light on you!" Marty said with a laugh. He lightly tapped my shoulder to let me know he was teasing.

"Hilarious," I said flatly and sarcastically. Then I slapped him on the arm to let him know I was also kidding.

"I was just thinking how you look like a werewolf, and I look like a vampire," I said honestly.

"Shut up! How do I look like a werewolf?" Marty said with a playful expression on his face. "I mean, I can see how you look like a vampire, with your white china-doll skin. I was hoping I could check out your fangs." He then took out his silver necklace from under his shirt and flashed his cross.

"Rar!" I growled and flashed my teeth and then turned my head away and hissed jokingly, as if the cross was going to burn my vampire face off. Marty laughed again. "I have a silver bullet in my pocket, so don't pull any crap, Teen Wolf," I said jokingly to him, suddenly thinking about Michael J. Fox hiding in the bathroom from his father, covered in hair, looking at his hairy hands with their gross yellow nails.

"Yeah, how do you think we got this keg? I'm the official beer getter. I just flashed my red eyes and told the old man to 'give me a keg of beer, now.'" He growled the line.

I giggled at the movie reference that flowed from his full lips. Movie quotes could pour from my lips like the beer flowing from a keg. I think movies are the parallel to our existence. If it wasn't for movies, I would have had no idea what to say at that moment (or in most conversations, for that matter). I wondered if this was normal and if everyone did this. It seemed normal right now, talking with Marty, and I found comfort in that. A faint smile was still lingering on both of our faces, and we caught each other's eyes and laughed. He took a deep breath and opened his mouth as if he was going to say something, but then he stopped. Then the smile suddenly left his face. The silence lasted for about two seconds but felt like forever, yet it wasn't uncomfortable. It was calming in a way. I searched my brain for something to say. I glanced over at Joy, who was still talking to Rich; they were much closer to each other now—less than a ruler's length apart—as if they were gazing into each other's souls.

"So, how much is it for a cup?" I asked him with a smirk.

"Oh, uh, I don't know. I'll get you one." Marty turned abruptly and walked toward the crowd. Like clockwork, Joy was immediately by my side, and I saw Rich walking over to the crowd, too.

"Wow, good timing," I said. "Did you get thirsty at the exact same time I did, or what?"

"Sort of," Joy said with a hint of exhilaration on her face. "I saw Marty walking, and I decided I needed a break. Our conversation has been really intense. Rich is telling me things that I've never heard Tommy say, and I've been with Tommy for two years. I don't really know Rich—well I didn't think I did—but he sure seems to know me." She licked her lips and ran her hands through her brown, wavy hair.

"Like what?" I asked excitedly.

"I guess you could say he really likes me and wants to date me. I can't explain it, but it's like he's giving me a proposition that's making it very hard to say no. I feel like I was just watching a presentation, and he was selling himself, trying to get me to buy him." Joy looked a bit confused but was smiling at the same time. This made me feel excited for her even more; I liked that someone was treating her this way. The fact that Tommy was cool, older, and a football player seemed to be all that was required in their relationship; he really did not do much else. It was like Tommy had picked Joy out of a lineup based on her looks and said, "I want her." She'd had no choice or say-so, so she'd just started to date him, as if she was socially mandated to do so: Tommy wants you, so you have to date him—it's just a given. To refuse would be social suicide. I'm sure the same thing was happening at college, and Tommy had no insight about what he was doing, because he always got what he wanted. Their relationship always reminded me of *Can't Buy Me Love*; Joy was similar to the character Cindy Mancini with her college boyfriend away at school. In the movie, Cindy had a big stand-up poster of her college boyfriend in his football uniform displayed in her room—which was about as superficial as their relationship was. Rich could be her Ronald Miller! Joy was much more than a trophy girl. She was a rare trifecta of brains, beauty, and sense of humor.

"That sounds cool, actually," I said encouragingly. I wanted Joy to be with someone who would appreciate her for who she was, not just because she was beautiful. She's way better than a trophy girl. "So give me some examples." I said this feeling relaxed now that the coast was clear of the guys who were still lost in the sea of testosterone surrounding the keg.

"Well, he kind of sounded like you, Mary Kate. I had to check his ear to make sure there wasn't an earphone with you coaching him and telling him what to say," she said playfully.

I smiled; this sounded promising. "Well, Rich is a genius," I said playfully back. We both laughed, and she slapped my arm. "OK," I said, "enough of this crap—they'll be back soon. Tell me the CliffsNotes version of it; the suspense is killing me."

"I don't know, Mary Kate, you know it's hard for me to say things like that; basically, he said everything that you've said to me," Joy said, looking at me with a mixture of shame and annoyance. She took my Zippo out of my pocket and lit a Marlboro. She inhaled deeply, and when she exhaled heavily, the smoke even had that black-light glowing appearance her shirt and my skin had. My hands were still shaking from the powerful moment I'd had with Marty. Joy's cigarette smelled good, so I lit one, too. I always feel more comfortable when I have something to occupy my hands; I'm not sure why. I'm definitely more comfortable when I have a beer in one hand and a cigarette in the other.

"You and Marty looked like you were having a good conversation. It was nice to see you smiling while talking to a boy, for once," Joy said, evidently trying to change the subject; she probably knew that if she pissed me off, I'd become distracted and stop engaging in conversation with her. This tactic didn't work for some reason, though. It was probably the adrenaline raging through my bloodstream, leaving me focused and alert from the crazy adventure we were taking part in tonight: the cemetery (trespassing), the drinking (underage), and being the only two girls hanging out with an entire good-looking male population.

"Knock it off, Joy. It's not like I'm clueless about the way things are with Gerry. I just don't know a way out. Can we talk about that later? I'm having a really good time, and you're being a buzzkill." I knew being called a buzzkill would sting. Who wants to be called that?

"Damn, OK, bitch!" Joy said, clearly shocked but smirking; she loved to banter. "Anyways, Rich said that he's always felt *something* around me and that there's *something about me*." She stressed the words and took a drag of her cigarette.

"Something? What's the something?" I asked impatiently.

"Simmer down over there, I'm getting to that," Joy said, sounding annoyed. The boys were going to be heading back soon. I needed to know this right now. I couldn't wait. She continued. "He said that there's something about me—more than being beautiful, smart, and funny—that there's something else he can't place yet, but he wants to hang out with me to figure out what this *something* is. He said that as of right now, this something is pulling him toward me like a magnet, and he keeps pulling away from it because of Tommy, but his body is being yanked toward me like a gravitational force. Basically he's saying he knows he's nuts for talking to me because Tommy would beat his ass if he knew. He said in his head he knows it's out of his control, but his body's drawn to me like an involuntary impulse." She said this unemotionally and detached from what she was saying, probably because she didn't believe it herself, as usual.

I thought I'd lighten the mood by giving her shit and making her laugh. "I've never said my body's drawn to you like a gravitational force," I said with a smirk. My vampire teeth flashed at her in a playful smile.

"Shut up," Joy said flatly. "You know what I mean." She said this in a mocking tone, as if to make fun of me for saying such a stupid thing.

"Sorry. I won't say such mean things to you ever again," I said, mocking her back. "I know I'm such a terrible friend, telling you that you're beautiful, smart, and funny. There's a lot to you—you're the whole package. You have many levels and layers. I love that about you, and I'm glad someone else saw that besides me, because you know damn well Tommy doesn't see that." I said this urgently, seeing the boys walking back. This was my payback for her comment about Gerry. We were both with guys who probably weren't good for us, but my problem was the opposite. Gerry knew and saw all the layers of me; he loved all my levels and depths. The problem was that he was obsessed with me in an unhealthy way. He always said he "doesn't want anyone else to have me" and wants to keep me locked up to prevent anyone from "seeing these things about me." Basically he was insecure with himself, and he was making his biggest fear come true: his fear was driving me away. His trying to control me to prevent anyone from seeing these things about me was actually having the opposite effect.

I took a long drag from my cigarette now; the light-headedness kicked in as it always did when I smoked. It counteracted the pang of guilt kicking in as I thought about what I had to do.

Joy still looked like she was processing what I was saying, with eyes moving around, forehead furrowed, a bewildered expression, and a blank stare at her cigarette burning down.

The boys were walking toward us now with four cups full of illegal sunshine: liquid gold, or, more importantly in my case, liquid courage. Perhaps the beer would help my brain work in this social setting. I nudged her; her long, gray cigarette ash fell, and she came out of her trancelike state. Joy dropped her smoke and stepped on it with her sandal. The boys handed us our beers, and we all took a drink of the foam—because, of course, since we were underage, no one knew how to properly tap a keg, so foam continuously shot out of the tap like shaving cream. I was familiar with the beer foam that my dad and grandfather allowed me to slurp off the head of their beer mugs. Foam wasn't a good thing, I was told, and they didn't mind letting me drink it. I thought the foam was delicious and never understood why it was considered bad. Now, looking at my cup of shaving cream, I started to understand. The mass of foam eventually melted into a carbonated piss appearance and was drinkable. It was ice cold, and I was grateful for the distraction. I finished my cup quickly, and the drink instantly tingled through me, making me feel giddy and electric.

"Slow down there, girl," Marty said to me, smiling and seemingly impressed by my slamming ability.

"Sorry, I was thirsty," I replied, wiping my mouth with the back of hand like they do in that Miller Lite commercial. Rich, Marty, and

Joy laughed, since they got my reference. We stood there, the four of us, looking in different directions and sipping our foamy piss. The white remnants of foam on our lips glowed under the blue moonlight. I looked up and caught Marty smiling at me. At this point I *really* got a good look at him, and he looked surreal and breathtakingly handsome in the radiant moonlight. His eyes were the coolest color blue I had ever seen, like a turquoise or teal with flicks of light green beneath sooty, long, to-die-for eyelashes. His face was chiseled, with a strong jawline and a small, slightly upturned nose that made him look boyish and adorable. His lips were luscious and full, with a distinct dark-pink hue against his light skin. His skin was smooth like marble, but his cheeks still had a blushing appearance. He took a deep breath in and looked up at the moon and took a sip of his beer.

"You know, I had a blast with you homecoming weekend. I never thought just talking to a girl could be that much fun." He sounded sweet, and he seemed sincere. I gasped inside, not expecting this.

"Plus, you're smokin' hot—I can't even take it. I'm dead serious— nobody cuter. Laughing with you *and* looking at you is like a gift." He winked at me, and I laughed nervously. *Holy shit!* He grabbed my cup and walked back to the keg to refill our cups. My mind lingered on what he'd said, as if the words hovered over my head like a balloon in a comic strip. I'd somehow forgotten about homecoming weekend, probably because I forced myself to in order to avoid the guilt. He returned promptly and handed me another cup of beer, which I slammed again. My mind traveled back to homecoming weekend and reminisced about our time together and how guilty I'd felt on the ride home, because it had seemed like I'd done something wrong, even though I technically hadn't cheated. I guess the fact that I'd wanted to was the source of the guilt. I glanced at Marty and saw that he was smirking at me. Our eyes locked.

"Soooo…any response to what I just said, or what?"

I stammered, mouth open, yet no words would come out. We stayed this way for what seemed like an eternity until we were interrupted by a flashlight waving in the distance. Luckily my eyes were not frozen, and my instinctive urge to react kicked in. Marty saw my eyes move and turned around to see what I was looking at.

"Aw shit! Cops!" He grabbed my arm and pulled me in the opposite direction. Rich and Joy's shared trance was also interrupted by us taking off like bats out of hell.

I turned around and saw Joy running, holding Rich's hand with one hand and still drinking her beer with the other. "Joy! Ditch it, come on!" I yelled. Joy probably didn't care; she never got into trouble anyway. Joy hooted with laughter. (It always seems she laughs her ass off whenever I'm stressed and nervous.)

I, on the other hand, was a nervous wreck and frightened, instinctively imagining myself behind bars and sobbing, with prostitutes singing the blues all around me. Marty's hand moved off my arms and to my hand. It was warm, strong, and soft. Running in the long, wet grass in the dark was difficult, and I found myself looking at my feet instead of straight ahead because I was afraid I was going to step on an animal or step inside an animal's burrow. Marty pulled me gently, and I looked over at him, looking straight ahead, determined and protective. He turned to look at me; he smiled a crooked smile, and his eyes glowed in the moonlight. We continued to run while looking at each other until, of course, I tripped on a rock (or something very hard) and wiped out. Marty unavoidably let go of my hand and fell, too, ahead of me. As I skidded across the mud, I heard Marty fall with a gloppy splash. I jumped up and saw Marty emerging from a small mud bog that had been covered by the wet grass and reeds.

"What...the...fuck?" he exclaimed. His eyes met mine and observed that I was trying my best not to laugh due to my usual incongruent reaction to situations. I wasn't sure if that was the right thing to do, but I felt euphoric when I heard Marty begin to laugh. I, too, then let go and began to release my deep belly laugh. When I saw his teeth and eyes now fluorescent under the moonlight against the black mud background, my stomach fluttered. He looked sexy as hell, being all dirty like that! Joy and Rich were laughing hysterically before they caught up to us.

"We totally saw your shadows ahead of us, and then all of sudden you disappeared!" Joy squealed. "I thought you guys got knocked down; I didn't realize you fell into a swamp. You look like the Loch Ness monster!"

"I was a werewolf earlier; now I'm the Loch Ness monster. It's like Halloween in June," Marty said as he grinned playfully at me. I beamed back.

"You dipshit, Marty!" Rich yelled, laughing. Suddenly I felt defensive of Marty, who just saved my ass from the po-lice.

"Uh, excuse me, Dick? I mean Rich. If you could run faster and got here first, it would have happened to you," I retorted. I glanced at Marty, who was smirking and gave me a wink. My heart skipped a beat.

"Oh snap!" Joy said, giving me a high five. Rich laughed.

"I have to admit, that was a good comeback, Mary Kate," Rich said.

The imminent-danger signal inside me subsided to the comic relief of the situation. We were near the fence of the cemetery on the other side, toward the entrance. I began to wonder where the rest of the boys were and why no one else was running toward us this way. We were near a busy street, yet I felt invisible because of my muddy camouflage. I was no longer fluorescent, since we were near a busy street and streetlights.

As the light emerged, I found myself gawking at Marty in front of me, looking at his muscular legs and ass in his cargo shorts, his back a *V* shape, wider at the top and sloped down into a *V* on either side to a smaller waist. He'd gone from a sweet-looking boy to a hot, grimy *man* smudged with dirt and mud. His wet, dirty shirt clung to his protruding back muscles. We reached the fence; Marty climbed first and caught his hand on the top sharp edge of the fence. He hissed in pain. Then he removed his shirt, laid it over the top of the fence, and jumped down.

"Here, Mary Kate, climb up and put your hands by my shirt so you don't cut yourself. It's sharp," Marty said. I was dumbfounded by his sweet gesture and also by his round pecs and lumps all over his chest. He had a smaller build, so he didn't appear to be as muscular as he was. I vaguely remembered him being in swimming, missing work for swim meets, which resulted in him having to quit. His body was a complete muscle, shredded and cut everywhere. The fact that he was covered in mud gave him more of a defined look, and I felt that familiar electrical sensation I'd had initially with Gerry shoot into my groin.

I was pretty good at climbing fences; as a child, we played all day outside with the boys on the block. Playing cops and robbers as a child definitely benefited me right now. I didn't want to look like a "total girl" trying to climb this fence. I threw my leg over the top of the fence, over his T-shirt, and felt the sharp pieces that Marty must have cut himself on; his T-shirt shielded my hand.

"Just jump down, I'll catch you," Marty said. He wiped the blood from his hand onto his shorts and held his arms up to me. It was a foreign sensation just then; I didn't remember trusting anyone to catch me before in my life. Anyways, I braced myself at the top of the fence, put both hands on his T-shirt, and was able to hold on and climb down. With my back to him, he pulled me off the fence as soon as my legs came into his reach. His strong arms around my waist felt strong but inviting, and a throb emerged between my legs as he touched me. My heart was racing. I surrendered and allowed him to pull me off the fence. He set me down gently and took my hands into his and looked at my palms, which showed the superficial scratches left by the sharp fence edge.

"I told you to jump, badass!" he said sternly. He lifted my palms to his mouth and kissed them each softly. My body quivered from his unfamiliar touch. I smiled and looked at his hand: it was a bad puncture wound that appeared deep, with blood dripping down the side of his arm. A kiss didn't seem appropriate for me to reciprocate, but I thought I should do something. I suddenly thought of how I looked like a vampire and smiled.

"I'd kiss your hand, too, but I might not be able to stop. Your blood looks dee-li-cious," I said, emphasizing "delicious" in the most flirtatious voice I could muster. He smiled, closed his eyes, and threw his head back and laughed quietly. I beamed proudly because I'd made him laugh. He ripped the sleeve off his T-shirt and wrapped it around his hand.

"Thanks for laying your T-shirt up there for me...but I don't bleed, remember?"

"Oh yeah! What the hell, man?" Marty said facetiously, looking up from his hand. He looked at me intently, his ocean-like eyes burning into mine. The streetlight glowing on his glorious body, accompanied by the shadows of night, gave him more definition, and he became the sexiest man I'd ever encountered in real life. His full lips looked soft and bitable. He licked his lips, put his nonbloody hand on the back of my neck, and pushed me close to him. I was surprised by this gesture but sensed a compelling draw to him; it was undeniable. I felt that *something* that Rich must have been referring to—this magnetic force you have no control over. We stared at each other for a long time, and I didn't want it to stop. His serene, breathtaking eyes were swallowing me whole. Oddly, I felt at peace and calm, as if time stood still.

"All right, all right, let's go!" Joy yelled from the other side of the fence, interrupting our trance. Rich was laughing, looking at her admiringly. I became aware of a sudden zap of electricity, like the power had just gone out. Marty and I immediately parted and began coaching them both on how to get down the fence, using his T-shirt so they wouldn't cut themselves like Marty had. Marty took the rest of his T-shirt off the fence and wrapped it around his hand. A small red dot began to emerge from the wound; he put his other hand on it and applied pressure. The four of us stood there for a moment, gaping at the fence, all lost in thought; a lot of shit had just happened. I think we all needed to regroup.

"I have my brother's car parked a few blocks down. I can drive you guys home," Rich said, lifting his eyebrows at Marty, motioning his eyes toward Joy. I assume this is the facial expression code for a buddy to make like a tree and get outta here.

"I smell like a sewer, and I'm all muddy," Marty said. "I don't want to get your brother's car all dirty. I don't live far from here; I'll walk it. See you guys later." And just like that, he was gone. His V-shaped, rippled, muddy back was all that I could see. Marty began walking quickly, and then he ran across the street. My heart sank.

I felt like a third wheel suddenly but followed behind Joy and Rich, who were still holding hands despite us no longer being in danger of having the police behind us. We walked toward a blue Honda four-door. *Pretty nice car to entrust to your little brother,* I thought suspiciously.

"How old's your brother?" I asked with a smirk. When I saw the coupons in the console, my suspicions were confirmed that this was his mother's car. Rich eyed me in the rearview mirror; I could see the smirk in his eyes. I shut up and didn't press it. It's less impressive to say, "I can drive you home in my mother's car."

Joy lived across the street from me; I wondered how this would work out to Rich's advantage. I saw Joy writing her number down on a piece of paper—a coupon. Slick maneuver on her part; she was probably thinking the same thing I was. When we pulled up to our block, I slid over to the passenger side. Joy got out first and pulled the seat forward, and I hopped out. I turned around and squatted down to see Rich in the driver's seat.

"Thanks, Rich," I said.

"Sure, anytime, Mary Kate, and uh, thanks for the skid marks," he said with a smirk.

I glanced back, and on the leather seat was a streak of mud from my clothes—basically a muddy ass-print. I blushed. I was about to climb back into the back seat when Joy stopped me. I climbed out, and when I stood up, both of our heads were above the roof of the car, out of Rich's line of sight. She motioned her head back and forth quickly toward my house; translation: I should vanish. I understood.

"I'll get something to clean this up, Rich," Joy said. "Go park the car. I'll be right back." Rich did as he was told, and I'm sure he was eternally grateful that I'd left muddy skid marks in his car. I stalked up to my sidewalk; as I turned to see Rich's car, I saw that he was grinning at me from ear to ear. I gave him a thumbs-up, as if this was all part of a master plan on my part to have a muddy ass. This did work out to his advantage. He gave me a thumbs-up back. I smiled back and went into my house.

My house was quiet and dark when I walked inside. I went to the bathroom immediately and stripped off my muddy clothes. I saw remnants of blood on my T-shirt, and my heart shivered euphorically at the thought of Marty. I began to wonder why he'd left so hastily. He did the same thing on homecoming weekend. Then I wondered why I was thinking about him with this bizarre longing feeling. I climbed into the shower and scrubbed myself with pumice scrub to get the dried mud off me. The water at my feet was gray from all the dirt. My hair needed to be washed three times because I continued to feel the grittiness of dirt on my scalp. When I was finally scrubbed clean, I emerged fresh as a daisy and exhausted. I put my clothes in the washing machine with extra soap. I knew my mother would probably freak out about that, since she had everything rationed out at the house.

I wrapped a towel around me and another around my hair. I went into the kitchen to get some water and saw that the phone was off the hook. The answering machine light was also blinking in my room. I had my own phone line in my room that I paid for myself. There were fifty-six messages on my phone. I thought I'd misread the numbers. When I pressed play, I discovered I was wrong.

Gerry had called shortly after our encounter today (the burger incident). He was angry and "demanded" I call him back. Multiple hang-ups, one message from my girlfriend Sam, then ten from Gerry, becoming more and more desperate. I'm sure the regret kicked in once he'd showered the ketchup and mustard off his face. He said, "Sweetie, I'm sorry. I don't know what got into me today. Please call me."

The last two sounded sincere; I realized he must be feeling remorseful for his behavior and that I should let him know I was home and I am serious this time. I called his house, and his mom answered sleepily. *Dammit, I hate doing this,* I thought. I turned on my record player and selected Van Morrison's *Moondance* album again. I listened to "Into the Mystic" and replicated the evening at the cemetery in my head. I moved the long phone cord toward the window and looked down on the cedar chest that I'd moved into this cove in my room near the window so I could smoke. I looked at the moon, and Marty's handsome face appeared in my head. I sighed, lit a cigarette, and dialed the phone.

"Hi, Mrs. McGrath, I know it's late, but Gerry called and said he needed me to—"

I heard the other extension pick up, and Gerry said, "I got it, Mom." She hung up.

I didn't even want to talk to him, so I cleared my through "Eh, em."

"Hi," he said back. "Please. Listen just for a second. I'm sorry, pumpkin; I don't know what came over me. I love you. I didn't mean to say that; I've been trying to figure out all night why I'd ever consider calling you that name."

"OK," I said quickly, annoyed; I'd heard this shit before. "Listen, I'm really tired, and I have to work tomorrow. Just wanted to let you know I'm home. I received all your messages. Please stop calling. It's over, let's not drag this out."

"That's it? We can't talk anymore?" he said, sounding hurt. I started to feel guilty about tonight, the incident with Marty—I guess me "feeling" something for him was grounds for guilt. It would kill me if I knew Gerry was having fun with another girl like that. I had to let him go. I had to move on. We were too young.

"I don't really feel like talking right now, and Maeve is sleeping," I said with a yawn.

"Where did you go tonight?" he asked. *Oh shit, here we go.* I sighed. He was unbelievable, like it was any of his business. In the past, I would be hesitant to even tell him; he'd get all pissed off, and I didn't want to tell him everything. He'd start asking me every detail: who I was with, what I did, who I talked to, what time I got there, what time I left, what I was wearing. It was exhausting. The jealousy and possessiveness were too much. He always liked to say, "You're mine," which I suppose I should have adored, but I didn't care for it. At first I'd felt like he was crazy about me, but now he seemed just plain crazy. Initially I felt like he idealized and worshipped me, but after a while, it began to feel more like I was his property. He felt threatened by anyone who talked to me. Then he'd flip out and somehow I'd feel like it was my fault. I didn't understand how this happened. Then the excuses would start about why he did this or what was going on for him to treat me like this. I couldn't live like that; I wanted to be myself. Instead, I was exhausted all the time. Gerry always seems to know how to wear me down until I gave in again. If I kept talking to him, I would end up in this vicious cycle again that I did not comprehend. I figured no contact at all was my only choice.

"Gerry, It's over. I'm serious. You are going away to college in the fall, so we would have had to say good-bye anyways. I am disconnecting my phone. Please do not call me anymore or come to my house. Let's just do this now," I said, kind of shocking myself because I really meant it. I didn't know how I was going to get through it, and I started to get a bit choked up when I thought about his family and how much I would miss them. I could hear him on the other end breathing heavily, and I didn't want him to talk because I knew I would lose it. "Good-bye," I muttered quickly and hung up. I began to cry, and the tears were shooting from my eyes. I never thought this would happen between us. I lay in my bed sobbing, knowing this is what I had to do, but I was scared. I was alone.

It hadn't always been like this; it had started so sweet and innocent. I don't know where things went wrong...

# 3

I had worked at the Greasy Spoon the summer before. He came in every day—they did have delicious food. One day he hung around longer than usual and was smiling at me a lot, like he had a secret about me. It was making me kind of paranoid. Finally I asked him, "What?" I flashed back to *When Harry Met Sally*, when Meg Ryan asks Billy Crystal, "Is there something on my face?"

He then asked me what time I got off work.

"What?" I asked again in my state of paranoia.

"Uh, I was just wondering what time you got off work today," he said shyly.

"Wondering why?" I said, annoyed. I was clueless. He had nice hazel eyes, which were exploring all around my face, and it kept making me nervous. I wiped the sides of my mouth, my eyes, and my nose.

He laughed and said, "I was wondering if you wanted to go for a walk or something."

*Walk? Walk for what? This is weird*, I thought. He was still staring at me intently.

"You know, like if I could walk you home?" he asked again, a little more nervously than before.

"How do you know where I live?" I asked, even more paranoid.

"Uh, I don't. I assume you live close. I just wondered if you would mind—you know, so we could talk a little. I haven't really heard your voice much except to ask me how my food was and to ring up my check." He smiled. I swear his tooth was shining for a second, like the "ding" you see in commercials. It was a really cute smile. My paranoia subsided a little. It was kind of sweet.

"I guess so," I said softly. It was the summer, so I usually got off around two, after the lunch rush. It was one now. My boss Billy was smirking at me from behind the kitchen window. His wife was smiling at him. *What's going on?* I thought. I told him to hold on a second and walked back into the kitchen. Billy and his wife turned toward me and said, "Yessss?" together, all sweetly and singsongy.

"What?" I asked them, annoyed.

"Oh, nothin', deary," Billy's wife replied.

"I was wondering if I could go home now," I asked softly. "It seems to have slowed down."

"It has?" Billy said. "It seems to be heating up in there to me." His wife elbowed him in the ribs.

"Sure thing, deary," Billy's wife said. She called me "deary," and I didn't know her name. I knew her husband's name: he insisted that I call him Billy, and he always introduced her as "my wife." So I never really addressed her as anything. In the morning, we just said, "Good morning," and in the afternoon I'd say, "See you later." It wasn't what I was used to; I was always expected to address grown-ups as Mr. or Mrs. and their last name. It didn't really work that way with these people. It was also payday, so I didn't really want to leave without my cash for the weekend. I stood around for a minute, and he said, "Oh yes, hold on." He got some cash from his apron and gave me a wad. *Yippee, cha-ching*, I thought like a typical kid who thinks she's rich, but it really wasn't much: fifty-seven dollars, mostly in singles.

I put the wad of cash in my pocket and walked out front. He was sitting at the counter staring toward the kitchen. When I came out, his eyes looked at me with a warm glow. It was really uncomfortable. All the regulars from the restaurant had silly grins on their faces. I looked around at them, my eyebrows furrowed; some of them giggled. One of the regulars—this old man with a trucker hat, short-sleeved, button-down shirt with two packs of cigs in his pocket, and plumber's butt—jumped up, pulled up his pants, and opened the door for us. He gestured toward the door, so I smiled and thanked him. When we got outside, I could hear the faint sound of whistles and laughter from inside. Now I got it. It clicked. I'm pretty slow when it comes to things like this; my cheeks burned. I guess I should have realized that when Billy Crystal was staring at Meg Ryan and she asked him that, he replied, "You're a very attractive woman." *Oh shit.*

I turned toward him and smiled nervously. He smirked crookedly back. His shirt had a logo that said "McGrath" above it. I couldn't remember his first name. I knew he had to work, because he wore this green polo every day to the restaurant. He probably knew my name from the name-tag plate I wore. That was all he could really know about me. I was puzzled as to why he wanted to walk me home. I'd never really talked to him, except to take his order and bring him the check.

He asked about school—the usual small talk. He was a caddy at the nearby golf course. I didn't know much about golf, except that gophers were a bad thing on a golf course, from watching *Caddy Shack*—so not much. He had to be at the course at six in the morning and was done by noon.

"I thought golf took like sixteen hours, because my dad would be gone until the next day whenever he had a golf outing," I said.

He burst out laughing. "I'm not sure where your dad plays, but playing eighteen holes usually takes four to six hours—nine holes, less than that."

"Ah, I see. Do they serve alcohol on the course?" I asked. I could hear Kenny Loggins singing "I'm Alright" in my head. I tried to push it out of my mind.

He laughed again. "At the bar they do, but not on the course usually."

"So this polo is your caddy uniform shirt? Is that your last name?" I asked.

"Oh jeez, yes, I'm Gerry McGrath. I'm sorry, Mary Kate. I assumed you knew my name. Sorry. Not to be a stalker or anything—I knew your name from people yelling it at the restaurant." His cheeks flushed.

I smiled and blushed, too. I didn't know what to say. It felt surreal. Usually in movies, when a couple is walking or driving, they normally have some music playing to show how much fun they're having. I could use some conversation pieces right about now. *Some Kind of Wonderful* popped into my head. The guy in that movie did seem like a stalker: the intense gawking at Amanda Jones, the way he asks her out when he's never talked to her before. This interaction with Gerry was giving me the same impression. The thought of the movie calmed me for some reason, because even though the guy in the movie seemed like a stalker, he really did like her, so I guessed that was a good thing.

"It's OK. I just checked out for a minute there. I can't get Kenny Loggins singing 'I'm Alright' out of my head," I said jokingly.

At first Gerry looked puzzled, and then he smiled with recognition. His eyes lit up; they were a warm hazel color, with thick eyelashes. He nervously took off his maroon baseball hat, scratched his head, and put it back on. "Smartass, I make good tips, too. I've got that goin' for myself," he said and elbowed me. "So does everyone say Mary Kate, or do you go by anything for short?"

"Mary Kate is really only three syllables, so nothing for short." I smiled and looked at him playfully. I was feeling a little more comfortable now that I had some kind of frame of reference. I liked that he was nervous, too. I didn't like arrogant types. I like confidence in guys, but not too much so they seem like total dicks. Saying "Hardy Jenns with two Ns" and giving the gym teacher the finger popped into my head. Another *Some Kind of Wonderful* reference—yes, I'm aware that I'm a freak.

"What's your last name, Mar-rie Kate?" he said, emphasizing the syllables. He pounded his fist into his leg at each syllable, like we'd learned in grammar school. I burst out laughing, a little louder than I anticipated. I was so nervous!

"I still use that tactic, one of the few things I remember from my Catholic education," I replied.

"Yes. Some of those things we will never forget. What parish you grow up in? Oh, wait, you still didn't tell me your last name."

"Danaher," I said as deadpan as I could.

"Shut up! Your name is not Mary Kate Danaher! After Maureen O'Hara from *The Quiet Man*? Get the fuck outta here!" He said this so enthusiastically that I hesitated to tell him my real last name now; it would be a disappointment.

"Nah, I'm messin' around. My dad loved that movie and named me after her. It didn't really work, though, because I have black hair. My sister has red hair; she should have been named Mary Kate," I said regretfully. "My last name is…O'Brien. Mary Kate O'Brien."

Who did I think I was—James Bond? Why was I talking like that? Bond, James Bond. Dork—ugh!

"I like it, Mary. Kate. O'Brien. MKOB. Kind of like BYOB." Gerry laughed and looked down. There were a couple seconds of silence; I had no idea what he was talking about.

"I'm sure you have other qualities like Mary Kate Danaher. I'm guessing you don't take a lot of shit from anyone, just like she didn't," he said with a wink. I was relieved and appreciative of the compliment. I let his words marinate for a while. It was a different kind of compliment, but I enjoyed it.

"You got that right," I said finally with a smirk. "Remember, before everyone had VCRs, and we actually had to watch a movie when it was on TV, and you had to run to the bathroom at the commercials? You couldn't 'pause' the TV! Man, that was hard! Well, I knew how much my dad loved *The Quiet Man*, even when I was like six years old. I had a tap and ballet recital, and my dad was torn because he wanted to go to my dance recital, but he also wanted to watch the movie. I told him he could stay home and watch it; I wasn't even mad," I said proudly, without thinking. Suddenly a wave of regret came over me when I saw the shock on his face. I was trying to show how cool a kid I was, and instead the astonishment on his face indicated that he could sense what kind of a man my dad was.

"Did he go to the recital or watch the movie?" Gerry asked inquisitively, eyes open wide.

I was kicking my own ass inside for telling the story now. I didn't want to tell the truth and be patronized. It hadn't bothered me when I was six, but it kind of stung now. I hadn't thought about that day in years. As my big mouth started to tell the story, my emotions changed quickly. He probably saw the enthusiasm fade from my freckled face.

"He did come to the recital after the movie was over," I murmured.

Gerry looked disappointed. His thin lips curled over his teeth, and he blew his cheeks out. He put his hand on the back of my arm lightly for a second and then pulled his hand back. I looked at his arm and realized that caddying must be a good thing; his arms were tanned and ripped. He busted me looking at his bronzed, cut arm. I quickly shut my hanging-open mouth.

"Are you looking at my farmer's tan?" he asked. He pulled his sleeve up to show the whiter, untan skin. He looked embarrassed. I felt like a jackass. My cheeks burned. Hallelujah—we were almost at my block. We turned down my block silently.

Gerry took a deep breath and said, "I bet you were adorable at that recital. Your dad had to be nuts not to see every minute of it."

*That took some balls*, I thought. He didn't know my story: if my dad was in the picture or not. I could have been offended that he'd just met me and insulted my dad, but of course I wasn't. I was beaming on the inside. It was just what I needed to hear to make that lingering sting go away. Either he was a genius for being able to read my emotions or a complete dumbass who didn't think before talking—like me. I didn't mind either scenario; he was a win-win in my book.

The sun was blaring down on my block, which didn't have a lot of trees. My sweat mustache was going to start coming in, so I needed to get into my house soon. Of course, Gerry had a sweat mustache, with beads of sweat all over his face, but it looked kind of sexy on him. Of course, if I sweat like that, I look like a pig; guys do it and they look hot. It's bullshit.

Meanwhile, speaking of hot, Gerry then lifted the bottom of his polo to wipe his face, exposing his whiter but equally chiseled abs with those two indentations on either side of his hips. How the hell do guys get those? I hadn't seen a real person with those—only celebrities in my *Big Bopper* magazine. *Ffffuuuuccccckkkk*, I thought. I felt a tinge of excitement in my belly and then my groin. What the...

*This guy must want some kind of tutoring or free food from the Greasy Spoon*, I thought. There was no way he was single. I thought I was decent; I wasn't hideous. I never really seemed to care how I looked or thought about it much until right now. I looked down at my feet and discovered I had a big, crusty blob of cheese from the cheese-fry machine in the middle of my shirt. *For fuck's sake! Good God! I need to get out of here. Four houses to go; this is torture. Four, three, two, one. Phew.*

"Well, this is my house. Thanks for walking me home. So, uh, who's going to walk you home?" I nervously joked.

I stepped onto the first step of my porch, leaned on the banister, and casually crossed my arms to cover the cheese stain. Outside I was trying to keep my composure, because I was shitting my pants on the inside—not literally but figuratively speaking. His eyes traveled from my Tretorn shoes to my face quickly and with this piercing look in his eye that made me feel like I was in trouble. I needed to keep it together, but I was vacillating. I never wanted to be in my stuffy, hot, un-air-conditioned house more than this moment in my life. He took his hat off again, scratched his hair, and put his hat on backward. *Aw shit, holy hotness*, as Joy would say.

"I'm sure I can walk myself home. I only live like a block down right now. I'm staying with my grandmother for the summer. She needs help at night. During the school year, I live maybe five miles away." He paused for a second. "I was, uh, wondering if you wanted to hang out tonight? You have a video of that dance recital? We could watch it," he said teasingly. He smiled, and I could swear his eyes glowed when the sun was shining on them. He needed to put that hat back the other way; I slowly sensed that I was being hypnotized. *You're getting very sleepy...very sleepy.* I shook my head. I needed to slap myself or put some cold water on my face. Now I knew what the expression "take a cold shower" meant. *What does "hang out" mean to him?* I wondered. I became suspicious about his ulterior motives. He wasn't after me for my money, so what was this all about?

"I mean, we could do something, but I don't really have any record of that recital. I think someone took a photo or two with a Kodak disc camera," I said jokingly. The cheese on my shirt was starting to melt with the sun blazing overhead.

"OK, cool beans. I can walk down like around seven?" he said with a smile.

"Um, sure. What do you want to do?" I asked, trying to tone down my cheesy grin.

"I'll think about it. See you later, then." He turned his sweet ass around and walked down the block. I caught myself smiling and watching him like a fucking loon. I ran to the bathroom, ripped off my cheese-crusted uniform, and looked at my reflection. My face was so greasy it looked like I'd wiped bacon on it, and my hair was plastered to my forehead. Son of a...

# 4

I wanted to shower immediately, but I knew I'd need to shower again around six because my house was Africa hot. My baby sister Maeve was in our room, coloring. Maeve was seven years old and cool as hell. She was my buddy. Maeve had the dirtiest feet of any kid I'd ever met, since she hated to wear shoes. Despite us making her take a bath every night, the dirt was embedded in her feet; it had become a permanent part of her anatomy. Her hair rocked, though: the best color red, with strawberry-blond highlights. She has two different color eyes, one is hazel, and the other is blue. Her eyes are striking, and overall she is a stunning little girl—plus, she's hilarious. Maeve is just plain cool all around, except for her dirty-ass feet.

"I saw you talking to that boy out the window," Maeve said to me, pretending to be nonchalant.

"Mmm, hmm," I replied to her. I was sure I knew where the little shit was going with this.

"How do you know him?" she asked without even looking up from her coloring.

"I just met him today at work; he's staying with his grandmother for the summer. She lives down the block." *Love this kid, but I'm not in the mood right now*, I thought. *I need to figure out what I'm wearing later.*

"Who's his grandma? What's his name?"

Maeve needed to know everything. "I don't know his grandma," I said impatiently. "His name's Gerry."

"Mary and Gerry sitting in a tree, K-I-S-S-I-N-G, first comes love, then comes marriage, then comes a baby in a baby carriage." Maeve was smirking and still coloring.

"Shut it, sister, or I'll beat you," I said jokingly. Maeve giggled, and I gave her a hug.

"Mmmm, you smell like cheese fries or grilled cheese or something," Maeve said. I usually brought her home something, but oops—not today.

My wardrobe consisted of jeans and jean cutoff shorts. My grandmother always got jeans at the thrift store, and we cut them off once they finally had holes in the knees. I had an Outback Red tank top from The Limited that I'd gotten for my birthday. It was one of my only first-time-owner items of apparel I had. The remainder of my wardrobe were hand-me-downs from family or from thrift stores. Of course, I normally didn't care, but today I did. I was excited to wear my new plaid low-cut Chuck Taylors that I'd just bought with my work earnings.

Our brother Michael was home, but Maeve was pretty independent, which was good, because he rarely came up from the basement to even check on her. Michael had this sort of sinister presence in our home, and I could almost hear the theme of Psycho playing when he did emerge from the basement. I could understand why Maeve preferred me being at home with her.

I realized that I was starving, and so was Maeve, of course—she was always hungry. I made grilled cheeses with tomatoes served with root beer. We kicked back on the couch in front of the fan with the TV tray and devoured our lunch. We both fell asleep watching *Tom and Jerry*. Maeve and I always took really good naps together. Today's nap lasted three hours.

I woke up to my mom slamming things around in her room. She'd just gotten home from work. I assume she was frustrated that Maeve had just taken a nap, because now she'd be up all night. I realized it was seven fifteen. I ran upstairs to shower. I quickly twisted my wet hair into a ponytail. I brushed my teeth, slapped on some Lip Smackers and blush, and ran downstairs.

"There's a boy at the door?" my mom told me and questioned me at the same time.

"Sorry, Mom, I didn't mean to fall asleep. I was going to tell you that I got asked out today." I proceeded to quickly catch my mom up to speed about the day's events. She looked skeptical and probably didn't want me to leave because Maeve would expect entertainment tonight while she was up late.

I shushed my mom and sister and opened the door. There was Gerry, who had a confused look on his face. Then he smiled at me. "Sorry, I thought I had the wrong house for a minute there," he said. He introduced himself to my mom and sister. Maeve was suddenly speechless and standing behind my mom, shy as can be. My mom appeared too tired to care.

"Mom, this is Gerry McGrath. Gerry, this is my mom, Mrs. O'Brien," I said, unsure of how I was supposed to do this. This was my first real semidate. I'd kissed a couple of boys playing spin the bottle at Joy's house, but that was about the extent of my love life.

"Be home at ten thirty, OK?" my mom said.

"OK, Mrs. O'Brien. Thank you, and nice to meet you," Gerry said politely. He gave a little wave to my sister, still hiding behind my mom. She was smiling and peeking from behind her.

"Hey," I said. Damn, I was nervous.

"Hey. I thought you were blowing me off today. I came by at seven, but no one answered the door."

"Sorry about that—Maeve and I fell asleep. She's my nap buddy. We slept like three hours; my mom is annoyed because Maeve won't fall asleep tonight until late again." I suddenly felt guilty for my mom.

"Would Maeve want to come with us? I was thinking we could just hang out at my grandma's. She has a lot of pets—two cats and a dog." As soon as Gerry finished saying this, the door opened, and Maeve said, "I'd love to!"

"Great. You have to wear shoes, Maeve," I said flatly. Damn the screen doors and no AC—you can hear everything. My mom waved gratefully at us; Maeve was awesome but she could be exhausting, especially when you were tired already. Maeve looked annoyed but went to put her shoes on. Interesting how quickly the shyness wore off; she loved animals of any kind. I was ambivalent about Maeve coming with, feeling a mixture of disappointment and relief. She might take some of the pressure off the conversation, but I wanted to talk with Gerry alone, too.

Maeve skipped back to us and held my hand, which surprised me. She's not a real touchy-feely kid. I was feeling nervous and excited, and Maeve appeared to mirror my mood. Gerry smiled and asked Maeve if he could hold her other hand, and he and I could swing her. We did this about fifteen times down the block to his grandmother's house.

The fireflies were starting to come out when we got to Gerry's grandmother's house, along with the mosquitoes. A tiny woman wearing a blue cotton dress was sitting on the porch, reading the paper with a small magnifying glass.

"Gerry, what do we have here? Introduce me to your lady friend!" Gerry's grandmother held her hand out to Maeve, who giggled. "Look at that head of hair this girl has—just gorgeous." She was a cute, frail woman, with the same inviting hazel eyes as Gerry, and they still had a sparkle. Her gray hair was in a loose bun, and I could tell she must have been a very beautiful woman in her time. Her face was still very attractive, with smooth skin. Her face appeared much younger than her body.

His grandmother turned to me and said, "You must be Mary Kate." She winked at me and held out her hand. I laughed and shook her hand, and I told her my real last name. "Please call me Ava," his grandmother said warmly. "Come in and meet the family." She introduced us to the animals, and Maeve was instantly occupied. I was grateful for this. I was also excited that Gerry had told his grandmother about me, and she apparently approved of my joke.

Gerry showed me around and pointed out different people in his family in the photographs throughout the house. I saw a photo of Ava and her husband at their wedding. She looked like a movie star, wearing a beautiful form-fitting satin wedding gown: perfect figure, skin flawless, gorgeous smile. Gerry resembled Ava more than his grandfather, who was also attractive in a less obvious way: tall, dark, and handsome, with a larger distinguished nose. I could almost imagine him shaking his head and saying, "Ah cha cha cha cha."

"That's my Buzz," Ava said.

"Buzz?" I asked. I was intrigued.

"We call him Buzz because of his big schnoz. He always makes me laugh," Ava said, beaming.

I looked at that picture of Buzz and Ava, and a wave of sadness came over me as I wondered if Ava was a widow. I hesitated to ask Gerry this, though, because part of me didn't want to know. Gerry must have sensed what I was thinking. I have zero poker face; everyone knows what I'm thinking or feeling at any given moment.

"Buzz is OK; he's been at an assisted-living facility because he had hip surgery. That's why I'm staying here for the summer. I'm helping my grandma out until he comes home, and I'll help the both of them when he does come home. She can't really care for him, and he obviously can't care for her right now. My grandmother is resistant to this; she's having a hard time," Gerry said sadly. His eyes glassed over, and he looked down.

"Having a hard time?" I asked. I wanted him to continue. I knew what he meant, but I wanted details.

"Well, they've taken care of each other for fifty-five years, ya know? It's hard for them to be apart; it's hard for them to understand aging. My grandma is in the beginning stages of Alzheimer's, and sometimes she thinks she's much younger and that Buzz left her.

Sometimes she thinks she can just get in the car and go, but the state wouldn't renew her driver's license—stuff like that. Every morning I have to remind her. Sometimes she talks to me like I'm Buzz." Gerry said this so solemnly that I had this urge to reach out and hug him. This surprised me, because I had just met this guy today.

"I'm sorry. This must be really hard for them, but for you, too. I can't imagine doing this. I mean, you're just a kid—well, not a kid, but just a teenager. This seems pretty intense. This just seems so grown-up for you to be doing this. I admire your selflessness," I said in spite of myself. He looked at me earnestly, as if he was hanging on my every word.

"Yeah, you look like you're having a blast, Mary Kate," Gerry said sarcastically. "You're working your ass off every day. I could say the same thing about you. Every morning I see you walking to work at the butt crack of dawn. You bust your ass all day at work. You're working like you have a mortgage." Gerry looked confused, but I could see a hint of approbation in his eyes.

"Thanks, I think," I said, not sure where he was going with this.

"I'm sorry, Mary Kate. I meant it as a compliment. I suppose you're right about what you're saying to me about caring for my grandparents. It doesn't seem fair that someone our age should be working as hard as you do. I don't really feel sorry for myself about my situation, since it's my grandparents—they mean the world to me. Someone has to step up to the plate; it may as well be me." Gerry said this with so much intensity that I felt goose bumps on my arms. "My parents both work, my sister's in college, and I'm not doing much with my summer except caddying, so why not? They're not going to be around forever."

I smiled at him in awe, and he reciprocated with a similar expression. I had a sudden connection to him—a connection I hadn't really felt with anyone, except maybe with Joy. Most of the kids my age didn't seem to be troubled with any kind of real issues that I knew about. Most people I met seemed to be making a living of having fun. It seemed like with all the friends I'd made, their parents were still married and still together, going on family vacations, and they seemed like normal families. They spent a lot of time shopping, hanging out, playing sports, seeing movies, going out to lunch—all these things seemed like a luxury to me, especially when their parents paid for these things. I tried not to judge or be jealous, though. My mom told me not to compare and that you never know what someone else's life is like until you walk in that person's shoes.

Because of my mother's wise words, I seemed to just accept my life for now; it is what it is. I knew deep down there was more for me. I noticed when I did compare my life to others, I became depressed and unmotivated. I didn't want to get out of bed. What good did that do? So I just did what I had to do: I kept going.

"Come on, let's go outside," Gerry said with a smile. I peeked around the corner and saw Maeve petting the dogs, with the cat on her lap. I followed him to Ava's backyard. I felt like I was walking onto the set of *Fantasy Island.* Tons of different exotic flowers were all around the yard, and white lights were wrapped around birch trees. A garden of different fruits and vegetables in the corner of the yard caught my eye; I'd been meaning to do this for my mom to maybe save on our groceries. A sense of serenity and tranquility came over me in that yard.

"It's peaceful back here, isn't it?" Gerry said appreciatively.

I nodded in agreement. We headed over to a screened-in patio with a swing hanging from an overhead balcony on the second floor. Buzz and Ava's place was a really beautiful and heartwarming abode. It truly gave off the feeling of home more than anywhere I'd ever been, outside my own residence. I could sense the love everywhere, which sounded foolish to me, considering I'd just arrived there. It was almost as if you could feel the affection radiating from this atmosphere and the life Buzz and Ava had made for themselves—a similar sentiment I'd had before my home became broken. This effect was stronger, probably due to the length of Gerry's grandparents' marriage and the length of their commitment to each other.

Gerry was looking at records on a table in the corner. I stopped abruptly. I hadn't seen another person my age holding a record in my life.

"What?" Gerry looked at me.

"I've never seen someone our age holding a record!"

Gerry gazed at me, his expression difficult to read. He was grinning and slightly shaking his head. His eyes were shining. "Well, this is my grandparents' house, so of course they have records. They don't know any other way—they're old school. They're set in their ways. My grandma says she's too old to figure anything new out," Gerry said fondly.

"I think that's cool. I have a record player with a tape player attached. I tape records. I'm sure that's very weird. It's normal to me."

"I think you're cool," Gerry said with a flicker in his eye. "I know we just officially met today, but I've seen you a lot of times. I see how you interact with people. You remind me of my grandmother. Everyone lights up around her, just like they do around you."

His words stirred something inside of me that I hadn't been aware of in a long time. I couldn't quite place what this sensation was, but it was comforting. When he was discussing his grandparents, it left a strong surge of empathy for him within me, I assume because I felt the same emotions about my grandparents. I had a tremendous amount of respect for both sets of my grandparents, and I admired them immeasurably. My eyes slightly welled up with tears as I thought about the inevitable mortality of my grandparents and how I'd someday be in Gerry's shoes; I'd most definitely be spending my summers with them as well. I hadn't cried in the longest time—in fact, such an extended time that I couldn't remember. I'd subconsciously built an invisible and impenetrable wall around me that protected me from feeling, period. I found my reaction odd and surreal.

"Thanks," I said, genuinely and completely touched. I shuddered at my susceptibility becoming exposed like a raw cut.

"No, thank *you*," Gerry said. "This is the first time I've come across 'normal' in a long time. I usually accept that I don't belong anywhere. Although in this moment, I belong right here, right now, hanging out with you. I know I just met you officially, but I drive past you each morning. I often get consumed with this overwhelming urge to pull over and escort you to wherever you're going. Watching you walk to work at six in the morning ignited a fire inside me to be chivalrous and gallant, like in the books we read as kids."

His words were so unexpected that they penetrated my heart before I had to chance to protect myself from…feeling. The vulnerability was still lingering from thinking about my grandparents; I didn't have a chance to reactivate the wall I had around me. His words were hanging over me like a cartoon bubble replaying in my mind. His words made me feel good—empowered.

I moved to the swing and allowed myself to go with it, to be in the present and enjoy it. I allowed myself to *feel* and to let someone in. It had been so long since I'd let my guard down. It was truly exhausting to function behind invisible bars, forcing myself to stay numb. I became aware of the enlightenment instead of bars surrounding me right then. It was liberating to have my wall disengaged. I closed my eyes and moved the swing back and forth as I thought of nothing except being in this moment. Gerry settled on a record and put it on the player, and I heard the crackling of the record.

Patsy Cline began crooning "She's Got You," and the nostalgia washed over me as I remembered my grandfather. I loved him so. He was the only man I trusted, and this was his favorite music. He was the only man who was ever honest with me, which I respected. He called me out if I was lying: "Quit yer fibbin'," he would say. My dad couldn't handle his honesty, and my grandfather couldn't tolerate my dad's bullshit. That's what made me have the utmost respect for him. The irony was that this was the first male I'd let my guard down around since my grandfather, and this guy just played his favorite music.

"I love Patsy Cline. How did you know?"

"I took a wild guess," Gerry said with a smile. His alluring hazel eyes lit up, and his thin lips turned up in a satisfied smile. He reminded me of my grandfather, too—there was realness about him. I wanted to say this but was hesitant. Without my wall up, it seemed like he could see right through me. He sat down next to me on the swing, and we rested there for a long time without saying anything. We just listened to the music. I was cognizant of the alertness inside me; I was alive with presence in the moment. I felt clearheaded. This was a rarity for me. I was alive. I had grown accustomed to a confounded state of detached being; it was my norm. Patsy crooned,

> I've got the records
> that we used to share,
> and they still sound the same
> as when you were here.
>
> The only thing different,
> The only thing new.
> I've got the records,
> she's got you.

I got the chills on my arms as I listened to her voice resonate outside in that beautiful yard. Gerry got up and decided on his next choice: Johnny Cash.

When "Ring of Fire" came on, I was just astounded. "No fucking way! You did not just put on Johnny Cash!" My grandfather and his brother both resembled Johnny Cash. I was already feeling nostalgic about my grandpa, and this just completely solidified it. I could no longer hold back. I began to speak; words poured out of me as if my floodgates had been opened. This guy somehow reached me. He smiled at me with a fulfilled expression, like he'd just guessed the right answer to a tricky question at school. Something inside me clicked, as if two wires that had been cut were now fused together. The detached sensation I usually had was now nonexistent, and I was connected. I was on!

"You have a genuineness about you that makes me feel very comfortable," I said. "You remind me of my grandfather, who's the most unadulterated and honest person I've ever met. Thank you for inviting me over." When I said this, I meant it with all my heart. I didn't want the night to end. I was afraid I'd wake up the next day and my wall would reengage itself, leaving me exhausted again, chained to the walls of my defenses.

He abruptly went inside the house and reemerged with two glasses of white wine. I was shocked: we were underage! Drinking at someone's house?

Gerry must've read my expression. "I told you, my grandmother thinks I'm Buzz sometimes. She won't know. My parents and our family have always allowed us to drink with dinner and stuff like that. It's no big deal. Hope you don't think I'm a pansy for drinking wine." He smiled.

"Maybe a little," I replied sarcastically. I nudged his arm to let him know I was teasing. The wine was sweet and sparkling. I loved it. I could have drunk it all in one long sip, but I attempted to control myself.

We rocked on the swing for a while and made small talk about the mundane daily details of our lives. These are the things that we should know about each other but aren't that fun to talk about usually—but it was with him, over wine!

He switched the music back to Patsy Cline, and "Walkin' after Midnight" began to play. He grinned at me and then held out his hand, and I took it. He pulled me up to my feet.

"Dance with me." He said this so seriously that I almost started laughing. I had no idea how to dance. I'd never danced with anyone except my baby sister. I was clueless. My mind searched for a movie that I could relate to. Adults would dance frequently in old movies. All I could think of right now was *It's a Wonderful Life*, when they're doing the Charleston and then fall into the pool. I let him lead. I was trembling yet giddy from the wine and his endearing company. I was only eighteen, and I was a lightweight.

Gerry wasn't much taller than me; he took my other hand and put them both around his neck. He put his hands on my waist. I was suddenly shy, looking at his chest and not wanting to look up at him. He took his forefinger and lifted my chin up to meet his gaze. His eyes were definitely more intense up close, and he smiled at me, showing

48

his dimples. My heart skipped a beat. My hands were still interlocked behind his neck. His hands traveled from my waist to my sides, my shoulders, and then to the sides of my face. He leaned in and kissed me lightly, leaving me wanting more. He opened his eyes, stared at me warmly, and smiled.

Of course, my mind was now wild with thoughts; the end of *Pretty in Pink* emerged, when Andie kisses Blaine passionately. I looked at him, smiled back, and pulled his face to mine. We kissed for a long time, with our lips exploring each other's mouths. My eyes closed, and attraction stirred inside me like it had been hidden under a rock somewhere and had now escaped. His tongue entered my mouth, and the intensity of our kiss began to evolve. My breathing increased with a jumping butterfly-in-the-stomach feeling. We were full-blown making out.

In my brain, I knew we needed to stop. My sister was inside the house; we were in his grandparents' backyard. Yet my soul knew that we were the only people in the world right now. I suddenly had this urge to do things to him and the desire to have him do things to me. In the past with the guys I had kissed, I was either grossed out or was going through the motions out of curiosity but was numb to any emotion. Since Molly Ringwald was already in my head, the scene quickly transitioned to the movie *For Keeps*, where she gets knocked up. Hence, the responsible side of me kicked in, and I knew I had to stop this. I removed my hands from his neck and pulled my mouth from his and looked down. He followed my lead and put his head down on my shoulder. Both of us panted heavily, trying to catch our breath.

"Wow. You're something else," Gerry said, looking at me with an impressed grin.

"Uh, yeah, you are, too," I replied, completely shocked at what had happened. "I better go get Maeve—she needs to get home."

Gerry held my hand and pulled me into the house. We walked down the hallway of pictures, and I stopped for a second to glance at the picture of Ava and Buzz.

"When will Buzz be home?" I whispered.

"In a few weeks, I hope," Gerry whispered back.

Maeve was still awake, of course, and watching TV. The cat was on her lap, and the dog was sleeping next to her. Ava sat in the recliner, walker in front of her, arms crossed and head down, asleep. My neck hurt looking at her. My grandmother did the same thing; I couldn't understand it. I've never been tired enough to fall asleep on my chest. Maeve smiled at us, and Gerry let go of my hand.

"Are we going now?" Maeve asked.

"Yeah, it's getting late," I told her.

"But I'm not tired yet," Maeve said with a frown.

"Of course you're not, but we need to go." I knew I sounded like my mother.

"Why?" Maeve asked. I was now getting irritated and could understand why my mother sounded so annoyed with her at times. Maeve must have sensed my irritation with her—I was very rarely irritated with her—because she stood up and grabbed my hand. We said thank-you to Gerry, and Ava still didn't budge. Gerry held out his hand to shake Maeve's hand; she giggled and shook his hand back. His expression changed from playful to serious when he looked at me. He gave me a kiss on the cheek, eyes gleaming. I blushed.

Maeve and I walked down the block, and I asked her about the animals. She talked about the animals the whole way home and said that Ava seemed pretty entertained with her there. We went inside our house; Mom was asleep on the couch, as usual with the TV on. Maeve was actually yawning and seemed ready for bed. She changed into her pajamas—my old pajamas—and curled into a ball on her bed.

"Mary Kate?" she murmured. "Would you lie down with me and play our song?"

When Maeve was about four or five, our dad yelled at her, and she came to me crying. This kid had the ability to melt my heart, no matter what, so I gave her a hug. At the time, I'd been listening to a Cyndi Lauper tape, which was one of the first cassettes I ever bought. I played "True Colors" and held my baby sister, her legs wrapped around my waist, her arms around my neck. I rocked back and forth, singing that song to her. I didn't want my parents fucking her up like they did me. I tried to encourage her to love herself. My parents didn't teach me that; it didn't seem like loving yourself was important in their generation. My mom was always positive, but I doubt she realized the message she was sending to her kids. Allowing my dad to walk all over her and not being assertive with him was teaching her daughters to be doormats in relationships. Her passiveness was also teaching her son that this was how you treat women. I have no idea how I was aware of this at my age; I believe it was partly innate, because I was strong-willed, and probably from watching so many movies where people learn what's the right thing to do. A quote from *Some Kind of Wonderful* stuck with me: "I'd rather be with someone for the wrong reasons than alone for the right. I'd rather be right." So I sang to my baby sister hoping she would learn to love herself,

> And I see your true colors
> shining through,
> I see your true colors,
> and that's why I love you.
>
> So don't be afraid to let them show.
> Your true colors are beautiful,
> like a rainbow.

My baby sister preferred not to be coddled, yet she allowed me to hug her and rock her; she even said, "Again, Mary Kate, again." Whenever she was sad, despite how tough Maeve was, she would frequently ask me to sing this song to her. I'd sing to her for a while, and once she was asleep, I'd go downstairs to have a much-needed cigarette.

Back in the present, I was sitting on my porch smoking and thinking about the day. I was hoping Joy would come out, but I didn't have the energy to throw sticks at her window. I was growing tired and stubbed out my cigarette and flicked it under my neighbor's tree when Gerry appeared out of nowhere.

"Hey," he said, smiling.

"Hey, stalker," I said, smiling back.

"Whatever—I'm not a stalker. I don't have your phone number, silly. I'd like to have your number so I don't have to be a stalker." He smirked. "I have a pen; just write it on my arm."

I laughed and wrote my number on his hand. He looked at it, and a wide grin appeared on his adorable face. "Thanks. I wanted to call you, but then I realized I didn't have your number. I was going to pull a Romeo and Juliet and throw rocks at your window, but of course I don't know which room is yours. I didn't want to wake your parents up."

"Yeah, good idea—my mom would have been pissed. What did you want to talk to me about?"

"I just wanted to tell you that I had a great time with you tonight. I felt really comfortable tonight; it's been kind of lonely staying with my grandma. She sleeps a lot."

"I had a lot of fun, too," I said. "Thanks for asking me to come over, walking me home today—everything."

"What are you doing tomorrow?" he asked, grabbing my hand.

"I'm actually off tomorrow. No big plans," I said hopefully, turning to face him.

"Wanna do something? I won't go caddy tomorrow."

"You can just do that? Just not go?"

"Yes—plus it's supposed to rain. So even if I did go, it may be rained out, and not many golfers will be there. Since it's going to rain, want to go to a movie or something?"

"Sure." My heart skipped a beat. He kissed me lightly on the lips again but didn't pull away. I closed my eyes and let him continue to kiss me. Inside I was like a fire, and with each kiss, I was quenched as if he was the oxygen causing me to grow. He stopped.

"Awesome," Gerry said. "I'll borrow my grandma's car. I better go. I'll call you tomorrow, like tenish?"

"Sure, a day date. Cool," I said teasingly. I went in the house, ran to my room, and dove into my bed face-first into the pillow. I was excited about tomorrow; I had no idea how I was going to fall asleep. I thought about the day's events, and it seemed like a lot had happened since the morning. When I'd left for work that day, I didn't have a clue what would be in store for me. Eventually I fell asleep with a smile on my face, which was the first in quite a long time.

I slept like a rock and awoke to butterflies in my stomach like Christmas morning. I quickly made breakfast, but I wasn't hungry at all. I tried my best to eat and told my mom what I'd be doing. She made a little squeal and teased me and told me to be careful. I showered and blow-dried my hair. I rarely do this, as a rule, but now I suddenly cared about how I looked. I settled on a white cotton skirt and pale-pink scoop-neck T-shirt and white Keds. I curled my eyelashes and put one swoop of mascara on each eye; it always ended up running if I did more. A bit of pink-tinted bubble gum Lip Smacker, and I was ready.

Gerry called at exactly 9:59 a.m. I'm sure he could sense I was totally beaming. I detected his eagerness through the telephone wires.

"So, can I come pick you up soon?" he asked with urgency in his voice.

"I'm ready when you are," I said, trying to act casual. I kissed my mom and Maeve good-bye and went and waited on the porch.

He pulled up in a humongous powder-blue Cadillac that was about as long as my house, with white leather hood and white-rimmed tires. My jaw dropped open, and I laughed with surprise. He got out of the car, walked around to the passenger side, and opened the door. He gestured for me to get in, and I walked to the car with a giggle and got inside. He closed the door, and it was so heavy that it didn't close all the way. He opened it again and had to slam it shut. I giggled again. The car smelled like evergreen trees. The seats were white leather and were surprisingly cold. Gerry got in the car and also slammed his door. He smiled at me and gave me a kiss on the cheek. Then he took my hand, raised it to his mouth, and kissed the top of my hand.

"What would you like to do today, milady?" he asked with a smirk.

"I thought we were going to the cinema?" I said, playing along.

"We are, milady. What cinema would you like to see?" he asked again, playfully.

"I really wanted to see *Goodfellas*," I blurted out without even thinking. This was the most assertive statement I had ever made in my life; I usually waited to consider what other people wanted to do before I made a decision. He smiled wide in response. I was pumped. I lifted my arms up in triumph and then rested them to touch the roof of the car; then I moved my hands to the back of my seat. As I did this, I caught him looking at me—well, not my face this time. He was looking at my sides and I'm assuming checking out the rack. When I glanced at him, he had a devilish grin on his face as if he was undressing me with his eyes. A surge of excitement streamed through my body. I was giddy again, intoxicated with infatuation.

"What?" I said, pretending to be clueless. He shook his head and started the car.

"Sweet Jesus," he murmured as he turned over the American-made engine.

When we arrived at the movies, he insisted on paying for us both. It was a nice gesture, but I felt awkward about it. I was unsure what to do and searched my brain for something to guide me. He interrupted my thoughts.

"There's no way in hell I'm letting a girl pay for me," he stubbornly said. "I wasn't brought up that way, and my mother would probably beat my ass if she found out."

"All righty then," I sheepishly replied. I didn't have money to be wasting on frivolous things like movies and things of that sort; my mom had some kind of sewage problem on the side of our house that was going to cost her a shitload, so I needed to help.

He grabbed my hand and pulled me to the concession stand, and we got popcorn, pop, and Sno-Caps, which he also paid for. *If you can't beat 'em, join 'em*, I thought. He was holding the Sno-Caps in his teeth and the popcorn and pop in a drink caddy he held with two hands. He stuck his left elbow out and was moving it up and down, motioning to me. I took the Sno-Caps out of his mouth. "Need some help there?" I asked jokingly.

"Well, yeah, but no, I wanted you to put your arm inside mine, silly," he said shyly.

"Oh," I said, my face sizzling.

I interlocked my right arm into his left, and he guided me to the theater. We sat in the back, of course, and we were early. I was fired up. I loved the movies. Joy would say to me frequently, "I love that you love movies," and I didn't know what she meant until right now. My enthusiasm was contagious, I'm assuming because Gerry seemed fired up, too. We turned to each other; he grinned widely, which I reciprocated.

"You have no idea how awesome this is," he whispered to me. I busted open the Sno-Caps. "Popcorn and Sno-Caps are delicious together, did you know that?"

"No," I said. "I wasn't aware. I usually sneak some kind of random snack I find at home whenever I go to the movies, which I don't do very often."

"What kind of snacks?" he asked, appearing to be genuinely interested.

"Gummy bears. They get real warm and soft when they've been in my pocket," I quoted.

"Rooney eats it." He quoted back *Ferris Bueller* to me, and euphoria kicked in. It was so great to be with someone I didn't feel like a complete freak with because of my weird memory for movies. It was obviously a quality that others could possess. I almost replied "I love you" to him, I was so elated. Which would have been nightmarish;

I meant it in a way that I'd say to Joy, like, "I love hanging out with you." But this wouldn't be good on my first real official date with him. I decided to offer the Lord a moment of silence in thanks for my engage-brain-before-engaging-mouth moment, which does not occur frequently for me.

We gobbled the popcorn and Sno-Caps; the combo was delicious, I must admit. Before we realized it, we had almost completely polished off all the snacks even before the previews were over. I now had to pee from slamming my pop. Pop was a rare commodity in my household. It was like heroin. Once we all got a taste of it, it was like we couldn't stop. We would tap our veins to signal to our mom that we needed more pop, like a heroin fix. I was now high on pop, sugar, and infatuation. I decided to make a break for it and run to the bathroom before the movie started.

When I stood up, about fifteen pieces of popcorn flew off my chest. I must have been eating like a savage. They always say to "be yourself" on dates, but I'm not sure scarfing down food like a homeless heroin addict would be the best way to win someone over.

I ran to the bathroom, peed really fast, washed my hands, wiped them on my skirt, and ran back to the seat in about one point five minutes. He glanced up when he saw me walking down the aisle.

"Damn, girl! That was fast."

I was glad my lightning-speed urinating skills impressed him. "Maybe if you go now, you might make it," I said in a competitive tone.

"Man, I should have timed you!" he said regretfully.

"It's not a contest. Just go so you won't miss anything."

"All right. Dammit," he said under his breath. He hopped down the wide stairs in the dark to the exit.

Unfortunately for him, the movie started. He took much longer than I did. Maybe he chose not to run, but it was his loss. My mind flashed to the movie *Lucas*, where Charlie Sheen and his girlfriend are making out in the movies. I remember thinking "what a waste" to make out and miss a movie. Now I was starting to get it, but there was no way in hell I was missing any of this movie—we had plenty of time to make out.

He strolled in with a disappointed look on his face. He looked so flippin' cute in his baseball hat that I started to reconsider my previous statement. "You didn't miss anything," I said.

"Yeah, OK, racehorse," he said.

The movie kicked ass, of course, just as I knew it would. Gerry and I began attempting to quote parts of the film, but of course we couldn't get them perfect. This art comes with practice and repetition of watching movies over and over. My engage-brain-before-engaging-mouth protection was now gone, and shit was spewing out of my mouth, shooting from the hip with improvisation. My best Brooklyn accent was butchered, but I did my best to impersonate Lorraine Bracco: "Yeah, apartment 2B, Janice Rossi—she's a whore."

Gerry laughed hysterically and did his best to impersonate Joe Pesci in an equally bad Brooklyn accent: "What, am I here to amuse you? What am I, a fuckin' clown?" I was crying with silent laughter. I loved it.

I was all riled up with adrenaline from the movie and the company and still high from the heroin (a.k.a. pop fix). We went to eat at a restaurant that was trying to be like the fifties with a pull-in area for your car; they attach a tray to your car, and a waitress brings you the food on the tray. It was a cool concept; I was wondering if the waitress would have roller skates. I always felt like I was from the fifties anyway with the way I thought, dressed, and ate. I was a big fan of chocolate malts and root beer floats. I loved *Grease*. Of course I watched *Grease* probably a hundred times as a kid, so I knew exactly what to do in a place like this. I ordered a burger, a root beer float, and an Eskimo Pie with a knife, assuming he wouldn't get the reference. The waitress scowled at me.

The waitress quickly came back with our order. She had red matte lips, drawn-in black eyebrows, a fake beauty mark, and matted dishwater-blond hair with a pink-and-blue nurse-style restaurant hat. She was the epitome of what you would imagine in a 1950s waitress. We fit right in, too, with his grandparents' old powder-blue Cadillac. I was starving, of course, despite making a pig of myself at the movies. I should have just gotten a strap and wrapped it around my head and attached it to the popcorn like a horse's feed bucket.

Gerry handed me the root beer float and said, "Here you go, Sandra Dee."

What? He did not just get my *Grease* reference. Of course I had to say something. "I'm just clarifying that you understood my *Grease* reference?"

"Of course I did. A hickey from Kenickie is like a Hallmark card—when you care enough to send the very best." He growled and bit my neck, just as Kenickie did to Rizzo. I giggled, and his breathing on my neck sent chills down my spine. "I have a sister, silly. Of course I know *Grease*," he said proudly. He just went up about five notches in my book.

"Damn. I'm impressed," I said. His face blushed, and his eyes sparkled. He grabbed the rest of our order and handed me my burger. I sipped my root beer float, allowing it to penetrate my veins like a heroin addict would—not that I'd know; I probably saw heroin used in a movie once.

"I was..." he began to say but then hesitated. His cheeks flushed.

"What?" I slurred without taking the straw out of my mouth.

"Nothing...it's nothing," he said. He looked embarrassed.

Now I had to know, of course. I cannot play it cool. "Come on, you can't do that! I won't tell any of your friends you like *Grease*. What could be more embarrassing?" He glanced over at me with a shocked expression on his face. *Aw shit. What did I say? Nuts.*

"My friends all know already. I was Danny Zuko in the play as a kid," he said, trying to look proud by raising his head up, nose in the air.

I didn't buy it. "No fucking way. You were not in a play!"

"Yeah, I love musicals. What can I say? I'm a total cheeseball," he said sheepishly.

It was a good thing I'd finished my heroin root beer float, because I set my Styrofoam burger box on the dashboard and felt a sudden impulse to jump his bones. The front seat was so spacious and all one seat: no console or middle divider. If the driver adjusted his seat, the whole bench-like seat went at once. I slid next him and then abruptly got onto my knees. I took my right leg and straddled him. He appeared startled and dropped his burger onto the seat in his container. I leaned back on the steering wheel, smiled wickedly at him, and ripped off his baseball hat and threw it in the back seat. His eyes traveled all over my body, and I could feel his desire for me radiating. I grabbed the sides of his face and kissed him hard. I could feel his mouth turned upward in a smile as I was kissing him, and he moved his fingers into the sides of ears and into my hair. Chills shot down my spine again as the sensitivity I always felt when someone played with my hair kicked in—although I'd never had someone play with my hair accompanied with stimulating kisses.

It was still light outside, and as a car pulled up next to us, the interruption triggered shame within me. I was embarrassed at my public display of affection, or I should say "sluttishness." We both opened our eyes, and he rested his forehead onto mine. We both smiled nervously. I sheepishly de-straddled myself and sat on the backs of my legs next to him; then I casually slid over, my feet still next to his legs and my legs straightened out, with my back against the passenger door. I crossed my legs, reached for my burger and my Styrofoam cup, and took a big annoying slurp to get the melted ice and last remnants of root beer. He was sweaty, and his eyes flickered, and he looked at me with a completely vulnerable look of shock, excitement, and head-shaking. He slapped his hand on my calf; I jumped, since I was on edge from the rush of emotions racing through me.

"Girl, you're something else," he said, and he lay his head back onto the car seat. He turned around and lifted himself up toward the back seat to get his hat. His shirt went up as he did this, exposing his boxers above his shorts and his cut abs. I blushed and turned away.

He sat back down with a look of complete satisfaction and took both hands to his hat, one on the brim and one on the back. He adjusted his hat repeatedly on his head for a second or two. I caught myself staring at him as he turned to look at me; I quickly moved my eyes to the car next to us. He followed my gaze.

"Who cares, baby?" he said sweetly and rubbed my calf. I hate that word "calf." Even looking at the word, I think of a cow. "I don't care what they think or what anyone thinks, for that matter," he said with a shrug.

"Of course you shouldn't!" I said, humiliated and shocked by my own behavior. "I'm the one who looks like a complete tramp. What choice would you have?"

His eyes darted at me. He looked angry. "Don't talk about yourself like that. I'd never think that of you. I was having a blast today, and that was the icing on the cake. It wasn't quite the reaction I expected when I told you I played Danny Zuko, but it was the best response I could imagine." He gave me a wink and a smile. He leaned over and poked my belly and laid his head on my legs for minute. I smiled at the affectionate gestures, and my shame subsided. We drove back to his grandparents' house. I wasn't sure what he had in mind, but I kind of hoped we were going to go out somewhere else; I was grateful at the same time to be out of the public eye. Not like anyone was look- ing at us, but what I'd done earlier was so unlike me. Either it was my heroin-pop addiction, or this guy was the real deal.

I was stunned how I'd reacted to my emotions in a way that was very impulsive for me. I hadn't been that in touch with my emotions in years and had never been in a situation like this. I always used to react to my father when he was on one of his tirades, and I took it upon myself to be the spokesperson for the family, since no one else had the balls. Everyone would sit there in a trance, frozen with vacant stares, but somehow I was immune and unable to fall under his spell. I often wished I could, but I remained alert and aware. My emotions were appropriate to the content. I'd confront my dad, because some- one had to. I paid for it dearly, though, and over time I conditioned myself to succumb to the tyranny. I was beaten down, and I forfeited, but I didn't give up. I temporarily surrendered when I realized it was a dictatorship and that I couldn't continue alone. It was a standoff, and then one day he left. We won.

Therefore, my current responses were usually distorted: I laughed when I was angry and cried when I was happy. I was (and still am) a total nut job. I sensed I should quit while I was ahead. I was sure I'd appear like a cocktease, but this was all new for me. For once in my life, I was being myself, reacting the way I wanted to without hesitation. It was liberating, yet petrifying. My gut was telling me to go home and take a cold shower. I assumed if things were to continue, it would be anticlimactic. *What the fuck is wrong with me?* I thought. I couldn't believe I'd just done that.

"Would you mind taking me home?" I asked quietly. He looked at me and sighed; he looked disappointed. I really wasn't that easy—I just made myself look like it. I'm sure I gave him the impression that he was totally getting laid that night. My sugar level was crashing, and my euphoria had worn off now, leaving me vulnerable, embarrassed, and tired. I needed to go home and regroup. I knew I needed to call it a night.

"I wish you would come over," he murmured.

"I bet you would," I said jokingly but sounding angry—which I wasn't—but that mood was lost.

"Come on," he said with his brow furrowed. He pulled up in front of my house.

"I'm sorry. I meant that as a joke. It didn't come out that way." I paused. "I had a blast today, I really did. Thank you so much." He smiled and looked down. He looked relieved.

"MK, you're the coolest girl I've ever met," he said genuinely. "I had a blast. Can we do it again soon?" His eyes sparkled. His smile was crooked and playful, and he had a hopeful look on his face. "Please go out with me again this week."

"Of course I will," I said, relieved as well. I gave him a kiss on the cheek and gathered up my strength to pull the lever and open the ginormous door. He lightly grabbed my wrist. I looked at him. He leaned over, looked down for a minute, and gave me a smoldering look that confused me, like he was impersonating someone. A nervous laugh arose in my throat.

"Give me a kiss," he said in a pleading voice. *Aw, shucks.* I leaned in and gave him a light kiss on the lips and hopped out of the car before he opened his eyes.

# 5

If you were watching a romantic comedy, especially one from the '80s, you would see the new couple doing all sorts of fun things together with a song playing to indicate how smoothly falling in love was going. A montage of moments with some cheesy song to show the progression of their romance: a couple walking along the beach holding hands, walking along the lake holding a balloon, playing miniature golf, having a water fight while washing a car...

Well, needless to say, this is how I'd describe the next few months with Gerry and me. We were together all the time, and we were having a blast. I turned into one of those girls I couldn't stand. My whole existence began to be consumed by him. I stopped calling my friends back. I spent all my free time either with him, thinking about him, or talking about him. At least the feeling was mutual. When his friends would say things like, "What did you do to this guy?" and "He's totally whipped," I'd act casual and shrug it off, but deep inside I was ecstatic to hear such things. We would talk on the phone for hours at night and spend our weekends together from morning until night.

One day, my long-lost little sister walked down to Gerry's grandparents' home looking for me. The guilt suddenly trumped the infatuation. She was visibly upset and wanted me to come home and put her to bed. What could I say? She was my baby sister. Seeing her like that was like someone waking you up from a daydream (even though it was real), and then bam! A slap of reality kicks in. I had a moment of clarity about what a jerk I was being to everyone else in my life. I cringed at the thought of facing Joy; I hadn't returned her calls for weeks. As for Maeve, I was surprised it hadn't happened sooner.

"What's wrong, Maeve?" I asked her.

"Please come home, MK I miss you," she said, and the guilt was on full blast.

"Sure," I said. I gave Gerry an apologetic look and took Maeve's hand and walked out the door. Maeve and I walked home in silence, which was scary, because this never happened unless something was wrong.

Once we got home, got into bed, and were snuggled up to each other, Maeve began to cry. "Oh, Mary Kate, Mairead's coming home," she said with a sob, referring to our oldest sister. I suddenly wanted to cry, too. I rubbed her hair, and finally she went to sleep. Unfortunately, I was *wide* awake. My mind drifted off to Joy and how shitty a friend I'd been. I looked at the clock. It was only nine fifteen; she would still be up. My hands shook as I picked up the phone to dial her number. I looked out the window and saw that their lights were on, but the phone just rang and rang. I didn't want to annoy her entire family, so I took a deep breath and went downstairs to go outside. At this moment I had a major urge for a cigarette. I was one of those social smoker types. Since I'd been with Gerry, I'd been high on emotions and hadn't needed any other kind of fix. Plus, he didn't like it.

I went back to my room to get my cigarettes out of my dresser drawer, along with my Zippo. Maeve was sleeping like an angel. It was pretty sad that the kid was petrified that her older sister was coming home. I couldn't think about that right now. I needed to talk to Joy. Just then the phone rang, and I jumped in response. I answered immediately to prevent waking Maeve.

"Hey," Joy said quietly.

"Hey," I replied, feeling like a dog that's just been scolded, with its tail between its legs. "Can you meet me out front? Want a smoke?" I asked Joy hopefully.

"Uh…sure," she said after a long pause.

"Cool. See ya in a minute," I said, nervous as hell. My mind raced as I thought what I was going to say to her. I walked outside to the perfect, crisp, early fall air. I took a deep breath. The fresh air soothed me; it was invigorating. She walked out of her house, hair on top of her head in a scrunchie, still looking beautiful while messy. Usually I waited for her on my porch, but I kept walking toward her. She kept walking toward me with a growing confused look on her face. My step sped up, and I wrapped my arms around her under the streetlight in the middle of the road. I hugged her hard. Tears welled in my eyes with shame and guilt. I loathed myself at that moment.

"What's this?" Joy asked. "What's wrong?"

I stepped back and looked at her. She looked at me with big eyes, looking puzzled.

"I'm an asshole," I said, looking down.

"Well, we already established that years ago," Joy said with a smile; she tapped my shoulder to let me know it was a joke.

"I hate myself right now. I've been a bad friend," I said.

"I get it, MK It's OK. I'm sure I did the same thing to you when I started dating Tommy," Joy said in an attempt to make me feel better. I vaguely remembered her being MIA for a while, but I worked a lot, so I didn't really notice. I still saw her for our evening smokes and talks.

"I don't really remember that."

"Well, I did. It happens. Life is going to happen; it will never come between us," Joy said, smiling.

"Wow. You're good. You should write fortunes or bumper stickers or something," I said, teasing her.

"Shut it."

"I don't know what's wrong with me. I feel like I was possessed," I said.

"Ah, that's what it feels like," Joy said. She took a cigarette from me and motioned for us to head into my backyard, because her parents were still awake. We both lit our smokes and sat on the back porch of my house. The house was falling apart. We had some sort of plumbing or sewage problem on the side of our house, and water continued to fill up along the basement windows. The siding was getting rusted and curling up on the end. The stairs on the back porch were creaky and loose.

"So that's what love feels like? Like I'm possessed?" I asked her.

"It is pretty powerful. I don't care, as long as you're happy, he's good to you, and he makes you laugh," she said as she took a long drag. "Just don't get knocked up." She smiled and blew the smoke from her nose. I was dizzy from not smoking for so long. It was good to hang out with her; it grounded me. I felt like I had control again. The last few weeks—months—had been a whirlwind. My head had been spinning most of the time.

"We haven't even done it yet. I'm not going to get knocked up, dumbass," I said, laughing back. "We've basically dry fucked—can't get pregnant from that. But the making out is getting out of control, and I have blue balls like nobody's business most of the time."

Joy giggled. "Wow, you're good," she said, clearly impressed. Now I could see why Joy had given it up to Tommy. I told her what had happened that night, how Maeve had come to Gerry's, asking me to come home.

"Why? What was she upset about?" Joy asked.

"Mairead's coming home," I said, taking a long nervous drag.

My oldest sister, Mairead, was away at college. She'd gotten herself a scholarship for volleyball. She'd been gone, like, forever. She didn't come home much, and I didn't blame her. I probably wouldn't either if it wasn't for Maeve. Mairead was two years older than me and thirteen years older than Maeve. They never really connected. Mairead said Maeve was a "pain in the ass" and "a little brat."

The summer before Mairead went to college, I came home to find Maeve hiding under the kitchen table with her hands in her mouth, petrified. She looked like Randy from *A Christmas Story*, hiding under the table from Black Bart.

"What's wrong, Maeve?" I asked her.

"It's…it's…Mairead—she's going to beat me," Maeve stammered. I choked back a laugh. She looked hilarious, and of course my brain was comparing this situation with Randy from *A Christmas Story*.

"You're silly, Maeve. She's not going to beat you," I said jokingly.

Mairead came into the kitchen; Maeve whined and hid behind me. Mairead looked pissed: her auburn hair disheveled, her forehead furrowed, and her green eyes wild. I'd always admired my big sister—she was usually kind to me—but we began to have issues whenever I stuck up for Maeve.

"What's going on?" I asked Mairead.

"It's none of your concern, MK She's going to get what's coming to her, and you have no say-so about it," she said furiously. She was a tough cookie, and you didn't want to get on her bad side.

"It is my concern, Mairead—she's our sister. Did you tell her you were going to *beat* her?"

"Yeah, I am. She needs a good ass whoopin'. I'm sick of her crap." She looked frustrated. Maeve grabbed onto me tighter.

"You're not her mom, Mairead; let her deal with it. You know as well as I do that beating her isn't going to do anything, and you're going to feel guilty," I said matter-of-factly.

Mairead looked annoyed; she was probably irritated because she knew I was right. This had happened before, and I'd caught Mairead crying in her room after she'd "taught Maeve a lesson." I'm sure Maeve had done something mischievous this time, too—she was a little rascal.

"Fine, whatever," Mairead said, and she stormed off. I heard a door slam upstairs, and Maeve clung to me like a baby monkey.

"Thank you, Mawie Kate," Maeve said; at the time, she couldn't pronounce her *r*'s yet. I hoped she never could. I loved how she said my name. I melted every time she said it.

"It's OK, you little rascal. What stunt did you pull this time?" I asked Maeve with a smirk on my face. I gave her a playful swat on the butt. She wrapped herself tighter around me and buried her head in my neck. I kept shrugging my shoulder so she would look at me. Maeve giggled.

"Um, I was just looking in her jewel box. When she came in, I wan away and then hid under da bed. She kept twying to get me. She went to get a bwoom to swat me, so I got out from unda the bed, and I've been hiding all ova the place. Until you came home to wescue me, Mawie Kate, thank you so much." Maeve gave me a hug. Her beautiful red hair was on my cheek, and I stroked her hair. I couldn't understand how Mairead could stay mad at this sweet girl; she was just a little kid. Our dad had left shortly after she was born, and I think Mairead somehow blamed Maeve for this. I'm sure Mairead knew it was ridiculous of her to be mad at a child, like it was really her fault. Mairead had to blame someone, so why not the baby who had "made her daddy go away"?

Finally, after Maeve was soothed, I put her in front of the television to watch cartoons. I went upstairs to confront Mairead. Her door was closed but not locked. I opened the door. Mairead was lying on her bed. I didn't want to get into it with her; I knew I had to be gentle. She was kind of touchy in those days. She'd been around the longest, so she'd seen the most between our parents; she'd also been close with our dad. She probably blamed Maeve so that she wouldn't blame herself.

"Mairead?" I said quietly.

"What?" she said, sounding annoyed.

"What's wrong?"

"That little shit keeps taking my stuff. I'm sick of it."

"You know what I mean," I said, both of us knowing this about Maeve and her curiosity. Mairead didn't say anything for a long time. She sighed and got up from the bed.

"I really don't want to talk about it, MK," Mairead said, appearing more calm now.

"You're my sister, too. I don't want us to fight. She's just a little kid, Mairead. It isn't her fault."

"What do you mean, it isn't her fault? She's going through my stuff—she knows better!" Mairead said, looking pissed again.

"I mean, it's not her fault that Dad left." After I uttered these words, Mairead reacted like I'd slapped her in the face, and she abruptly turned her head to the side. My words lingered in the air over us like a comic-book balloon. I couldn't take them back now; what I said was out there now. I couldn't stand the way our family had been separated; I wanted us to be close. He wanted us to be against one another. It seemed like he was always pitting us against one another by talking about the one who wasn't at home. Someone was always the scapegoat.

"Get out," Mairead said flatly. I knew she was furious because she always becomes very quiet and stone-faced. This was what I'd been afraid of. I didn't want to fight with her. However, it needed to be said; her alienation of Maeve had to stop. Maeve needed us, her big sisters, to teach her—to take the place of the absent parent.

"Please, Mairead. I di—"

"Get out!" Mairead screamed. Tears welled up in my eyes, and I turned around and left. I was going to leave, but I was afraid to leave Maeve with *her*. I was mad at Mairead, but at the same time, I knew why she was acting like this. It was *his* fault. He fucked us all up and then left us behind like we were a wrecked car in an accident. We were the mistakes he couldn't be around. It hurt too much. He had to know deep down that he was a shitty father, and instead of being a man and facing it, he left. He left my mom to take care of four kids. He did this to punish her for the mistakes he'd made. He blamed my mom for the mistakes he'd made, and he believed the only suitable punishment was to walk away. Walk away like a fucking coward.

As usual, my brain traveled to a movie for comic relief. I couldn't just stay mad or sad; my brain wouldn't allow me. It had a trained defense mechanism that kicked in and automatically began scanning the memories in my brain to help me cope. I began to hear Keanu

Reeves's voice in my head, from *Parenthood*: "You need a license to drive a car. Hell, you need a license to catch a fish. But they'll let any butt-reaming asshole be a father." I smiled. I couldn't help it. My hurt vanished like a cloud of smoke.

I got up from my bed and walked down the stairs to hang out with Maeve. Then I remembered another scene from *Parenthood*, after the little boy trashes his dad's dental office. His mom says, "Gary, you're a great kid. You're a great kid. You just have a shitty dad. I think we'd all be better off once we say 'the hell with him.'" I said this quietly to myself: "The hell with him." It felt good to say it. I wanted to scream, "The hell with him!" but that's not my style; I didn't want Maeve to ask what I was talking about. I wanted her to forget about my dad; she would be better off.

Since that day, Mairead had been distant from me, but I found some sort of closure with our dad's absence. It didn't hurt anymore. I didn't care. I knew it wasn't my fault—hell, I was just a kid. I wasn't a mistake, and I was going to make damn sure he knew that. I was going to take my anger and allow it to motivate me. Every step I took through life, through high school and beyond, I was going to show that piece of shit I was not a mistake he could just walk away from. He did me a favor. It gave me motivation, a drive inside me to prove him wrong. Maybe deep down, my dad knew we would all be better off without him—less damaged. Maybe he didn't want to do anything to mess Maeve up. Maybe that's why he left. All I knew was that I was glad he did.

According to my mom, Mairead was coming home for the summer. That's what she'd said last year, and then Mairead had "decided" to take a class up there and hadn't come home.

The same thing had happened at Christmas break. I was skeptical whether she would really come home or not, but then I heard a car door slam out in front, and I saw Mairead walking up the porch. My heart jumped. She looked beautiful. Her face had filled out a little; she'd looked a little gaunt when she'd left. Her peach skin looked radiant and healthy. Her green eyes sparkled, and her auburn hair looked shiny and full. I was so happy to see her that I almost jumped into her arms. I stopped myself. I didn't know how she felt about me. I didn't know where we stood in her mind. I decided on a subtle approach. I walked slowly up to her, smiling, and I gave her a big hug right when she walked in the door. I gave her a kiss on the cheek. Her eyes glossed over, she put her bag down, and she hugged me back. We embraced for a long time, and I was focusing on all the emotions I felt for her, hoping it would penetrate her wall and that she would trust me again. I missed her so much.

"Hey, little one," Mairead said to me with a smile.

"Hey, big one. I've missed you," I said back with a smile.

"I've missed you, too," Mairead said back, sounding sincere.

"You look good," I said genuinely. Mairead was going to respond, but something behind me caught her eye.

Maeve stood in the doorway of the family room, eating an apple and looking at us. I didn't know what Maeve even remembered about Mairead, since they hadn't seen each other in a long time. Maeve used to say "Maiwead" back when she couldn't say her Rs. She'd outgrown that since, I was sad to say.

"Hey, Mairead," Maeve said flatly. Mairead eyes changed; she'd looked surprised at first when she saw Maeve. Her eyes warmed, and she smiled. She walked over to Maeve, knelt down in front of her, and gave her a hug around her waist. Mairead's head was against Maeve's little belly. Maeve looked shocked and then glanced toward me. Tears welled up in my eyes, and I smiled. I walked over to the two of them and put my arms around them both, and we hugged and cried. Maeve looked happy, but I doubt she knew what was happening. All Maeve needed to know was that she was loved; and she was.

# 6

Surprisingly, Mairead began talking to me and asking me to do things with her. We didn't talk about what I had said yet there seemed to be an unspoken acknowledgement that Maeve needed us and we needed each other. Mairead and I hung out every day; we rode bikes on the trails, we went shopping, we watched movies, and we even brought Maeve with us most of the time. We didn't talk about anything that had happened. My sister was back, and I needed her. I had a million questions to ask her that I couldn't ask my mom. She told me about college life, and I told her about high school life. She told me about the guy she'd been dating. I told her about Gerry.

"So have you guys done it yet?" Mairead asked. I slapped her in the arm with a shocked look on my face, but deep down I was grateful she'd asked. I needed some guidance.

"No, not yet. It's getting close, though, and I'm scared."

"What have you done so far?" she asked casually.

"We've made out a lot—a lot of touching. I don't know what you mean, exactly," I said nervously.

"You know, like first base, second base, hand job, blow job, sixty-nine—stuff like that?" Mairead rattled this off like a grocery list. She was speaking a foreign language to me. I had no idea what she was talking about. I'd heard people saying things like that, but

I didn't know for sure what they meant. I'd asked Joy, and she didn't know, either. I'd asked another friend of mine, and she said, "I think it means like licking his fingers and blowing on it." I doubted this was true, but it wasn't like I could ask my mom for clarification.

Mairead explained each of these acts to me, and I'm sure my face was all over the place: confused, surprised, disgusted, grossed out, grimacing. None of it sounded good. When I told Mairead about what I felt when Gerry and I made out, some of the things she said started to seem possible.

"My boyfriend told me that his dream is for me to go down on him while he's sleeping," Mairead said. I wasn't down with the lingo just yet, so I had to ask her to explain again.

"Why would he want a blow job while he's sleeping? What's the point of that? He wouldn't even know what was going on," I asked, bewildered. Mairead burst out laughing and patted me on the head like I was some stupid little kid.

"He would obviously wake up, silly," Mairead said in a condescending tone that I didn't appreciate.

"Oh, I see," I said, still not completely getting it.

Mairead had me watch *Fast Times at Ridgemont High* that night for the tutorial on the blow jobs with the carrot. I think I understood after that. She kind of showed me herself and told me to put my hand at the base of his shaft and play with his balls, and she explained what guys liked. I felt a little more confident about what to do, but I was confused and unsure if I actually wanted to do any of these things. That night, Mairead was going to her boyfriend's house, and she packed both of us a little supply kit of condoms. She said she was going to take me to get on the pill next week. I laughed—we hadn't even done it yet. She told me not to take any chances. I listened, because this was what I needed to hear.

Gerry was sitting on his porch when I pulled up with Mairead. She got out of the car and walked up to the porch and introduced herself. Gerry smiled, clearly relieved to meet her finally. I had told him a few stories that I think made him intimidated by her. Mairead raised her eyebrows and gave me a wink and left. I guess that was her stamp of approval.

"Hey," Gerry said, putting his arms around my waist. "I couldn't wait for you to get here."

"Me too," I said, feeling the condoms in my purse, and I blushed.

"I have a surprise for you," Gerry said excitedly. He took my hand and pulled me inside. I saw some new medical equipment in the living room that hadn't been there before. I looked at Gerry, confused, until he came out of the bedroom. It was Buzz!

"Oh my goodness! Who is this beautiful creature standing before me?" Buzz said playfully to Gerry. Buzz was still handsome, with a nice, friendly face; his big nose still made me think he was going to say, "Ah, cha cha cha cha." I walked up to him and held out my hand to shake.

"Get outta here, I want a hug. I've heard all about you, Mary Kate Danaher!" Buzz said with a smile. I smiled back, feeling giddy that Gerry had told him about me.

"It was just a little joke. I was surprised that Gerry knew what I was talking about," I said.

"Knew it? We've watched that movie fifteen times here—every Saint Patrick's Day, of course. My daughter bought that for me when she bought us the VCR. I don't understand technology, but I sure do like it. How wonderful is it that you can own movies and watch them anytime you want in your own house? I don't know why anybody leaves their house anymore," Buzz said, full of life.

I was impressed. Since he'd been in a nursing home all this time, I thought he'd be frail and weak. He seemed healthy and strong. He stood steadily with a cane, wearing brown dress slacks with a belt and a white tank top.

Ava was in the kitchen, looking radiant. She looked much younger today, and I wondered if her frail state lately had been because Buzz hadn't been home with her. They looked happy. Ava was making homemade tomato sauce. She was standing at the counter, cutting up garlic, and Buzz was standing behind her with his arms around her waist and his head resting on her shoulder. They were giggling like they were kids. Watching them made me feel all warm and fuzzy inside. Gerry and I looked at each other and smiled. He grabbed my hand and pulled me downstairs to the basement. He closed the door behind him. He pulled my hand to the couch downstairs and picked me up and laid me down on the couch. He collapsed on top of me, kissed me, and groaned.

"You feel so good next to me," Gerry said sensually. "I've been thinking about you all day." I smiled, and we began to make out like crazy. His hands were feeling every part of me and running up and down my sides, my waist, my legs, my butt. His thumbs were moving toward my breasts each time he ran his hands down my side. I started to want him to touch them; I liked the way it felt with his hands on my breasts. I became more and more excited and began to have the urge to move my hips against his legs between mine. His hands slowly moved to my breasts outside my shirt, and I felt a twinge of pleasure between my legs. I started to wish he would rip my shirt off and put my breasts in his mouth. (*What?*) I was shocked at the erotic urges that were entering my mind. I had never felt these types of sensations or my body reacting the way it was. The familiar ache in my groin was there, and it had not yet been satisfied.

"What about your grandparents?" I asked.

"They both don't really come down here—they don't use the stairs. That's how my grandpa broke his hip," Gerry said, looking serious for moment. Then his expression changed into a wicked grin that made me want to growl at him. (*What?*) "Why do you ask, sexy girl?" he said in a different tone of voice that made wetness emerge in my underwear.

I thought about what my sister said: Gerry wasn't sleeping, but that would never happen. I was fresh from the lesson today, and I needed to get this done. Whatever was raging through my body was giving me confidence and motivation to "get off." We were intertwined together on the couch, hips moving, and we fell onto the floor, still wrapped in each other's bodies and kissing madly. He began to kiss my neck;

his hands were caressing my lower back and waist. Slowly he began to pull my shirt off. Gerry was on the floor on his back, and I took the opportunity to straddle him. His face looked intense, his eyes blazing over my body, his hands cupping my breasts. I looked down at the fly of his cargo shorts and unzipped them. A sound escaped his lips that sounded involuntary and shocked: "Oh!"

I wasn't expecting this to happen so quickly and for Gerry and me to be making out so heavily and engaging in such heavy petting five minutes after I'd arrived. I still had gum in my mouth that I'd pushed to the side of my mouth, between my gums and my cheek. I wanted to take it out, but I didn't know where to put it. I chose to not ruin the moment and pulled the elastic of his boxers down, and it popped out like a pup tent. Now I knew what my sister meant, because I actually *wanted* to do this. I leaned down and opened my mouth and was about to put the tip in my mouth when my tongue grazed the top of his penis and I heard a scream in a high-pitched voice: "MK!" I jerked up in reaction to his yelling, my mouth still open, completely bewildered and nervous that I'd done something wrong with my teeth or something like that. I saw it for the first time: sperm. Yes, his spunk, love juice, man milk, shooting all over like a sprinkler. I was mesmerized by it and couldn't turn away. Gerry's eyes were closed, and he was rolling side to side with a look of anguish on his face. He was moaning loudly, "Ah, oh!" I stared in amazement at the reactions that were happening to him: the jerking and shaking of his body, his facial expressions, and the ejaculation! Jeez. The whole thing turned me on, and I wanted to do it again.

"I'm sorry. Are you OK?" I asked, concerned. Gerry looked as if he was trying to suppress laughter.

"Hell yeah, I'm OK. I'm more than OK. That was amazing! You're going to give me a heart attack, Mary Kate!" I wanted to hump him. He was lying on the ground, wet spots all over his T-shirt and khaki shorts. He sat up, leaned on his elbows for a second, took one hand, and reached behind my neck. He pulled me to him and kissed me with so much passion that I felt like the room was spinning when he stopped. He put his forehead on mine, and our noses were touching. My eyes were closed, and when I opened them, I felt his eyes burning into mine. His eyes looked different: warmer than I'd ever seen them. I smiled at him, and he kissed me gently on the lips.

"I'm going to, uh, change my clothes real quick in the laundry room," Gerry said, sounding a little embarrassed. I got up and lay down on the couch, crossed my legs at the ankle, and had my arm over my head as I stared at the ceiling. I heard the water from the washing machine start, and then I heard, "Ow, what the—?" I walked to the laundry room, and Gerry had on his boxers and was pulling the elastic out as he looked down at his penis. I suddenly became nervous. Did I do something wrong?

"Is it broken?" I asked jokingly.

He laughed. "Uh, no. Did you have gum in your mouth today, by any chance?" I was confused, but then I realized that I didn't anymore. Oh, shit! Gerry watched my facial expression change from confusion to guilt.

"Yeah, that's what I thought," he said with a laugh. "I need to get some scissors." My face was as red as a beet, I'm sure. I was mortified. The gum had fallen out of my mouth into a sea of pubes! I'm sure it was killing him, pulling on his hairs surrounding his most sensitive body part. I felt so stupid. *Note to self*, I thought. *From now on, buy Tic Tacs!*

He came downstairs grinning in a fresh white T-shirt and plaid shorts, his maroon hat on backward. "I suppose I needed a little trim," he said jokingly. "It makes me look bigger." I blushed. We'd never talked like this before, and it was exhilarating but surreal. He picked me up and threw me onto the couch and mounted me like a vise, clenching me down and pinning me between his legs. He looked different to me with the huge, sinful sneer on his face. I could feel him harden again next to my leg; I didn't know it could do that again so quickly.

"Now it's your turn, baby doll," he said forcefully. I didn't understand what he meant. Was he going to put half-chewed gum in my pubes? He began to kiss my neck and slowly moved down. He lifted my T-shirt and began to kiss my belly, my waist, my sides, and moved down to my pelvic bone, which made me jerk uncontrollably. It tickled!

"Oooh, you're ticklish there. I'll have to remember that," he said seductively. He unbuttoned and unzipped my shorts.

"I'm sorry about the gum! Please don't do it to me. Please!" I blurted out, panicking. Gerry began to laugh and kissed me on the mouth.

"That's a good idea, but I wouldn't do that to you, baby," he said sweetly. He pulled down my shorts, and I was incredibly nervous. I had gotten some underwear from some random Contempo store with elastic strings on the sides, still full coverage in front and back. This pair was white and had little pink hearts on them. Gerry pulled the elastic and touched my pelvic bone again. I jumped and squealed. He laughed.

"I like these panties," Gerry said, looking wicked again—wickedly sexy. He kissed my belly, hips, and sides again and pulled my panties down with his teeth. I felt so uncomfortable at the exposure of my privates. I had no idea what he was doing. He started kissing my hips, my upper thighs, and then my inner thighs. I was petrified I might fart in his face. I was worried about how I smelled down there. Why was he doing this?

Then he began kissing me all over *down there*. I was flabbergasted. My sister hadn't mentioned anything about this. Gerry took my leg, lifted it up, and put it behind his head and then did the same with the other leg. My legs were in a diamond shape, with him in the center. This was the most exposed predicament I'd been in. I felt vulnerable. He looked intensely at my privates, took a deep breath, and gently began touching me there and kissing my belly and then my hips and then down there. I peeked down at him doing this to me, and I was in such a weak position—like I was at his mercy. At first it was a little too much right in the center; the uncomfortable pressure almost hurt. I moved and told him that it was hurting me a little bit. He smiled and kissed me again around my inner thighs and then lightly outside, which felt so erotic, dirty, and *holy shit*.

I started feeling electric, tingly sensations and then more and more until my hips clenched and I was moving my hips involuntarily. I had my hand in my mouth to prevent myself from screaming. It felt so fucking good! Gerry somehow was able to keep up with my rhythm, which I was surprised about, because I was moving so wildly. I felt a small flicker of pulsing, throbbing pleasure that continued to grow until I was feeling the tingling, mind-blowing, head-to-toe euphoria that consumed my body from top to bottom. My body was then lethargic from the extreme release that I hadn't known I'd needed until *it* happened. He was smiling from ear to ear. I was panting, my head was spinning, and I pulled up my shorts, suddenly feeling ashamed. Gerry stood up and smiled at me. He went to the laundry room again and came back wearing a different outfit. I looked at him, confused.

"I needed to change again," he said, looking embarrassed. We both burst out laughing.

# 7

It was dark. I blinked my eyes a few times to recognize where I was. My head was on Gerry's bare chest, his right arm cradling me from behind and enveloping me to him; his hand was wrapped around me and resting on my waist. He either was Plastic Man with ridiculously long arms, or I was very tiny. I felt small next to him. We'd never slept together before. My mom would kill me if I didn't get my ass home soon. I tried to remove myself from this tight squeeze, but each time I moved, his arm grew tighter, as if rigor mortis had set in. He was impossible to move. I had to wake him up. I shook him—nothing. I said his name a few times—nothing. I attempted to move his arm; he rolled toward me and wrapped his other leaden arm around me. Now it was like the coil of a boa constrictor—not that I'd ever been squeezed by one, but I imagined that this was how it would start out. It was also sweet and satisfying, so I paused and looked at his sleeping face (because I had no choice, for one), but I gave up on trying to wake him and decided to just "be" for a moment. His biceps around my neck and forearms were strongly embracing me; it was peaceful. His long, dark lashes looked fuller while his eyes were closed, which made him look like a little sleeping angel. He had such a baby face compared to the rest of him, which seemed grown-up, well-built, and solid.

I could lie here all night, I thought, but I knew my mom would end up walking over there if I didn't come home soon. I was still able to turn my head at least, and I saw the remote above Gerry's head on the floor—typical guy, always needing to have the remote close. I slid my arm out from his clutches and got ahold of the remote and turned on the TV. David Letterman was on, which meant it was almost midnight. Gerry stirred and rolled onto his back. He let me go, and when I got up, he started mumbling. As I was putting on my shoes, his eyes slowly opened, and he glanced to his right, pulled himself up to his elbow, and looked around the room. His brow was furrowed and squinting from the TV's glow in the dark basement. He caught my eye and smiled.

"Hey, babe, I thought you left me," he murmured.

"No, but I do have to get home," I said reluctantly.

"Oh man, I wish you could stay longer," he said, crawling toward me. He put his head on my lap and his hands around my waist. I was sure my stubbly legs were scratching the shit out of his face. I cringed at the thought. I ran my fingers through his hair a few times and said I had to go. He sat back and grabbed his gym shoes and started to put them on. I zoned out for a second there, just staring at him in disbelief that this guy was mine. He looked up sleepily, eyes droopy, hair messy, and face innocent, with wrinkles from something indenting it; my heart leaped. He busted me staring at him and gave me a crooked grin.

"Come on, I'll walk you home." He held his hand out for me to hold.

"Thanks," I said happily as I grabbed his hand.

We walked down the block holding hands, feeling content without having to talk. I welcomed the silence. My mind was recapping the evening, and when I peeked over at him, I guessed he was doing the same, since he was looking down at the ground, corners of his mouth turned up, deep in thought. When we reached my house, I stood on the first step on my front porch. He was still holding my hand, and I turned around to face him while he was still standing on the ground so that we were at eye level. He rested his forearms on my shoulders; we put our foreheads together, and our noses touched. He kissed my eyelids. I gave him a hug, my cheek resting on his shoulder and my nose to his neck as I took his scent in.

"Sorry about the gum," I said shyly, face buried in his neck. He laughed quietly. My armpits were sweating a little in my nervousness.

"It's OK, sweetie," he whispered. "I had an excuse to do some grooming, and now I like it. It only hurt for a few minutes." He giggled in my ear and buried his head in my neck. We were both like a couple of ostriches, and *Looney Tunes* popped into my mind.

I didn't know what to say next; my anxiety was rising, and my mind searched for what to do next, what to say. The first thought that came to me was from *Some Kind of Wonderful*, and on a whim I blurted out what came to my mind. "You always hurt the ones ya love," I said, laughing timidly. He raised his head up, and I did, too, simultaneously. He looked into my eyes and kissed my mouth passionately; my eyes closed in response, as if in a trance.

"Aw, sweetie, I love you, too," he said.

*What? What does he mean, "I love you, too"? Oh-my-fucking-gawd! Did I just do what I think I did? Son of a—! I just somehow said I love you first! Oh man!*

"OK, bye," I said abruptly. I turned on my heel and stumbled into the house. What the hell was wrong with me? Why couldn't I be normal? My whole flipping brain was a bunch of fucking pop culture citations! I had no frame of reference for anything. I stormed up the stairs and busted into Mairead's room. She was lying on her bed wearing a long-underwear long-sleeved shirt and flowered underwear, ass up, lying on her stomach on the bed, talking on the phone. She looked like a total cliché of a teenage girl gabbing on the phone with one of her girlfriends. All that was missing was the fucking lollipop. She glanced over at me with her peripheral vision, barely turning her head. Her huge green eyes looked at mine from the corner of her eye. She must have caught the mortified look on my face and told whomever she was talking to that she had to go. She slammed the phone down and smirked at me.

"What...the...fuck...happened...to...you?" she said haltingly.

I threw myself on her bed and took her pillow and rolled around with the pillow over my face so I could moan and convulse for a few moments without waking everyone up. When I removed the pillow, she was still smirking, her head resting on her hand, propped up by her elbow. "Are ya done?" she asked, appearing bored with my dramatic display.

I spewed out the night's events: the good, the bad, and the ugly. I slapped her arm when discussing the good: the mind-blowing what-I-suppose-was-an-orgasm I'd had when "he'd gone down on me," as she said, and she told me now that this might happen. She was impressed that Gerry had performed cunnilingus without being prompted. She was also impressed with his quick response to my attempting to blow him and my not really having to do much of the dirty work that's usually involved, but she said she'd tell me about that later. This led to the bad: the gum stuck to his pubes. She snorted, then snickered, then began cackling for I don't know how long, but I was annoyed because I was still at just the "bad," and she couldn't even contain herself. I was frustrated and walked out of the room. I didn't need to go on, because I'm sure she probably thought this was what my look of disgrace had been about. I was sick to my stomach and didn't want to disclose anything further.

I wanted to cry from embarrassment, but I wasn't mad or sad enough; I was still a tad exhilarated by the evening. I had my head down in my pillow, and Mairead slapped my butt; she was sitting on the edge of my bed. I had the urge to say something mean to her, to make fun of her somehow, but I couldn't say anything. I just glared at her and tried to look as unamused as possible. Her expression appeared benevolent. I was guarded, feeling unsure whether this was genuine compassion or was meant to reel me in to humiliate me some more.

"I'm sorry, sis," Mairead said, sounding kind. I was intrigued but didn't respond; I was still cautious. "That's hilarious," she said, "because I did the same thing. That actually happened to me, too! It was so funny to me that it happened to you on your first time, and you weren't even drunk." I smirked a little. Of course this would take place in my sister's sex life. Why not? It was like the house was full of a bunch of blundering fools. Of course, she was drunk at the time—at least that was her excuse. I had none, except that I was a moron.

"It's cute, sis," she said sweetly.

"Don't patronize me, please," I replied back, wounded.

"I don't mean it that way; I'm sure it sounds that way. The night sounded really great overall. You said he was laughing about it, so it doesn't sound like a big deal. You looked like you saw a ghost when you initially came in here," Mairead said.

I was annoyed now. "I'm glad you think it's 'cute,'" I said snottily, using air quotes around "cute." I added, "There's more to the story, but I don't feel like getting into it with someone so juvenile and ignorant. I need to go to bed to escape this misery and humiliation. Please go away."

"MK, please, I'm sorry." Mairead said this so amiably that it tugged at my heartstrings a little. But I was too stubborn and hurt. I lay there with my back to her for a long time, until I finally heard her sniff, sigh, and tiptoe out of my room.

Maeve was sleeping in her bed, and I was astounded at how soundly she slept. My constant presence at Gerry's lately had eventually led to her being able to sleep on her own. I guess I'd been enabling her all those years whenever she'd said she couldn't sleep by herself. She was apparently just pretending because she didn't want to sleep by herself. My mom no longer had the patience for it, and I didn't blame her. Working all day does take a toll on you. I lay down next to her in bed and smelled her hair. I think it's fascinating that everyone has a certain smell; my sister's scent was sweet and fresh, like watermelon or raspberries. Her scent soothed me, and I tried to think about the positive events of the evening and eventually drifted off to sleep with thoughts of strawberry shortcake or lemon meringue in my mind instead of gum wrapped in pubes.

# 8

I woke to the sweet smell of pancakes and coffee and Maeve's big eyes staring at me. I hugged her again, and we both went downstairs for breakfast. My grandmother was over; I could smell her perfume immediately: "Charlie." She always smelled minty fresh of Doublemint gum (only half a piece, as she would say). This was my maternal grandmother, who'd lost her husband five years before to a brain aneurysm and had learned how to drive when she was sixty-five. She'd worn a beehive hairdo for the last forty years; she thought it made her look taller. I wasn't crazy about her beehive, although the rest of her was always dressed to the nines. Today she had on a smart camel blazer and a brooch with a golden antique sun. Underneath she wore a white ruffle blouse, matching camel pants, and plaid flats.

She'd always say that she had to "put my face on," but really it wasn't much makeup: red lipstick, powder, and filled-in eyebrows. She wore tortoiseshell cat-eye glasses, so she didn't bother with the eye makeup. Her nails were always long and painted—coral in the summer, orange in the fall, red in the winter, hot pink in the spring—she didn't veer from the red family too often. Maeve and I were half-naked in boxer shorts and tank tops from sleeping with no air conditioning in the summer, and here was our grandmother wearing a business suit. We loved seeing our grandmother; she was fun and sweet and always,

always, always had something for us. My mom and grandmother were sitting at the kitchen table having coffee.

"Oh, hel-lo," our grandmother said in a singsongy voice, and she gave us a little wave. She was fabulous and screamed class. She also couldn't hear jack shit. This was annoying as hell, but it wasn't her fault. I'm usually sensitive to sound, too, so if something was to go on me when I got old, I'd hope it would be my hearing, too. Maeve and I gave her hugs and kisses, and she patted our butts gently. She would always say, "You girls have such nice butts; I never could get mine to fill out my pants." My grandmother was ninety pounds soaking wet. She loved to watch TV with us because she wanted to see what the "gals were wearing now"; she didn't care that she couldn't hear what they were saying. I adored that my grandmother got all gussied up for us "just to visit," as she would say. It made me feel special. I heard the front screen door slam shut, and Joy busted into the kitchen. She loved my grandmother, too. My grandmother giggled as Joy pushed us aside to hug her.

My grandmother wasn't rich, although one would think she was, the way she presented herself. Her secret was that she was confident in herself, never gained weight, and took care of her clothes. She was a "digger" at resale shops and thrift stores who always found fashion gems for herself and for us. Another one of her famous sayings was that "money can't buy class." She didn't have a lot of money, but she sure did have a lot of class. I knew she was a genius when I thought about my neighbor, whose father was an owner of a chain of restaurants and obviously very well-off. His only daughter was spoiled rotten, and her wardrobe was packed with name-brand threads from Nordstrom, Lord and Taylor, and Bloomingdale's. She flaunted herself around like she was some kind of fashionable diva, but in reality she looked gaudy, overdone, and tasteless. She wore gobs of makeup and too much perfume. The outfits were over the top and included a whole lot of fashion "don'ts." Sometimes, less is more. Having poor fashion sense could be fixable, but she was also rude, had no manners, and was completely disrespectful to everyone. Yep, sheer genius, Gram: money cannot buy class. This girl was the epitome of how money cannot buy class.

While Joy, Maeve, and I were gushing over my grandmother and talking about the most recent J.C. Penney catalog; my mom excused herself to go do laundry. Since we were perpetually broke, our washing machine was off-limits to us. My mom was terrified that someone was going to break it, and she was afraid we would use too much gas if we used the dryer. My mom usually could be found in the backyard hanging clothes on the clothesline or else taking them down. She soon came in with two baskets of laundry, and I realized that my mother had hung my underwear outside, and my cheeks blushed with humiliation. My grandmother motioned to us to assist my mother with the laundry. We were reluctant, but we all started folding. My grandmother's eyes lit up, and she held up a pair of my hot-pink bikini briefs. I'd gotten a six-pack of Hanes undies from the neighborhood department store; they were not Victoria's Secret by any means. My grandmother held them up and said, "Whose little numbers are these?" My face looking like a beet, I grabbed them, and we all giggled. I laughed as well but felt a tinge of humiliation. When we were done folding, I took my basket of clothes upstairs.

I went to my room, my mood suddenly crashing like an ocean wave, pissed off that we were so fucking poor. I was sure there were poorer people out there, but it would be a lot easier to live around other poor people. Not neighbors who owned a chain of restaurants and a spoiled daughter who had outfits that cost as much as my family's mortgage. I plopped on my bed and buried my head in my pillow and screamed into it. A quiet, muffled sound emerged despite the level of anger I had. I was furious that my mother didn't have the sense to hang my underwear inside if she was so concerned about the gas bill and using the dryer. When my parents had been married, I guess we had fit in around here, but now my mom was only making probably half of what my dad was making. He got out of most of the child support and pension she was supposed to get because they had so many bills. After the divorce was final, the bastard filed bankruptcy and got out of most of those monetary obligations. My mother had hired a cheap, shitty lawyer because she had no other choice. She got screwed.

I remembered my mom bought a pair of cheap costume earrings at the same neighborhood department store where I'd bought my hot "numbers." She'd actually bought plastic earrings, put them in, and asked me, "I'm going to wear these to the divorce hearing. Do these make me look rich?"

I tried my best not to laugh and said, "Of course not."

She went to the bathroom mirror and began laughing and glanced at me from the reflection in the mirror, and when I saw that she was laughing, I broke into laughter as well. Soon we were both in hysterics. I was so grateful for my mom and also thankful that she'd seen the humor in that: she'd thought some cheap department store earrings would make her look rich and that the lawyers might not think she was eligible for my dad's money. Both of us were giggling and punchy, silently laughing from our guts till the tears came from laughing so hard. We hugged, and my mom's laughter suddenly turned to tears; the next thing I knew, she was sobbing on my shoulder.

This seemed illogical to have my mom hugging me and me consoling her. I was the kid—wasn't I supposed to be getting consoled by my mother? This was the way things were "supposed" to be, but I truly didn't care. Her tears just filled me with anger and motivation to get revenge. Our massive success would be our revenge. That day I vowed to myself that I'd never *ever* be dependent on any man, and I'd make damn sure I'd get educated, make money, and show that motherfucker he hadn't broken us. I'd make sure Maeve would follow suit, so this would never happen to us, and if it did, we would be prepared.

My mother graduated from high school, got married, and ten months later had a baby. That's what they did in those days. Fifteen years later, she was completely vulnerable, dependent 100 percent on my father for everything: transportation, finances, and our future. In her defense, she didn't know—that's what everyone in her generation did. When things got hard, my dad just left. I don't think it ever oc-curred to her that this would happen; if anyone was going to leave, it should have been her. She never would have, though, because she was too Catholic and too naive. She wasn't a big rule breaker and not a big one for thinking out of the box. She didn't use birth control because it's against the Catholic religion, and each pregnancy was another nail in the coffin of her dependency on this man.

I let her cry for a long time that way, on my shoulder. She needed it, and it had been evident to me that she'd been walking around in a daze from the shock of the situation. I was glad she was now in tune with reality; the shit had hit the fan. I could feel the anger rising inside me, and her bawling and sniveling started to disgust me. I could no longer tolerate it and said something my mom would consider horrifying: "Fuck him, Mom." My mom flinched and reeled backward, clearly stunned by my language. She wasn't a big fan of the F-word, and I knew it. I, on the other hand, am a big fucking fan of it.

"What did you say?" she gasped, brow furrowed, tears streaming down her face.

"You heard me. I said Fuck. Him." I said it slowly, annunciating the "ck" sound like I'd learned on *Sesame Street*. She stood there look-ing at me like I had ten heads.

"Mom, he's a coward. He walked away when things got hard. He's treating us like a totaled car in an accident—like he can just walk away and start over. We're human beings. He's the one making the mistake, not you. The mistakes you made were in being too nice to him and not telling him to go 'pound sand,' as he loved to say. You not kicking his ass to the curb years ago is the other mistake. He did us a favor. I know you're scared, but in ten years, Mom, things will be reversed. He'll be the sorry one. He'll be the one sobbing. We will succeed. We will be OK." My mom stopped crying then; she appeared to be listening and intently processing what I was saying. Then she went to her room and shut the door. I knew I'd been heard.

For the divorce trial, my grandmother searched every resale shop and thrift store for an ensemble that would allow my mother to appear tasteful, respectable, desirable, and classy—which she did. My mother looked smashing but in a "less is more" kind of way. She wore a navy pinstripe suit. She wore a pencil skirt that stopped right above the knee with a small slit on either side; the blazer was a flattering crossover style with a belt, and a crisp white blouse with a pointed collar peeked out from the blazer. My mother looked sexy yet classy without showing a thing. She got her hair cut, which was tied back in a low ponytail. She had just the right amount of makeup on.

"I betcha those lawyers are going to look at your mother and think your father is absolutely nuts," my grandmother said proudly.

"You got that right, Grams," I said. I smirked to myself and noticed that some of my anger had subsided. I turned my head on my pillow and thought about how things seemed to have been in the past. I thought of my widowed maternal grandmother's marriage of forty-two years, my paternal grandparents' marriage still going after forty-five years, and Gerry's grandparents making it for over fifty years. I remembered Buzz hugging Ava the night before like they were teenagers, still very much in love. How does love last that long and stay so strong? How come some people's marriages don't survive and others do? I lay there deep in thought until my phone rang, which scared the shit out of me.

"Hello?" I murmured.

"Hi, pumpkin," Gerry said sweetly. My heart fluttered, and my groin twitched, followed by an imminent urge to cry. This was a sign my period was coming soon. *Jeez, the mood swings females have to go through*, I thought.

"Hey." I said this quietly and in a choked-up voice. I could sense my eyes welling up with tears, and I knew I had no control over myself to stop them.

"What's wrong, sweetie?" Gerry asked, sounding panicked. I tried to talk, but the tears were pouring out. I didn't want him to know that I was crying—how embarrassing. I stammered again in my attempt to speak; instead, an obstructed groan came out. "What is it?" he said, even more urgently now.

I was in full-blown tearfulness mode now. Son of a bitch. I took a deep breath and attempted to shake it off. "Nothing," I said in a whiny, nasally voice that I hadn't intended, but it was the best I could do.

"Oh my God!" he yelled, and he hung up. He must have thought I was a total nutjob at that point. He was probably wondering what the hell I was crying about.

Two minutes later, Maeve was hollering up the stairs, "Emmmm Kaaaay! Your boyfriend is heeeere!" I wanted to splash some cold water on my face and pull it together quickly, but I could hear my grandmother's little ballet flats clicking along in the hallway. This wasn't how I intended her to meet him. I wiped my nose on my forearm and flew down the stairs. Gerry had on the maroon baseball cap that I loved with a green T-shirt that said "Kelly's Pub." His eyes were full of fear when he looked at me. I smiled genuinely at him, hoping this would signal that I wasn't upset with him. He smiled back and appeared a little more relieved.

"Oh, hel-lo," my grandmother said to him in her singsongy greeting again. She gave him a little wave. She looked at me and said, "So who is this tall drink of water?"

"Grandma, this is my friend Gerry," I said to her proudly. I got the impression she approved, especially after her charming "who is this tall drink of water," said in her best Mae West–style seductive tone. She held out her hand, and Gerry shook it gently. "Gerry, this is my grandmother, Mrs. Olsen."

"Please, call me Cecilia," my grandmother said, scolding. She wasn't crazy about the term "grandmother." As a child, every year I'd ask my grandmother how old she was, and she would reply that she was twenty-nine. Finally, when I caught on and said, "Hey, you were twenty-nine last year!" she said, "You should never ask a lady how old she is—it isn't polite." She wasn't the type to grow old gracefully; she was going to fight it. She slept with Vaseline on her face on a silk pillowcase, because "it prevents wrinkles."

"Well, OK," my grandmother said. "It was nice to meet you. I'll leave you two alone to chat." She winked and scuffled into the kitchen. Gerry's eyes bored into me. His eyebrows furrowed—his eyebrows turned into almost-grins. He looked concerned. He put his hands on my waist as I stood on the bottom step of the staircase.

"What's wrong?" he asked, looking so sad that I felt bad for making him so concerned, even though I knew it wasn't my fault—it was just hormones.

"Nothing to do with you; I was just frustrated here with my mom," I said, trying to sound convincing. I wasn't sure if I was supposed to disclose hormonal issues with a guy, but my gut was screaming no! If I were to ask my grandmother, it would be a definite no. She never thought it was proper to discuss things like this; her theory was that "there should always be some mystery, no matter how many years you've been married." Gerry and I were only dating, so I'd assume this was a definite no.

"Let me take you out today. Whatever you want to do, it will be a Mary Kate day," Gerry said with hopefulness in his voice. I was touched by his idea, which of course made me want to cry again—fucking hormones.

"Awwww, thanks," I said. "I need to shower and stuff. I'll call you when my grandma leaves."

"OK, sweetie," Gerry said sincerely, and he gave me a peck on the lips. "Hurry up." He smiled and walked out the door, breaking into a jog as he got down the block.

I took a deep breath and went into the kitchen. My mom, grandmother, Joy, and Maeve were all sitting at the table smirking at me. "He's handsome." My grandmother said, which only she could have said without sounding condescending. I blushed. Joy shook her head, gave me nudge, and walked past me in the hallway and headed home. She obviously knew I'd be hanging with Gerry that day. Her boyfriend, Tommy, was coming home that weekend anyways, so I didn't feel guilty. Maeve looked glum for a moment, until my grandmother reached into her tote and pulled out a few little packages for her. I smiled and went upstairs to shower.

I had no idea what I wanted to do today, but I was glad to get out of the house. I decided on my default favorite thing to do: going to a movie. *Thelma & Louise* was playing, and I was embarrassed to admit that I wanted to see it; plus, in my hormonal state, it would be right up my alley. I called Gerry, who answered on the first ring.

"Yel-lo," he answered jokingly.

"Hey," I said.

"Hey, hot stuff. What's the good word?"

"I'd love to go to a movie with you, if you want to."

"I told you, baby, anything you want to do. What do you want to see?"

"I'm kind of embarrassed to say, but I want to see *Thelma & Louise*." I could feel my cheeks blush as I said this, and I could hear Gerry sigh on the other end.

"A chick flick?" Gerry asked. "I'm kidding. Of course I want to see a movie with hot chicks."

He laughed. "I said whatever you want to do, baby," he said, sounding like he was smiling on the other end. "Hold on a second." I heard muffled voices; he must have had the phone to his chest. "My sister's here. I was going to have you meet her, but now, since I mentioned chick flicks, she knows exactly what we're doing, and she wants to come with." He said this sounding disappointed.

"That's cool," I said. I did want to meet his sister; she was older than Mairead, and if she wanted to see the movie, too, then I must not have been that big of a nerd.

I took a shower and felt much better, but I was still tired. I settled on black shorts and a white T-shirt and stuffed my purse with Kotex super-plus tampons, and Gerry was already at the door. His sister was the female version of him but in a good way—she was pretty and cute and had a big smile on her face when I got in the car. She had the same color hair as Gerry's, but her hair was curly, and she had blond highlights.

"Hi, Mary Kate! I'm Shelley. I've heard so much about you!" Shelley said, and my heart jumped. Gerry gave her a look and started the car. Shelley was two years older than Mairead and a senior in college. She seemed very positive—one of those people it was impossible to stay in a bad mood around.

When Shelley got out of the car, I noticed that she was taller than Gerry. Gerry grabbed my hand to help me out of the car. I walked between them and felt incredibly short next to them both.

"Wow, I feel really short next to you Shelley. I feel like you guys are my parents taking me out for ice cream," I said jokingly. I usually like to make fun of myself before other people have a chance to.

Shelley cackled, and Gerry smiled. "OK, honey, what kind of ice cream would you like? You've been such a good girl this week, and you cleaned your room, so you can get any treat you want."

I couldn't help but laugh when Shelley played along. She added, "Thanks for letting me come with you guys. I've wanted to see a good movie for a long time, but my boyfriend would never see this with me. Plus, Brad Pitt is soooo hot."

Gerry rolled his eyes, and I smiled. I didn't even know who she was referring to. Gerry opened the door to the theater for us both.

"Why, thank you, little brother," Shelley said sarcastically.

"Thanks," I said flatly. "I'll be right back." I needed to make a break for the bathroom. I'd stuffed the tampons in my purse but had neglected to put one in, and I'd just felt a gush and wetness in my underwear. I was imagining blood trickling down my leg as I speed walked to the bathroom. Luckily I caught things just in time. As I was putting a dime into the maxi pad machine, just in case, Shelley came into the ladies' room.

"Oh boy! Buying maxi pads from a machine! That's the worst!" Shelley said this a little too loudly.

"Yeah, unfortunately I may need to take a couple bathroom breaks for diaper changes," I said, smiling and then blushing.

"I hear ya—I've had plenty of days like that. Then I started the pill, because I was so heavy that I wouldn't even leave the house on my first two days." Shelley said this matter-of-factly. I was surprised that we were discussing menstruation details after I'd just met her half an hour before.

"Wow," I said. I was actually surprised. It had never occurred to me to not leave the house when I had my period; it must have been pretty bad for her. I also wasn't aware that the pill did anything for menses. I made a mental note to look into that. "OK, I'll see you out there."

Gerry was sitting at a table with three pops, two ginormous buckets of popcorn, and Sno-Caps. My stomach growled loudly. I was craving those Sno-Caps already. He smiled wide when our eyes met.

"I'm sorry that my sister crashed 'Mary Kate Day,'" he said in a sweet, childlike voice.

"It's fine. Your sister seems cool," I said sincerely.

"Yeah, she's all right. She came over to visit our grandparents last night and decided to stay the rest of the week. I do like hanging out with her without my parents around. Not so much when my parents are present, though—Shelley and my mom butt heads. Once they got into a fight, and she pushed my mom, and she fell down the stairs." Gerry said this while laughing nervously.

"Whoa! Holy shit! Was she OK?" Shelley seemed so optimistic and laid-back; I couldn't imagine her becoming that angry. But then again, mothers do have ways of pushing our buttons.

"Oh yeah, she was fine. They were carpeted stairs. My mom was more humiliated and pissed off at Shelley's disrespect than anything. My sister didn't come home again from school for six months."

"Wow. Jeez, what were they fighting about?"

"I think they were fighting about her going on birth control. My parents are very Catholic and don't condone it, especially since she's not married." Gerry looked deep in thought.

"She just told me in the bathroom that she's on the pill—she said it helps with her periods." This came flying out of my mouth before I could stop it. My face blushed, and so did Gerry's.

"Uh, yeah," Gerry said shyly. "That's what she was telling my mom, but my mom doesn't care—it's nonnegotiable, according to her." I sensed he wanted to change the subject, and so did I. He added, "Wait, she just met you like five minutes ago and told you she was on the pill?"

Fuck.

"Uh, I don't know," I stammered. "It's not a big deal."

"How did that topic come up?" Gerry asked with a furrowed brow. "Actually, never mind, I don't want to know."

Shelley came up to us, and Gerry looked at her with a confused expression and shook his head. We sat in the back row. I went in first and sat down, crossing my legs on the seat. Gerry sat next to me, and Shelley sat next to Gerry. It was freezing in the theater. I loved air conditioning, since we didn't have it at home, but I was also not used to it. My legs were getting goose bumps, and the hair on my legs was already growing back. My legs were spiky already. Gerry held my hand.

"Your hands are freezing," he said as he handed me a bucket of popcorn and the Sno-Caps (*yes!*). "I'll be right back," he said.

Shelley moved over to sit next to me. She had her own bucket of popcorn. She started shoveling popcorn in her mouth and gulping down pop like she was ravenous. "Are you going to bust open those Sno-Caps or what?" she asked.

"Oh yes, sorry," I stuttered. Man, we'd just sat down like one minute ago. I handed her the Sno-Caps, and she poured them directly into her mouth. I stared at her mouth open, completely appalled. I'm not usually concerned with people eating from working at a restaurant, but she was grossing me out. Plus, I needed my chocolate fix.

Gerry came back, took the popcorn from me, and covered my legs with his fleece zip-up coat. It was all warm from the car and felt like it had just been taken out of the dryer. I leaned over and kissed him on the cheek. He put his arm around me and shoved Shelley's head; she slapped his hand. I laughed and leaned over and lay under his arm. His deodorant smelled really good; he was warm and toasty, and I could hear his heart beating. He kissed the top of my head, and I felt so cozy that I almost could have fallen asleep, but I was like a kid in a candy store at the movies. I didn't get out much.

I was so into the movie, I didn't eat much. I definitely paid attention to who Brad Pitt was! Sweet Jesus. I looked down and observed that Shelley's entire bucket of popcorn was empty, and the box of

Sno-Caps was crumpled up and discarded inside the bucket, too. *Sheesh, she can really pack it away*, I thought. Gerry played with my hair and caressed my scalp with his fingers. I got the chills again, but this time not from being cold. I must have looked like a dog getting its belly rubbed, because I was completely at his mercy. I was tired, hormonal, emotional, and vulnerable.

When the movie ended, I was mind-blown. I had never watched a movie like that before. Gerry held my hand as we walked to the car, and Shelley went to the bathroom. Gerry pulled me by the hand into the parking lot. I had begun to ask if we should wait for his sister when he grabbed the sides of my face and kissed my lips hard. I was taken aback by this sudden exhibit of passion in the daylight in the middle of a parking lot. Since I was exhausted from crying and hormones, I gave in to his kisses and was soon putty in his hands. Soon, my head was spinning from his tongue being in my mouth so vigorously and the intensity of the session. I lowered my head to catch my breath. He lifted my chin up with his index finger and then kissed me gently.

"Your lips are so full right now. I've never seen them like this. I just want to keep kissing them—maybe bite them. You're delicious." He said this with a slight growl in his voice.

He was turning me on. Then I remembered that Shelley was with us and that I had my period. I sighed and moped to the car. He opened the passenger door for me and kissed my hand before he let it go. He got into the driver's side, and we both slid toward each other on the leather seat. In seconds, we were devouring each other, his mouth all over my face, kissing my eyelids, then down my neck. I had this foreign urge for him to move his mouth down to my breasts. I wanted his mouth on them. This craving became unbearable, and I grabbed his hand and placed it on my breast. The sensation was transmitting pulsing pleasure currents throughout my body, and I could feel myself getting wet. My thigh was pressed against his pants, and I could feel him hard as a rock, jabbing into my leg. He was sucking my neck now with both of his hands under my shirt, his thumb inside my bra and stroking my nipples until they were hard and protruding outside my bra.

I was sliding down the seat until we were sprawled out on the bench of the front seat. We were making out wildly, his hands all over me, under my shirt, rubbing my upper rear thigh. The evidence of his arousal was digging into me at the exact right spot. We were grinding and basically dry fucking until I was throbbing and pulsating. He continually kept trying to put his hand there, but I continually moved it away. I wasn't ready to discuss female issues with him. I moved away from him. We were both somewhat relieved—well, at least I was. We were both panting and trying to catch our breath.

"What happened to Shelley?" I asked at last, very glad she hadn't come back to the car.

"She was planning on staying here to meet up with her friends at the mall." He grabbed my hand and kissed the top of it. I blushed. He was so sweet. Then he looked me in the eyes, kissed the tip of my nose, and said, "I love you, Mary Kate."

I smiled at him, kissed the tip of his nose, and replied, "Ditto." I laughed from quoting *Ghost*. He pinched me. Then I reciprocated. "I love you, too," I said, and I meant it. I believed he meant it, too. I could see the love in his eyes. His warmth and affection were beaming out of his eyes, and mine were toward him as well. I was on cloud nine.

"I realized how much more I love you today when you were upset," Gerry said with a pouty lip and a smirk. "It was like a knife in my heart." He smiled wide and put the car in drive. I felt relaxed, with the end of summer wind blowing in my hair and our first normal "I love you" in the way it was supposed to happen. I was content with how it had gone down. I began to think about our make-out session. This was the second time we'd gone feral in this big-ass car. The car was like an aphrodisiac. I could easily lose control, and I needed to get some protection. I thought about Shelley and the pill.

"What would you like to do next?" Gerry asked.

"Lunch and ice cream?" I asked hopefully.

"Whatever you want, I told you."

At lunch, both of us were quiet and lost in thought. I was thinking about the pill and condoms. I wondered what Gerry was thinking about.

"So, Mary Kate." He cleared his throat: *ahem.* "I've been thinking that we probably need to look into some sort of protection. My parents would kill me if I got you pregnant."

I smirked to myself that he was thinking the same thing I was. I was feeling ballsy and wanted to give him shit, so I said playfully, "Pregnant? You have to have sex to get pregnant, don't you?"

"Uh," he stammered. His cheeks flushed. He took a big gulp of his Coke.

"What makes you so sure you're getting laid? Just because we dry humped doesn't mean I'm givin' it up to ya." I raised one of my eyebrows as a convincer. He looked down at his plate, looking ashamed. Now I felt guilty. "I was just kidding, sweetie," I said sincerely. "I was thinking the same thing you were. I won't get pregnant. I absolutely cannot get knocked up." I took a bite out of my sandwich—nervous eating.

"I've never had sex before," Gerry said quietly. I choked, then coughed. I took a big swig of my Coke and swished it around in my mouth.

"You? You have never had sex?" I whispered. "I can't believe that not one girl has snagged you yet."

"Nope," Gerry said proudly, which confused me. "I'm Catholic. I'd always planned on waiting until I got married."

"Me, too," I said, also proudly. He smiled, blushed, and looked down at the table. He looked up at me with a smoldering look and grabbed both my hands in the center of the table. I kicked off my flip-flops and moved my feet under the table and rested them on the inner part of the chair between his legs. "Well, we aren't getting married anytime soon," I said. "We could keep doing what we've been doing. It's been fun. We could still wait until marriage." His face sank. I moved my right foot and nudged his inner thigh. He raised his eyebrows. He put his hand on my leg.

"Ha. Your face just looked like Ralphie when Santa Claus told him, 'You'll shoot your eye out, kid!'"

He laughed and said, "Yes, having sex with you and getting a Red Ryder BB gun are totally in the same ballpark." I blushed. He tapped my leg playfully.

"You shaved today?" Gerry asked.

"Yeah, what the hell is that supposed to mean?" I asked facetiously.

"I'm just teasing, sweetie. I was just saying that because you joke that your hair grows back in seconds when you get goose bumps or cold." He sounded apologetic.

"Yeah, whatever," I replied flippantly. He rubbed my calves.

"I love your muscular little legs. You have such a cute little body," Gerry said in a sweet little voice. A sideways grin emerged on my face. He knew how to make me smile. I was turning into a sap.

"Let's get some mint chocolate chip," Gerry said, and he put his arms around me. I knew my mom loved me and my grandparents, but this kind of love—to have someone adore you—kicked ass.

# 9

The next day, Mairead was home and wanted to hang out. Joy came over, and the three of us decided we needed a girl day. We rode our bikes on the trail and went to lunch at The Greasy Spoon, since I always got a good discount there. We all lit up a cigarette and exhaled simultaneously. My counterpart, Ruth, an older woman, single mom of three kids, came to take our order. She was tall and thin and was the queen of giving shit to the old guys who came in every day.

"Hey, Ruthie, how are you?" I said.

"Well, well, well, what do we have here? Can't get enough of this place, huh? Coming in on your day off?"

"We do have excellent food. It's a good sign if you eat the food where you work."

"If you say so. So what are we having?"

"We'll make it real simple for ya," I teased. "We'll all have the same thing: three cheeseburger baskets and three Cokes."

"You got it, sweet pea." Ruthie nudged my shoulder with her hip and put our order in at lightning speed. I watched her walk briskly toward the kitchen, all the cooks were looking at us through the order window. I wasn't sure if I should wave or what.

"So you guys have to come visit me up at school in October," Mairead stated with manic eyes. "Homecoming weekend last year was amazing—it was a blast! So get the weekend off, MK"

"What weekend is it? I hope it isn't the same weekend as Tommy's homecoming," Joy said, thinking out loud.

Mairead rolled her eyes. "October twentieth. I'm telling you, you *have* to come!" Mairead was very convincing.

I was pumped that she wanted me to visit her; I hadn't visited her the previous two years because she'd basically been MIA and we'd been estranged. I wouldn't dare miss it, because I knew she might not ask me again. Joy and I went to separate high schools: she went to public high school, and I'd be finishing my last year in an all-girls Catholic high school. I'd grown accustomed to rolling out of bed, throwing my uniform on, and going to school. I didn't know how Joy did it—going to school with boys and having to pick out her outfit every day.

"I cannot believe we start school in a week," I said to Joy and Mairead. "This summer has been a blur." They both groaned and nodded with agreement and then lit up another smoke. I hadn't really thought about what would happen when Gerry and I both started school again. We were both seniors now. I was at an all-girls Catholic School and he was at another all-boys Catholic high school.

When I got home, I called Gerry's grandparents' place. "Hey," I said when Gerry answered.

"Hey!" Gerry said. I grinned. I loved that he sounded happy to talk to me. "Are you home?" he asked. "Want to come over?"

"I thought you'd never ask," I said flirtatiously. "I'll be over in a minute."

I rode my bike down the block. Gerry was waiting for me on the porch. My heart leaped when I saw him. His eyes sparkled as I approached him.

"You look so cute on your little bike," Gerry said with a smile.

"Shut up," I said back.

"What? You do. My grandparents made dinner, and they wanted you to come. I'm kind of sad I won't be down the block from you anymore." He made a pouty frown face.

"Yeah, me too—I like that you're so easily accessible," I said, smiling. "Luckily, you don't live that far. I could even ride my bike to your house."

"I have my mom's car, silly," Gerry said to remind me.

"I'll miss you picking me up in the Caddy. That's one sweet ride."

"Buzz and Ava will let me borrow it anytime. I definitely like picking you up in that car." He winked at me, and I blushed at my behavior in that car. There was something enchanting about that car; it was like I was possessed when I was in it.

"That car makes me do crazy things. It's like the Stephen King movie *Christine*," I joked.

Gerry snickered. "Christine was jealous of the guy's girlfriend and tried to choke her and tried to prevent him from getting laid." He said this and then his face flushed; he probably hadn't meant that literally, since he'd only gotten to first base so far in that car.

"Oh really, get him laid, eh?" I teased. We hadn't discussed our consummating our relationship again, which I was relieved about. I figured that once I gave it up, I could never go back. I liked things the way they were and was petrified to be on that level. I assumed Gerry was on the same page, because he hadn't mentioned it again. I didn't want to tell him I had taken the bus to a clinic one day after school that was confidential and it was called "The Pubescent Center" that my friend Sam told me about. I was supposed to start the pill the Sunday after my period. I also got a huge lecture from a counselor about still using condoms at all times because the pill does not prevent against STD's. I was mortified. Gerry and I are both virgins. Did I have to worry about this? The lady I met with told me some terrifying stories about getting genital warts when she was engaged. I escorted myself out with my head down feeing sheepish.

"Uh, you know what I mean," he stammered. "Let's go see if dinner is ready." He held out his hand and led me into the house. I still stopped in the hallway of old photographs whenever I walked by—all those photos were so cool. I felt like I took a DeLorean back into the

1940s whenever I was at Buzz and Ava's place, as if I'd been transmitted to a different era. I admired the style of clothes, the cars, the black-and-white and sepia photos. It was a different time, and quite frankly, I wasn't down with the fashion in my day. Flannel shirts and the grunge look weren't really my thing. I was enamored with the skirts, heels, hats, hair styles. It seemed like everyone took pride in their appearance and respected themselves and others. It appeared to me that the trend of the nineties so far made everyone look like a bunch of slobs. I wasn't into it.

Dinner was almost ready, and the aroma was spectacular. My stomach growled intensely when I stepped into the kitchen. Ava had made her special homemade tomato sauce. I was impressed, since Gerry had told me she had Alzheimer's, but she was able to recall that recipe without blinking an eye. Gerry said she had been doing great since Buzz had been back at home. Their routine was now intact and back to normal, which he said helps Alzheimer's patients: familiarity and routine are good for the disease. My heart swelled thinking how selfless Gerry had been to spend the summer with her, and my heart ached for their family having to watch her slowly deteriorate.

The menu included homemade dressing, salad, garlic bread, gnocchi, and Ava's special sauce. Buzz was stirring the sauce, wearing his usual outfit of white tank top, suspenders, and brown slacks and dress shoes. Ava was wearing a seersucker dress and red flats while tossing the salad. I stared at them in awe that they still dressed like that and were so devoted to each other. Faint sounds of Frank Sinatra emerged from the patio record player through the screen windows. Ava and Buzz hummed along, half-singing, half-humming. I assisted Gerry in setting the table. Shelley then strolled in looking disheveled, as if she'd just woken up from a nap. She plopped down at the table and yawned.

"Wassup, MK?" she said through a yawn.

"Not much, Shell, what's up with you? Tired?"

She scoffed. "It's so calm and quiet here; it makes me sleepy. It's also kind of boring," she whispered with her hand by her mouth. I acknowledged what she said; I understood that it was probably boring for her, since she was a busy extrovert.

Buzz rubbed his palms together, looking thrilled for this well-prepared meal. The atmosphere was vivacious with Buzz around, as if an aura of life and vitality encircled him. Of course my mind flashed to the movie *Cocoon*, wondering if they had some alien chrysalis in the basement.

Buzz poured red wine for all of us and winked at me; I was taken aback at first, but my grandparents let me drink the foam from their beer, so I supposed it was similar. Buzz pulled a chair out for Ava, slid her in, and raised his wine glass.

"Salud," he said wholeheartedly. We all replied "salud" and toasted our glasses. I wasn't aware of this tradition but followed suit. I sipped the wine; it wasn't what I expected. The flavor was bittersweet, with no resemblance to a kiddy cocktail, which is what I'd hoped for. Once I anticipated that the wine was going to taste like absolute shit, the essence improved. My cheeks burned shortly after a few sips, aglow with fever. The food was delicious. The wine went down smooth, and the room was abuzz as we kept the momentum going. Buzz was telling stories that any audience would consider comical. The laughter was continuous, and the wine was flowing freely. Gerry's eyes glistened, and my eyes were wide open as I took it all in.

Ava observed Buzz quietly with a flicker in her eye and a warm expression. She hung on his every word despite probably having heard these stories countless times; Buzz was an enchanting storyteller. His speaking style reminded me of Morgan Freeman or Alec Baldwin, whose narration abilities captivated their audiences and made them thirsty for more. Buzz would periodically touch Ava on the hand or the shoulder or pause to gaze at her. I was conscientious of this, and it warmed my soul. My eyes welled up with tears. My invisible wall that surrounded me had not been resurrected, and lately I'd been more susceptible to sentiment. For years I'd been numb, unable to be penetrated by pain, which was good, but I was incapable of giving or receiving true affection and intimacy. Tonight, by witnessing true love, I understood the benefit of being vulnerable and receiving all forms of emotions.

When Buzz was out of stories, we went to the living room to watch *Pretty Woman*, which surprisingly is a big favorite of the geriatric population. Buzz and Ava were enamored with this movie apparently, and I enjoyed watching it again with them. Shelley seemed ready to get shit-faced, because she opened another bottle of wine and poured it into all of our glasses. As for me, I was more buzzed by the effects of the continuous laughter and atmosphere, although I'm sure the wine was coursing through my veins and doing its job. When the movie was over, only Gerry and I were still awake. Buzz and Ava were holding hands, snoozing with the top of their heads touching. Shelley was snoring. We both laughed. Gerry and I remained on the couch holding hands and began talking about Shelley and college drinking, which reminded me.

"Oh! Guess what?"

"What?" Gerry smiled and turned to face me, appearing intrigued.

"Mairead wants me to come visit her at Eastern's homecoming weekend! I can't believe it. You know how Mairead and I are! She's never wanted anything to do with me. I really feel like things are changing. I'm so excited to go and hang out with her."

Gerry's face darkened, and he let go of my hands. "Oh, I see," he replied flatly.

"What? You don't think that it's awesome? You want to go too?"

"Uh, maybe." He got up and went to the sink and began to do the dishes. I went over to help and kissed him on the cheek. His mood seemed to improve while he washed and I dried.

After Gerry and I had finished cleaning up the kitchen, we resorted to spinning towels into strips and whipping each other. Every time there was a snap or crack on the ass or thigh, we laughed. Gerry seemed buzzed to me and was growing goofier by the minute. He proceeded to wet the corner of the towel, and it made the loudest *whack* so far, but it also stung the most. It grazed the bare skin on my thigh as he aimed for my shorts; it was a sting that increased and triggered a retaliation response within me. I was pissed.

"Bastard!" I grimaced and punched him in the arm. He crossed his arm over his chest and wrapped his hand around his arm where I'd jabbed him. He was still grinning and not responding in the way I had hoped. I inspected my leg and saw that a raised pink welt was forming.

"Oh, you want to play rough, baby? We can play rough." He said this in a tone I didn't recognize and scooped me up and threw me over his shoulder and smacked my ass. Taken off guard, I squealed, then quickly covered my mouth. I was ambivalent about where this was going. He seemed playful, but I hadn't seen this side of him before. His facial expression was not congruent with his inside mood; he was smiling but while seeking revenge. I laughed with a touch of apprehension. Gerry stomped down the basement stairs and plopped me on the couch and mounted me, holding my wrists as I tried to push him off. He held my wrists over my head and grinned. I attempted to utilize my legs to push him away with my foot, but he extended his legs over mine. I'd underestimated his strength, and now I was completely helpless.

"Come on, baby, wrestle with me!" Gerry said, sounding somewhat normal again. I relaxed a little, sensing that he was just teasing. I attempted to twist my wrists, but his grasp tightened. He laughed. I moved my legs, but the muscles clenching in his legs pinned me more. I was enveloped under him like a corset. He began kissing my neck and face, but I couldn't get into it. This trapped, claustrophobic feeling was eliciting a rage inside me, and I wanted to escape. I let my body go limp for a moment while he was kissing my neck. He seemed to loosen his grip in response and rubbed his chest against me. This might have turned me on if I hadn't felt so threatened and guarded by his mood swing. I quickly twisted my hips and turned my body sideways and fell to the floor.

His expression looked surprised and possibly impressed; this swiftly changed to a sneer, and he pounced on me. We rolled around on the floor, struggling, and at one point I was able to mount him, and I kneeled on his arms. I glared at him triumphantly, and he was expressionless; I couldn't read him. My legs were strong but not strong enough to pin him for long. He also appeared to be enjoying this, and instead of fighting, he lifted his head and licked my inner thigh and then nuzzled his face between my legs over my shorts. I was caught off guard; the intense pleasure it gave me immediately made me powerless, and I relinquished the battle. The wine, adrenaline, and vulnerability were leaving me fiery and passionate.

"I'm totally just teasing you, pumpkin," he said in a sexy, growly kind of voice. "You're so fucking hot! You turn me into an animal."

Gerry bent his legs so his thighs touched my back and used the momentum of his own weight to rock himself up, and I slid down into the crevice of floor between his legs. Since his hands were now free and I was now putty in his hands, he put his hands behind my back and laid me on my back on the floor; he kneeled above me, pulled his shirt off by the back of his neck, and began kissing my belly. He was rougher than usual, and his stubble was contributing to the intensity. He unbuttoned my shorts and licked my panties, then the sides of my inner thighs. He slid both of his hands up my shirt while his mouth was growing closer to the area where I ached and throbbed. His hands were deliberate, and he groaned and sighed as he licked me, and I was paralyzed. I wanted to yell out or groan—the urge was growing, and the pulsating and throbbing were now in tune with his stimulation.

"Oh, baby," he said breathlessly; the sound of his voice was the icing on the cake, and I climaxed, room spinning, hips rocking wildly. The orgasm was so intense that I wanted to growl and attack him like a rabid animal. He collapsed below me and I crawled toward him with my pulse still racing. I unbuckled his pants and pulled them down. He popped out like a catapult and winced briefly, and I made up for it by kissing him first and then putting my mouth around him, and he was now paralyzed and powerless. I had no idea what I was doing, but I was sure anything warm and wet would do the trick as long you didn't bite them. He was jerking and quivering fairly quickly, and this time he was able to warn me so I could remove myself before being fired upon.

Both of us collapsed on the floor, completely incapacitated, panting, and with hearts racing. I didn't see that coming, no pun intended, but it was welcomed and unexpected. The intensity of pleasure had definitely increased. I lay there, bewildered at how it all had gone down. We both remained there halfway clothed, disheveled, and unable to move. He turned onto his side to face me. I turned on my side to face the opposite way, and we lay in a spoon position. I really had no interest in kissing him until we both engaged in dental hygiene. Then, with his arm resting on my waist and his hand inside both of mine, we were satisfied.

"That was fun; I mean, more than fun—amazing. I love you," Gerry whispered to me, and he kissed my cheek. I had to admit it had been fun. I had second thoughts about starting the birth control, since I couldn't imagine anything better than what we just did!I was beyone content with what we were doing so far and not having to worry about fertilization. However, I assumed I might not be able to stop myself and with his strength, I had a fleeting thought that I might not be able to stop him! I shuddered at that thought and put it out of my mind for even thinking that and I attempted to shake the slight fear and uneasiness I'd had earlier and focus on how good I felt now after that orgasm instead! I was still mindblown that my body was capable of such a thing and that he could do that to me.

# 10

Reluctantly I put my school uniform on and got ready for my long journey to school. I walked about a mile to the bus stop, waited for the bus, and rode the bus until I reached my stop to take a second bus that deposited us in the school parking lot. By the time I got to school, I was exhausted. It was like a full day before I even started school. All of us did enjoy utilizing public transportation so we could smoke between stops. I found myself daydreaming of Gerry on the bus and lost in my thoughts. In years prior, I remembered girls would call their boyfriends from the payphones at school while they were at lunch. I thought it was bizarre and ludicrous at the time; they could have called from home in a few hours. Now I understood and found myself longing to hear his voice. *I'm whipped*, I thought. I started to imagine movie montages where guys would be watching their beloved from afar while music played. I continued to think he could see me at school, which was weird but made the day go by faster.

Ever since my freshman year, we took a certain hallway to get to our study hall, and every week someone was tossed in the garbage. I was small, so it seemed I was tossed in most frequently. Sometimes my classmates would tell me we were getting someone else, so I'd reach for that person's leg, and then I'd end up in the garbage. It was a bitch to get out of the garbage cans they had. I tried to be a good sport about it, but sometimes I wondered if I was a glutton for punishment.

On the third day of school, I ended up in the garbage; in the past this hadn't bothered me—remember, my barricade was up permanently, and I was numb, so nothing was a big deal to me. I was so laid back that I was almost comatose, just going through the motions and not engaging in my life. This day was different: when I was tossed in the garbage can, I felt shame and humiliation. I was annoyed. My uniform was twisted, and my shirt was untucked in the back, and on the way to study hall, I got a detention from the disciplinarian officer. Man! Then I got to study hall late and was scolded for that, so I ignored everyone. I was furious, and I decided I'd no longer take that hallway after class or toss anyone in the garbage again. Yes, it was a lot funnier when it wasn't me, but with how I was feeling, I didn't want any part of making someone else feel that way.

I tried to shake off the negative feeling I had all day following that incident, but I was sour grapes now and unable to stop. I thought about Andrew Clark from *The Breakfast Club* disclosing the story of why he was at detention for taping that kid's butt cheeks together, and now I no longer thought it was funny. Before, I never thought it was such a big deal, but now I comprehended why he felt so bad. I shuddered to think of the people I'd bullied in the past and the mean shit I'd done. It was always like I wasn't in my body when I did those things, like I had no soul. I realized the magnitude of the disconnection between my body, brain, and emotions. I remember my friends would tease me that I didn't have a soul: I laughed at everything and never got upset, and none of them ever witnessed me crying. Life had been a hell of a lot easier when I was numb. Now I could feel, and it sucked.

By Friday, I came home from school exhausted, collapsed on the couch, and passed out immediately. I was worn out. I slept so long that when I woke up, it was seven thirty and dark outside. I jumped up frantic, thinking it was morning and that I was late for school. I'd also had a lot more energy when I didn't feel anything. What the hell was going on? I was about to go to my room to call Gerry when I heard a knock at the door. When I opened it, I saw an anxious expression on Gerry's face.

"Where have you been?" he asked, sounding angry.

"I've been asleep on the couch. Why?"

"Well, could you let me know next time? I've been calling you on your phone." Gerry sounded uptight and was acting like a worried parent instead of my boyfriend.

I started to get defensive. "Let me get this straight. You want me to call you to tell you when I'm going to take an unexpected nap?" I sighed. "What's wrong?" I asked, wondering what the urgency was.

Gerry hesitated, his eyes moving around my face and staring at me blankly. He'd moved back to his parents' home, and I saw through the window that he'd driven his mother's hatchback over. Faint wisps of smoke appeared to be coming from under the hood. His face softened, and he pulled me to him, gave me a hug, and buried his nose into my neck.

"I guess nothing. I was worried about you. I suppose I shouldn't worry, huh?" His voice was slightly muffled from talking into my neck. "I couldn't stop thinking about you this week; it's been torture being at school away from you."

"Absence makes the heart grow fonder, right?" I said, not knowing where that came from. "We have talked on the phone, though."

"Yeah, but you know it's not the same," he said. "I wrote you a few notes this week."

"Huh? Really? I wasn't aware guys wrote notes. I thought that was just a girl thing. I got busted writing a note last year, and my teacher read it to the class, so I haven't been writing notes much since."

"Shelley told me to write you a note; she thought you would like that," he said sheepishly. "After the first one, I wanted to keep writing to you. It also made me miss you more." I was touched. He was saying things I needed to hear. I'd had a shitty week coping with this new concept of "feeling." I didn't want to explain it to Gerry—probably too deep. Guys are simple, from what I'd been told, so I kept it simple.

"I missed you, too. I thought about you at school a lot," I said truthfully. "I could try writing you a note. I'm pretty cursed, and I'll probably get caught, but I'll make an attempt."

He pulled out four square-folded notes from his pocket and gave them to me. "Read them later, OK, when I'm not around. You know, you haven't officially met my parents, and they're dying to meet you." I tensed up instantly. "So will you come over for dinner tonight?"

Well, I had to meet them sometime; at least I was refreshed from my four-hour nap. Sheesh. My mom wouldn't allow a boy in my room—justifiably. So I ran upstairs to change and brush my teeth while he waited. Maeve was starting to warm up to him by this point, and when I came downstairs, he was coloring on the floor with her. I wished I had a camera right then. My heart swelled with love and pride; he was a good guy. My shoes scuffed on the bottom step. They both turned around, and Gerry lightly pinched Maeve's nose.

"See you later, Maeve," we both said to Maeve, and we waved to her. She waved back to us but was looking out the window; her friends from next door were out in front, so she followed us to join them outside. We got into his mother's hatchback. I was nervous. Gerry took my hand and kissed the top of it. I was slightly trembling. I'd chosen a loose cotton black eyelet skirt my grandmother had given me and a purple T-shirt and black sandals. I was amazed at the stuff my grandmother found at thrift stores, and I was grateful to not have to wear jean short cutoffs again while meeting his parents.

"What are you nervous about? They're going to love you. How could they not?" Gerry smiled. I felt a little relieved.

His mom and dad were how I imagined they would look. His father was very tall, stout, solid, and handsome, with a ruddy complexion, and his mother was much shorter but had Gerry's face. They were both out in front sitting in lawn chairs drinking beer when we pulled up.

"I'll open the door, OK?" Gerry said hastily and kissed me on the cheek. My hands were cold and clammy. My mind flashed to *Ferris Bueller*, when Ferris instructs the audience to lick their palms. I wiped my hands on my skirt. Gerry opened the car door for me and took my hand. He held my hand as he escorted me up the driveway. Both of his parents had their heads cocked sideways, accompanied with sweet grins on their faces, as if they were saying "awwww" inside. They both looked like they were hiding something: smirking and eyeing each other, sipping their beers, and trying to suppress their laughter. I held out my hand to each of them and addressed them by their last name, the way I was raised to. His dad held my hand a little longer and looked me straight in the eye; I shuddered, as if he could see right through me. His expression softened, and he pulled me to him to give him a hug.

"Buzz has told me all about you, miss," Mr. McGrath bellowed. His wife smiled at him.

Buzz had told him about me? Not Gerry? What was that about? "Yes, they're incredible people," I said. "I'm grateful to have met them." His dad rose slightly in the chair, and a proud expression emerged on his face. Gerry's mom smiled but remained silent.

"Well, then, let's go eat," Mr. McGrath said. I had no idea what his mom made, but it was yummy. I think it was some kind of breaded chicken with mashed potatoes and green beans and for dessert, apple pie. I'd eaten better that week with his family than I had all year at my house. His dad asked the usual questions; his mom didn't say anything except to pass something to me. His dad resembled Buzz and had the same captivating appeal about him—anything he said held my interest. Gerry had his hand on the back of my chair as he drew circles on my shoulder blade with his thumb.

Then the conversation turned to a topic I wasn't expecting. His mom began to ask Gerry questions about football: when it started, when the practices were, when the games were going to be held. His mom went from a mute to loquacious in a matter of minutes. It was surreal to witness. Gerry squirmed a little in his seat and removed his arm from the back of my chair, my back now cold from where his arm had been. From what I gathered, Gerry was on defense and would be having something like tryouts, but he'd already made the team, so I wasn't sure exactly what this was. I watched football on TV or my grammar school team so I did like it; but I didn't understand the game.

"When's homecoming?" his mom then inquired. I was astounded at her interest in this topic, and it was fascinating to see the dynamics of his parents' marriage unfold. His dad appeared to be the more emotional, talkative, nurturing type, while his mom seemed more like a traditional guy, drilling the son with questions about the football details and not talking much or displaying much emotion. I was engrossed with the conversation and completely absorbed by his parents' role reversal. So far what had transpired was that Gerry would now have football practice Monday–Thursday after school and a game on either Saturday or Sunday.

"Homecoming's October twentieth," Gerry said sharply, looking down at his hands.

*No! Son of a bitch! The one fucking weekend my sister asks me to do something. Dammit!* No wonder he'd behaved so weird when I told him. Between my job, my family, my school, his school, his family, and now football, coordinating our schedules was going to be a nightmare. How the hell did married people with kids do this?

# 11

Gerry's mother instructed him to take me home before midnight, which was when my mom typically expected me. I'd gotten away with coming home later, because she was usually conked out every night by ten while watching TV. I also didn't think my mom had the energy to ground me at that point. I was eighteen, a legal adult, so I thought she'd be able to start letting go. I was somewhat relieved that his mom had set some limits with us, because it seemed that he liked to push the limits my mom gave me. Also, because I'd lost my self-control recently and hadn't been ambivalent about my behavior. Gerry and I had begun dating in June, and it was now September. I was appalled at what I'd done with him physically and where we were emotionally. I'd always believed that I would wait until I was married to have sex. We hadn't done it, per se, although we had ventured close to that point. With Gerry those boundaries were fuzzy, because I had such intense desire, emotions, and trust in him, and to be honest, I'd been enjoying my slut self immensely.

My concern was that it might be revealed in some way that I was a sleaze, but the only person who could do have done that was Gerry, and he seemed like a private person—but what did I know? I was sure I was just "in my head" and analyzing things too much, which I always tend to do when I feel like I'm losing control. I was losing control—being in love means feels completely out of control. I'd done things lately that never even would have crossed my mind before I'd met him. Part of me was scared, I suppose; he said he loved me, he acted like he loved me, he introduced me to his family, so what was the problem? Girls are so fucking dumb! Do we all do this? Create drama where there isn't any? Question things that don't need to be questioned? I was totally overthinking this. I wished I was a dude.

"Sweetie?" Gerry asked while driving me home. I had to get my head out of my ass—or my vagina out of my head—whatever. I hated being a girl right then. I just wanted to enjoy what was happening instead of ruining it by thinking too much.

"Yes, sorry. I feel bad that I didn't know you were on the football team and that it was such a big deal to your mom," I blurted out.

Gerry sighed and cracked the window. I stared at him in the darkness. He had such a cute profile. I was watching his face change with the shadows of the car against the streetlight; I took a deep breath and exhaled at how handsome I thought he was. I found it fascinating that I couldn't imagine my life without him and how it was impossible to go back to the way you were before, because now you know too much. When you don't know what love is, you don't know what you're missing. Then, when you find it, how can you live without it?

"You know, I'm not sure why I didn't mention it. I guess I was glad to not have to discuss it. I'm sure you could tell that we discuss football quite often at home. I find it relaxing to be with you and not have to talk about it and that you don't ask me a million questions. You are a breath of fresh air for me. I love football, but it's kind of a lot of pressure." He looked tense. The sides of his jaw were clenching as he turned down my block. I was at a loss for words. Sometimes less is more, so I decided to keep my mouth shut and make a quick getaway. When we pulled up to my house, I gave him a peck on the cheek and exited the car before he could protest. I briskly walked into my house without looking back. I heard him pull away after I closed the door.

I washed my face and brushed my teeth on autopilot, lost in thought about the evening. Mairead's light was on, so I went into her room and saw that she was packing; duffle bags and boxes were all over the place. She was going back to school that weekend, leaving Saturday afternoon. Mairead looked frazzled: her hair was in a ponytail, and baby hairs were sticking up from her ponytail. She had bags under her eyes and looked like she might pass out. Her lips were chapped.

"Hey," I said quietly. She glanced up from her bag.

"Hey," she replied with a sigh.

"Need help with anything?" I asked, hoping she would say no.

"Nope. You arrived just in time, when I'm pretty much done. I could have used your help earlier," she said sarcastically.

"So...I...uh...just found out that Gerry's homecoming is on October twentieth as well."

Gerry hadn't said anything about it, but I got the impression that he'd been disappointed when I'd told him that Mairead had invited me to come up that weekend. After tonight, it made more sense. I wanted to process this with Mairead because I was unsure of what to do.

"Yeah, so what does that mean?" she asked with her hand on her hip.

"Nothing."

"Well, you're still coming to visit me, right?" Mairead's eyes darted into mine; she was the type who always cut to the chase.

"Yeah, tonight was weird. I met his parents. His dad was really friendly, and I felt at ease around him, but his mom didn't say very much. Then she began interrogating Gerry with questions about football. I wasn't aware that Gerry even played football. The other day I told him how I was excited about visiting you for homecoming weekend, and he behaved kind of strange about it but didn't say anything. His mom asked about homecoming specifically. What is homecoming, anyways? I don't get it." I unloaded all these thoughts out loud.

"Oh, yeah, homecoming's a pretty big deal. Alumni come back to visit, and all the athletic teams play on our home field. They'll have a parade, plus the football and rugby games. Then, lots of fun activities will be going on—tons of parties. You'll have a great time.

Plus, I'm not sure how much longer I'll be at Eastern, so I really want you to come this year. I may be transferring out to Columbia next fall."

I was impressed with her planning ahead; she usually wasn't a big future-planning kind of person.

Mairead had asked me first, and Gerry hadn't said anything about that weekend, anyways, so I didn't want to cancel with my sister and then have him not have any big plans. I was so touched that my sister, whom I'd been estranged from for almost two years, wanted me to come visit her. I had to do this, because I knew she might never ask me again. She was family, and blood trumps friends. I needed my sister now more than ever. The only problem is I do not have a car and neither does my mom.

It was kind of an ongoing inside joke, because my dad was the only one who drove in our family. My mom had nervous parents who didn't want her to have a driver's license. Over all the years my parents were married, she never followed up and got her license, and now she was petrified to drive. Her mother, my grandmother Cecilia, had recently gotten her license at age sixty-two, when her husband died. My dad was usually half in the bag, so it was not a good idea for him to take her for driving practice. Mairead and I both found it crazy that our mom wasn't dying to get her driver's license and a car. We both couldn't wait to find someone to let us use their car and get our licenses. Normally, teenagers could rely on their parents for this; we had kind of a bizarre setup.

I still think my dad had to have been off his rocker to leave my mom; the dude had it made. She did everything for him. She did his laundry, made his lunch, and made sure his dinner was on the table when he got home. She was Wilma, and he was Fred Flintstone. Once, my dad was about to leave for work when he discovered that Mom had forgotten to make his lunch. So what did he do? He got back into bed. When my mom asked what he was doing, he replied, "It must be Saturday, because my lunch isn't made." My mother scrambled into the kitchen to whip his lunch together. Like I said, she was nuts.

Mairead and I just looked at her with awe; either she was a saint or the dumbest woman on earth.

One day the summer before, Mairead and I had vowed we would make sure to get our driver's licenses after witnessing an incident with our mom. It was a Sunday, and our dad was hungover as usual, lying on the couch all day while she served him breakfast and lunch on a TV tray. Mairead, Joy, and I were sitting on the front porch, and my mom rode out from the backyard on her ten-speed bike. She said she would be right back. About an hour later, at about five in the afternoon, we were still sitting our lazy asses on the front porch listening to radio. Maeve and a couple of the kids on the block wanted us to play running bases with them; basically, they wanted the big kids to chase them. Mairead and Joy were throwing the softball back and forth. Maeve, the neighborhood kids, and I were the runners in the game. I was running toward Mairead, and she was looking down the street with this dumbfounded expression on her face, mouth drooping open. I turned around, and my mouth dropped open, too.

It was dusk, and the sky had that pinkish-orangey glow. I had this random slow-motion sensation come over me. I could vaguely hear the *Chariots of Fire* song in my mind, and my mind flashed to *Mr. Mom*, when all the grown men are doing the obstacle course. In the distance, a silhouette of a woman riding her bike, holding the handle bars with one hand and the other arm extended above her head balancing a tray over her head in the other. As she became closer, I recognized it was my mother carry a rectangular box of a Little Caesars double pizza deal in her hand while riding a bicycle. Initially I was impressed that she was able to balance that big rectangular box while riding a bike. Then I looked at our car out in front and thought, *Why didn't she ask my dad to drive her?* My mom was approaching us and doing fine with her balancing act down the street. As she needed to maneuver her bike up the curb and then take a sharp turn toward our house. We all gawked at my mom as if we were at the circus watching the performer ride the bike holding the pole across the tightrope. It was as if we all were frozen, staring at her in slow motion and not knowing what to do. Then Maeve yelled, "Yeah, *pizza!*" She charged my mom, who started to wobble. I covered my mouth with my hand and hissed as my mom inevitably dropped the pizza.

My mother's expression was of pure anguish as she watched the pizza soar to its demise. My mom was so upset about watching the pizza that she yelled in slow motion, "Ttttt-hhhh-eeee pppp-iiii-zzzz-zzzz-aaaa!" She hit a bump and crashed to the ground—ironically, next to my father's car. Maeve intercepted the pizza box from hitting the ground and ran into the house. Mairead, Joy, and I all stood there with our hands in different places on our faces. My hand was over my mouth, Mairead's fingers were in *V* shapes over her eyes, peeking out, and Joy's fingers were interlaced together on top of her head, elbows meeting in front of her eyes. The bike was crooked, wheel still spinning but now bent. My mom sprawled on the ground sobbing, her head in her hands and one leg over the bike. Mairead, Joy, and I looked at one another and began to slowly walk toward my mother. The three of us were biting our lips, trying not to laugh. I knelt down next to her and put my hand on her arm and whispered, "Mom, are you all right?"

My mom, trembling, sniffling, crying, her hair damp from sweat and tears, lifted her head to look at me and then got one look at her bike and just began to laugh. It was a nervous, awkward laugh, but to the relief of us all, it was a laugh. Mairead, Joy, and I all began to laugh a little with her, and then it increased to that silent, tears-coming-out-of-your-eyes laugh. In unison, we assisted in helping her up. She limped into the house, where my dad, and Maeve were already eating the pizza.

The pizza survived the fall, but the second one had slid on top of the first one, so it was like a double-decker pizza.

"Where did we get a double-layer pizza from?" my dad asked. We all laughed again. I laughed for a different reason I assume than everyone else, I laughed at him for being so clueless.

"Mom had a coupon for Little Caesars, but they don't deliver, so Mom'll have to disturb your nap next time, and you'll have to pick it up," I said to my dad, and the four of us laughed again and each took a double slice of pizza and imitated the Little Caesars man saying, "Pizza, pizza."

The next day, I signed up for driver's ed classes at school.

# 12

So I had my permit for about a year but no car to drive or responsible adult to supervise me, so it expired. Gerry stopped over after football practice during the week. He was sweaty and smelly, but I liked how he looked. He preferred us to talk on the front porch or stairs in my house so he could stand on the ground and I could stand on the bottom step so that our faces would be even and he could put his arms around my waist.

"I'm really glad to see you," he said, hugging me as I got a big whiff of him.

"I'm glad to see you, too, and to smell you," I teased.

"I'm sorry, I hate showering there. Everyone has athlete's foot or some things I would rather not see. I can shower at home."

I wrinkled my nose, grossed out. "I wish I could drive over to watch you practice sometime."

"Do you have your license?" Gerry asked with a confused look on his face.

I laughed. "No—shut up," I replied. I then went on to tell him the pizza and bike story and how I now had an expired permit. I laugh harder and harder every time I tell it, and he was laughing hard, too.

"That's hilarious. Well, you know I've had my license for two years now, so I could take you driving in the cemetery and stuff to practice sometime."

He sounded like he was trying to impress me. It worked. I jumped up and down. "That would be awesome. I don't want to be picking up food for my kids someday on a bike."

"I'd never allow you to do something like that," Gerry said.

I raised my eyebrows, trying not to think too much about what he'd just said—"allow."

"Thanks," I replied and quickly changed the subject. "So...how about this weekend?"

"Sure," he replied. He looked up at the sky and shook his head and then leaned in to kiss me. I was smiling when he kissed me. "I have something else to show you—that's why I stopped over." He took my hand and walked me to his car. He leaned into his car and pulled out his football jacket. It was in his school colors: blue and yellow. Various patches and symbols were on the coat, with his name and number on the front-right side.

"I saw a girl wearing her boyfriend's coat today and thought it would be cool if you wore mine," he said excitedly. "I think you would look adorable in it."

I tried to look excited. I was moved by his sweet gesture and that he wanted me to be part of something so important to him. I'm not someone who should ever play poker, though, because my emotions are always written all over my face. I'm a terrible liar and equally terrible at hiding my thoughts or feelings. His face sank in response.

"What?" he asked, looking wounded.

I felt like a jerk. "It's totally sweet and thoughtful of you to do this. I feel really honored that you'd want me to wear something so important to you."

"I feel a 'but' coming," he said, and he lay the coat back inside his car.

"No 'buts'—I love the idea. I was just a little caught off guard by the extremely bright color combination. I'm sorry that I didn't look excited at first." I said this hopefully.

His eyes lit up again. "So you'll wear it?"

"Of course I will," I said, trying to concentrate on what I was feeling and how sweet it was, not how fucking ugly the coat was. He reached into the car to get the coat out and smiled proudly as he wrapped it around me.

"You're turning me on wearing this coat." He smiled as he tugged the coat and pulled me toward him. My stomach jumped with excitement; I could feel his attraction for me with the way he pulled me to him and kissed me passionately. His eyes looked at me dreamily and affectionately. Whatever this was, I didn't want it to end. If wearing his coat leads to these feelings of euphoria, I'll suck it up and wear it.

"I love you," he said, still looking at me with this look that I never wanted to go away. I smiled shyly and blushed and told him I loved him, too.

"I'm crazy about you, you know that, right?"

"I'm pretty crazy about you, too," I said honestly.

"I like that you wear my coat—it makes me feel good letting people know you're mine," he said sweetly.

My nonpoker face was unable to deflect the confusion I felt when he said this. "Mine? I mean, I'm yours?" I inquired, with a twinge of some kind of irritation inside. I wasn't quite sure what this was— maybe like putting a leash on a dog.

"Well, you know what I mean; you are my girlfriend, aren't you?" I nodded. "So, like you're taken—you're my girlfriend. You know how someone wears a wedding ring so you know they're married? So you wear this coat to let others know we're dating."

I understood what he was saying, but it was still nagging at me, like a tiny feeling of humiliation that was making my defiance flame fire up. "I see what you mean," I retorted, "but I don't need any kind of brand to let people know this. I only want to be with you. I don't need anything else."

"Of course, and I only want to be with you. Maybe I just want to keep the other boys away," he said with a smirk.

I laughed. "Oh yeah, I had lines of them outside my house before I met you," I said as a tease.

"See, this will keep them away, then," he teased back.

I sighed and gave up this battle. I smiled and kissed him. "What day is your game next weekend?" I asked excitedly.

"It's at noon on Sunday," he said, a bit flatly I thought.

"Awesome. I'm off! I'll be there, and I'll wear your jacket with pride!"

He smiled; then, arms intertwined around my waist, he pulled me to him and hugged me. I hugged him back and kissed him on the cheek.

I then decided to bite the bullet and tell him about going up to see Mairead in October—like ripping off a Band-Aid, quick and painless. "I'll wear it with pride when I go visit Mairead on October twentieth as well," I blurted out at lightning speed. I looked down, my mind flashing to Ralphie from *A Christmas Story* as he tells Santa Claus that he wants "a Red Ryder BB gun with a compass in the stock and this fing that tells time." When I lifted my head up, Gerry's eyes were lifeless; he was staring vacantly and had a flat expression on his face. I took my hands and placed them on the sides of his face to have him look at me in the eye.

"I'm sorry. I'll go to all your other games, but I need to visit my sister. She really wants me to come that weekend," I said, and I was sincere. He nodded his head in agreement and looked away. He gave me a brief hug.

"OK. I have to get going," he said dismissively. My heart sank. I felt guilty. Even though I knew in my head that I wasn't doing anything wrong, I still felt guilty and didn't understand why. He briskly walked to the car, turned over the engine, and took off. I could still smell his scent on me, and tears welled in my eyes. I guessed he was disappointed I wasn't coming to his game that day. I moped into my house and plopped on the bed and cried for no real reason, except that I felt bad. "In his anger and his shame...I am leaving, I am leaving..." These words were suddenly in my head, and I wasn't sure what song they were from. I sang them to myself for a while until the rest of the words came to me. I found the album and put on Simon and

Garfunkel's "The Boxer." I listened to it over and over until my guilt subsided. Then I had an idea.

I decided to make Gerry a mixtape. It would probably sound like shit with the record crackling on a tape, but it's the thought that counts, right? I put "The Boxer" as number one, "Paint It Black" as number two. Then I was at a loss for songs. I didn't want to be cheesy and put a bunch of sappy love songs on there. I wanted it to be cool and inspiring for his football games. I did have some tapes, so I flipped through those. I found Whitney Houston's "One Moment in Time" and thought that would be cool because of the Olympics, I don't know. Then I taped over "The Boxer" and "Paint It Black" and dubbed "One Moment in Time" as number one. I decided I wouldn't have my first mixtape to him be all crackly from records. I'd stick to the tapes we had. I did have a single, "At This Moment," by Billy Vera and the Beaters. My mom and I loved the song from *Family Ties*, when Alex P. Keaton realizes he loves Ellen.

I decided I had to go to the dungeon and ask my brother for help. (Psycho theme playing in my head.)

# 13

I wasn't close with my brother. He was the oldest and the most fucked up of the four of us. He'd been around and conscious when things got bad with our parents and now was able to remember what had happened with them. He was the scapegoat; he'd stuck up for my mom and had caught the majority of the abuse from my dad. I felt for him, but he was such a butthead, it was hard to feel bad for him. He had a severe authority problem, he smoked weed, and he was now getting his GED. I had to admit, he did have kick-ass taste in music, and I knew he would have some tapes down there. He was also in a cover band, not sure what music he covered. Most of the time it was just noise, but sometimes I could hear them playing actual music, and it sounded pretty damn good.

I slowly opened the door to the basement; it creaked, and I grimaced. I don't know what I was afraid of—well, actually I do. In one of our most intimate sibling moments, my brother had hung me on the back of this door and had closed it so I wouldn't tell my mom about the party he had. I was shitting in my pants hanging there, with duct tape over my mouth as I stared at the flight of stairs before me. I was a stubborn little bitch, too. He would rip the duct tape off my face and ask, "So are you gonna tell Mom?" and I'd respond, "Yep!" over and over again until I almost fell. I kicked the door with the back of my heel and bawled. He eventually unhooked me and gave me a hug, and I never told our mom. Basically I never even mentioned my brother's name again to my mom. (As in *Christmas Story*—"Flick? Flick who? Michael? Who is Michael?") I don't believe I'd said ten words to him over the past five years.

I went downstairs and knocked on his door. I didn't hear anything. I was sure he was out. I would have heard him snoring if he'd been asleep. His door was open, so I peeked inside. It smelled of stale cigarettes, beer and crushed velvet. He had a lot of Led Zeppelin posters that were that fuzzy black material. It had a certain scent to it. I could dimly see beer cans scattered throughout with ashes in the tops of the cans and ashtrays overflowing with cigarette butts. His bed was empty, his comforter twisted into a teepee shape. Then I saw it: his monster stereo system. The stereo was incongruent compared to his room and our house. This thing didn't belong in this place; it was some killer sound system, shiny and new. Man, making a mixtape on this thing would be awesome. He had drawers full of tapes, and 90 percent of them were albums I had upstairs.

What a dick, I thought. We have a sewage system problem on the side of our house that my mom cannot afford to get fixed, and he has a stereo that probably cost as much as a mortgage payment. Then I thought for a moment and realized that he probably didn't pay for this and that these were all hot items. I found Simon and Garfunkel, the Rolling Stones, the Doors, and Led Zeppelin! He also had a new band's tape, Guns N' Roses! One of the newer bands that I actually liked. I definitely had to dub these bad boys for myself. I closed the door and tiptoed back upstairs. The coast was clear, so I turned the corner, and *fuck!* I smacked right into my brother's chest, and the tapes fell on the floor—luckily just on the carpet. His brown eyes were wide and intense. He had on a Metallica T-shirt with a knife sticking out of a toilet that said "metal up your ass." He had smoke coming out of his mouth and was holding a cigarette in his hand. His hair was disheveled. I've been told he is "too good-looking," whatever that means. I find him revolting.

"Uh…what…the…*fuck*…do you think you're doing?" Michael asked. I felt like I was two feet tall.

"Uh, hi, Michael, I went downstairs to see if you had some songs, because the albums I have crackle. Can I please borrow these?" I picked the tapes up off the floor and put them back in their cases.

"It appears that you've already helped yourself there," he said with sarcasm. "Maybe if you would've asked me first without taking them, I'd say yes." He swiped them out of my hands and stomped down the basement stairs with his black metal-toe combat boot Doc Martens. My heart sank. I didn't realize how excited I'd been until my project was taken away. I needed to do this. I went upstairs, got some money, and brought it back downstairs. I swallowed my pride and knocked on the door to Michael's room.

"Go away!" he bellowed.

"When the Levee Breaks" was playing in his room, muffled behind the door. "Please, Mike. I, uh, need your advice," I said, not realizing that I needed his advice until it came flying out of my mouth. The music went off. He opened the door with a cigarette hanging out of his mouth, now wearing a black baseball hat on backward. His brown eyes sparkled, and his eyebrows turned into little *U* shapes.

"You need my advice?" he said, muffled through the cigarette between his lips. I shook my head and sighed. He opened the door wider to allow me to pass inside.

"I'm sorry for coming in here. I had an idea, and I wanted to ask you about it, then I saw your killer stereo system." (Flattery never hurts.)

"And?" I could tell he was growing impatient, but he beamed proudly at his fine piece of equipment. I wanted to say, "And I can't believe you're such an asshole having something like this in our house when Mom is struggling to pay for our utilities." But I didn't, because he would just shut down and I wouldn't talk to him again for five years. His fuse was always pretty short.

"And I wanted to make my boyfriend a mixtape because he's mad at me and I don't know what to do—I can't stand it." My voice cracked. Michael smirked, put out his cigarette, and plopped down on the edge of his bed. He grabbed a baseball and began to spin it in his hands.

"You…you have a…boyfriend?" he asked.

"Yes, his name is Gerry McGrath," I said proudly. He looked like he was trying to suppress a laugh.

"Really? How old are you?"

I snorted. "You don't know how fucking old I am, weirdo? I'm your sister!"

He laughed and nudged me. "I'm teasing; I know you're sixteen."

"You don't know shit—I'm eighteen, for your information."

He smiled again, looking impressed. "Well, aren't you the little firecracker!" he said with a smile. "I guess I should remember that with your stubborn little ass hanging on the door, stuck there with duct tape."

"I took an hour to cave dangling above my death," I said, giggling and impressed with myself. "I don't think I've talked to you since that day. You scared the crap out of me."

"Yeah, sorry 'bout that," Michael said humbly, looking down at his lap. "You can borrow these tapes to make your *boyfriend* a *mixtape*," he said in a teasing voice.

"Thanks, man," I said modestly, even though I was doing cart-wheels inside.

"So, uh, what did you need my advice about?" he said with a curious expression. I didn't really need his advice, I don't think. I needed his tapes.

"Oh, nothing. I kind of feel weird talking to you about it, since we actually haven't talked in like five years." I was being a smartass. Everyone likes a smartass, right?

"Come on, try me," he replied, appearing genuinely interested.

"Well, I'm going to visit Mairead on October twentieth for home-coming weekend and—"

"Wait, what? *You* are going to visit Mairead at Eastern? No fucking way!" he said, smiling. "I want to go!"

Oh jeez, not what I expected to happen today. "OK," I said impatiently. "You'll have to talk to her about it."

"Sorry, go on," he said, putting his hand on his chin to indicate that he was truly paying close attention to what I was saying. I smacked his arm, amazed at how quickly we'd resolved this five-year-long grudge.

"So it's Gerry's homecoming weekend that weekend and—"

"Who's Gerry?" he asked.

"Are you serious?" I replied. "My boyfriend, OK, hello McFly?"

"Oh yeah, sorry," he replied sheepishly.

"So it's his homecoming weekend, and he seems disappointed that I'm going to visit Mairead, but he hasn't really said anything—he just looks strange when I talk about it," I said finally.

"Strange how?"

"Well, he gets real quiet, and his eyes get dark. What do you think that means?"

Michael played with his beard and appeared to be deep in thought. "What was the question again?" he asked innocently.

"Oh Lord! Forget it McFly." I sighed and left his room shaking my head. I couldn't be too bad because I had an armful of gold to make a non-cracking mixtape.

Michael came upstairs later on that night, I am not sure if he has ever walked up those stairs. Apparently, he eventually caught on to what I needed advice about and just needed a "few hours" to process it. He didn't offer much advice about my question about Gerry's behavior. He did offer me the use of his stereo system; I couldn't believe it! I almost hugged him but was able to stop myself, because that would have been too weird. He then said something somewhat profound. "Your guy shouldn't be mad at you because you are visiting your sister. Family's more important than friends" and "blood is thicker than water" is what Michael told me. I thought this was ironic, considering we hadn't spoken in five years because he'd had a party with his friends. Surprisingly, Michael then offered to drive me to Eastern. He'd apparently called Mairead earlier, and she was shocked but OK with him coming to visit; she was also shocked that he would be escorting me. I asked Michael to drive me to Gerry's house after school tomorrow, and he agreed.

School dragged all day. I couldn't wait to get home and bring Gerry his mixtape. I was excited. I was very pleased with my work. Everything was annoying me today because I was totally impatient. In religion class we discussed sexuality, and I was very uncomfortable. One girl (who frequently had hickeys) in the class decided that this was an opportune time for her to disclose her "statutory rape" situation at school; she was seventeen and he was eighteen. I didn't have the patience for it. I had already heard the other side of the story on the bus aka "the gossip train". Apparently, this was just her excuse to be a victim, when she really had just given it up and her parents had found out, so she claimed he'd raped her when in fact she was fully consenting and they were only a year apart—maybe six months. She cried and snuggled up to the nun in class, who stroked her hair. I thought I might vomit.

Then, in gym, we were discussing our previous teams for tennis. The majority of my gym class population was African-American girls. They were all hilarious, and they actually distracted me with their entertaining stories and their own lingo. I adored their expressions for things. I could listen to them all day. Well, during the previous classes, we'd been divided into teams by color: four girls were red, four girls were blue, four girls were green, and so on. My team was the color black. We now had to tell the gym teacher what teams we'd been on over the last month, because she was going to rotate us. So one girl said she used to be on red, and one girl said she used to be on blue. When it was my turn, I shouted out, "I used to be black!" The entire class roared with laughter. The African-American girls were shaking and squeaking. They all patted me on the back, like I was the funniest person on earth. I actually didn't realize it was funny until

I'd said it. I don't think I'm a funny person, and I'm often surprised that people laugh at what I say. I was just saying what came to mind without any intention of being funny. But if people want to think I'm witty and clever, I won't argue.

*Finally*, the end of that treacherous school day arrived. The bus was, of course, extremely slow getting home and made about fifty more stops than usual. The African-American girls were singing "Bust a Move." Even though it was a fairly new song, I couldn't enough of them singing and dancing to it. I tried to join along in the singing to distract myself sounding ridiculously Caucasian. I was shaking my leg rapidly, I was so on edge. I accidentally hopped off the bus one stop early; after I kicked myself in the ass, I ran the extra two blocks to my house. Michael's car wasn't out front. I whipped off my uniform in a flash, put some deodorant on, brushed my teeth, and sat on the couch waiting for Michael. After about fifteen minutes, I stormed into the bathroom and put on some lip gloss, then mascara and blush. What was I doing? I heard Annie Potts from *Pretty in Pink* in my head reply, "Wishful makeuping." This was ridiculous; I had to get out of there. So I decided to walk it.

Fucking five miles later, with a sweat mustache and sweaty armpits, I ultimately arrived at Gerry's house. I rang the doorbell, and his dad answered the door. He had a surprised expression on his face. "Hey, Mary Kate, come on in." The house smelled glorious, and I was starving. He offered me something to drink—their fridge was stocked! Another one of those things where you don't realize how poor you are until you go to someone else's house and they have central air or pop in the fridge. I excitedly had a root beer, and he gave me a personal Home Run Inn cheese pizza. His dad luckily made himself two, and I was done eating mine before he sat down.

"Holy smokes, Mary Kate! You can eat! I love a girl with a healthy appetite!" he exclaimed.

I appreciated this. I wasn't skinny or fat; I thought I was just right. But of course, I was unsure if this was a good thing and if I should in fact be skinnier. His Dad asked me questions about school and began disclosing some stories about his high school days. The conversation with him just flowed with ease. His dad was an excellent conversationalist, and I truly enjoyed talking with him.

He asked me about my family and I found myself telling him about my Dad leaving, my mom's situation and my siblings. He appeared very engrossed in what I was saying. We were interrupted by laughter, and Gerry opened the door with Shelley right behind. His face dropped. My stomach lurched. I wasn't sure what to make of his expression. Then he smiled with a gasp and gave me a hug. I'd missed him so.

"Mary Kate and I have been having a lovely chat; I was hoping you'd never come home, Ger," his dad said with a wink. I blushed and giggled. Gerry grabbed my hand and pulled me into their dining room and their "parlor." People who are rich have a family room with a TV and then another room with furniture for "company." It was beautiful. He pulled me on the couch with him and kissed me madly. My heart leaped with relief. It had been agony since he'd left so abruptly the day before.

"What are you doing here? How did you get here?" he asked, kissing my cheek and pulling my legs onto his lap. My legs ached, and elevating them felt nice. He began rubbing my leg. I closed my eyes and leaned my head back like a dog that's getting its belly rubbed.

"I walked, silly," I replied. Gerry's eyes bulged open. "My legs ache, so that feels nice."

"You walked! Get out of here!" He massaged my legs. "How come?"

"Because I wanted to give you something I made." I was thrilled: the moment was finally here! I reached into my pocket to give Gerry the tape, and then I realized that I'd never taken the tape out of the cassette player. Son of a bitch! My face sank, and I handed him the case, burdened with disappointment.

"A mixtape? You made me a mixtape!" he responded with an impressed look on his face. He read the songs I'd written on the insert.

"Yes, but I forgot the tape at home. I'm a moron," I replied flatly.

Gerry slapped my leg. "Don't talk about yourself like that. It's the thought that counts. The fact that you're here is enough." I looked down, ashamed at his scolding. He took his two fingers and lifted my chin up to meet his eyes. His eyes were filling with moisture. I admired the thick eyelashes that framed his gleaming eyes, which were about to erupt with tears. *Holy shit!*

"This is the sweetest thing anyone has ever done for me," he said passionately. He buried his head into my neck and nuzzled under my ear. "I love you," he said in a muffled voice. I closed my eyes and leaned my head against his ear. We sat like that for a long while.

I think we both may have dozed off, because it was dark by the time we woke up. They had a grandfather clock that chimed, and I counted seven dongs. Gerry raised his head up, appearing disoriented for a second. I'd just been wondering if it was morning or night.

"Hey," I said.

He pushed himself up and then held his hand out for me. "I'll drive you home, OK? I have a shitload of homework to do," he said sadly.

"That sucks. I forgot that I do, too."

We climbed into his mother's hatchback.

"I'll run in when I get home and get the tape, OK? I'll be quick."

"I'm in no hurry; I'll probably be awake late anyway, with that little catnap." He smiled. I noticed that his mom had a cassette player in their car. I grinned, hoping he would listen to it on his way home.

Gerry pulled up to my house and got out; he put his arm around me, and we walked arm in arm to my doorstep. He lightly swatted my butt when I ran into the house. On my way back down, I saw that Michael was standing by the stairs.

"Hey, sis. I'm sorry. I got stuck in traffic," Michael said by way of explanation, looking grungy in his flannel shirt and Chuck Norris T-shirt. He always looked kind of dirty; I thought he worked in construction, but I wasn't sure.

"No big deal," I replied. I should have known better than to depend on him. I made a mental note to find another ride to Eastern; I couldn't have my brother bail on me.

"Is that your guy out there?" he asked curiously, smoothing his hair.

"Yeah. Would you like to meet him?" I said, growing impatient. He always seemed like he was in slow motion.

"Uh, OK," he said hesitantly. I walked out with Michael following. Gerry's eyes were looking at Michael with a confused expression. I did the introduction. They shook hands, both appearing to be shy. Michael quickly walked back into the house.

"I didn't realize he still lived here. You rarely talk about him," Gerry said.

"Yes, kind of weird story. I'll fill you in later," I replied. "OK, I'll let you go. I don't want to delay your homework any further."

Gerry frowned. "Mary Kate, you made my day, baby." My heart fluttered. I watched him walk to his car, and when he got inside, he slipped the tape in the cassette player, and I heard the beginning of "One Moment in Time" start. I know that music choice was probably cheesy, but what the hell, it was from the Olympics. That had to inspire everyone. After all, he was a football player!

I strolled into the house, satisfied with the day's events and relieved that things were "fixed." I didn't like having that uneasy feeling like he was mad at me or that I was disappointing him. I went to my room and began to do my horrid algebra homework; my brain literally ached with stabbing pains while trying to figure these out. I always struggled with math, and it was hard for me to keep my mind on my assignments. I continually caught myself checking out and daydreaming about Gerry and his sweet little face. After about an hour of this nonsense, I was finally done with algebra and was mentally exhausted. My phone rang, which jerked me out of my spaced-out mentality. I picked up quickly.

"Hey, baby," Gerry said on the other end of the line. An automatic sappy grin emerged on my face.

"Hi," I said quietly, still smiling like a cheeseball.

"I love my tape. Thank you so much. I'm completely in awe of you. I have no idea how you compiled something like that. It's just so..." he said sweetly, his voice trailing off.

"So?" I probed.

"I don't know the word for it. The mix is amazing, and the fact that you did that for me is so thoughtful. I love all the songs, including some of the songs I didn't even know I liked. I feel pumped up when I listen to it, and oddly, I can't wait for my game on Sunday. You inspired me," he said calmly, and I beamed like a dork. "My mom and dad can pick you up for my game on Sunday."

"OK," I said nervously. Being with them alone would be challenging: his mom was very difficult for me to read. "I can't wait to watch you. It's going to be so cool!"

"I'm kind of nervous for you to watch me. I didn't care that much before about my performance. Now I feel like I want to do well—you make me want to be a better player. I want to impress you," he said shyly.

I had a warm, fuzzy feeling growing in my chest. "I love you so much," I blurted out in spite of myself.

"I love you, too," he replied softly.

"I have to work the next three days after school, so I'm not sure if I'll have a lot of time to talk."

"That sucks. I wish you didn't have to work and that I could just take care of you," he said sweetly.

"Uh, thanks," I said awkwardly. "It's no big deal—I'll just miss you."

"I'll miss you, too. I'll also be busy, with practice and homework. My parents will pick you up around nine on Sunday."

"OK, then. See you Sunday."

"See you Sunday; I love you."

"I love you, too," I said back. We both sat there for a while, not saying anything. I didn't want to hang up.

"You hang up," I said teasingly.

"No, you—I can't," he teased back.

We did this back and forth for a minute, which was adorable to me, but I'm sure it would have been sickening to witness for an outside party.

"Let's hang up at the same time, OK?" I said.

"Good idea," he said back. "On three: one, two, three."

I laughed and hung up. God, I'm a dork.

# 14

I had to work the next three days after school and then did homework, so the remainder of the week flew by. Sunday arrived at last,
and I awoke to that flurry of nerves in my stomach. I was stirred
up with joy and newness. I'd never attended a high school football
game. I was wearing Gerry's jacket, anxiously awaiting his parent's
arrival on my porch. I kept a lookout for his mom's hatchback.

A giant, insanely huge white van was heading down my block and
stopped in front of my house. It was an RV. His dad honked the horn
with an obnoxious melody and got out of the driver's seat. He was
giggling and opened the door for me. I climbed inside; I'd never seen
such a thing! A van equipped with a bathroom? It had electricity and
a kitchen; it was so weird and cool at the same time. When I entered
the RV cab, I saw seats behind the driver's seat and passenger seat. I
sat behind his dad on the driver's side. His mom was reading a book
in the passenger seat.

"Hello, Mary Kate," his mom said curtly.

"Hi, Mrs. McGrath," I replied. She went back to reading her book.
Mr. McGrath smiled at me in the mirror of the RV. I breathed. I wasn't
sure what to do. The radio was on a sports station. It calmed me for
some reason; my grandparents listened to the same station, and it
reminded me of them. We didn't talk much on the way to the game. I
had no idea what to say or do in that situation. My mind searched for

some kind of script, but nothing was coming. My mind was blank. I didn't want to be annoying or a chatterbox while his dad was listening to the radio and his mom was reading. So I just sat back and enjoyed the ride. Mr. McGrath would ask me random questions and appeared to be pondering my answers with great thought because there was a long pause between my answer and his next question. He asked me if my mom had a car and was blown away when I said my mom did not have her license. He asked how I got to school, he seemed more shocked that I told him I took the bus. I found myself nervously telling them about my mom and the pizza story. Mr. McGrath laughed. Mrs. McGrath smiled.

When we got to the game, I asked his parents if they needed help, and I carried the portable seat cushions. It was dreary and windy outside. I like wind, and I prefer dreary to sunny weather due to my stark-white skin. I usually get sunburn even while wearing sunscreen. The stadium was enormous; the band played drums, tapping continuously. The sun peeked through the clouds occasionally, which made for a beautiful fall day. The atmosphere was invigorating. I didn't understand the concept of football, but I loved the ambience of it and how passionate everyone was about it. I think it was also because Sunday football was usually a good day in my family; my dad would be very into the game or not home at all, watching the game somewhere else. Football equaled relaxation at my house.

We climbed onto the platinum-colored bleachers and found a perfect spot in the middle where you could see all the players in a row on the sidelines. I stared at the players as I tried to find Gerry and sat down on the ice-cold bleacher. My butt immediately froze, and I jerked involuntarily. His mom was looking down at me and laughed in a sweet, motherly way.

"Here, silly. That's why we brought the cushions you're carrying," she said warmly. I smiled sheepishly and distributed the cushions to his parents before they wisely planted their asses down. My face blushing in response to her somewhat patronizing tone, I looked up again at the sidelines and sensed her looking at me. I turned to her, and she was smiling with an "it's OK; everything's going to be all right" kind of expression. I smiled back, and in that moment it seemed a layer was removed from her harsh, steel-coated shell. Her face appeared much different when she smiled. It lit up her whole face. A whistle blew, and we both turned toward the field.

I spotted Gerry looking up at the stands. I'd forgotten to ask him what number he was, but I could recognize his stance and of course his sweet ass in those tight navy-blue pants. His jersey was daffodil yellow with navy writing; McGrath was written on the back, number fourteen. When our eyes met, he removed his helmet, revealing his messy hair and black horizontal lines under his eyes, and he winked at me. My stomach did backflips. My heart palpitated, and a surge of energy shot me below the waist. He looked so handsome—hot, actually. The brutal ride here had been worth every minute. He kissed his hand and waved. I kissed my hand and blew a kiss back in reaction before realizing how cheesy I looked. His parents were waving, too, so that kiss could have been meant for them. His mom didn't blow a kiss to him, which would have been socially acceptable for her to do; my cheeks burned with embarrassment. Everyone tolerates mom behavior.

I heard some obnoxious female laughter behind me, and when I turned around, I saw three girls laughing and whispering to one another. They were all breathtakingly gorgeous, and I immediately thought of Cindy Mancini and her two follower sidekicks from *Can't Buy Me Love*. They were all completely beautiful, of course. I shuddered because I sensed that chicks like that were Bad News Bears. I'd definitely be avoiding those broads at all costs. I turned back around and realized I had a few questions about football. These would make lovely conversation pieces for his mother, because I otherwise had absolutely nothing to say to her usually. Since she was a big football fan, I thought it might help to break the ice.

I asked her why they had those black lines under their eyes. I asked her certain questions about the game and if Gerry was going to score a touchdown. She laughed sweetly at times and at other times spoke to me in a condescending tone, like "you're such a stupid girl who doesn't understand the game of football." She explained that Gerry was on defense and that he blocked the other team from scoring. I sort of understood. I said to her, "So he's kind of like Mike Singletary from the Bears?"

She raised her eyebrows as if she was surprised and said, "Exactly." I beamed like I'd gotten the last word in the spelling bee correct. Impressing this woman was challenging, but it did have its rewards. She asked me if I had to use the ladies' room and suggested I go before halftime, and then she immediately explained to me what halftime was. I was slightly insulted—I at least knew what halftime was. Sheesh.

When I came out of the stall, that striking blond Cindy Mancini type was standing at the sink. She smirked in the mirror when she saw me come out of the stall. She was wetting one of those stiff, coarse, brown paper towels, which she then wiped her face with to remove the windblown dust from the field. Of course, this illuminated her radiant skin and emphasized her flawless, supple cheek with its natural rosy hue. I caught myself gawking at her like a guy in awe of her beauty, except that I was a female and jealous as hell. My skin was so pale that it was almost blue from the veins showing through. I had to always wear sunscreen and tinted moisturizer, or else I'd even startle myself when I looked in the mirror, as if I'd seen a ghost. *Yikes—oh, it's just me.* I was so amazed that her skin could be so naturally perfect that my bluish shade now turned green with envy. When our eyes met in the mirror, my mind immediately flashed to *Ferris Bueller* and his sister Jeanie's eyes meeting in competition; Jeanie was so vindictive and envious and wanted her brother to get caught ditching school so badly. The flawless, piercing, sky-blue eyes and beach-tussled blond haired girl sneered atme and sighed.

"You must be Mary Kate. I'm Michelle." She said with a condescending tone.

"Hi, Michelle," I said. Michelle was staring at me still, looking me up and down with an evil sneer. "What?"

"Oh, nothing," Michelle said with a satisfied sigh. "I'm just pleased to see that you're a step down." Then she chortled in a way that sounded like a catlike purr that made the hairs on my neck stand up. I was so intimidated that I stood there paralyzed with my usual go-to "deer in the headlights" expression and vacant brain. The evil bitch strutted out of the ladies' room; in the mirror I saw the reflection of her perfect derriere. I was completely flabbergasted at the audacity of this broad telling me right to my face that I was a step down. I assumed that meant not equivalent in looks to Gerry. It stung because I knew it was true, despite Gerry telling me otherwise.

I processed this interaction and left the bathroom feeling dazed and confused. I sighed painfully when I saw the three of them leaning back on their elbows on a ledge and thrusting out their overly padded boobs. I tittered to myself, no pun intended, that I was voluptuous and au naturel in the breast department. The one brunette with mega-lipstick-coated lips blocked my walkway—her tarantula eyes adorned with every color of the rainbow eye shadow that Wet n Wild had to offer—and speared herself into my space. She invaded my personal space and was three inches from my face.

"You like to blow kisses, baby? How 'bout we play peek-a-boo, too?" The other two girls giggled. "You look like Little Orphan Annie doing that," she continued, and the other two brats snickered loudly with their fake, obnoxious laughs. I was in my frozen state as usual, but then a flicker of anger blazed forth when I caught a whiff of her Bubblicious breath. I clenched my jaw, and then…something came to me. My mom had always told me to "kill them with kindness" whenever I told her a bully story from grammar school. The older I became, the more I realized that my mother was a genius.

"Oh, really? Thanks!" I said enthusiastically. "You remind me of Dee Dee McCall from the TV show *Hunter*." I said this trying to sound as sincere as possible; she did resemble a forty-five-year-old woman, wearing all that makeup. From her expression, I'd say she'd never watched the show or knew who I was talking about. It was on Friday nights, so I was sure she was never at home watching TV like I was. I walked away before the three of them could get a word in. I walked back to my cushioned seat, relieved that finally I'd been able to stick up for myself, especially to those kinds of girls. I had Gerry's coat on, and for the first time, I was wearing it with pride.

⤳

I came back to my seat to find his mom and dad jumping up and cheering. His mom was yelling all sorts of different instructions, profanities, and comments. She was cracking me up; I'd never seen a woman so passionate about something, let alone football. This time, she caught me looking at her.

"What?" she asked.

"Nothing; you're just funny," I replied.

"Funny? Funny how? Like a clown? Am I here to amuse you?" she said with a Brooklyn, Joe Pesci accent—a woman after my own heart. His dad was looking at us now, smirking but staying quiet.

"You saw *Goodfellas*?" I asked her, surprised.

They both laughed. "Yes, Gerry recommended it after you guys saw it, so we went to see it, twice!" his dad said.

"No, I'm serious—how am I funny?" his mom asked, speaking now in her own voice.

"I guess not funny like I'd laugh *at* you—funny in a good way. Your comments during this game are humorous. I'm also impressed with how much passion you have about something, especially football," I said genuinely. His dad grinned and looked back at the field. His mom had a humble and agreeable expression on her face. Her gumption and vigor were contagious, and soon I was cheering and leaping along with them.

Gerry's team won. According to his mom, Gerry played well. Every time he blocked someone, I winced, while his mom shouted approval. All I could see was pain.

We exited the bleachers in good spirits and walked to the ginormous RV. I was listening to his mom explain something to me about defense, but my thoughts were distracted by wondering what would happen now. Would Gerry meet us and drive home with us? While thinking this, I felt a groping around my waist from behind and felt myself being lifted. I laughed, assuming it was Gerry. He put me down, and I turned around and saw that it was indeed Gerry, now kissing me all over my face. I secretly hoped those evil bitches were watching. His parents continued walking, I presume feeling uncomfortable with their son's public display of affection. I didn't care what anyone thought right then, because I was on cloud nine. When he finally stopped, I looked up at him lovingly, and he reciprocated. He was remarkably good-looking, especially when sweaty and glorious in his uniform.

"Thanks for coming to my game, baby doll," he said gratefully. His voice was hoarse and raspy from yelling during the game, and it was turning me on.

"I am so glad I could make it!" I said truthfully. "Seeing you in that uniform was worth it."

He smiled shyly. "I wish I could ride with you, but I have to take the bus back with the team. Will you meet me at my house?"

"Of course I will," I replied.

I felt much more at ease on the ride home than on the commute there. I speculated that his mom was just one of those people whom it takes a while to get to know. She wasn't reading and was talking to her husband about the game but would glance back at me periodically, as if I was part of the conversation. The traffic exiting the parking lot was congested, and the ride home took a long time. I was growing sleepy from the fresh fall air and now being in the warm, cozy RV. I attempted to keep my eyes open and was trying to look out the window. My eye started twitching. It was a weird sensation.

"Tired, Mary Kate?" his mom asked quietly.

"Yes. Is that why my eye is twitching?" I asked her, wondering. She started to laugh.

"You're a funny girl, Mary Kate," she said sincerely. Again, I'm funny, but I wasn't trying to be. I was really wondering. Whatever—I was too sleepy to care. "Take a little nap, Mary Kate. There's a bed in the back, which is what this RV is for—road trips." She smiled. I was perfectly content where I was, because I couldn't move from exhaustion. Two hours later, we finally arrived at his parents' house. I woke up when the ignition was turned off.

"Wake up, missy. Man, you were snoring!" his dad said teasingly. I laughed, but then I was worried that I really had been snoring. I could never tell with him; it seemed he was always being facetious, but he was also hard to read, with his deadpan affect and big build. Gerry pulled up in a car packed with men like a clown car. I beamed when he squeezed out of the car. He was showered and wearing a baseball cap, track pants, and sleeveless shirt and carrying a big duffle bag.

"Yay! I'm glad you're here!" he said with so much zeal that I blushed and giggled. He wrapped his arm around my neck, pulled me to him, and kissed the top of my head. Of course, his mom had dinner ready before she left with instructions for Shelley to put it in the oven. Mrs. McGrath was one of those organized, plan-ahead types I couldn't comprehend but admired. Shelley was home sleeping and woke up when we came home, probably starving. Dinner was a pot roast with potatoes and carrots, and it smelled mouthwatering. I was ravenous. I wolfed down food at lightning speed, and it hit the spot—they always had the best dinners. It was delicious. His dad was smirking at me as he watched me eat again. When I caught his glance, I giggled and blushed.

"Like I said, Mary Kate, you can sure eat! I like a girl with a healthy appetite."

After we finished eating and had loaded the dishwasher, his parents asked Shelley, Gerry, and me to watch the Bears game. They had videotaped it while we were at Gerry's game, and while watching the game, his mom and dad would pause the game and point out different plays and rules about football. I could have found this condescending, but I found it endearing and thoughtful. The game did begin to make more sense after their explanations. Following the game, an excerpt from the "Super Bowl Shuffle" played on TV, so

I began singing along unconsciously. Gerry appeared shocked and puzzled at hearing me; his eyebrows were raised.

I explained we played the Superbowl Shuffle quite frequently all year round when I was growing up, since my dad had gotten a VHS copy of it for Christmas one year. When I told Gerry that I knew every word of the "Super Bowl Shuffle," he scoffed in disbelief.

"I do!" I exclaimed with a smirk.

"No way," he replied, rolling his eyes.

Shelley was eavesdropping now. "What can you do, MK?" she inquired with a yawn, still looking half-asleep.

"I told Gerry that I know every word of the 'Super Bowl Shuffle,' but he doesn't believe me."

"Hell—that's like a Bible verse around here. Let's hear it," she said with a smile.

"I can sing some of it right now, but I'd need to be prompted with the music," I answered.

"Well, let's hear some of it then," she said encouragingly. Gerry was sitting back with his hands behind his head.

"Well, I haven't quoted it in years. Man, I never should have said anything."

"OK, sing one of the players," Gerry said, tickling me in the ribs. I laughed and slapped his hand away.

"My name is Sweetness and I like to dance, runnin' the ball is like making romance," I quoted. I sang horribly and began to giggle uncontrollably. Singing this was making me shaky inside, and my stomach wrenched. Thoughts of my dad plowed into my head, along with memories of watching this over and over. Thoughts of my most humiliating and embarrassing memories flooded into my mind, and I trailed off. I took a deep breath and blew my cheeks out. Gerry and Shelley looked at me with anticipation, thirsty for more.

"Come on! Keep going!" Shelley said. Gerry tickled me again, which irritated me this time instead of making me laugh.

"I...uh...really need the music. I feel really stupid right now. Can we just forget it?" I pleaded.

"You brought it up, sweetie," Gerry said, cupping his hand around my neck. He kissed me on the cheek and then whispered in my ear, "I like how you sing; your voice is turning me on for some reason."

I blushed, and my ear throbbed; goose bumps traveled down my spine. I smiled, and I felt calm again. "Maybe another day," I whispered back. "I just can't continue."

"Oh jeez, get a room! Come on, MK!" Shelley said with annoyance. I couldn't continue singing; those shameful memories flooded me when I sang, and I didn't realize that bothered me until now. I must have blocked it all out. I should have kept my big mouth shut and not bragged. This was the kind of crap that always happened to me whenever I thought for myself and spoke on my own. I always made a fool of myself.

"All right, you guys. I forgot all about this until I started singing, but in that one Walter Payton sentence, I felt flooded with the most embarrassing and humiliating memories of my life. I must have blocked it all out. I didn't mean to be a showboat; I was just trying to impress you, but this totally backfired on me," I said sheepishly.

"Aw, MK, I'm sorry," Shelley said, sounding sincere. Gerry rubbed my back and kissed me on the cheek. "Well," she added, "it can't be worse than my most humiliating childhood experience. I got my period for the first time while on the American Eagle at Six Flags Great America—either that or that ride busted my hymen." Her face flushed, and she laughed nervously. Gerry shook his head and covered his eyes with his hand. "When I exited the ride, blood went down my leg and into my sock!"

I tried to be empathetic because that's truly a horrifying experience for an eighth grader to go through, knowing that everyone for years to come will remember that incident: "Remember when Shelley McGrath got her period at Great America?" I thought that would be rough, but that was nothing compared to mine. It was no fault on Shelley's part; that was an accident, an act of God, and it could have happened to anyone. My situation was embarrassing because I should have known better but didn't. It was all self-inflicted. I trusted Gerry, and since he was being so encouraging and supportive, I figured, what did I have to lose? I'll tell them this story; maybe it would be good to laugh about it. Shelley had just unloaded her most embarrassing moment, so I felt compelled to do the same.

So in 1985, the neighborhood was on fire with Chicago Bears fever, and everyone broke the commandment *Thou shall not have any false gods before me.* Mike Ditka was a legend. People worshiped him. Our school got into this team spirit, and the entire school was encouraged to enter a "Super Bowl Shuffle" competition. Each grade had to split into groups and perform. I so wished we had assigned groups, because I knew no one would ask me to join their group because I really didn't play with any classmates outside of school. I was usually grounded and unable to go anywhere with friends. As I mentioned before, the more isolated I was, the more I struggled socially. Plus, I was in that awkward eleven-year-old stage. Despite my being a total social outcast, most of my classmates were nice to me, probably out of pity. One of the girls in the popular clique, Rachel, seemed to go out of her way to be welcoming to me and asked if I wanted to be in their group. I was thrilled! It was probably the first time I was really excited about anything at school.

I told my mom the second I walked into the house. My dad even got into it because it involved the Chicago Bears. I said I needed to wear a Bears article of clothing hoping my Dad would take me to Venture to buy something. Instead, my dad had an idea to make me a jersey out of one of his old white T-shirts. My mom had some blue felt, and we glued a number fifty on this T-shirt because I was supposed to sing the part of Mike Singletary. I wore this homemade jersey to school with my brown corduroy uniform pants.

When I arrived at school, I was shocked to find that every student was wearing jeans, gym shoes, and store-bought Chicago Bears T-shirts and jerseys! I saw that the group I was to sing with all were adorned in cute jeans and different official Chicago Bears jerseys and matching blue-and-orange scrunchies in their hair. Some kids had had their faces painted or Bears helmet stickers on their faces. Even the primary grades wore child-size jerseys or Bears T-shirts with jeans and gym shoes. I was mortified and embarrassed. I was angry at my parents for making me go through this.

When I got to my classroom, I didn't want to take my coat off. I wanted to pretend like I was sick and go home. I was also aware that this wasn't a possibility, because my parents never picked us up from school, I mean no matter what unless I was puking. My Mom would have to walk there and it usually took her forever to leave work so it was not even worth it. My father would just ignore the call because "it wasn't an emergency." I couldn't cope with the guilt of my mom picking me up on foot or riding her bike when I was already feeling disgraced.

Due to the "level of participation," as he said, the principal had to inflict some rules on the competition and put a limitation on how many students could perform at one time.. I guess because I hadn't made it to practice, the decision had been made to cut my sorry ass. Rachel walked up to me with sheer repentance on her face, which increased as she got a look at the dingy white homemade Bears costume. Rachel said in a patronizing tone, "Hey, MK I'm really sorry—we tried to call you this week to let you know the day we were practicing, but your phone was busy or there was some recording that it was disconnected." I believed her because I didn't yet have the mental capacity to see through people's bullshit; my bullshit meter was already on overload listening to my dad every night. Also, we frequently didn't pay our phone bill, so I was sure it was true. I wondered briefly why they hadn't notified me at school, but what was the point? I toughed it out and watched in horror as my class did a choreographed routine. They were like Chicago Bears cheerleaders, and it was awesome. A part of me was grateful, because I'd have looked ridiculous up there with them. I'd have stood out more with my homemade jersey. The *Sesame Street* song played in my head: "One of these things is not like the others; one of these things just doesn't belong."

The other girl who'd gotten cut, Kristina, was fired up and furious. I had no idea why. I was already in the beginnings of my numb stage, where I really didn't give a shit about anything—no point in getting pissed off. Yet I could feel embarrassment still, and it was gnawing at my soul. Kristina was very persuasive and somehow talked me into doing "our own routine" to show them. Again, I was clueless; whatever, sure, I said. It didn't occur to me in that moment that we had absolutely nothing planned as Kristina stormed up to the sign-up desk and wrote our two names down.

The group I was initially supposed to have performed with was spectacular, of course. It wasn't possible that they had choreographed and planned that routine in one day, I realized, feeling foolish. They all looked cool and pretty, and they were great dancers. None of the girls sang any of the parts; they just did more of a cheerleading routine. My time memorizing all the players' little ditties was a waste of time, and I became conscious that I was going to be cut anyways and wasn't considered a part of their group. I grasped the concept of how big of an outcast I was. I was certain that Rachel had asked me because she was nice like that, without consulting with the other girls, and when she told them that she'd asked me—well, adios.

I think I blacked out temporarily following their stellar performance, and I vaguely remember walking on stage. It was a distant memory until the following Friday, when they played all the performances on the recently installed classroom televisions. It was a school-wide event. I watched in horror as grades K–6 all looked cool and fun in their store-bought threads and up-to-date sneakers. Everyone clapped during each performance—especially the cheerleading squad that Kristina and I were supposed to be with—which also included whistling by the boys. Basically every girl in the class was on that stage except me, Kristina, and two other girls we all assumed were girls but who reminded me more of Allison from *The Breakfast Club*: basket cases. This was also my first realization that I was classified in this genre of students—the outcasts.

Kristina and I immediately followed the cheerleading squad, which exacerbated our terrible performance. We looked exceptionally shorter due to the small TV in the classroom, and we had just followed the biggest, coolest, hottest group of girls—who also played basketball. Looking at twenty girls onstage and then in the next scene seeing only two really intensified the horror of what Kristina and I were about to endure. Our social lives would be nonexistent following this event. Both Kristina and I had complete stage fright and stared blankly at the camera. At least for Kristina, she looked presentable in her official jersey and jeans, unlike me, with my dad's yellow armpit-stained XL T-shirt with a felt number fifty glued to it.

It seemed like an eternity for the music to start, so there we stood with the microphone humming; the entire class was silent. Eventually I could no longer hear the humming because every room in the school was echoing with hysterical laughter; I could hear the laughter echoing down the hallway. I was frozen and horribly humiliated, and yet I was unable to not join in the laughter. I slowly glanced toward Kristina, whose face was beet red and laughing, too, hiding underneath her desk's cover, so I did the same until I heard my atrocious voice singing Walter Payton's part. The laughing diminished from people trying to hear my Walter Payton impression. I even attempted to sing the words the way he did. I could no longer bear watching myself and put my head under the desk cover again. I wanted to put my hands over my ears. Thankfully, they stopped playing the "Super Bowl Shuffle" after the Walter Payton part. Who knows, I probably would have kept singing, since I knew all the parts. When it was finally over and the next routine had begun, I lifted my head from beneath my desk and saw that everyone in my class was staring at me.

I shuddered at the memory as I stared at my hands, my cheeks burning. After a long, uncomfortable silence, I looked up at Gerry and Shelley. Shelley's mouth was hanging open with a knock-the-wind-out-of-you expression, and Gerry's lips were curled under his teeth as if he was trying not to laugh or to prevent himself from saying anything. His eyes looked at me with a pitiful expression that made me want to slug him.

"Uh, MK, you won!" Gerry said and patted me on the back. I was confused; my eyebrows furrowed in bewilderment as I tried to figure out what he meant.

"That story has to be the most humiliating and brutal experience I could ever imagine," he continued lovingly. "And that's another reason why I love you so much: you can laugh at yourself, and you can tell that story and know it's not the end of the world. You're an amazingly strong girl."

I no longer wanted to hit him, and then I had an ache come over me. I was desperate for a hug. Gerry pulled me to him and kissed my forehead, and then I felt his body trembling. I looked at him, and he was silently giggling as he looked at Shelley, who was also silently shaking with tears coming down her face. I had no choice but to laugh. Shelley ran over to the couch and hugged my back. I felt safe and comforted despite my junior high nightmare that sealed the deal of my social-outcast status until graduation. It didn't matter now; I knew that all this stuff and drama meant nothing once high school was over. Just getting through it was the bitch of it all. But that childhood humiliation triggered that little fire of anger inside me, Scarlet O'Hara popped in my head. "As God as my witness I will never go hungry again!" *Note to self,* I thought with as much passion and fury as Scarlet. *If I ever have kids, they're getting fucking store-bought Chicago Bears jerseys, so help me God.*

# 15

The following week, Gerry was very preoccupied with football. I was OK with this, since I was struggling with work and school, although I had been feeling his absence lately; even when we had been together, he wasn't exactly all there. He was there physically but not mentally. I did my best to understand and knew I'd have my love's undivided attention back again as soon as football season was over. I was lost in thoughts of him when the phone rang. I flinched, and my heart jumped.

"Hello," I answered a little too excitedly.

"Hi, pumpkin," Gerry murmured.

"Hi!" I exclaimed before slamming my hand over my mouth; I must have sounded like a jackass with how overzealous I sounded.

"Wow! Are you that excited to talk to me, or what?" he asked playfully.

"Yes, actually. I miss you."

"I miss you, too, baby. Almost done—I know I haven't been a very good boyfriend lately."

The sound of "boyfriend" still always made me feel giddy. "When can I see you?" I asked impatiently.

"Well, on Friday there's a big party at—"

"Stubby's?"

"Who? Stubby's? Oh yeah, big party at Stubby's. *Breakfast Club* again. You're silly. No, there's a big party at Eddie's. His mom is away on business, so it could get really crazy. You're coming with me!"

"Um, OK, sounds fun. I just have to work on Saturday morning at seven. But I'll just go in tired, no big deal," I replied disappointedly. I'd been looking forward to hanging out with him alone, but a party would suffice.

"Aw, come on. Can't you call out? His party's going to be huge!"

"I wish I could, but Ruth has been helping me out a lot with weekends so that I can be at your games and stuff. I'll go to the party with you. I'll just go to work tired and go to bed when I get home on Saturday."

"Oh, OK, I guess. I'm so sick of you working. I wish you didn't have to work. I can't wait until I make enough money for the both of us." Gerry sounded let down.

"What? When we're twenty-five? Get outta here, silly. *No* big deal. I have to work—you know that." I was becoming annoyed with this conversation; it was getting old. "So can you come over tonight at all?" I asked pleadingly. I craved his hugs.

"I wish I could, baby, but I have a paper due tomorrow, and of course I blew it off until the last minute. How 'bout tomorrow?"

"I have to work tomorrow," I said, frustrated because I knew we were back to the work issue, and somehow this was my problem. He could have worked harder during the week to get his papers done on time.

"Dammit! See? This work bullshit is getting on my nerves. I wish you could just be a normal eighteen-year-old girl instead of having so many adult responsibilities. I know your family needs you, but I need you, too. Do you ever think of that?" He said this sharply, and it stung like salt in a wound. I was dumbfounded by his statement. I didn't know how to respond. My mouth hung open next to the receiver, but nothing would come out. I thought of the squeaks Allison makes in *The Breakfast Club* when she buries her head into her coat on her desk. I put my hand over the phone receiver, afraid that something to that effect would exit my mouth. Uncomfortable silence...

"Sweetie? I'm sorry. I didn't mean it the way I said it. You're nor-mal—I just meant that it isn't fair that you have all these responsibili-ties, and so many other girls don't. You deserve to be having fun, not feeling responsible for your family." Gerry said this sounding heart-felt, but I still felt wounded by his words. I sensed some resentment in his words, and although it wasn't my fault, he sounded like he was justifying what he'd said instead of apologizing. With that, I decided to let him go.

"OK. I'll see you Friday, then?" I responded flatly.

"Yes, Friday, honey," he said sweetly. "I love y—"

I had hung up. What the fuck? Did he think I liked to work? No. I'd rather be having fun, too, but what could I do? I couldn't com-pare myself to others because then, of course, I'd get depressed and resentful. It had happened before. My mom was right, and I didn't want to feel like that; it didn't do any good. There's no point to that. Wishing for something that isn't going to happen right now is point-less. I'd taught myself not to worry. My school counselor once told me that "worrying is like a rocking chair: you rock back and forth, but it doesn't get you anywhere." I thought of this advice a lot; it soothed me and prevented me from wanting to give up. I decided I needed to go see my counselor at school the next day.

My counselor at school gave me a lot of exercises to let go of what she called my "control issues." I didn't really want to control any-thing in particular, but I seemed to have trouble handling things that were out of my control, such as the weather, people's behavior, and the unfortunate events that seemed to plague my existence. Once she pointed out that I did this and I began to recognize my behavior, she offered an alternative way for me to think of it. She elaborated that, instead of wasting my time trying to control things that I couldn't control, I should learn to accept them and make the best of it. She used metaphors and encouraged me to come up with a solution, like "you can't control the wind but you can…" and I'd have to fill in the blank. The first time, I responded with "go inside." This answer, I suppose, was wrong or not exactly what she was looking for, because she kept inquiring about it. She explained that going inside when it was windy would be avoiding or hiding from whatever event was out of my control. She wanted me to learn how to embrace it. At the end of each session, she used that metaphor until my answer became what she was looking for. After about three sessions, she began with "you can't control the wind, but you can…" and I responded with "wear a windbreaker." She laughed and explained that this would be preparing for the wind but not embracing it. I was becoming irritated.

Finally, at our fourth session, a light bulb went on in my head, as if that part of the "think for yourself" part of my brain had been hibernating for the past ten years. I thought of wind and Mary Poppins emerged in my head, so I responded to her wind question with "fly a kite." She smiled genuinely and said, "Exactly. That would be an excellent way to embrace the wind, wouldn't it?" I asked what she would do, because I was curious how long it would take her to figure it out. Of course, she didn't answer the way I wanted her to, either. She replied, "It doesn't matter what I would do, but flying a kite would be a fun thing to do on a windy day." I replied, "Whatever"—which translated to "fuck off" in adolescent language—and walked out frustrated with her lack of disclosure.

The following week, she asked me a metaphor: "You're at the beach, and the waves are very strong, you could…" I tensed up immediately and felt nauseated. I had the sudden urge to punch myself in the stomach to make this yucky feeling go away. I'd gone to the beach once, and it hadn't been a pleasant experience. It was the first time my dad had allowed me to bring a friend to anything, so of course I asked Joy to come with us. Joy wanted to walk down the beach, which sounded fun to me. When we came back, my dad asked us, "So did you enjoy strutting your stuff like prima donnas?" As usual, I was totally clueless and had no idea what he was talking about, but Joy knew exactly what he was talking about. The contemptuous glare she gave my dad signaled to me that he was being a dick again. My dad didn't like her because she went to public school, he claimed. I thought this was a horrible and unfair reason to not like someone. Who cares where a kid goes to school? What's the difference I thought? Then it clicked, I knew the real reason. It was because he couldn't control her, and she saw right through him. He couldn't hit her or make her do anything. He tried to keep me away from her by isolating me and grounding me for months, but she didn't give up on me.

Later that day, we were having a blast jumping up and riding the waves from the lake, and I was laughing and having some good carefree fun for once with a friend. My dad abruptly grabbed my arm and pointed down at my privates and said, "What the fuck is wrong with you? That bathing suit is see-through! I can see your nipples, belly button, and pubic hair!" I saw that people were glancing at me and I felt humiliated. Again, I was clueless. I didn't know that this bathing suit was going to be see-through. It had pink and white stripes, and obviously when it was dry, it wasn't see-through. At the store, they don't let you dump water on yourself before you buy a bathing suit. This was just one of those examples: I wasn't a parent, but what the fuck? Could you give your kid a little respect and the benefit of the doubt? Speak to them privately and ask them what happened or point this out to them without talking to them like they're stupid. Therefore, waves and beaches weren't a fond memory for me, and I remained silent during most of our session that day.

Toward the end of the session, the therapist said the metaphor again, and I just got pissed off. She asked me what was difficult for me with this metaphor. I figured, what do I have to lose? So I told her the beach story. I'm not sure if a therapist is supposed to do this, but her eyes shined for a second as if she was about to cry. Her expression, of sheer compassion but not pity, was oddly comforting to me. I felt validated by that one reaction, and I could see she was saddened by what I had disclosed to her. I sensed she understood how hurtful and demeaning that must have been for me, and I felt her empathy.

She said with a small crack in her voice, "Wow. I'd think that would be—"

"Humiliating? Degrading?"

She nodded slightly. "Damaging," she replied softly.

"Uh, yeah," I replied. "You could say that."

# 16

Friday came at last, and I was wearing some new clothes my grandmother had bought me from a real store: The Gap! Yeah! I didn't feel like such a loser and was now looking forward to attending this party. New threads really do make a difference. I put my hair in rollers and applied more makeup than I usually did, thinking about those evil bitches who would most likely be attending. They were the team's cheerleaders, unfortunately. I needed to stand tall and feel like I could hold my own around them, and a little lipstick could make the difference. When I opened the door, Gerry gasped.

"Holy shit! You look hot, baby!" he said hungrily.

I smiled proudly to myself. "Yeah, I clean up real nice, don't I?" I responded with newfound confidence delivered by Maybelline.

"Clean up? You're smokin', girl!" he exclaimed with lust in his eyes.

Pleasurable surges pulsed below my waist. That look was worth the effort; I wished I could have frozen it in time. I wanted to take a picture of it.

"Don't move. Keep looking at me like that!" I yelled and ran to the kitchen to grab my mom's Kodak disc camera. I was sure she wouldn't be pleased, when she got the pictures developed, to observe this "I want to jump you" expression on my boyfriend's face. I decided to bring this camera to the party and to develop the pictures myself to prevent a *Parenthood* moment when the mom develops Julie and Tod's love-sex photos. I imagined Julie's mom laughs at one of the nude pictures and says, "This is one for my wallet." When I came back to the family room, his look was still present and even more alluring.

"Your ass looks fantastic in those jeans—sweet Jesus!" Gerry said passionately. I wanted to jump him and pull him upstairs, but I at least wanted to make an appearance at the party. I grabbed his hand, and we walked to his car. As we walked, his hands were all over my waist, hips, and ass. I giggled, and when I opened the door, his mom had been waiting for us. Oops.

"Oh my gosh! Mrs. McGrath, I'm really sorry to have kept you waiting. I had no idea you were in the car. I thought Gerry drove over," I said, blushing.

"Mary Kate! I can see why Gerry kept me waiting! You look sensational."

"Doesn't she?" Gerry replied, clearly still mesmerized with me. I thought I looked OK, but I felt like the most beautiful girl in the world from the way he was staring at me. I liked this.

The car ride was challenging, because Gerry was still ogling me and throwing his head back and looking up at the sky playfully. I was laughing. This was some much-needed attention, and I was grateful for his interest, which I so badly missed. He exited the car first and took my hand to assist me out of the car. He kissed my hand. I was beaming. His mom displayed that "awwww" look again. I blushed. He put his arm around me, and we walked into the party, arms around each other, his hand in my left ass pocket.

"You're not leaving my side tonight, girl. If I knew you were going to be looking like this, I'd have changed plans. Hell with this party!"

Jackpot: these were the magic words, and I was putty. I was ready to jump him right then and there, right in front of the house. I would allow him to deflower me. It felt like we had waited a long time. We had stopped by a tree in front of Eddie's house when Mrs. McGrath pulled away. I pushed his back toward the tree and stepped on his feet for some height. I could feel his arousal jab into my belly button.

"Keep talking, baby, and you may just get what you wish for," I said salaciously.

"Oh man, show me the way home, honey," he said, mock *Top Gun* style. "Now, don't tantalize me right now; we'll be in front of people, and I may just have to disrobe you in front of everyone."

"Oh, really? Disrobe me, huh. You want everyone to see me naked?"

His face softened. "Actually, no, but I'm finding it more difficult to resist you and your seductress ways." He looked down at me with lust in his eyes.

"A seductress? Me? Really? That's a new one. You're the one who's seducing me, with your beguiling words and bewitching looks," I said, grabbing his shirt collar. He laughed, kissed my forehead, and smelled my hair.

"I know, you can feel me right now—you're aware of what you're doing. You and your titillating ways—no pun intended," he replied, sliding the tip of his tongue to the bottom of his teeth and eyeing my breasts.

"They're spectacular, aren't they?" I concurred with his reference and jokingly complimented my own rack.

"Oh yes, they are. I haven't been able to see much of them, and I miss them deeply. I want to speak with them about a matter of great importance." He smirked sexily and glanced down at the bulge in his pants. Fuck, I wanted him so badly. My mind was racing with escape routes and transportation possibilities before we got spotted. The night I'm ready to give it up, and he doesn't have a car. They did it for the first time in a car in *Say Anything*…Therefore, it must be OK, I rationalized.

Then I heard her voice. Son…of…a…bitch.

"Well, well, well; look who's here. Are you going to join us or dry hump by the tree?" Michelle said mockingly. She was the ultimate buzzkill for me, and I glanced at Gerry, who rolled his eyes.

"Who is that chick Michelle?" I asked.

"She's just a cheerleader for us. That's all. She has zero personality. She thinks she is hot shit because she is Eddie's cousin," Gerry replied.

He grabbed my hand, and I gratefully allowed him to escort me into the house. Excessive warmth hit me in the face, and music pierced my eardrums. Apparently, Eddie was in a band, and his band-mates were "jamming," as people were calling it. My sober ears were not ready for such noise, and I needed a beer or a stiff drink immediately. Michelle was acting as a gracious hostess and handing us cups, which I knew was for appearance only. She wanted to make herself seem more important to this party than she actually was. She had an inflated sense of importance in my eyes, but I doubted anyone else was aware of this, since most people viewed her as the hottest commodity in this group. She seemed to be the most sought-after female of the group, and for some reason, she wanted the one person she couldn't have.

"So, are you excited about the big game tomorrow, Ger Bear?" Michelle asked Gerry in a tone that made me gag. Gerry sipped his drink, grimaced, rolled his eyes, and put his arm around me. I graciously accepted his touch, sipped my drink, and grimaced as well. Then I snuggled up to him to signal to Michelle—back off, bitch. I would have pissed on him to mark my territory if that would have kept her away. The drink was brutally strong, but I needed it to tolerate this broad.

"No, I'm not really excited at all, Michelle," Gerry said in a dead-pan voice. I pinched his butt in encouragement, hoping he would keep it up. I was elated with his responses; I was ready to blow him. I'd finished my drink already, but there was no way in hell I was leaving these two alone to go get us something. Gerry also gulped his drink down, and of course Michelle was right on that, ready to fetch it for him. I handed her my cup as well, assuming she'd probably spit in my drink. She came back quickly, holding all three cups in a triangle shape in her hands. She handed me the first one, but I nudged Gerry to take that one. Whichever one she wanted me to have, I wouldn't take it. I'd seen *The Princess Bride* too many times for that. She obviously hadn't built up immunity to iocane powder, and I doubted she'd spat in all three. I took the next cup graciously and gave her the most sickeningly passive-aggressive thank-you I could muster. Yet she stuck around, talking in her nauseating tone, and I continued to sip the vicious jungle juice.

Tom Petty's "American Girl" began playing, and I yanked "Ger Bear" into the middle of the room. I could no longer tolerate her baby talk, and I had no qualms about being rude at this point. The alcohol agreed with me and made me ballsy. I began to encourage him to spin me, and I was doing stupid dance moves I thought were amazing because of my booze goggles. I rolled into his arm so that his arm was enveloped around me, and then he spun me back out. Gerry was laughing and appeared giddy as well from the punch. It doesn't take much alcohol at the age of eighteen to get a good buzz going; the atmosphere and probably the lack of oxygen from the number of people there were also working in our favor.

I glanced over at Michelle, whose eyes were darting at me like Stephen King's *Carrie*. I heard the freaky musical score from *Carrie* in my head and imagined that some object was going to fly across the room and decapitate me. I whispered to Gerry, "Look at Michelle—she's reminding me of Carrie right now."

He looked over at her and smiled and put his forehead against the side of my head. "I love you," he murmured to me and kissed my ear. Then he looked up at the ceiling and said in a slurred voice, "I hope no buckets of pig's blood fall on us."

I giggled at his reference. "I love you, too," I said, slurring my words as well. He grabbed my face and started kissing me in the middle of the room. I was too buzzed to care what people thought and secretly hoped that bitch was watching. People were bumping into us and pushing around now, dancing to "Pump Up the Jam." I pulled away from Gerry and sang along to this song that I actually despise when I'm sober.

I backed into Eddie, a tall, lanky fellow who resembled Jimmy Stewart, and I immediately liked him. Also because he was drinking his jungle juice from a glass stein. I found this hilarious, and I began talking to Eddie. He knew who I was already, and I knew who he was, although we weren't introduced properly. We conversed like we knew each other forever.

"You remind me of George Bailey!" I yelled over the music.

"Oh yeah? Well you're...you're screwy! I'm going home to see Zuzu!" Eddie replied.

I was so excited that Eddie just quoted *It's a Wonderful Life* to me without skipping a beat. I clapped and squealed like the biggest nerd and hugged him. Unfortunately, my breast knocked his mug out of his hand, and it crashed to the floor. I stared at the wooden floor and watched the glass pieces explode all over the room as if in slow motion and mumbled "ohhhh fudddggee" like Ralphie when he dropped the nuts. Only, I didn't say fudge, I said the word. "Oh *fffuuuuccckkk*." I slowly looked up at Eddie, guiltily waiting to be scolded for my clumsy stupor. I noticed instead of looking irritated or angry, he was smiling and had an impressed look as he stared at my breasts.

"Sorry, man, they have a mind of their own," I replied jokingly.

"That's awesome!" Eddie laughed and gave me a high five. "Well, it isn't a party until something gets broke." He laughed, quoting *St. Elmo's Fire*.

I laughed. "Nice, Eddie!" I said and gave him a high five back.

I bent over to pick up some of the glass shards, and Eddie and Gerry began to assist me. Gerry was staring at my chest with an angry expression on his face. When I bent over, I had some significant cleavage showing, and Eddie was licking his chops. I blushed and stood up abruptly. I decided to use the ladies' room and regroup and obtain more jungle juice. Unbeknownst to me, Gerry was right at my heels and followed me into the bathroom. The bathroom was small, one of those hidden powder rooms that rich people have. The door almost touched the pedestal sink, so he had to maneuver me and himself around to slam and lock the door. He appeared pissed off. I could see his jaw clenching. I was leaning with my ass on the back of the sink, with him facing me. His hands were next to my hips as he leaned on the sink.

"What?" I inquired innocently.

"You like that? Guys looking at you like that?" He asked this in a jealous, arrogant, and cocky tone.

"Uh, yeah. Right. Guys looking at me? I have to watch people drool over you, but someone looks at me once, and you get all hot and bothered?" His look was a mixture of anger and arousal, like he could fuck me with his eyes. "Don't give me those eyes," I said, trying to sound joking.

"I'll look at you any way I want to. You are mine. You are my girl." He was a combination of aroused and angry, and in my drunken state, it was doing it for me. I liked the combination of angry, aroused, passionate, jealous, and lustful in his face. I was getting booze muscles and talking with more confidence than I ever had before. I leaned into him and had my face right up to his; I shoved my chest into him until our noses were touching. His eyes were piercing mine, and his breath was hot and fruity from the punch but tantalizing. He tried to kiss me, and I pulled away, teasing him. He gasped, and I grew more turned on by his reactions to me. I felt powerful and seductive. He cupped the back of my neck and pulled me toward him. I resisted, and he groaned and smiled. I smiled back and continued to keep my neck tense and playfully resisted him. He held my face, and I turned my head to withstand his kiss; he countered by kissing my neck, and I began to succumb to his persistence. I looked up and turned my head. He kissed the back of my neck, and because this was my ultimate weakness, I surrendered to his powerful, intense kiss and had waves of stimulation streaming inside me. I could feel him aroused and throbbing, digging into me.

My loins ached, and I wanted him inside me, and the urge was becoming unbearable. All rationality was leaving me; I was becoming reckless, impulsive, and animalistic. I began to have empathy for those girls who ended up knocked up in high school; now I could understand the power that infatuation, love, lust, and arousal could do to a person—not to mention alcohol, which destroys all judgment and inhibitions. It was suddenly as if we were no longer this cute, sweet couple who were crazy about each other. The high school "liking" each other was gone. At this moment, I felt like a woman, a legal adult, with my own emotions and feelings. I felt mature and sexual. My entire life I'd planned to wait until marriage to lose my virginity; now, with the power he had over me, I was ready to give it up at a high school party in a bathroom. I didn't feel cheap but empowered, which was a foreign feeling to me.

He moved his hands from around my waist to beneath my ass and lifted me up to fit perfectly inside this small, round pedestal sink. I was leaning against the mirror, and his hands were wildly moving all over me. My legs wrapped around him, and my feet crossed in the small of his back. I was dizzy with arousal, and his kisses grew stronger as he devoured me. I was going to a place that was impossible to turn away from. This erotic power of attraction was turning carnal and paralyzing. I felt like I'd wet my pants or just gotten my period. This thought suddenly brought me back to reality. I needed to empty my bladder, because the enlargement and stimulation were becoming painful from having to urinate. I didn't want to stop, but I had to.

Gerry was going to town on my breasts and neck, so I felt bad for being such a cocktease. Truly, if I hadn't had to pee, I totally would have given it up right then and there. Nine months from then I probably would have been regretting that decision, so I thanked God in my head for sending me a warning sign before I could make the biggest mistake of my life. I was also kicking myself for not going to a clinic when Mairead told me to get on the pill.

I whispered in Gerry's ear, "I'm sorry, baby; I don't mean to be a tease. I want to so bad, but I have to go to the bathroom." He was almost delusional with covetousness. It was like he couldn't hear me, or else it was selectively ignoring. I repeated myself, and he groaned sadly and put the top of his head to my chest bone. He was breathing heavily and making sounds like he was going to cry and was wincing in pain. I felt badly for doing this, although technically it wasn't my fault—he'd followed me in here.

"You know what? I don't mind a golden shower," he said, half-laughing and half-serious. I didn't know what that meant initially, but I could guess by the "golden" part.

"Uh, no. Plus, it wouldn't be a shower; it would be like a firehose."

I jumped up, pulled down my pants, and began peeing as if I'd held it in for three hours on a road trip. There was no tinkling sound; it was more like a flood of liquid from a hose. He watched me intently, one eyebrow raised. The pee slowed down, and then, when I pushed and used my vaginal muscles, the firehose happened again.

He began to laugh and looked somewhat impressed. "Wow, you must have some strong muscles down there," he said teasingly.

The intense emotion that was in this tiny little bathroom was subsiding, and I began to calm down physically. The moment had vanished as fast as it had arrived. I looked at his jeans, which now had a circular wet spot, and I had a twinge of guilt. He caught my eye and adjusted his pants.

"I'll go get on the pill this week, OK?" I said sheepishly as I pulled up my pants.

"Yeah, it's becoming more difficult to stop. I really am glad we stopped, though; I didn't want our first time to be in a situation like this." He looked down, appearing defenseless and powerless. At least that jealous, angry side of him had disappeared. Shame and awareness had set in as I thought about what people would be thinking when we emerged from the bathroom together. He began to undo his pants and stood there for a moment, but nothing happening. I looked at him in confusion.

"Stage fright," he said and smiled. "Um, it's kind of hard to, uh, you know, when I'm hard." He blushed, and I caught on.

"Oh, OK. I'll go out first—meet you out there," I said abruptly, and I walked out of the bathroom before he could object.

When I exited the bathroom, I was hit with the moist hot air from the body heat of the million people now at the party. I went virtually unnoticed until I caught Michelle's eye, as if she had been on a surveillance team. It was creepy, in a way, how she watched us like a predator observing her prey. This Mexican standoff continued until Gerry emerged from the bathroom and bumped into me. He put his arm around me and shoved the person in front of us out of the way. He had his arm hooked around me like I was glued to him. I liked the protected and safe way I felt when he held me this way. I could feel Michelle's eyes piercing my back like Superman with his laser vision. I actually felt cooler when I entered the dining room area, since it seemed that every junior and senior in every high school within a twenty-five-mile radius was in the front room and kitchen of this house. I caught Eddie's eye when we arrived in the dining room; he was holding some kind of funnel over his head attached to a hose that was leading into another guy's mouth. Eddie grinned at me and had this goofy expression on his face. I couldn't help but reciprocate. In my periphery I caught Gerry glaring at me. When I turned to face him, he appeared sullen and was clenching his jaw again. *Oh jeez.* I nudged him.

"Will you knock it off already? I was just about to give up my most prized possession to you in the powder room, goofball! I'm nuts about you. There's nothing to be jealous of. Don't you want your friends to like me?"

His face softened briefly, as if he was considering what I was saying, then it tightened again. "I don't want anyone liking you like that. He likes you—like, he has a crush on you," he said grudgingly.

"So what? Michelle has a crush on you. I don't act like it's your fault and get mad at you. We can't control other people's behavior," I said, impressed with my acute ability to stick up for myself with a rational comeback. Gerry was quiet and appeared to be processing what I said, at least. I released myself from him and went to the punch bowl. Eddie handed the beer bong to someone next to him.

"Hey, MK Want a beer bong hit? It's fun," Eddie said encouragingly. I instantly turned toward Gerry but then immediately regretted it. "What? You have to ask your boyfriend for permission. Is he your dad or your boyfriend?" His smartass remark made my cheeks hot and my throat sore, and I was fuming. Mentioning my dad and implying that I had to ask a man for permission was a combination of fuel to my innate fire. I shoved him aside and grabbed the other end of the beer bong. This guy Rich was holding the funnel, and he winked at me. Luckily they were just pouring cans of beer into the bong instead of the jungle juice, which would have been like liquid heroin at that speed. I kneeled down on the ground and looked up at the beer bong; then, rotating my eyes to meet Gerry's furious gaze, I pivoted my vision away. Then I caught Eddie eyeing my cleavage, which made me want to laugh until I had a mouthful of foam that took me by surprise. I did my best to swallow without choking. Eddie, Rich, and the other guys were cheering as I finished. I held up the end of the beer bong and laughed. Eddie slapped me a high five, and when I turned triumphantly to Gerry, I saw that he had vanished.

# 17

"You're one cool chick!" Eddie said, pulling me up and kissing my hand. Out of instinct I turned to where Gerry was standing and saw that he still was not back; then I played it off by tilting my chin toward my shoulder and wiping my mouth off. Rich patted me on the back and gave me a high five.

"She's the only one who could do it! All the other broads choked or spit...they didn't swallow." Rich smirked and nudged me. I elbowed him back, shocked at his vulgar innuendo. Rich and Eddie put their arms around me, holding their cups up, and some guy wearing a gray newsboy style cap took the picture, smirking at me. Then he handed me a cup and instructed me to hold my cup up in a "cheers" pose with Rich and Eddie. This guy took another picture of this pose, and I laughed because Rich and Eddie were so tall and lanky compared to my short stature. I kept looking at Rich instead of the camera because Rich was hilariously making faces and dancing while the gray-cap guy took pictures. Rich's face was warm and inviting, like someone who makes you feel comfortable enough to sit next to him on the first day of school. His eyes shone when he smiled, and I caught myself gawking at him. The beer was fizzing inside me, and I was starting to feel woozy. Something jolted a reminder to me that I needed to go soon; the smell of the greasy pizza arriving sent a reminder that I had to work the next day.

I pushed Eddie aside and stumbled into the front room, scanning the room for Gerry. It was a struggle because I was now seriously intoxicated and it was dim in the front room. Then I spotted Gerry and Michelle talking in the corner of the room. I could see her mouth moving, and he appeared engrossed in the conversation (as opposed to how he had reacted earlier). My stomach seethed with anger, and jealousy stung me, but I wasn't mad at Gerry. I knew that the evil bitch was up to her conniving ways, yet I sensed a hint of betrayal when I observed Gerry's behavior toward her. His usual aversion to her had now been replaced by a tender, almost captivated look. I slowly glided toward them, oblivious to those around me, as if I'd been hypnotized into not taking my eyes off them. Then I witnessed something, and my body became immobilized.

This almost occurred in slow motion. I watched Michelle whisper something into his ear and saw Gerry's arm lifting and touching her warmly on the shoulder, paired with a subtle, compassionate look. I stood there for a moment in shock. Watching him give this look—my look—to someone else gave me a knock-the-wind-out-of-me sensation. The deer-in-the-headlights syndrome was back, which restricted control over my limbs and seized my ability to process anything. I didn't want this evil bitch to know that she affected me and longed for that confident frame of mind I'd been in when I arrived. Apprehensive and scattered, I turned my back to them, desperate to regain my composure. I maneuvered my way through the making-out couples and dirty-dancing, grinding people who now made me sick. I belted up the stairs and heard Eddie yell out, "If you got to puke, don't go in the master bathroom!" I cringed at the "master bathroom" part. These rich people—how many bathrooms are really necessary?

I found what I presumed wasn't the master bathroom, because it wasn't attached to another room. This bathroom was decorated in a masculine way; I inferred that it was Eddie's domain. I cringed when I saw my reflection. I was now pale, disheveled, and oily. I looked out of it. The person I'd presented myself as when I arrived at this party was now gone, to be replaced by my insecure, clueless self. I suddenly flashed to Say Anything…and recollected the curly-red-haired drunk guy who has a meltdown in the bathroom mirror when he realizes for the first time how repulsive he is. I imagined Lloyd and Diane driving him around for three hours trying to find out where he lived so they could drop his pathetic ass off. I did not want to end up like that guy. I didn't have to puke. Then I realized a couple was making out in the stand-up shower. I attempted to find another bathroom.

I found another half-naked couple in the king-size bed in Eddie's parents' room. I walked past them unnoticed and closed the door to the master bathroom. The lights were dim and soft in the gleaming marble bathroom. The cream and brown granite was something you would see in a magazine, not in real life. They had one of those huge, beautiful footed bathtubs of shiny porcelain that briefly made me want to date Eddie so I could utilize this tub. The lighting in this bathroom was much more forgiving than Eddie's harsh fluorescent bulbs.

I stared at the porcelain tub and then thought of Michelle and her beautiful skin and devious ways and decided to open the drawers of Eddie's mother's private lair. I justified that this was for a greater cause and that his mother might agree with me.

Of course, she had the best of the best makeup and some kind of magical ceramic brush that gave my hair the soft, lustrous appearance of a Pantene commercial or Julia Roberts in *Steel Magnolias* on her wedding day. OK, not really, but that's what popped into my mind when I used the brush. I decided to help myself to everything. I used a bottle of foundation of some kind that erased my mascara from under my eyes and left my skin dewy. I spotted a glass pot of bronzer that caused my lifeless skin to appear bright and glowy. I couldn't find any black eyeliner (she only had purple), so I settled for this, and ironically, it made my golden brown eyes pop. I made a mental note to ditch the black eyeliner from this point forward. I applied some of my own Lip Smacker and used some "Beautiful" perfume and began to feel that confident person coming back.

My head was starting to ache, and I realized that I needed to go to bed or drink water or both. I heard come commotion from outside the bedroom. Immobilized with shame and fear, I stood there for a while, not sure what to do. Luckily, I thought to flush the toilet, and I walked out to find Eddie escorting the couple out of his parents' room. As I was walking toward the door, he was walking back into the room. He looked startled.

"Creepo!" he said jokingly. "Where did you come from? Was this a *ménage à trois?*" He cocked one eyebrow and smirked devilishly. My cheeks burned with embarrassment, and I was speechless. "You didn't puke, did you?" he asked, sounding panicked.

I cleared my throat. "No, I just needed to use the bathroom, and the other one was...tied up." I attempted to say this confidently.

"Oh. Sorry. Well, you don't look like you puked. You look, uh, actually you look really good." Eddie did look astounded. "Considering you just did a beer bong, too!" he said with a smirk. I smiled back. He appeared taken aback and looked a little too long at my eyes.

*Oh jeez, he knows. How humiliating.* "Uh, the party was really fun," I said out loud. "Thanks. I'm going to get going—I have to work tomorrow. See ya," I said abruptly and turned toward the stairs.

"Wait! Going? NO! It's just getting started." Eddie said.

"I might stay a little longer, but six a.m. comes pretty fast." I responded feeling sorry for myself a bit. He walked toward me and extended his arms out to give me a hug.

I halted. *Oh shit.* I attempted to give him a quick hug. He squeezed me a little harder than I'd expect, which caused my breasts to press against him. I caught on, ironically feeling relieved—as long as he didn't realize that I'd fluffed with his mom's stash.

"Good to see you, MK You're always welcome, especially without *him*," Eddie said, sneering.

"Uh, thanks. OK," I said hurriedly.

Eddie's expression was bewildered, and his brow was furrowed. "Hey, MK, you smell like...my *mom!*"

Bile burning in my throat, I laughed nervously and ran down the stairs. I walked through the dining room, past the beer bongers cheering, and into the kitchen. I downed a glass of liquid courage and walked toward where I'd last spotted Gerry and Michelle. I cringed at saying their names in the same sentence. "Smells Like Teen Spirit" was playing, and more of a crowd had gathered and was dancing pit style, but of course there were Michelle and Gerry, still talking in the corner. I strolled confidently toward them, with Michelle's back to me; Gerry looked up, and we locked eyes. His expression indicated that he was aware he was doing something he shouldn't—a kid caught with his hand in the cookie jar. Before I could reach them, Gerry patted her on the shoulder dismissively and paced toward me. She turned to look his way, appearing disappointed, until she saw me, and then her face shifted to a contemptuous glare.

He put his arm around me, and we walked outside without skipping a beat, as if he'd read my mind. The sudden cold air whipped into my face and made me feel alert. I didn't have anything to say; I was at a loss for words anyway. Gerry appeared to be speechless as well. Sometimes, things are better left unsaid. We walked to the closest busy street to use a pay phone. He called his house, and luckily Shelley answered the phone. She left right away to pick us up, but the tension and silence between us made it seem like an eternity. I had no idea what to say or how to say it. My mind raced for something, a movie, a memory—anything—but nothing came. I imagined *About Last Night*, when Deb and Dan get into a fight and are waiting for a train and don't talk, either; she just looks at him longingly with a hopeful expression. I wondered if I should do this. I wanted him to talk; I felt he owed me an explanation. I'd said enough at the party. I glanced over at him; he appeared to be lost and was staring at the ground. I thought about how long he had been talking to her and became flooded with feelings of betrayal and jealousy

"So…what was that about?" I inquired impulsively.

"What was what about?" Gerry asked, playing dumb.

"If you want to be with Michelle, be my guest," I replied, feeling disheartened. Gerry's expression wasn't what I had anticipated, and he remained silent longer than I'd have hoped.

"You know I don't want to be with her. I was talking to her—that's it."

"But you know how she feels about you, and I told you that I don't get mad at you about that. Tonight seemed different. I sensed that you enjoyed talking to her."

"You seemed to be enjoying yourself when you were doing a beer bong with Eddie."

"That's not the same thing. You and Michelle were in a corner, and the way you were looking at her and how you were touching her... I'm not mad at you. I guess you could say I'm hurt."

"I touched her arm," Gerry said dismissively.

"Like I said, I'm not mad at you. I'm trying to convey that if we weren't together and someone saw you at the party, I think they would have thought you were into her. It seemed intimate," I said with a crack in my voice. "I don't know, I get the impression that you're attracted to her, and I don't want to stand in your way." I prayed for Shelley to arrive soon.

My prayers were soon answered when Shelley pulled up. I climbed into the car, surprised to hear Whitney Houston's "One Moment in Time" playing. Gerry buckled himself in the front seat and ejected the tape from the player—my mixtape. Shelley pushed it back in.

"I love this song. This is an awesome tape, MK," Shelley said with a smile that was quickly erased when she saw my gloomy expression. "What's wrong, guys?" she asked. Neither of us replied. We pulled up to my house as I was fighting back the tears. I felt it in my gut that I was right about what I'd said, which left me discontented and hoping I was wrong. When Whitney ended and Billy Vera's "At This Moment" began to play, I started to lose it. The tears were in my eyes, and I had a lump in my heart. Gerry unbuckled (because he had to in order to let me out), and his eyes changed from vacant to compassionate when he saw my face. He took my hand and pulled me to him, hugging me.

Then he put his arms around my backside and picked me up. We walked this way to my front door, and my heartache lifted slightly. He set me down on my front stoop and faced me.

"I'm sorry, baby," he said genuinely. "I don't know what's wrong with me. I love you. You're my girl. I guess I got jealous when you went by Eddie—even though I told you he had a crush on you—so when Michelle pounced on me, I felt entitled to talk to her. She's scheming and manipulative, and I know that."

I didn't feel satisfied. "Thanks. I did a beer bong with Eddie because I didn't like what he said to me about having to ask your permission. It had nothing to do with you. That was a dig toward me. I wanted to show him up. It wasn't to make you jealous. He also implied that you were my dad, and that pissed me off." I was grateful to be able to clarify myself. Gerry seemed to have a pang of conscience and hugged me tightly. I still had a lingering sense of unease, though, despite his affection. "So like I said, though, what was that about? How do you feel about her?" I couldn't help but ask. I thought I knew, but tonight everything had changed when I saw them together.

Gerry was quiet at first, which left me feeling uncomfortable. "I told you, baby. I love you. I think she's a conniving bitch. I was drunk and pissed off, and she's so pretty and all up in my face, and I guess I got lost in the moment." Gerry slowly inserted a knife into my chest with his words. I winced in pain. "I'm sorry. You know what I mean."

"I obviously don't know what you mean."

"You're my girl. I love you," he said again. "I was pissed and being dumb—like I am right now. Listen, I'll call you tomorrow. I don't want to say anything else. I don't want to hurt you, and I'm talking like a sausage." Gerry kissed me and paced to the car.

Arrested by his words, I stood there, solid and heavy. When he pulled away, I attempted to lift my leaden legs from the steps and go inside. Those words replayed over and over in my head: "she's so pretty and all up in my face." I dragged myself up the stairs, set my alarm, and crashed on the bed, thankful for the alcohol because I knew I never would have been able to sleep otherwise. Ruminating and sobbing, I fell into a troubled, restless sleep and woke up abruptly two hours before my alarm went off. Something was amiss, and I sensed it in my gut, but I knew I had to go to work soon. I tried to put the apprehension out of my mind and go back to sleep.

Miraculously, I woke up for work feeling all right. I took a shower and went to work in robotic mode without thinking too much about what I was doing (or what I wished I was doing) and just focused on the present: I had to go to work and get through the day. I did my best to stay in the moment and not get too in my head, as they say. It was busy, which I was grateful for, since that made the day go by faster. Once I punched out and left work, I allowed myself to feel tired, concerned, and lost in my thoughts. I hoped that Gerry would surprise me and I'd find him waiting outside for me to drive me home, or maybe he'd be waiting in front of my house. He wasn't. When I arrived home, I called his house, but the answering machine came on. I didn't leave a message. I showered again and lay down on my bed, hoping he would call.

I woke up abruptly at 6:00 a.m. on Sunday morning. No call or message from Gerry.

I called Gerry at 10:00 a.m. on the dot because my mother always told me to never call anyone until after ten. His mother answered cheerfully and said that Gerry was at football practice. I was tired of lying around my house and sick of waiting for him, so I went for a run, which cleared my head. I knew I needed to stop being pathetic and go out with some friends. I called Joy, but she was not home. Then I decided to call my friend Sam and see if she wanted to hang out. She always made me laugh. I met my friend Sam freshman year in high school. We shared a locker, and I was always mesmerized by her name-brand cool stuff: Esprit backpack, Liz Claiborne purse, coats from The Limited—you name it. My stuff was usually a hand-me-down or from Venture, so I drooled over her things. Sometimes she would throw me a bone and let me borrow something or even give it to me, because "I've grown tired of it," as she would say. Sam and I hit it off right away, and I had no idea why she took a liking to me, but she said I made her laugh. I'm no comedian by any means, and she was always laughing when I talked; I wasn't sure at first if she was laughing at me or with me. She invited me to do things with her and was nice to me, so eventually I assumed she was laughing with me. Sam was another tall, lanky, blue-eyed blonde. Why my short and stocky self continued to hang out with tall, skinny chicks who exacerbated this difference is beyond me. She also had a car and was always willing to pick me up and take me anywhere. She genuinely seemed to enjoy my company. I didn't understand why, so I asked her one day.

Sam said, "That's why you're so funny, because you're always saying or doing things that are hysterical. There's something like innocence about you that I find refreshing."

*Oooh OK, whatever,* is what I thought at the time.

Homecoming weekend was now just a few days away. Sam had talked me into getting my hair done by her stylist, Ari. Sam had just had her hair highlighted again about a month before; she always looked like a polished model, and I looked like a frumpy mess, as usual. Sam openly admitted that she no longer had any idea what her natural hair color was. She'd gotten lowlights, highlights, and all-over color for the last three years. I had not yet ever done anything to my hair. My mother had me brainwashed that dying hair was bad, because her best friend "had the most beautiful auburn hair, and she went and dyed it blond like a fool. Her hair turned to straw!" I could hear my mother's words echoing in my mind. My mom always said that she would dye her hair only when she turned gray, but of course, she still wasn't gray at all. I'd just ripped out another gray hair the other day, so I succumbed to Sam's pressure to get my hair done. I was afraid of my father's genes, which would mean I'd be gray by thirty.

"Ari's fabulous. He'll make you look like a movie star," Sam said. She looked like a movie star, so I believed her. "I'm just getting a touch-up; meanwhile, you sit down and look through his books to pick a hairstyle and color you'd like." *Jeez, Sam,* I thought, *I've gotten my hair cut before, at Fantastic Sam's or BoRics. I'm not Amish.*

We arrived at Ari Alexander's Beauty Boutique, and I was already getting signals from my gut that this wasn't a good idea. I started to object, but Sam just got out of the car, went to the passenger side, and yanked me out. We walked into the purported boutique, but it wasn't so fabulous on the inside. There was furniture everywhere. "Ari's in the process of moving to a new salon, so things are a little disorganized," she said.

"Samantha, my dear, how are you?" A man resembling Fabio appeared and air-kissed Sam on each side of her face. "Who is this lovely creature you've brought with you?" His accent was intriguing, and I couldn't help but blush and smile. I wasn't sure what nationality he was—Italian, Greek, I had no idea—but he was definitely Mediterranean. Ari came over to me and gave me a hug and started to do air-kisses on each side of my face. I stood there motionless and didn't reciprocate. He began touching and examining my hair. The way he was holding out my hair reminded me of how someone would hold a dead rodent. I wasn't sure if his expression was one of disgust or concern, but it left me feeling foolish.

Now, my hair had not been cut for some time, and I started to feel embarrassed by how bad a shape my hair actually was in. Although I'd had pin-straight hair my whole life, during puberty my hair sometimes started to take on a wavy, curly look if I let it air-dry. I wasn't crazy about it, but it did look better than being pin straight. I didn't really give my hair much thought or even take the time to blow-dry it.

"Ari, this is my friend MK I want you to make her look fabulous!"

"Sure, sure, Samantha, I'll make her look like a movie star. I'll fix her up!" Ari replied as he was going through a few books. He wore a white silk shirt that was unbuttoned, exposing his chest hair, and some kind of shiny black pants. I wondered if they were satin, silk, or sharkskin. I'd never seen anything like them and had to stop myself from reaching out and touching his pants.

"Here you go, darling. You look through these books and pick out what you like, OK?" Ari said, and his accent was so endearing that I decided to do whatever he said. I felt like he was my master and that I was his obedient little doggie. I casually watched Ari painting Samantha's head like a masterpiece and her talking away to Ari, her nails shining and eye shadow shimmering.

I flicked through the first book, which reminded me of a Mediterranean Vidal Sassoon or VO5 commercial. All the styles would require me to actually style my hair, use a curling iron and blow-dryer, and do all the rest. We never had the money for those things, so I'd never really used them. I struggled to find a hairstyle that was realistic. A lot of the models had beautiful makeup and clothes on; I started to slide down in my seat, feeling more and more inadequate as time went on. After about four books, I grew tired. I saw a photo album on the end table next to me. I decided to take a break from "fabulous."

I flipped through the pages of this photo album, which looked professional. The photographs were eight-by-tens and had white borders around them like postcards. The pictures were so clear that they looked like they belonged in a travel book. A few photos were of beautiful fountains and monuments. I started to think that they were postcards until I saw Ari in some of the photos.

The next few pages were pictures on a white beach, with clear teal water with a cliff in the background and houses (or something) built into the walls of the cliff. I had only seen pictures like this in an encyclopedia. Ari was on the beach wearing a white blouse, similar to the one he was wearing now, and shorts. He was alone. I was expecting some hot Grecian goddess next to him. Maybe she was taking the pictures. In the next few pages, Ari had his shirt off and was posing in different stances: the discus thrower, the thinker, and what have you. I started to wonder if this was his model portfolio.

As I turned the next page, I started to sweat. Ari was running on the beach and was no longer wearing anything. My brow furrowed as I tried to comprehend what I was seeing. I felt like such a creep but couldn't look away. The morbid curiosity kept my eyes glued to the pages. The next few pages were of Ari jumping in the air, his package in full view. I was now looking at full-frontal nudity. I started to wonder if this was illegal. I was the most puzzled by his penis. I really had never seen many before, although I had changed a lot of diapers as a kid. If my memory served, none had resembled anything like this. I'd seen Gerry's that one time following the gum incident. I'd never seen this wrinkly, toilet-paper-roll-resembling penis. I could feel the bewilderment consume me and my cheeks get hot. I found myself wanting to examine things more closely. Then I was completely appalled and confused by the situation: he had a photo album on a coffee table, on display for anyone to look at, and he was naked, exposing his peculiar-looking penis to everyone. I was extremely uncomfortable and could feel tiny beads of sweat emerge on my face. I glanced over at Sam, who was looking at a magazine with her head painted bronze. Now it was my turn, and I wasn't sure I was up for it.

"Oh, those are photographs of my vacation pictures from Athens. Aren't they beautiful?" Ari asked as he stood before me. He startled the hell out of me so badly that I jerked my body, and the portfolio fell to the floor. I began to pick up the nude photo pages and handed them to Ari, who was still standing, and I was now face to face with his package underneath those pants. He raised one eyebrow at me (I'd kill to be able to do that), and I immediately felt panic and shame, as if I'd been doing something wrong. I'm not sure why I ended up feeling like the kid whose hand had been caught in the cookie jar just by his one sneer with a raised eyebrow. (*How does he do that?* I wondered.) He ripped the photos from my hand and in his haste elbowed me in the eye. Then he walked away! The bastard didn't even apologize. If I had a car, I would've been so outta there. The anger triggered a memory from *Ferris Bueller*: "I ask for a car, I get a computer. How's that for being born under a bad sign." Instant smile. I didn't get a computer either, however, I was grateful that my brain did this trick for comic relief. Man, that John Hughes is a fucking genius!

I obviously didn't know Ari very well, but I could sense he'd been totally annoyed with me from the start. Perhaps it was the way he held my hair like it was a dirty rag that tipped me off. I was not beautiful like Sam. He was definitely *not* giving me the movie-star treatment. He basically pushed me into the chair, strangled me with the cape, and aggressively began spraying my hair with water. I hadn't even told him yet what hairstyle I wanted, and he'd already started cutting like *Edward Scissorhands.* I was facing away from the mirror and was wondering what he was doing. But because I felt uncomfortable and stressed in his presence, my "deer in the headlights" speechless self took over, and I did nothing to stop him from butchering me. Next thing I knew, he was painting my head and pushing my roller chair back to Sam. Then he affectionately put his hands on Sam's shoulders and slowly brought her to the shampoo bowl. They were both laughing, and he was gently soaping up her hair.

I scooted my chair over to see my reflection, but all I could see was my hair plastered to my head, looking like dirt had been painted on my head. As I was wheeling back my chair, Ari looked up, and his eyes were daggers. The music from *Carrie* popped into my head, and I was afraid Ari also had mental telepathy and would make scissors fly and stab me. While Samantha's hair was getting styled and blow-dried, I was getting claustrophobic under that cape, and my scalp was beginning to sting and itch. If this was what being a movie star was all about, I didn't want any part of it. I wanted to get the fuck out of there *now!*

Samantha now turned around, and I saw that she resembled a nineties Farrah Fawcett. I began to calm down, hoping that maybe I'd resemble one of the other two (brunette) Charlie's Angels. That pleasant vision was extinguished once Ari slammed my head onto the shampoo bowl; suds were all over my forehead and were sliding down and starting to sting my eyes. He sat me up and was drying my hair while grinning and staring at Sam as if she was a giant steak. I started to reach my hand up to feel my hair, but he slapped it down. Samantha looked up from her magazine at me with a surprised expression, and

Ari put his show back on: "Now, no peeking, girls! I want you to be surprised." I could read Samantha's expression—which was a combination of surprise and horror—that the end result of my makeover wasn't going to be good.

Since Samantha was now curious and watching, Ari now handled me with a tender touch. His round-brushing of my hair was slightly relaxing, and I started to forget about Ari's weird tube-penis photos on the coffee table and his mysterious hatred of me and thought about how I'd be able to get home soon. I smiled to myself. Then, Ari slowly spun me around to face the mirror, whipped off the cape, and yelled "*voilà!*"

The smile was slapped off my face by my reflection as I saw what he had done to me. My natural long, wavy hair had disappeared; my hair now resembled Demi Moore's style from *Ghost*.

Ari looked at my expression and must have thought I was shocked with joy, since he said, "I know! Gorgeous, right? I tell you, I make you look like a movie star, yes? You look like movie star now! I cut your perm out, and we start fresh, OK? You look fabulous!"

His accent was no longer endearing, and I wanted to tell him the proper way of speaking English. Fabulous I wasn't by any means. My face was too fat and my cheeks too chubby for this short, bowl cut, or whatever the hell it was. It appeared to resemble Dorothy Hammill and the mushroom cut I had the majority of my childhood. Ffff-uuuu-cccc-kkkk!

Sam attempted to appear positive and in awe of my new look, but I knew her and knew that this was totally bogus. I was quite aware of her phony look. I appreciated her effort, but it was unsuccessful in convincing me. I stared at the reflection of myself in the mirror, my fat cheeks trembling with anger, my teeth grinding in fury. I was no longer numb—I was furious.

"This is on me, buddy," Sam said to me and patted my hand. For some reason, this act of kindness seemed more like pity to me, and I felt like I was about to blow my top.

"Sam, don't give this guy a fucking dime for this massacre! He totally just wants to get in your pants, so he treats you like a movie star, yet he was amazingly rude—actually, abusive—to me. I've been violated by being here. Did you see his pornographic photo album he has over there?" I exclaimed, foaming at the mouth.

"Shhhh, keep it down, MK He's harmless, and he's the cheapest hairstylist around. My hair would cost like two hundred and fifty bucks somewhere else. I'm sorry you don't like your hair, but it's really becoming on you. You're just not used to it."

Sam sounded sincere, and I began to calm down. This girl could persuade me to do anything; she should have been in sales. I made a vain effort to keep it together until we left. Unfortunately, Sam was too trusting and left me alone with Ari to use the washroom. Panic and anger consumed me when she closed the bathroom door. I was launching daggers at Ari, and his eyes met mine with a playful and arrogant expression, like a bully who's taken a kid's lunch. Thankfully, Sam finished in the bathroom quickly and came out. Ari's smiled changed to looking innocent and sweet, and he slapped his hands together, Mr. Miyagi style.

"You two movie stars have a lovely evening, and I'll see you next time!" he said, sounding sincere, but I was onto him. He gave Sam air-kisses on either cheek. *If that motherfucker comes near me, I swear to God...*

Then, like clockwork, *Ferris Bueller* invaded my head again, unwanted: "If you touch me again, I yell rat!" I was too angry this time for my brain trick to work. I was getting bad vibes from this dude, and I yearned for the opportunity to beat his ass or kick him in his creepy penis. Then Ari made a crucial mistake and touched my head; the hair on my now-exposed neck was standing up like a cat ready to pounce.

"See, milady, aren't you glad you cut that wretched perm out? And you now look like a movie star." He said this slyly and then whispered, "I told you you'd *look* like a movie star, but I didn't promise that you'd look good." This guy was un-fucking-believable.

"It wasn't a perm, you bastard, and don't you ever touch me again!" I screamed. "Keep your hands and your weird gross turtle dick away from Sam, or I'll call the police to inform them that you're showing pornographic photos to minors!"

Sam stared at me in shock. Ari looked bewildered. I stormed out of his shadysalon. As I walked to Sam's car and sat on the curb, I was shocked at my rage and assertive reaction without hesistation. I gave myself a light punch in the arm like Brian in The Breakfast Club after he composed his masterpiece to Mr. Vernon.

# 18

I was now feeling foolish and depressed. My hair was now atrocious, and it didn't cheer me up. It made me feel worse. When I got home, there was a message was on the machine from Gerry, at least, so I called him back.

He answered on the first ring. "Hello?"

"Hi," I replied flatly.

"Hey. Sorry I didn't call you last night. I kinda drank too much and passed out when I got home," he said softly.

"Oh, I see. Was the party fun?" I asked, not really wanting to know about another fun party I'd missed.

"Yeah, it was OK. You didn't miss anything." He sounded distracted. "What are you doing?"

"Nothing, really. I just got home. Sam talked me into getting my hair done by her guy. He butchered me." My voice cracked as I glanced at myself in the mirror, and I almost cried.

He snickered. "What do you mean? You don't like it?"

"It's really, really short. I hate it. I look ugly." I was starting to tear up.

"I'll be right over," Gerry said, and he hung up.

*Huh?*

Five minutes later, Gerry pulled up in front of my house. I was sitting on my porch having a cigarette and trying to calm down. I was running my hands through my hair over and over. Feeling the short, tiny hairs on my exposed neck was surreal. I'd never really felt all that pretty or sexy before, but now I definitely did not. I looked like a boy, and my cheeks looked bloated. I put my head in my lap as Gerry walked up. I could see his feet beneath me in his shower shoes.

"Holy shit!" he exclaimed as he touched the back of my neck. "Come on, baby, let me see."

I reluctantly lifted my head and looked at him sulkily. I felt very young and childish. I knew it was just a haircut, but it was a drastic one. He smirked and looked at me closely. He pushed one side of my hair behind my ear, then the other. He lifted my chin with his index finger and examined me again.

"Stand up, please," he said sternly. I flicked my cigarette, sighed, and stood up. He placed his hands on the sides of my face, kissed my lips softly, and then slid his hands slowly down my neck. "Turn around; let me see the back." I obeyed his instructions, feeling curious. "It's fucking hot, baby. It's sexy! I love it!"

I was completely confused. I thought all guys loved long hair. What the...

"I love that I can feel your neck. I love that I can run my fingers through it and grasp it, like this." He slid his fingers from the base of my neck to my scalp and then clenched his fingers closed around my hair and pulled me to his mouth abruptly. I got goose bumps at first, then it hurt slightly, but it turned me on in a way. His gentle force-fulness and passionate kisses were lifting my mood and making me feel presentable again. I smiled shyly and looked down. He lifted my chin again to meet his gaze. I was standing on the bottom step of the porch, and he stood on the ground, as we always did so that we would be all lined up (eyes, nose, and mouth).

"I do. I love it. You look amazing. It looks cool," he said sincerely as he placed one arm around my waist and the other around my neck and kissed me harder and more intensely. I could feel him harden and press into my belly button. His arousal turned me on, and I felt sexy again in his presence. "Damn, girl, I'm all worked up. I just want to throw you on the couch and rip your clothes off right now and run my fingers through your hair and hold you next to me." I was blushing and throbbing at his words. He pressed his forehead to mine. "I'm glad he butchered you, as you said. It looks hot on you. You look older, like a college girl or something." He smiled and nudged me.

"Well, I guess that's good for homecoming weekend—that I look older and like a 'college girl,'" I said, using air quotes. "Thanks, baby." I smiled and nudged him back.

His demeanor changed instantly, and I could sense a sudden coolness between us. He stepped back, and the mood was lost. "Oh, yeah. You're leaving Friday, right?" he asked in a flat voice.

"Yes," I replied equally flatly, confused by his sudden change in mood.

"Well, you be a good girl, OK?" he asked, his eyes looking vacant.

"Of course I will, silly," I replied, now realizing that he was jealous again. "I love you."

"I love you, too," he replied, still in a flat voice. "Well, I'll be at practice, and then we have homecoming as well, so…I…uh…guess I'll talk to you when you get back," he said nervously. I nodded and smiled. He gave me a quick peck and briskly walked to his car.

*Holy mood swings. I thought bitches were bad on the rag—sheesh, boys are just as bad.*

Homecoming weekend finally arrived. School dragged all day; two fifteen couldn't come fast enough. Sam drove us home from school, with her car already packed with her weekend things. To my surprise, though, my brother and his friend TJ were loading up another car and had assumed they were driving us. TJ had his mother's new Toyota Camry, which looked as if it was in pretty good working condition. Sam wasn't crazy about driving on the expressway, so she was fine with allowing someone else to drive. Plus, TJ was kind of cute, and Sam started her little giggle, which usually indicated that she was interested. We loaded up the trunk and were soon on our way. I was looking forward to seeing my sister—it had been quite some time since I'd last seen her.

Gerry's behavior had been extremely aloof and standoffish whenever I mentioned this weekend. I knew he wasn't crazy about my going, but my sister would have been pissed if I'd missed it. Like she said, she might not be there the following year and it was important to her that I come—she's my sister, and I was sure I'd regret not going. I also had no idea why Gerry didn't want me to go; what would *he* be afraid of? He wanted *me* to be a good girl; I assumed he was concerned about me cheating. Yeah, right. Me? I should have been more worried about him. After all, he was the first real guy to have asked me out. My past kisses had basically come from playing spin the bottle, and going out in seventh grade really didn't amount to much. My past encounters had looked nothing like Gerry, either. I was the one who should have been concerned.

We arrived relatively fast, and it was cool to hang out with my brother, too. Mairead no longer lived in a dorm room and instead rented a house with three other girls. It was liberating to see how my sister had been living. I was impressed. The house was small and had that stale day-after bar smell (I knew that smell because I used to help my dad clean some bars in my neighborhood on Saturday mornings), but it was a house nonetheless. They had a small kitchen with a table and four chairs, a living room with couches, and a decent-size TV, and each girl had her own room. My sister had been working at the school cafeteria and a bar to pay for her rent, food, and other stuff. Apparently you could afford to drink cheaply at parties: cups were usually three bucks each, and you could drink all night. All the bars had nickel beer night two or three nights a week. I immediately wanted to go away to college. Walking in the door of the house equaled fun.

Mairead looked fresh and pretty; she was also turning twenty-one this weekend, so she had a bit of a birthday glow. Her smile beamed, and she hugged me very hard. She was wearing plaid pajama bottoms and a hooded sweatshirt with Eastern's school logo. Her hair was in a high ponytail, and she looked adorable, like a college bookstore model. She even hugged Michael, followed by a punch in the arm. Kinda funny because Mairead and Michael are technically "Irish twins," born eleven months apart. Michael would be twenty-one in eleven months, and I think it drove him nuts that Mairead was older than him and could now buy alcohol. She introduced me to her three girlfriends, who all appeared cool and friendly. Sandy was a tall, lanky model type with a more exotic face and olive skin. She wore her brown hair in braids and was wearing a cowboy hat, and of course she looked good—hot, even. Nora was short with brown bobbed hair and an athletic build, and she was also wearing head-to-toe college attire and Birkenstock sandals. Colleen was blond and curvy, with a pretty face and a friendly smile. Sandy apparently knew Michael, because Michael walked right over to her and sat on her lap on the couch. Sandy wrapped her arms around his waist and kissed him on the cheek. *Oh jeez*, I thought. *Here we go already*.

I went into the kitchen to get some water, and Mairead filled me in on things in general, plans, and Michael. Last semester, Michael had visited Eastern impromptu with his buddies and had hooked up with Sandy; not knowing she was roomates with Mairead. Now it became clear to me Michael's true motive for coming to visit; and here I'd thought he was just trying to be a good brother. He always had something up his sleeve. From an outside standpoint, I guess Michael would have been considered a good-looking boy, and since he'd grown up with three sisters, maybe he did treat his girls well. Mairead rolled her eyes at Sandy and Michael on the couch looking so cozy; Mairead appeared grossed out. Sandy was one of those flawless-beauty types, like Cindy Crawford, and I caught myself staring at her. Mairead motioned to me to come to her room, and she closed the door.

"Nauseating, isn't it?" she asked, looking disgusted.

"Yes—revolting and repulsive," I replied, humoring her. I was more shocked and impressed than anything, but Sandy wasn't my friend, so I could see why Mairead would be grossed out.

"Anyway," she said, "we're going to go for dinner and drinks and then hit this bar, Monti's." Her face lit up. "It's gonna be a good time!"

I was perplexed about how I was going to pull off getting into a bar at eighteen, so I voiced this concern to Mairead. Her roommate Nora had the connection: her brother was the bouncer at Monti's, so I was good on that front. I hadn't drunk too much alcohol in my life at that point, so I doubted it would take much. I was so excited for the night anyway that I was riding on adrenaline.

The rest of the afternoon, Mairead, Sam, TJ, Nora, and I went for a walk around campus, with Mairead showing me all her prime spots. It was a sunny and fresh fall afternoon, and I was enjoying the weather and feeling rather proud of my sister. Michael and Sandy did not join us, I assume they wanted to be alone. After campus tour, we headed back home to shower and get ready. Sam and TJ had disappeared, and I just didn't have the patience to look for Sam.

Monti's was a shithole, but they didn't card at the door. Twenty-five-cent bottles on a Saturday had the place packed with college kids, all of whom had that bloated look from the freshman fifteen. The beer was tough going down at first, but slowly I became immune to the bitter taste; soon it was going down like water. I felt like I was fresh meat with the way all the bloated dudes were looking at me. I must have looked out of place: unbloated, innocent, and young. I was in sheer ecstasy that I was eighteen years old, in a bar, drinking with my sister.

A deejay started playing, and soon the dance floor was packed with all the women in the bar. To my surprise, they began to play all the old stuff that was right up my alley: the Jackson 5, the Beatles, the Rolling Stones. When Ike and Tina's version of "Proud Mary" started, Mairead grabbed me, and the next thing I knew, we were on the tiny little stage next to the deejay booth. Mairead and I used to roller-skate for hours listening to records, particularly the song "Proud Mary." My mom even videotaped one of Ike and Tina's concerts for us; we watched it over and over, memorizing every line. Mairead was impersonating Tina by mimicking, "Listen to the story now," and I was doing Ike as only I know how: furrowing my brow and singing low in a bluesy style.

Mairead was enthralling; it seemed like half the bar was mesmerized with her. She had such finesse and charisma. I glanced over to see Michael sitting at the bar with Sandy standing between his legs; they were leaning up against the bar stool, both grinning at us and looking completely shocked. This gave me more encouragement, so I nudged Mairead to do the dance moves we had practiced for years while roller-skating in the basement. We began bending over and throwing our hands forward and back, singing, "Rollin'! Rollin'! Rollin' down the riva." The alcohol gave me confidence, and my sister was like my self-esteem. We were alive with adrenaline, faces glistening with sweat, and the music overtook us. Other girls began to join us, and soon Michael and Sandy were beside us as well. Mairead grabbed Sandy's cowboy hat and put it on, and Sandy began swirling her hair around. I was overheated, so I whipped off my sweater and started twirling it over my head. Sandy and Michael were laughing at us, and Sandy removed herself from between Michael's legs to take pictures of us. Of course Mairead and I began posing and being ridiculous for the pictures.

The songs continued, and I knew every word. I was sweating, and the dance floor was getting more crowded. A few guys had now caught the drift that, if they wanted to hook up tonight, they would need to take it to the dance floor. Next thing I knew, I was being whisked into the air by some big football player. Mairead was also being spun around by some other husky-looking male. I just went with it. It was freeing to just be me, without a care in the world. Thoughts of Gerry were far from my mind, and I embraced the night and went with the flow. I wasn't doing anything wrong; I was dancing, drinking, and having a good time. I worked hard, and I knew I deserved it. Eventually I had to stop to use the ladies' room. The big football player asked me what I wanted to drink and was totally looking at my breasts when he asked. I was so tempted to tell him what *they* wanted to drink, but I actually enjoyed the attention, though I would not admit it. I liked the way he was looking at me. Other than Gerry, I'd never entertained the idea of any male talking to me, and I avoided such encounters at all costs. Now I was aware of myself, my attractiveness, and my sex appeal, all of which Gerry had unleashed. I let go.

Mairead grabbed my hand and pulled me giggling and stumbling into the bathroom. I looked in the mirror and realized what I had on underneath my sweater: a worn, near-see-through white T-shirt with slightly yellow pit stains. You could totally see my white bra and hard nipples right through this top. No wonder that football player had looked at me like I was a steak. Mairead had a tank top on under her sweater and looked like she had just finished working out. We both peed violently next to each other in the stalls, laughing about whose pee was louder.

"I...am...really...glad...you...came...up!" Mairead said through hiccups.

"Me too!" I replied excitedly.

"Isn't it fun?" she said, slurring.

"Yes, a blast!"

We exited the stalls at the same time, washed our hands, reapplied some lip gloss, and dabbed out faces with toilet paper. Mairead put her arm around me, and we walked out arm in arm to the bar to acquire more beer. It felt like every guy at the place was looking at us, and I couldn't figure out why.

"Les do a schot," Mairead said, slurring. "Two redheaded sluts and two beers!"

My head was spinning, and I couldn't stop laughing. I was euphoric. My big football player dance partner came up behind me and put his hands around my waist. I was startled by the sudden and foreign touch. As the bartender served us the drinks, Sandy came up to us. "Oh, Lord have mercy—shots, girls?" she asked with a laugh. She took more pictures, which I graciously posed for. Mairead and I became huge hams and intertwined our forearms around each other and slammed our shots. It went down smooth, surprisingly. Sandy took more pictures, while Mairead and I put our arms around the big football players. My dance partner had his hand right under my breast, and he briefly grazed my nipple with his thumb. I jerked away, feeling uncomfortable and slightly violated. It was my fault, encouraging him to put my arm around him and letting him spin me around while dancing. He looked at me with a scolded-boy expression.

"Back off, man," I said to him, and I moved to the corner of the bar. Mairead and Sandy had disappeared. I began to panic. I searched around the bar, attempting to find someone else, when I caught a familiar-looking face smirking at me. He had bright-blue eyes, porcelain skin, braces, and a gray newsboy cap on backward. I couldn't recall where I knew him from because of the unfamiliar atmosphere and my drunkenness, although the way he was looking at me had me tempted to walk over to him and introduce myself. It felt as if we had stared at each other for a long time, and *West Side Story* popped into my mind, when the entire crowd becomes fuzzy, and the only clear figures are Maria and Tony. My fucking brain. I was just about to begin walking toward him when Mairead grabbed my arm. I looked back, and the mysterious smirking dude was gone.

"It Takes Two" began to play, and Mairead, Michael, Sandy, and I retreated to the dance floor. Random boys were flipping me, spinning me around, and tossing me around like a doll. Soon the bartender called last call, and the hellish fluorescent lights went on. We put our sweaters back on and exited the bar. Mairead and I walked arm in arm behind Michael and Sandy, who were walking intertwined with their hands in each other's ass pockets. Mairead and I were about to vomit, so we covered our eyes and speed-walked in front of them.

"Just wait till the after-party at my house!" Mairead said excitedly.

I was exhausted suddenly and feeling woozy. "I gottagobed," I slurred.

"Here, let's stop at this place and get you a Coke. You can't miss the after-party—that's when shit goes down." We went to a 7-Eleven and got bags of chips and pop. I guzzled the pop, and I did feel better instantly. When we arrived at Mairead's house, people were everywhere. People were sitting on the porch and on the roof smoking cigarettes, the music was blasting, and the windows were steamed up. Her other roommates, Nora and Colleen, had stayed home and smoked bongs all night. They preferred to stay home and have the party come to them, Mairead told me.

It was a sauna in their house from all the people. I went to the bedroom to remove my see-through, armpit-stained undershirt and put on one of Mairead's tank tops. I glanced in the mirror and grimaced at the reflection of some kind of hell staring back at me. My face was greasy, and my hair was sticking up every which way. I was about to fix myself and then thought: fuck it. I was having fun, so who cares.

I reentered the party room, which was about twenty degrees hotter than the bedroom. It was dim and was wall-to-wall people; the room was filled with moist body heat. I scanned the room until I found Mairead sporting Sandy's cowboy hat again. She looked cute but sloppily drunk now as she stumbled into the kitchen; she set in motion more craziness by spraying the kitchen floor with water. "Smells Like Teen Spirit" began to play loudly, and people were slipping and sliding around on the kitchen floor. A pathway spread open, as if automatically, and guys began running at charging speed and diving onto the wet floor on their stomachs and crashing into the cabinets. Someone opened the back door, and another guy slid on the kitchen floor right out the door.

Through the crowd of sweating, drunken fools dancing all over Mairead's living room and kitchen, I spotted a guy wearing an Irish-style cap. My eyes widened excitedly, hoping it was the mystery man from the bar. The crowd tightened suddenly, because the same jackass was charging through the room to dive out the back door again, with people screaming and cheering him on. Being so short, I couldn't see anything except the shoulders of the people around me. So I stood on my tippy-toes to see if I could get a peek at the boy in the cap. As I was rising up on my tippy-toes, the guy in front of me was clapping and raising his hands up and down and cheering for the fool. His elbow came crashing down on my cheekbone, which stung like hell.

As I put both my hands on my right cheek, another guy's elbow came down right onto the bridge of my nose. That hurt twice as much as the first blow, and tears welled up instantaneously. My nose started to run straight away. I covered my head under my hands as if rocks were falling from the sky. I went right to Mairead's bedroom and collapsed on her bed, sobbing like a bitch.

# 19

I woke up with the sun glaring in my eyes and some kind of vise on my head. Ouch—pounding headache. I turned to lie on my side—ouch! Fuck, I'd just remembered the elbow to the cheek and the other elbow to the nose. I struggled to sit up and stumbled to the bathroom, now feeling queasy from the sudden movements. I jolted when I caught a look at myself in the mirror. My short, butchered hair was sticking up on one side and flat on the other. I had streaks of blood under my nose, on my chin and chest, and on Mairead's tank top. I had a large black-and-blue contusion on my right cheekbone that radiated near my eye. My nose throbbed with pain, and my cheek pulsated with a stabbing pain that went straight to my head. I washed my face and chest with cold water and then with hot to remove all the blood and put a sweatshirt on. I was sweating but freezing. Then the nausea started, and I ralphed urgently and violently. Deliriously, I staggered back to bed and was soon out cold.

I spent most of the morning lying around. Unfortunately, Mairead's room was right next to the bathroom, so I had the treat of hearing random people moan, throw up, and pee all morning. *Why do we do this to ourselves*, I wondered, but then I answered my own question when I remembered how much fun I'd had the night before. I was replaying the great night in my head when Mairead, surprisingly chipper, greeted me and went into the bathroom to shower. I was unexpectedly distracted by the glorious scent of bacon, and I needed to be downstairs immediately. When I got up, I did feel much better and no longer nauseated. Only the remnants of throbbing pain from my facial injuries remained. I marched into the kitchen, ravenous, my stomach growling madly, to find Sandy at the stove looking hot even when she just woke up.

"Hey," she said with a croak, "have some bacon; it's the best hang-over cure in the world." She pointed to a pound of already-cooked bacon on a paper plate on the table. I devoured five pieces in thirty seconds. It was delicious. "Have a Coke, too," she said and placed a red Solo cup with ice and a can of Coke in front of me. I slurped it down without breathing. It soothed my throat and quenched my thirst in an amazing way. "What the hell happened to you?" Sandy inquired with a raspy voice.

I held my finger up, since I was drinking the Coke continuously and didn't take a break until it was gone. "Long story," I eventually replied. "I got elbowed in the face last night. I don't know exactly." I grabbed some toast and two more pieces of bacon. This was quite possibly the best breakfast I'd ever had.

"Ouch. You want to shower next?" she croaked again. Whiskey pipes.

"Shower? For what?" I asked, confused. Sandy smirked as she looked at my greasy hair. I giggled. "I mean, where are we going? Of course I need to shower," I said.

Sandy, with her tan body in a white tank top with navy-blue jog-ging-pant cutoffs, looked like a model. Her sandy-blond hair looked after-the-beach ready. She had like ten pieces of bacon on her plate and three pieces of toast as she slurped her Coke. I was amazed at how much food she could put away yet still be so hot and skinny; ge-netics are just not fair sometimes.

"It's homecoming, silly—we're going to the game, then parties," Sandy said excitedly. Some of her voice had recovered, thanks to the Coke.

"Ugh," I replied. I wanted to go, but my body and head were saying no, and I needed another nap. "I need to lie down for a little bit longer." Sandy handed me two Advil and another Coke. It was nice being taken care of and having my hangover nursed.

"I'll wake you up in an hour. After your shower, put some red lipstick on that shiner, and it'll tone down the blue in the bruise. Then put some foundation on it." She smiled and winked.

"How do you know that? Gotten your ass kicked lately?" I asked sarcastically. She laughed.

I crashed and woke up feeling better and ready to go. I jumped in the shower, and the hot water soothed my aching body and face. I tried to style my hair parted on the side so the thicker side would be covering my cheek, which was now purplish—lovely. I hooked the other side of my hair behind my ear. I followed Sandy's instructions about the bruise and put more makeup on than I usually wore to balance it out—and because I looked like a victim of domestic violence. I put on some holey, shredded jeans, black Chuck Taylors, a T-shirt, and a gray zip-up hooded sweatshirt. I wasn't sure what else to wear. I grabbed money, a fake ID, and some Lip Smackers and was ready to go.

Mairead and Sandy were dressed in similar ensembles as me. Sandy lifted my hair up to inspect my bruise and makeup job. She nodded her head and grinned, indicating to me that it looked good. She proudly put her arm around me, and we walked outside. We all forgot sunglasses, so we went back to get those. Sandy forgot her purse, so she went back inside. Mairead forgot her ID and had to go back inside again. I was surprised that I hadn't forgotten anything. It was another beautiful day, with fall on the way and not a cloud in the sky. The weather was perfect sweatshirt weather, with no possibility of sweating—or a sweaty mustache—my favorite kind of forecast.

The stadium atmosphere was instantly intoxicating. People were tailgating in the parking lot, with different music blaring from people's cars. The three of us walked past a line of cars with hatches up and guys sitting in the trunk. They were all gawking at Sandy, of course. Mairead and I rolled our eyes at each other. My brother, Michael, was at the end of the row, sitting on the back of his car; he held an Old Style in one hand and a cup in the other. Sandy slithered right past everyone and gracefully ended up next to him on the back of the car. Bloody Mary mix and a bottle of vodka were sitting on the cooler, along with a plate of cheese cubes and salami. I did a double take; it was out of character for Michael to have such a spread prepared.

"Hair of the dog, MK—want a bloody?" Michael asked. He had a navy-blue baseball hat on backward, a beard lining his jaw, and pilot sunglasses. He also had ripped jeans, Chuck Taylors, and a blue hooded sweatshirt. In this moment, I saw my brother in a different light and could totally see understand why Sandy liked him. He had what it takes to bag a gal like that.

"Sure, brotha, thanks!" I said enthusiastically. It did look really scrumptious. I looked at the platter suspiciously. Michael followed my gaze. "Want some snacks? Sandy bought them and stocked my cooler. She's the shit." He gave her a big Maverick-from-*Top Gun* grin and blew smoke out of his teeth and nose.

Sandy beamed. "The cheese and salami are like another little appetizer designed to cure your hangover," she said. She was cool, too. *Dammit, where do these bitches come from?* I thought. I guess she couldn't help it that God had given her everything. She sat on Michael's lap; suddenly I felt uncomfortable and turned away.

I looked around at all the college kids and admired their lifestyle. I decided right then and there that I was destined to go to college and experience this. My eyes landed on a gray hat heading toward us. I stopped breathing for a second. He was walking right toward us. He was wearing sunglasses and smiling straight ahead; I caught myself staring and smiling at him as he walked past me and slapped Michael a high five.

"Wassup, Martay?" Michael asked excitedly as he stood up to greet him. They hugged briefly. I was shocked that my brother would associate with someone so...so...good looking.

"Not much, just here visiting my brother. You?" He smirked and took a sip of his beer. I could see a faint shimmer of tinsel on his teeth. I tried to contain myself as I realized that this *must* have been the guy from last night.

"Just visiting my sis, Mairead," Michael replied, lighting up a Marlboro Red. He motioned to Mairead and introduced her to Marty. "And *this* is my other sister, Mary Kate." Michael held his arm out for me to come to him. He put his arm around me and showed me to Marty as if I was for sale. Michael still had his arm hooked around my neck when I made eye contact with Marty. He smiled at me and shook my hand; neither of us took our eyes off each other. His eyes were stunningly bright and shining in the afternoon sun. It was so intense that I had to break our gaze abruptly. He also turned away and took another sip of his beer. I was sitting on the bumper of the car, grateful that Michael's arm was still around me. I took another peek at Marty from behind my hair; he was wearing an Irish-style cap, and his profile was strong. He was adorable and cool. I nervously put the sides of my hair behind my ears.

"Jesus! What the fuck happened to you, MK?" Michael asked me, looking concerned and a little pissed. Everyone suddenly glanced my way. My cheeks burned, and I gulped a big swig of my Bloody. I blew out my cheeks and searched for a humorous answer, but my mind was blank as to what had really happened. I was sure it was a boring or embarrassing story.

Then a different response came to me, and I smiled. "I didn't do the dishes, remember?" I joked. Everyone laughed, even Marty. I blushed and took another big gulp of my delicious Bloody Marty, I mean Mary. Michael gave me the suspicious stink eye and smirked at me. He pulled me closer to him with his arm around my neck, as if he was about to give me a noogie.

"Come on, for real, what happened?" he asked again, appearing actually concerned. I couldn't remember exactly how I'd gotten the bruise on my face. I was beginning to catch a buzz, though, because I was becoming giggly. I slyly looked at Marty while laughing, and then what had happened came to the surface.

"This is what you get in my house when you spill paint in the garage," I said with a smile. Mairead smiled, too. Michael took his arm off me and shook his head, now annoyed with me, and he opened another beer.

Marty looked at me with recognition, and his bright-blue eyes lit up. "You know what I got at my house for Christmas? A carton of cigarettes." He said this nonchalantly, smiled at me, and took another sip of his beer. I was impressed. Sandy looked at us, looking confused.

"Hey, smoke up, Johnny!" I replied immediately, grinning at him. He grinned back. Butterflies in stomach…

Marty walked over to me and sat on the edge of the cooler that was next to me; my stomach was doing backflips. I gulped more Bloody Mary and wondered if he could smell my gross, spicy breath from where he was sitting. I grabbed one of Michael's cigarettes out of nervousness. It was nice to focus on this for a second; just having this guy next to me was making me quiver. Michael was chain-smoking and lit another one the second he'd put the first one out.

Marty looked at me and Michael and then lit a cigarette, too. He took a big drag, and then a crooked smirk emerged on his breathtakingly cute face. "You don't smoke, Mairead?" Marty asked my sister, who was staring at him with the same shocked yet impressed expression I was. She shook her head no.

"That's because the chicks can't hold da smoke; dat's what it is," Marty said in a squeaky voice just like the brainy Anthony Michael Hall character from *The Breakfast Club*. I was utterly awed by his ability to effortlessly work this in to the conversation. He smiled at me again, with my stomach jumping as a result. What the hell? He then stared at me silently, eyes intense, apparently waiting for me to respond.

"What's your poison?" I replied back, relieved that my brain was on.

"Vodka," he immediately replied.

"When do you drink it?" I said coyly.

"Whenever," he said smugly. I blushed. It was like he was whispering sweet nothings in my ear, and I was feeling like we were flirting through movie quotes. It was bizarre. We continued quoting *The Breakfast Club* to each other; I was becoming gigglier by the moment, as if I'd sucked on a helium balloon. I couldn't stop laughing. When I caught Sandy's bewildered and judgy expression, I stopped for a second as if I was in trouble.

Sandy apparently couldn't take it anymore. "What the hell are you guys talking about? It's like you have some secret language or something." She looked irritated. She appeared to have it all—except possibly the sense-of-humor gene.

"We're speaking the international language of love," Marty said, deadpanning *Better Off Dead* with a Spanish accent; he winked at me.

I liked it. Beaming proudly at him, I yelled, "Nice! Get that shit up." Marty slapped me a high five, and we both took another gulp. "Hey, I want my two dollars!" I said, quoting the movie back to Marty. He held his hand up for me to slap.

"What?" Sandy asked again, looking totally bewildered. Jeez, why was she getting so mad, I wondered? I suppose this would be pretty annoying if you didn't know what the hell we were talking about. But how could you not? These movies were classics. I was raised on this shit.

"Sandy, maybe you would like some fronch fries and fronch toast," I said. She sighed and stomped away. Michael, who seemed to be pretending that he didn't know what we were talking about, nudged me with his elbow. We caught eyes, and he smiled at me. He got up to follow Sandy.

"That was awesome," Marty said to me, looking alive and cool as hell in his gray wool cap and red plaid flannel over a cream long-sleeve thermal shirt that clung to his chest. I tried not to stare, yet my eyes were drawn to it.

"Very. I was just wondering why she's getting so mad. Sheesh!" I replied.

Mairead, ahead of us, motioned with her arm to follow her. She yelled, "Game's starting! Let's go!"

I nodded, my attention immediately back to Marty.

"Totally," Marty said as he began walking, not taking his eyes off mine.

"Totaled, man. Me hitting you, you hitting the floor," I replied and grinned.

We continued with this dynamic as we walked to the game and during the game, completely oblivious to everyone else around us. I felt closer to him with every movie quote, as if this was connecting us—which was totally weird. It *was* as if it was a secret language, just like Sandy had said. I was also enamored because he was making me laugh, and I'd never met anyone who could keep up with me. I thought I was the only freak who did this type of thing for this long a time. I could quote movies all night. Gerry did sometimes, but not for this long of a time. I was trying to keep Gerry far from my mind right then. I distracted myself by thinking about how Sandy had been so cool this morning, but the more annoyed she became with us, the less attractive she appeared to me. She was probably flustered because Marty truly had paid no attention to her at all. This connection was also bizarre, because I knew nothing about him but his name. I was having a blast.

The next few hours were intoxicating from laughter more than from alcohol. Marty and I hung out the entire game; he escorted me to the ladies' room, and I waited for him when he needed to use the facilities. It was odd how deeply engaged and intently focused I was on our conversation. He was like a drug; I was hooked on our conversations.

I had a permanent grin on my face the entire time I spoke with him. Somehow the football game ended, and we all walked to the bar, but I have no recollection of anyone else except him. We laughed and talked without interruption or awareness of the people we'd come to visit.

"So, Mary Kate, how's the Greasy Spoon?" Marty inquired with his smirkish expression.

I was puzzled; how did he know I worked there? "Uh, good. I mean, it's a job. How did you know I worked there?" I asked. He began laughing and shaking his head. It was suddenly irritating me that he wouldn't answer me. I am not sure why this fired me up so much. If he hadn't looked so adorable, I would have punched him.

"You really must not have known that I used to work there, too. Apparently I was invisible there to you." Marty smiled and winked at me.

I suddenly recognized him; I remembered seeing him through the rectangular window of the restaurant, his back to me, consistently cooking the hamburgers as I put the order tickets on the clips. Embarrassment suddenly kicked in when I remembered the first time I'd seen his face. The owner told me that the breaded chicken sandwiches took the longest to cook, so he said to yell those out right away as I was putting up the ticket as a cue to the cooks to drop a chicken right away instead of waiting for the ticket. It was my first chicken order, and I wanted to do a good job. I yelled, "Chicken!" so loud that all the cooks jumped, completely startled. I cringed at the memory of Marty knocking over a couple of pans as a result of the ear-deafening "chicken!" I'd belted out. He looked up at me, and I remember him saying, "Jesus! I think they heard that over at Popeyes." (Popeyes Chicken was located next door.)

"Man, Marty, we should have talked more when we worked together. It would've been much more fun."

"I always meant to talk to you there, especially after you nearly pierced my eardrum and broke all the windows yelling 'chicken!'" He burst out laughing hysterically, as if he'd been meaning to give me shit for this for years. My cheeks burned, but I couldn't help laughing, too, when I saw him silently giggling like a kindergarten boy laughing at someone who'd just farted in church.

"Shut it, Marty. I was nervous, man. Everyone always says I'm a low talker and that they can barely hear me. I obviously didn't mean to yell so loud that they could hear me at Popeyes." I said this with my eyes dancing, knowing I'd just gotten him back, too.

"*Touché*, pussycat!" Marty said sarcastically, eyes looking down and cheeks slightly blushing. "You remember me saying that, huh?" he said with a pang of regret on his face.

I looked sincere and said, "You know I was just joking with you." My mind froze up, not knowing what to say again. Marty didn't say anything for a long time, and I kicked myself on the inside for killing the ease of the good conversation we'd been having. When I looked at him, he was still looking down. "Listen, I don't care. I can laugh at myself, OK? I'm quite aware I'm a jackass." I said this calmly and nudged him. He then looked relieved. I added, "Nice bosses, huh? They don't even really make sure we know everyone we work with. I was so nervous that I barely paid attention to any of the other employees there."

"Yeah, obviously," Marty replied, nudging me back and taking a big swig of his beer. I took out a cigarette, and he immediately lit it for me. He lit one for himself, and we smiled at each other for a long time. I shook my head at him in disbelief that he'd known we'd worked together and that we'd hung out for hours before he'd mentioned it.

"I had to quit because of my swim meets. So how is old Billy, anyway?" Marty asked, referring to the boss at the Greasy Spoon. I filled him in on work gossip—not that there was much.

Marty remained standing next to me, leaning on the corner of the bar. I was sitting on a bar stool with my right leg crossed over my left, my ripped jeans exposing my knee. When I talked, his eyes would travel from my eyes and face to my exposed knee. His eyes seemed fixated on it, even when he responded to me. He was staring so intently at my unclothed knee that I started to feel paranoid and wanted to feel it to make sure I had shaved it. I adjusted my legs and crossed the left over my right, which seemed to shake him out of his trance. He looked up and smiled at me, which caused me to blush and left me tingly and throbbing in my loins. He leaned over to the bar to order us another round. I slyly put my hand on my bare knee to feel for any stubble. Luckily, I'd done a pretty good job of shaving earlier, knowing I'd be donning ripped jeans. My knees and ankles are usually prime areas for missed shaving spots. I often leave patches of bristly stubble, which is quite unattractive on a girl.

This break in the conversation kind of made me aware that I hadn't seen my sister in what seemed to be hours, and I had no idea what time it was. I decided to go to the ladies' room and regroup. I went straight to the mirror, and to my surprise, I looked good: wild and alive. My eyes were bright and shiny, and my makeup was still in place. The bruises were still disguised, and my hair was kind of growing on me. The Demi Moore *Ghost* haircut was kind of sexy on me, I supposed, in a weird way. I styled it a little messier than she did and more on the side. There was a mirror on the back of the bathroom door and one over the sink, so I could see the back of me. I liked having my neck exposed; it made me feel mature and alluring for some reason. My eyes appeared bigger, which gave the illusion that my face and cheeks were smaller than they really are. Or perhaps I was just wasted. This new onset of sex appeal and feeling positive about myself was definitely unfamiliar territory.

I checked my teeth, looked up my nose, reapplied lip gloss, and went back out there to face that sexy motherfucker. I opened the bathroom door and could see Marty surveilling the ladies' room. His eyes traveled up and down my body as I sauntered toward him. His eyes appeared riveted to my body, and he seemed to be drinking me in. The way he was looking at me induced a racy and arousing sensation. I smiled smugly at him as I sat down, and he handed me a beer without breaking eye contact. I thought I could sit there forever allowing him to look at me like that; it was vivacious, in a carnal kind of way. His tranquil periwinkle-blue eyes with flecks of white and yellow under his thick black lashes were captivating me and causing me to feel uneasy in my seat. The *West Side Story* image appeared in my brain, just as it had the night before. I longed for the light, airy, comfortable chemistry we'd had earlier in the day while quoting movies and laughing. This degree of sexual chemistry was consuming me, and without acting on it at this point, I was unsure how to proceed with regular conversation.

The band at the bar began to play, which redirected our attention; I was completely content in his presence without talking. The band was playing the REM tune "Losing My Religion," which you can sing along with, but it's definitely not a dancing tune, slow or fast. I was temporarily engrossed with this band because I'd never seen a band perform this fairly new song, and they were pretty good at covering it. I could sense Marty looking at me, and I fought to not meet his gaze. He'd become so oddly quiet over the last hour since he'd been gaping at my knee. Were knees sexy? I wasn't aware of this. I was successful in not looking at him until the song was over. I turned toward him and smiled, and his crooked smile left me dizzy. It was becoming too much. I either had to attack him or get out of this situation.

The recognizable melody of "Into the Mystic" filled the room, and before I knew it, Marty had grabbed my hand and pulled me out onto the dance floor. I'd only listened to this song a thousand times on a record, with all its crackles and skips; I'd never heard it live, and it was dangerously sensual. We danced effortlessly and, despite my never touching him before, it was serene and easy. His body was strong and fluid against mine, tantalizing and tempting me. The magnetism between us was getting ignited by the enchanting music of Van Morrison. We gazed at each other with upturned lips, and he twirled me outward, only to pull me back closer to him. This guy had lured me in earlier with movie quotes and was now seducing me without saying a word; his eyes said it all. I was completely oblivious to everything around me and was under the spell of his seductive silence. The bewitching song ended with his dipping me and flipping me up to be nose to nose with those amazing eyes and very kissable lips. I gasped at being so close to his face, and the electricity between us was radiating everywhere. Unfortunately, some drunk dude knocked into us, and the moment was lost.

The band then sped things up by playing more danceable tunes, and more familiar faces emerged on the dance floor. Mairead appeared out of nowhere, and we hugged as if one of us had gone missing. Michael, Sandy, and some of Marty's posse also gravitated to the dance floor. We all danced continuously to '80s tunes until closing time.

I hadn't seen Marty again in a long time; I kind of got lost in the songs and moment with Mairead and Michael. I'd had a little too much to drink, and I was starting to feel woozy. I sat down at the bar and asked for water and a Coke. I slammed them in five seconds each. Suddenly, I had a brief moment of clarity in which thoughts of Gerry appeared in my head. The day's events flashed through my mind, and I thought of things from Gerry's perspective. How would I feel if he was talking to another girl for hours? I thought that, quite possibly, my behavior that night may have been the exact reason he hadn't wanted me to come up there that weekend. Shame burned on my cheeks, and I was grateful for the drunk dude bumping into Marty and me. Mairead found me and was all slurring and stumbling, so I ordered her a water and Coke as well.

"Water? Ewww. That's kryptonite right now for my buzz. No thanks," she said, slurring. "So anyway, where did that boy go you've been ditching me all night for?"

My cheeks burned again. "Yeah. I don't know if I should keep talking to him—you know, Gerry and all. I wouldn't like him talking to some girl all night if I wasn't there," I said sheepishly.

"Oh gimme a break. Puh-lease!" she exclaimed. "You're a kid, for fuck's sake. You're supposed to have fun. You're not gonna marry Gerry and be just like Mom, are you?"

*Aw shit. That stung. We're heading into some dangerous territory here.* Before I could even respond to that statement, the horrifying fluorescent lights blared over us just then, and the screaming bar-tenders told us all to get out: "You don't have to go home, but you can't stay here!"

We shuffled out of the bar, and I heard Mairead inquiring about after-parties; she put her arm around me, and I cringed. Truly I just wanted to go home: my real home. The shame and guilt were kicking in. I wanted to feel safe again, with Gerry's arms around me. I was totally done with this college scene.

# 20

The ride home was long and quiet, the air full of the alcohol emanating from all our pores. I sat in the back, quiet as a mouse. Sam sat in the front passenger seat, beaming at TJ, and they were holding hands. Michael was next to me, passed out, probably exhausted from all the booze and sex he'd enjoyed this weekend. My mind traveled to Gerry, and I couldn't wait to see him, although memories of the weekend with Marty continued to emerge in my brain. I caught myself smirking a few times and tried to shake it out so that I could focus on Gerry. He loved me, and maybe he'd been acting so strangely because he was afraid I was going to meet another dude, flirt, and hook up. I had never considered this was a possibility for me. Although Marty and I didn't hook up, the fact that I did want to was what scared me. I imagined Gerry with another girl, and waves of jealousy and rage traveled through my veins. I was also confused because I never could understand cheating before this. I always wondered, if you were in love, then why would you even want to be with someone else? After this incident, I guessed it was part of temptation and having weak moments. Gerry and I had felt disconnected lately, partially because of his odd behavior over the past few weeks. My mind wandered back to Marty again, unwillingly, and I wondered what had happened to Marty the night before. Marty and I had a good conversation and I was attracted to him, but that was it. I tried to sleep so that I could end this inner dialogue with myself and this annoying battle of wits I wasn't going to win anytime soon.

Hallelujah—we finally pulled up to my house, and I felt as if I couldn't get inside the house fast enough to call Gerry. I walked in the door, dropped my bag, and raced up the stairs. I dialed his number quickly. The phone rang and rang until finally his sister picked up.

"Hello?"

"Shelley? Hey, it's Mary Kate. Is Gerry home?" I said this so fast that I could barely understand myself.

"Uh, yeah. Hold on a second, please," Shelley replied, sounding strange—not her usual friendly self. Weird that she didn't say hi to me, I thought, and my heart started pounding fast. I was unsure why. After what seemed like an eternity, I heard his voice.

"Hello?" Gerry said curtly.

"Hey!" I squealed, sounding unbelievably cheesy.

"Hey," he replied flatly.

My heart was racing faster but also sinking. A long, uncomfortable silence lingered until I couldn't take it anymore. "I missed you," I murmured, feeling sheepish. This was exacerbated by a long pause. *Uh oh.* Heart still pounding.

"I missed you, too," Gerry finally replied, sounding emotionless.

My insecurity was on full blast at this point. "You did?" I replied, sounding shocked.

"Yeah...I did. Maybe I'll just come over? Is that OK?" he asked.

My heart jumped now. I was feeling hopeful. "Yes!" I exclaimed, sounding dorky. *Being a teenager in the 1990s is fucking unbearable,* I thought. What the hell did our parents do? This was torture having feelings like this.

I was pacing and restless as I waited for him to arrive. I was short and curt with my mom and Maeve. Alcohol withdrawal and Gerry withdrawal were making me irritable and edgy. My mom was asking a million questions about the weekend and acting slick about my sister, trying to get me to spill something. Maeve was all lovey-dovey and affectionate, but I was in no mood. I tried my best to have patience with her, but I was quickly running out. I needed Gerry here now. It was weird—the mix of emotions I was having. I was excited, scared, horny, and having intermittent periods of cold sweats, probably from the alcohol. Most of all, I felt horrendously guilty. I felt like I'd cheated, even though I'd only thought about it. I even considered telling him for a brief moment but then came to my senses when I quickly realized that doing so would make a big deal out of nothing. It seemed to take forever for him to get there. My mom was grateful for my coming home, she said, because she had to leave for work shortly and had been considering sending Maeve to Gerry's grandparents' place or to her friends' place next door until I'd arrived home.

I finally surrendered to my sister hanging on me and sat on the couch with her and watched *Tom and Jerry*, completely not paying attention and ruminating. I slowly started to realize that perhaps he hadn't missed me as much as I had and that he hadn't seemed excited to see me at all. An hour and twenty minutes went by of this torture, and by that time I was furious and feeling stupid. I went to the bathroom and looked in the mirror. I looked disgusting. I probably smelled disgusting. I decided I should shower. The showers at the college had done the job, but they hadn't been relaxing. Juggling travel bottles of toiletries and continuously dropping them in the shower—and then noticing the disgusting ring around the tub or the thousand-legger that ran by and nearly killed me—was definitely not a tranquil experience. So even though I'd showered over the weekend, I didn't feel clean. The water wasn't the fabulous city of Chicago water I was used to but some peculiar-smelling well water. I shuddered when I thought about the whole experience. I put the water on as hot as I could stand it, and calmness slowly washed over me. I was able to clear my head and compose myself. I made a mental note to remember that a hot shower in your own home does assist tremendously after a drinking binge. This hot shower also helped me lose some of my irrational thinking. I shaved everywhere and exfoliated in an attempt to remove the film that the unusual water had left on me. I stepped out of the shower feeling very clean and somewhat myself again.

I lotioned my body up, and a montage of Marty thoughts exploded in my head. I was wondering what he would think about my body and imagining the way he'd looked at me, as if he'd been devouring me with his eyes. I shook my head and tried to stop those thoughts. Just before the shower, I'd been pacing and agitated as I waited for Gerry. I felt extremely confused. I also embraced this new sexiness I now felt about myself that hadn't been there before; when I put on my bra and panties, I actually checked myself out, instead of doing my usual "throw on my clothes on autopilot" or self-loathing routines. It was nice to feel wanted. I brushed my hair slowly and allowed the lotion to dry on my body.

The sound of the screen door creaking open and slamming shut startled me out of my foreign state of mind. I threw on some maroon mesh shorts that Gerry had bought for me and a white T-shirt and walked down the stairs in my bare feet.

Gerry was sitting on the arm of the couch with his green baseball hat on backward and a gray T-shirt that was one size too small for him. It stretched across his chest and slightly exposed his tight pecs. His arms looked strong and cut. He had on maroon mesh shorts (same as mine) and was twirling his keys in his hands. He slowly turned to look at me, and I smiled at him. An hour ago, I would have dived into his arms and wrapped my legs around his waist. Now I was hesitant and nervous. He smiled at me. I stopped on the bottom step, and he stood up to meet me. Our eyes were even; his eyes flickered into mine, and I sensed a small throb in my groin. He put his arms around my waist slowly and slid his hands on my ass. A deep exhalation escaped his mouth, and I found myself holding my breath. He kissed my lips softly, his sexy eyes met mine, and he kissed me again. His lips were strong against mine, and my body melted. Then he buried his face into my neck. Relief checked in, and I put my arms around his strong shoulders. He was speaking into my neck, but I couldn't understand what he was saying.

"What are you babbling about?" I joked and nudged him.

He took a deep breath. "I was worried," he said with a grimace on his face.

"Worried about what?" I asked, already knowing what he was going to say. Guilt...

"I guess about everything—that I couldn't talk to you, you driving there, you hooking up with some college dude. Some college dude raping you, or some college dude wanting to rape you, and then you being OK with it. I don't know; my mind was racing with all kinds of different scenarios. I couldn't stand it." He sounded sad.

I took a deep breath and chickened out. "I didn't hook up with anyone," I said in a solid tone.

"You get drunk? Do you remember everything?" Gerry asked, sounding angry now.

"No—I went to a college campus, and we talked and watched movies," I replied sarcastically. "Of course I got drunk, silly, that's what you do, isn't it?"

His hands disappeared from my waist, and he stepped back. He was gritting his teeth. "So you were whoring around, all drunk?" he hissed.

Anger erupted in my chest. "Are you calling me a whore?" I asked coolly but feeling completely shocked on the inside. Ambivalent feelings of wanting to punch him in the face or cry were fluctuating inside me. My eyes darted toward Maeve as I realized that I didn't want her to hear this conversation. I sped past him and went out onto the front porch. He followed me outside. He was right on my heels.

"You didn't answer my question. Don't answer a question with a question!" he barked.

*What the fuck?* I thought. I didn't see this coming. "Well, it didn't really sound like a question to me. It sounded more like you were accusing me of something, not asking," I said proudly. The surge of anger inside me made me feel invincible.

"I'm just calling it like I see it," he replied bluntly.

"Oh, really? So if a girl gets drunk, she's automatically a whore. Is that it?" I replied, now seething.

"That's usually the case," he said with a smirk.

Now I really wanted to punch him. "You know what? I'm now completely disgusted with myself. I completely missed you, and I actually was ecstatic to see you. I couldn't wait to get home. And this is what I'm greeted with? Fuck you," I said briskly, and I stormed into the house. I told Maeve to go to outside and play. She obeyed immediately, probably never having seen me this way. I stormed up the stairs into my room and slammed the door, completely baffled about this whole interaction. I started to second-guess myself. Had I whored around? That was definitely not my intention. I was just talking to other men.

The door whipped open, and Gerry squalled in, his face flushed, eyes wild. He grabbed my arm and pulled me toward him. His arms were behind me, and then he pulled my hair down with his other hand and lifted my face toward him. I wanted to spit in his face. He kissed me hard and passionately. I attempted to turn away, and he grabbed the sides of my face. My anger slightly subsided, and my inner thighs throbbed involuntarily, which confused me. His tongue entered my mouth, and my body was trapped within his arms, which were still holding my hair. We made out wildly, unable to stop. His kisses were so concentrated and intense that it felt like he was devouring me. My nipples throbbed and hardened. Between my thighs was swelling and wet. I'd been so angry with him a minute ago, and now my intense desire for him was mysterious and forceful. He picked me up with one arm under my ass without taking his mouth off mine. He threw me onto the bed and was immediately on top of me. Between his legs was hard, throbbing, and pulsing against me. He lifted my top up and began kissing my chest and my nipples. My legs ached, and I was throbbing so powerfully that I couldn't think.

"You're mine, baby. I love you. This body is mine," he said teasingly, while slowly running his hands along my stomach and hips. He slid down my shorts. His mouth was on me, licking greedily, and I was powerless, unable to stop. He slid his finger inside me which intensi-fied everything. He said, "This is my pussy. You got that?" I nodded as "his" pussy tingled and throbbed until waves of pleasure overcame my body and my mind. His tongue was now inside me and on my clit until my orgasm was full-blown and I was coming in his mouth. Then he kissed my stomach roughly and put his mouth on my breasts. I could feel him throbbing between my legs. I was still swollen and wet from the massive orgasm he'd given me with his mouth. He was on top of me, thrusting with his shorts on.

"I fucking love you," he said in my mouth as he groaned and moaned and his body shook. His reactions were turning me on so badly, and I felt my body tingling again. I exploded again when he did. He collapsed on top of me and I could feel the warm wetness from him on my leg. He was panting for breath and I could feel his heart beating rapidly on my chest. My head was spinning, my body tingling and throbbing everywhere.

After a few minutes, he moved his face toward mine and kissed me and moaned at the same time. I kissed him back, feeling euphoric, yet my mind was starting to realize what we'd just done and wonder-ing how it had just happened. I didn't know what I should do. Should I say something? What was with all the possessive "you're mine" crap? How come in that moment I liked it? What was that about? I cannot stand the word "pussy" either, however, that aroused me. What the hell was going on?

"Baby?" he murmured sweetly. "What are you thinking about? Your forehead is all crinkled up." He smiled and kissed my forehead.

I hesitated and realized I should say something, since he did ask. "I guess this whole situation is just confusing me. A few minutes ago, you were implying that I was a whore. The next minute we are ... doing that!. I'm totally mystified. How did I let this happen?" I said, completely bewildered.

"I'm so sorry, baby. I get crazy sometimes, thinking about you with other people, and that's not fair to you. You're my girl. I didn't mean it," he said, sounding sincere.

"Well, if you love me so much, then why would you say or do things that would hurt me?"

"You always hurt the ones you love," he said with a smirk. Wiseass, his referring to the first time I'd said "I love you" accidentally because I was quoting a movie and was unsure of what to say at the time. I smiled back and spanked his ass.

"Ooh, I like that, baby," he said playfully and rolled off me to lie on his back. Then he sat up and retrieved his boxers and shorts from the floor. I watched as the muscles in his back contracted and moved. Then he stood and slid his boxers over his perfect ass. He turned sideways and smirked at me and then lay back on top of me.

"I don't know if I could ever get enough of you," he said with a smile. His blue-green eyes shone unsteadily, and he rested his cheek against mine. My heart was pounding and raging with love in this moment, but in the back of my mind was a little sense of concern that I seemed to have no control over myself or my emotions with him; what just happened was a perfect example. My eyes welled with tears.

He slowly lifted his head and wiped my cheek. "Sweetie? Oh my God! What's wrong?" he asked anxiously.

"I don't know. I'm scared. I was kind of scared of you earlier, and I'm kind of scared of myself," I replied, now sobbing.

"Angel. I love you. I. Am. Really. Sorry. I didn't mean it. I don't know how to handle how I feel about you. I've never felt like this before about anyone. I guess I don't know how to handle how I feel about you. Please forgive me," he said, sounding sincere.

My heart leaped at his charming and engaging way, and his words did comfort me. "Yes, I forgive you," I said sincerely but with a touch of uncertainty. What else could I do? He beamed and kissed me lovingly, which left me breathless.

For the next few weeks, I was madly in love again, and Gerry was on fire with the romance. He sent me flowers at school (which had all the other high school seniors swooning in jealousy). He wrote notes and mailed them to me. I flashed to the movie *Roxanne,* beaming all day from the love letters and attention I was receiving from my amazing boyfriend. I'm sure my friends were gagging with all my Gerry, Gerry, Gerry talk. When we weren't together, we were talking on the phone. I arranged my work schedule to go to all of his games or I worked in the evening instead. His games were so important to him and his family, and I wanted to be there. My mind became completely consumed with Gerry. The feelings of love were so powerful and intense; it was euphoria. I lost myself again, yet I could not stop.

One Friday night, Gerry's parents invited me over for dinner and I graciously accepted. I wore the jeans Gerry bought me with a black long sleeved shirt, my short hair styled a little messy and I wore silver hoop earrings. Gerry came to the door and was smiling playfully. He looked cute in his polo and jeans.

"What?" I smiled back knowing he was up to something.

"Nothing." Gerry smiled. He gave me a kiss on the cheek and we were driving.

Gerry pulled in the cemetery and parked. I looked confused. He got out of the car and opened my door. "I want you to drive." I immediately tensed up. "It's okay baby, no one will be in here. Dinner isn't ready yet anyways." Of course I imagine Say Anything... when Lloyd shows Diane how to drive. I got the chills and smiled at the sweetness of this moment. Gerry was staring at me intently while I was in the driver's seat.

He told me to turn on the lights since it was almost dusk and I ended up popping the hood. Gerry laughed and got out to close the hood, still laughing. Once I figured out how to turn on the lights, driving was fairly easy. Gerry kept staring at me the entire time I was driving.

"What? Aren't you supposed to be supervising how I drive?" I asked playfully.

"I like looking at you. You know what you are doing. It's just like riding a bike."

I sighed and continued to drive with ease around the cemetery 4 times.

"Ok, I want you to drive to my house." Gerry said calmly. I stopped abruptly and clenched my jaw. "You will be fine sweetie." I had sensations in my tummy like going on a roller coaster, nervous and excited at the same time as I pulled out of the cemetery. The first couple lights, I stopped too soon and Gerry laughed. He explained how to slow down before coming to a complete stop and how to allow the steering wheel spin through my hands. Finally we pulled up to his house and I was so relieved but couldn't wait to drive again.

"My Dad and Mom want to take you driving too so you can get your license. It's important" Gerry said. *Driving with his parents?* I made a panic face.

"It will be okay pumpkin, they love you." Gerry said sweetly as he put his arm around me as we walked up his driveway.

"They DO!" I exclaimed!

"Yes, I think they like you more than me sometimes."

"Get outta here silly." I punched him in the stomach.

"I'm Serious. They really love you." He pecked me on the lips before opening the door to his house. As usual, the house smelled wonderful and delicious. Mrs. McGrath smiled at me and gave me a hug. Mr. McGrath got up from the recliner and gave me a hug as well.

"You ready for some steak Mary Kate?" Mr. McGrath bellowed above me as we hugged.

"Hell yes!" I replied licking my lips. Mr. and Mrs. McGrath both laughed. Gerry rolled his eyes and smiled at me. "See?" he whispered in my ear.

Dinner was amazing and I could not stop talking about it. I would've licked the plate if I wouldn't have resembled Oliver Twist or a homeless child.

"Thank you so much for dinner Mr. & Mrs. McGrath! I have never had more delicious food in my life! I appreciate it so much." I said sincerely. Mr. & Mrs. McGrath smiled and looked at each other warmly. Mr. McGrath took a deep breath.

"Mary Kate, we want to help you. We want to help your family." Mr. McGrath said. I felt my forehead crinkle up wondering what he means.

"We are not really sure how yet, but we were thinking the first step is getting you a driver's license and a car." Mrs. McGrath said. I laughed. A car? I would never be able to afford a car.

"Thank you. Gerry told me that you guys want to drive with me to practice and get my license. That will be awesome. But, I have no idea when I would ever be able to afford a car and insurance and all that stuff." I replied with my cheeks burning. They all looked at each other and smiled.

"We know Mary Kate, that is why we want to give you a car. Nothing fancy, it is Shelley's old Chevy Malibu. She will be getting a new car." Mr. McGrath said and smiled. My eyes were wide with surprise. A car? I would be a car owner! I couldn't believe my ears. My eyes welled up with tears and I jumped to give his Mom a hug, then his Dad.

"Mary Kate, it's the least we could do for you and your family." Mrs. McGrath said and smiled warmly. I was so touched. I could take my mom grocery shopping, drive her to work, take her to pick up a Little Caesar's deal. My head was spinning at all the possibilities. I attempted to sit back down in my chair, but Gerry pulled me onto his lap and I hugged him. I was trembling. I was completely in shock at their kindness and now tears were streaming down my cheeks. Gerry smiled at me and wiped the tears away with his thumbs.

"So let's pass that driving test so you can take the car out of the garage. I got plans for this garage." Mr. McGrath said playfully as if I am doing him a favor by taking the car. I laughed through the tears. I got up and hugged them both again with true gratefulness.

We walked out to garage together to check out my new wheels.

I went out driving with Mr. McGrath after Gerry's game Sunday. I thought he was going to fail me, but he said I was "very cautious and that's good." Mrs. McGrath took me to take the driver's test Tuesday. She brought a rosary and said she will be praying the whole time I was taking the test. The stern male I drove with said "You are very cautious, that is good. Most kids do not drive like you." I was very glad I practiced with Mr. McGrath because I was a lot less nervous. I beamed in my driver's license picture! Mrs. McGrath and I drove back to her home with big grins plastered on our faces. I stared at my driver's license in disbelief the enter way back.

Mr. McGrath was sitting at the kitchen table reading the paper when we arrived. He was wearing black reading glasses on the tip of his nose and glared at me when I walked in. I was thanking God in my head that I did not fail this test because just his look made me not want to every disappoint this man.

"Well?" Mr. McGrath asked as he folded his newspaper. I contemplated playing a trick and telling him I failed, but I am the worst at lying and so I just shoved the license in his face. He jumped up and yelped and pulled me to him. He was gave me a big bear hug and lifted my feet from the floor. "I am so proud of you!" He said into my ear. My cheeks blushed and a weird sensation arose in my chest. I could not remember the last time my parents said that to me, or if they ever did but it felt wonderful.

Mr. McGrath placed me back on the floor and brought me to the table. He pointed to a sentence written on notebook paper. It stated "I, Mary Kate O'Brien is purchasing this 1976 Chevrolet Malibu from Mr. Gerald McGrath Sr. for $60 as is." I looked at Mr. McGrath and laughed, it seemed so formal. His handwriting was bold and slanted. Mine was small and curvy. He shook my hand and we both laughed. Gerry was still at football practice and I contemplated waiting for him, but I also was so excited to drive this car home and show it to my Mom and Maeve!

"It's all yours Mary Kate!" Now go on home and show your mother. You guys deserve it." Mrs. McGrath smiled and patted me on the back. I couldn't believe I was now a car owner! My hands were shaking as I backed out of their garage down their driveway. I was shitting in my pants, terrified that I was going to hit something or run on their lawn. I am sure I was driving with a petrified grimace on my face. I stopped at the end of the driveway and looked back toward the driveway. Mr. & Mrs. McGrath had their arms around each other waving at me. I beamed and waved to them and headed home feeling like a new woman.

$$\mathcal{Q}$$

I think my Mom thought I was kidding or going to fail because when I arrived home with my driver's license and the car, she looked somewhat irritated and stressed.

"What's wrong?" I asked my mom.

"Nothing's wrong. I guess I didn't expect this to happen so fast. I can't really afford to help you with this. I hope they don't expect you to owe them anything." My mother's face now crinkled up with worry.

"I know Mom. His parents gave this car to me so I can help you. They think it is terrible that you have to ride your bike to the store or to work." I said, hoping to reassure her. She looked anxious and stressed when I thought she would be happy and relieved. My mom then turned and went into the basement. I was disappointed in her reaction and felt so bewildered. My heart sank.

Thankfully, the streetlights came on and Maeve arrived home promptly five minutes later. Maeve jumped into my arms and fed my broken soul for a minute.

"Want to go for a ride in my car?"

"What!?" Maeve's head thrusted back in surprise, her eyes wide and she squeezed my cheeks. I put her down and she ran to the car and got into the driver's seat and began to turn the steering wheel.

"WOW!" Mary Kate whispered loudly. I beamed at her reaction feeling and was feeling very grateful in this moment. "What's this number in here Mary Kate?"

"That is the amount of miles on this car, so this car has driven 106,054 miles so far." I told her laughing to myself because I had asked Mr. McGrath the same question.

I decided to drive to an ice cream place about 6 miles away, Rainbow Cone. I have never had one but it always seemed silly to me to take the bus there. I was blown away at how easy things seemed now with a car. Maeve buckled in the passenger seat and was staring at me most of the time, watching me drive. At a stoplight, I looked in the rear view mirror and saw that there was a police car behind me and I immediately tensed up; my mind racing at what I could have possibly done wrong already.

"What's wrong Mary Kate?" Maeve exclaimed.

"I see there is a cop car behind me." I said softly and grimaced.

"I knew I smelled bacon." Maeve replied without skipping a beat and smirked. I sat there in silence for a couple seconds, not under-standing her reply. Then I got it and began laughing hysterically. Maeve grinned and appeared proud of herself for making me laugh so hard. Tears were now coming out of my eyes. I was scared to drive when the light turned green; I had never drove laughing yet! I drove through the intersection, still laughing, looked behind me and put on my signal to change lanes to the right side of the road. I changed lanes and the cop car passed me by. I put my hazards on and pulled over to the side of the road to gain composure. I finally stopped laughing and stopped replaying her statement in my mind; amazed at her wit.

"Where do you come up with this stuff Maeve?" I inquired wiping the tears from the sides of my eyes.

"The show Cops." Maeve said with a grin. "The bad guys are al-ways calling the cops pigs and stuff like that." Maeve giggled.

"Oh my God." I said under my breath, placing my hands over eyes. I laughed again. "I need to start spending more time with you and get back to watching Different Strokes and Family Ties re-runs."

I began driving again surprised at myself that I knew how to get to this ice cream place by following the street signs. I realized tak-ing the bus the last four years did pay off in learning the City of Chicago street system. It was now dark outside and the lights from Rainbow Cone were gleaming. Maeve was clapping when we arrived.

I felt like a little kid myself, mixed with feeling quite grown up and independent. Both of our eyes bulged and mouths dropped open as we received our HUGE original rainbow cones. I do not think either of us had ever had that much ice cream at one time. If we ever had ice cream or pop, my mom would hide it and give us a tiny, round scoop in a bowl and we felt like kings. We all wanted to eat slowly and savor every bite but then we would all devour it and lick the bowls as kids. I remembered Michael would be licking all around his mouth when done and would sit on the couch with chocolate ice cream on his nose for hours because Mairead and I would not tell him. I laughed at this memory as I haven't thought of this in years. I wanted to tell Maeve this story because this was before she was born; but I had a scrumptious ice cream meal to devour.

Maeve and I licked around the circumference of the top of the cone where the ice cream began to melt. Our eyes widened as we shared a look of "Holy shit, this is delicious!" Then we proceed to consume them like feral animals, occasionally locking eyes and smiling at each other. When we both finished the last bite of the cones, we sat back and sighed, patting our bellies completely satisfied.

"That was so good!" Maeve exclaimed. "Can we get another one?"

"Maeve!" I retorted then laughing because I was kind of thinking the same thing. Maeve giggled. "No! We will be so sick if we eat another one!" I contemplated bringing Michael and my Mom home one, but I decided against it because Maeve would end up eating them. Maeve and I walked out holding hands and when we reached the car, Maeve put her arms around my waist.

"When I grow up, I want to be just like you Mary Kate." Maeve said looking up at me. I stopped and gasped at the thought of her growing up anymore. My chin quivered and I smiled, breathing through my nose in fear if I opened my mouth to speak, I would cry. I hugged Maeve tightly and we got into the car. I turned over the engine and turned on the radio thinking of how to respond to my baby sister.

"Thank you Maeve." My voice cracked a little. "I don't want you to grow up, but when you do, I want you to be you. Because YOU are amazing." Maeve's shoulders shrugged up her ears as she smiled, appearing uncomfortable or shy. It was adorable. We drove home together in a content silence. Maeve looking around at everything as I drove. I kept looking at her and smiling to myself. I wanted the best for her and her future and I will do everything I can now to make that happen.

I was exhausted when we arrived home and I assumed Maeve was as well because she was so quiet. My Mom was sleeping on the couch with the TV on as usual. I set my alarm for school and decided I still would take the bus despite having a car because I enjoyed hanging out with my bus posse. Secondly, I was not exactly sure on how to drive to school and thought of it made me anxious. The bus was familiar to me and easy.

Maeve and I both brushed our teeth and climbed into my bed together. Maeve was asleep in seconds. I wanted to sleep immediately, but my mind began running about everything I had to do this week so I could attend Gerry's game. I had to go to school and then go straight to work the next three days. I took some deep breaths and reminded myself to take things day by day. Listening to Maeve's deep breathing, I was fast asleep in a few minutes with a smile of gratitude on my face.

School dragged the next day but I attempted to pass the time by composing a letter to Gerry's parents for the car. I cannot explain how different I felt knowing that I had options and I did not feel so trapped. I felt like I had the power to help my mom and myself. Everything did not seem so overwhelming. My future looked bright for the first time. They gave me the gift of hope and opportunity. They gave me the gift of independence. I wrote all this in the letter and mailed it right after school on the way to work. Luckily work was busy and it went by fast. I did not have time to think. Ruth drove me home from work and I felt silly because now I had a car, but I did not have time to go home after school before work. I called Gerry when I arrived home, but it was busy and I was so exhausted, I laid down and was asleep before I hit the pillow.

The next day was the same and when I arrived home from work Thursday night, my phone was ringing as I walked in the door."Hello!" I answered hoping it was Gerry. Nobody replied. "Hello?" I repeated. I heard him sigh.

"Hey." He said softly.

"Hi!" I exclaimed excited to hear his voice.

"So now you have a car so you don't need me anymore?" Gerry said softly, kind of an eerie tone in his voice.

"HA! Get outta here! You're silly." I laughed.

"This isn't a laughing matter." He replied.

"Oh jeez, c'mon don't be silly. I have school and then work. I called you last night when I got but it was busy."

"Yea, that's convenient." He replied sounding sarcastic. I sighed.

"What's the matter?" I inquired puzzled.

"(Tsk) I just told you. My parents give you a car and then I don't hear from you for days. Kinda convenient isn't it." Gerry retorted.

"Yea that was my evil plan all along. I was only dating you for a car. C'mon don't be ridiculous. You know I have to work more during the week so I can come to your game on the weekends." I replied.

"Okay, whatever. Subject change. There is party tomorrow night at Eddie's, do you want to go?" I sighed again.

"I would love to. But I have to work." I replied sadly. Now he sighed.

"This is bullshit. I am so sick of this." I shook my head, now getting annoyed.

"What are you sick of?" I replied.

"Just...this. I never get to see you. You are always working. Now you have a car so you pay me no mind. I see where I stand."

"That is not true! C'mon! I have to work, I don't have a choice. Now that I have a car, I will need to work more actually because I need to afford gas and insurance."

"Oh! Sorry that the car is such a burden now too. You are unbelievable!" He replied, sounding as if he was laughing. My cheeks burned with shame and frustration. I was too tired to think anymore or argue with him. Nothing he said made sense or had any truth to it. He sounded…paranoid.

"Listen, I don't know what to say. Nothing you are saying is true at all and it is not my fault I have to work. Thank you for making me feeling guilty." I replied exhausted.

"I just call it the way I see it." He replied and I was ready to hang up on him.

"It's been a long day, I will talk to you later. Have fun at the party tomorrow." I replied.

"Don't worry I will." He replied with a laugh and hung up. I slammed the phone down.

*EW. What the fuck?* I laid in my bed so frustrated that I began to cry. I was so confused.

Next thing I knew the alarm was going off for me to do it all over again.

# 22

His parents picked me up because it was an away game. They would drop me off at the school afterwards to meet up with Gerry because they had to attend a benefit. The Game was pretty disheartening, they lost pretty bad and everyone seemed down in the dumps post game. His parents did not say much on the car ride to the school. They dropped me off and I waited for him —out in front. I wore his jersey and coat in hopes that he would come to his senses about all of his silly accusations and realize I do care about him and he is extremely important to me.. I watched most of the players exiting the building, some patting me on the shoulder, some saying, "Hey, McGrath's girl." Part of me liked this, but part of me was like, "I do have a name." I was growing impatient and wondering what was taking him so long. Then I saw him, walking slowly with his head down out of the door. Concern washed over me; he appeared either really down that they had lost or like he was injured.. He looked up and he froze when he saw me, and I ran to him and embraced him around the shoulders. A muffled moan came out of him, and I pulled away with apprehension that I'd hurt him further. His face was ashen and pallid, the blood drained from his cheeks. His expression was of anguish and fear. My eyes widened and my brow furrowed in reaction to whatever his emergency was.

"Oh my God! What's wrong?" I inquired fearfully. Tears welled in his eyes, and his mouth opened but no sound came out. "What is it, baby?" I asked again. I went to hug him, but he held his hands up to block me and stepped back. This frightened me, and I felt a lump in my throat at his sudden change of demeanor. The suspense was killing me, and the silence was torture. I had this urge to shake him. He looked down and began to speak in a soft tone.

"I can't look at you and say this. Please don't make me look at you," he said sheepishly. Alarm kicked in all over my body, and I tensed up—as if this would protect me from what he was about to say.

"OK," I replied hesitantly.

"At the party last night, I, uh...ended up hooking up with Michelle...and I spent the night at her place. We didn't have sex but..." He confessed this and then looked up; tears were in his bottom eyelashes. He stuck his thumb and forefinger in his eyes and rubbed them. When he removed his hands and I looked at his face, my fight-or-flight response kicked in, and I found myself involuntarily cocking my arm back and decking him with all my might. I blacked out for a second from the magnitude of my fury.

When I came back to consciousness, I was walking out of the school parking lot. I do not remember walking there. It was bizarre that I blacked out like that. Mixtures of emotions were flaming inside me and creating a monstrous stabbing pain all over my body, but mostly my chest. I was heartbroken, I was devastated, I was furious, I was hurt, I was humiliated, I was sad, but most of all I was...relieved. Oddly, I was relieved he'd told the truth and that he'd confessed that to me. I was so alert and hypervigilant that I could focus now. This is what came to my mind with clarity and briefly soothed me: I found relief in his visible dishonor and abomination with himself.

In my pain, I imagined *Some Kind of Wonderful*, when Hardy Jenns is secretly cheating with a girl at school after he's basically just had sex with Amanda Jones. He then goes on to bullshit her, and she looks stupid and humiliated. I was grateful in my state of fury that he hadn't done that to me. I was thankful that he was noble and honest and allowed me to have some dignity. Rage rose up in me again when I remembered what I was wearing. I ripped off his jacket and jersey and screamed, thinking that I'd worn *his* clothes the whole game, and half the people in the stands had probably been at that party the night before. It was cold out, but I couldn't wear those clothes. My first instinct was to throw them in the garbage, but there wasn't one around because I was cutting down side streets so that I could sob furiously without as many cars witnessing me.

I heard a car idling next to me, and I saw that it was Gerry looking humble and sad. I had my arms crossed over me and was kicking myself in the ass for just wearing a lacy camisole under his jersey. His jacket and jersey were under my arms. He got out of the car, and I seethed with rage. In a storm of frenzy, I whipped his coat and jersey at his face and took off running. The ice-cold air made my nipples hard, and it was painful to run with them rubbing against my top. Sadness was now kicking in, and the hurt and pain were unbearable. Exhaustion consumed me, and I just wanted to collapse. I wanted to crawl into a ball and disappear. That wall that had protected me all those years was gone because I'd trusted him; I'd let him in. Despite all my doubts and fears, I'd let him know me—the true me. I'd allowed him to love me, and I'd allowed myself to love him. I cringed with regret and shame at my stupidity for believing that all men weren't bad and for permitting myself to fall in love with someone who would inevitably hurt me.

I finally arrived at my house and dragged myself to my room. My body felt like a fifty-pound weight was sitting on my chest, and I was struggling to breathe. My skin was solid and stiff from being exposed to the cold. The sudden change in atmosphere stung my body, but I welcomed the warmth. I put my men's flannel pajamas on over my clothes and crawled into my bed. My face was full of anguish and longing for tears, but they wouldn't come. Deep down, I was aware that the relief I so desperately craved wouldn't come from tears but from time. I collapsed inside as I tried to fathom how I'd get through that time. This pain was intolerable and was leaving me despondent. I frantically searched for something to bring me some clarity in this moment of hopelessness. Instead, a fatigue overpowered me, and I passed out cold within seconds.

I awoke to the sun coming into my room. I took a deep, cleansing breath and felt revived; I stretched with my hands above my head, and then it hit me. The memories of the night before came crashing down on me like a wave in a storm. The hollow pain inside me returned, and I was under the pressure of that rock again. I imagined a gray and black sky with thunder and lightning above me as I was in the middle of the ocean, alone. My wall had crumbled, and what had made it crumble, in a good way, was gone, and I was alone, naked with my vulnerability. An exposed sensation shuddered through me as I realized I was alone with no protection and no coverage—just bare. The pain was deeper than Gerry and Michelle and the high school drama; all the hurt and humiliation from my past years came full-throttle charging at me. I'd hidden behind that wall for years, and finally I had to face it; I had to *feel* it. I shook my head to myself, petrified: I can't do it. I just cannot do it alone. *Yes you can*, a small voice whispered inside me. I clenched my eyes shut and tried to make it go away. I was incurably a fighter, and I despised myself for it. Just give up, for fuck's sake, my brain would say to myself, but my heart wouldn't stop.

I was defeated, alone, abandoned, and beaten down, just as I had been all my life. Despite the pain, it was familiar to feel this way, and I welcomed it. I was more uncomfortable being happy, in love, vulnerable…the unknown. It was easy to gravitate toward the known. I was always the one who never gave up. My mother submitted, then my brother submitted, and then my sister. I stood by and watched them all fall, one by one, to the dictatorship and control. When I saw the most courageous people I knew collapse in defeat, I became stronger. I became angrier. My divergence was relentless, my will was infinite. I could see everything clearly, despite knowing no other way. Somehow in my soul I'd known that what was happening in my house growing up was wrong. I'd had this innate knowledge that what was occurring on a daily basis was a fucked-up level of dysfunction. Somehow I knew without being told. I was exhausted and beaten down in every aspect of my being. My body was lifeless and lethargic. But my fucking heart persevered, again. Dammit!

No one believed me in my family: *no one*. Not my father's siblings, not his parents, when I told them. Well, I guess they did believe me, but they did *nothing*. They confronted him but with caution, because they knew what would happen and who would end up paying for it. I eventually realized their hesitation was to protect me, not because they didn't care. I didn't realize it at the time that every time I fought, every time I did what was right, someone else suffered. My mom paid dearly, then my sister, then my brother. When he couldn't break me and he went after Maeve, I finally caved and surrendered then. He won. I submitted myself because I couldn't have him hurt Maeve. She was my weakness and he knew it. To my own disgust, I gave in for the survival of my family. I realized there was a limit to what people could do when dealing with a ticking time bomb, a psychopath. It was at that moment when I realized that sometimes being right doesn't matter. I tried to comfort myself in the thought that "what goes around comes around."

Eventually I was right, and he did get what was coming to him. He was revealed for what he truly was: a coward. He gave up. His leaving his family was him giving up and *me winning*. I'm sure the shame and guilt overpowered him, and luckily he had enough sense to leave. What was killing me right now was that, despite winning, we were still suffering. Every time we allowed this suffering to consume us, my dad won again. I wouldn't let him win. I would survive. My mother's favorite song began playing in my head, and I admired her for it. I inherited that will from her, and my dad probably felt inadequate because of it. She never gave up, she dealt with the cards God gave her and overcame those obstacles with flying colors. Although at times like this, I saw no flying colors and wondered why life had to be so fucking hard.

A lonely image of Duckie flashed in my mind of him sitting on the pavement, leaning against the wall of the record shop, rain pouring down on him, and him feeling crushed. Crushed that the girl he loved (and his best friend) went on a date with someone else. Soon after this memory of Duckie came a glimmer of hope. *Yes, you can.* Then I remembered the happy ending: Duckie is there for his friend and accepts that they are friends, nothing more, and he supports her. Duckie ends up finding someone for himself in the end. A small smile emerged on my face—a smile? How could I smile at a time like this? I decided I needed to cry and I needed to smile, so I decided to watch *Pretty in Pink* for the ninety-ninth time. Watching this movie now in my wounded and vulnerable state was a different scenario. It was as if my innocence was lost, and suddenly I saw a lot more of the sad parts to the movie that had always gone over my head before: how depressed her father was and how his wife had left him. His wife deserted him with a child, a girl, to care for on his own, and then she had to make her own clothes. What the fuck? Steff, the evil (as always) James Spader, was so good at being bad, and he really liked her? He was incredibly rude to her. Life is confusing. I sobbed, I laughed, and I smiled. It was cinematherapy.

Suddenly I realized that no one was home. What the...I'd been so self-absorbed that I hadn't noticed that Maeve and my mom weren't home. Aching for them, I looked around the house for clues about where they could be. Hugging my sister always consoled me, but facing my mom would not. I was always the one comforting her, not vice versa. I didn't feel like I could tell my mom what had happened. I couldn't turn to her for support; it just felt *wrong.* I was her rock, so if I fell apart, what would happen to her? Remnants of my conversation with Gerry the day before continued to penetrate my consciousness, and the pain crept slowly back into my chest. I became fatigued again and no longer cared where my family was. This exhaustion was over-powering, and I was defenseless against it. I heaved myself back up the stairs into my bed and passed out.

It was dark outside when I woke again, and I was dying of thirst. My eyes were heavy, as if I'd been drugged. I felt disoriented and won-dered what day it was. It was surreal to be sleeping this way—as if I had the flu and didn't know what day it was. I was sick with a broken heart. I was weak from the pain. I hunched over in a fetal position in my bed and found comfort temporarily. My mom appeared with a tray with hot black tea and toast. The hollow pain of hunger reacted, and despite my head saying no, my body was craving some kind of liq-uid. It was suddenly just what I needed (but didn't know I'd wanted). I was grateful for her presence.

"Hi, honey. You've been really sick," my mom said with a face full of worry. "You were dead to the world, sweating but cold, incoherent. I was worried. How are you feeling?"

Tears began to well in my eyes, and I buried my face in my pillow. "I'm OK, just weak and lethargic," I replied, muffled in the pillow.

"OK, you need to rest. I'll report an absence with school now so you can stay home tomorrow. I unplugged your phone when I real-ized how sick you were. It was ringing a lot, but you seemed like you needed to rest. It was weird, too, that you didn't stir at all when it rang. I was scared." My mom looked at me sadly.

I drank the tea quickly. I wanted so badly to hug my mom and sob into her shoulder and tell her what had happened. I wanted her to tell me that everything was going to be all right. This sensation of wanting my mom's support was new and strange. I'd always been her rock; now I felt like I couldn't fall apart. My mom smiled at me while I was drinking the tea. She appeared proud of herself that she'd done something right by taking care of me and bringing me tea and toast. I lay back down on my pillow and fell asleep again.

I dreamed that Gerry was there next to me, stroking my cheek and telling me that everything was going to be all right and that he loved me. His touch was so calming that I couldn't stop him. I let him tell me he was sorry, he loved me, and that it was a mistake. Then Michelle appeared behind him and put her arm around his neck to pull him away from me, and suddenly he was out of my reach. I jerked awake to the sight of Maeve next to me with her hand on my cheek. Her eyes were pools of fear, her face full of concern.

"You were having a bad dream, Mary Kate," Maeve whispered. "You seem so sad, Mary Kate." Tears welled in her eyes.

"I'm OK, sister. I'm tough. Don't you worry about me—everyone is sad sometimes." I tried to sound as convincing as possible. Maeve got up and pushed play on the cassette player, and "True Colors" played. I beamed at her in awe, and her face softened, mirroring mine. We both gazed at each other and listened to the song. She hugged me, and I hugged her back. In that moment, no one needed to tell me that everything was going to be all right, because I knew it would be.

# 23

*School? Ugh,* I thought. How was I going to get through that? The anguish must have been evident on my face, because my mom's expression quickly changed to a frightened look. Poor thing probably thought I was dying of botulism, when really I'd just fallen in love with a total asshole, just like she had. I was annoyed with that relentless glimmer of hope that was still shining inside of me—that he wasn't a total asshole. Annoying voice: He told you the truth, after all, and that took courage. He wasn't a coward. *Aw, shut up,* I told that part of myself.

I suppressed that tenacious hope and optimism that struggled to come out. I imagined I snuffed it out like a candle flame. It needed to be stopped, because I wanted to be angry, resentful, and hateful—because it felt fucking good. It was exhilarating. It was motivating. The anger was tolerable; the hurt and pain weren't. Every time that hope escaped, I ended up hurting. I didn't deserve to hurt any longer. I wanted to resurrect that wall and be numb again. I decided to start taking the birth control pill and carried the condoms with me in case I had an opportunity for a revenge fuck. I thought of *Say Anything...* Find a babe that looks just like her, bang her and dump her. Except it would be a guy in my case. Mission: Find a dude that looks like him, bang him and dump him.

Unfortunately I attended an all-girls school and took the bus home with girls so the chances of me meeting any dude were slim. I walked into school feeling different now, and for the first time I realized what a shithole it was. It was plain and dreary and filled with false promises and imaginary hope. All that was real now was misery. I looked at my classmates with pity. I saw how pathetic they all really were. We were all a bunch of suckers led to believe there was happiness beyond these walls, but really, it was just a holding area until we were released into the dark trenches of life. Anger seethed through me now. I was angry that I had to be here like this. I was fired up, and I wanted to hurt someone. I was hurt, so why not hurt someone else? Then I spotted my target, and my lips curled as I found my prey. Stand by Me's "Lard Ass" popped in my head as I saw her. The overweight girl in our class was innocently standing next in line for the water fountain. My pain was erased temporarily and replaced with an evil sense of joy. A scathingly brilliant idea sprouted, and I went to the ladies' room. I whipped out a dime and purchased one of those ginormous maxi pads from the dispenser. I walked to the art room and got a red marker, and I giggled to myself as I wrote "Kick me" on the diaper-size pad.

"Move it, fat ass," I said to her, and a twinge of guilt pinched me, but I shook it away. I tapped her back with the graffiti maxi pad, wings and all. She walked down the hall, and everyone laughed at her. I laughed as well accompanied with a hollow, empty feeling inside. It actually made me feel worse to hurt someone else. I thought it would make me feel better. The rest of the day, I remained in this dark, irritable state of mind with evil surging through me. I hated myself, yet I couldn't stop.

I walked out to the bus after school head down and wearing headphones. I didn't want to make eye contact with anyone. I didn't want to speak to anyone. I hated everyone. Most of all, I despised myself. I felt someone tap me on the shoulder and retracted my shoulder in disgust and kept walking. Then someone pulled my headphones off. Led Zeppelin's "Babe I'm Gonna Leave You" blared from my Walkman.

"Hey, what the—" I hissed. When I turned around to shove the person, I was shocked to find it was Gerry. I froze. *Son of a bitch.*

I turned to storm toward the bus as fast as I could, but he was too big and stood in front of me. I continually tried to get around him, but he was too quick. After all, the prick played football.

"Please, Mary Kate, please. I just want to talk to you for a minute," Gerry said, pleading. He looked just as shitty as I did: dark circles under his eyes, pale lips chapped and cracking.

I was filled with fury, yet my mind was blank. I was speechless and frozen but ignited with intense anger. It was the most bizarre sensation. Immobilized, I stopped this ridiculous dance in the school yard and glanced at my bus. It was still there. "I'm going to miss my bus. Please let me go," I said, trying not to sound like a baby.

"I'll drive you home. Please, just let me talk," Gerry said, begging. "Please."

My will was softening, but the thought of being in the car with him made me really fucking angry—and therefore feeble. "Fine, whatever," I said. I stared at him, coldly and vacantly.

"Let's go to my car. *Please!* You can even sit in the back seat," Gerry said with a hint of a flicker on his face that I was just about ready to slap off. I marched to his car, climbed in the back seat, and lit a cigarette. I didn't give a fuck what his parents' rules were about the car; *fuck* them, and *fuck* him. He jogged to the driver's side and got in. I heard the locks go on all the doors. I shot daggers at him in the rearview mirror and took a huge drag of my cigarette. It was actually making me nauseated, but I kept smoking because it occupied my mind.

"I'm sorry; I just don't want you jumping out of my car again. I promise I'm just taking you home. Please hear me out." His eyes looked full of hope at me in the back seat, and I rolled my eyes back at him.

"Listen, Mary Kate, I've been in agony the past few days. I'm lost without you. It was a stupid fucking mistake. It was a mistake. The worst mistake I've ever made in my life. When I think about it, I feel sick to my stomach. When I think of what I did to you, I feel like I want to kill myself. It's the worst feeling in the world, guilt," he said, sounding sincere.

Something about his words calmed me so that my seething anger subsided briefly and my brain could engage again. I smiled when a flicker of rationalization became clear to me. "Oh, I see. So the guilt of what you did is unbearable, so you're here to beg me for forgiveness to make this easier on yourself. I get it. You're such a selfish prick," I said sharply, and I took a long drag as I regained my fake composure.

"No, no, *no!* Mary Kate, that's not it at all. I assume you'll never forgive me. I just believe I owe you the satisfaction of knowing where I'm at—that I'm a fucking puddle. I'm a wreck. I'm not saying this so you'll take me back. I'm saying this because I want you to know this. I don't deserve any of your tears. I don't deserve any of your pain. I'm a piece of shit." He said this all with some convincing self-loathing. This sparked my interest, and the giver in me was already on alert, ready to start fixing. I took another long drag and thought, *Stop that nonsense.* His words did something for me, possibly made the gaping wound in my heart a little smaller. Now I wanted to make him feel better. *I'm such a fool,* I thought.

"Well, after all, you are a guy," I muttered stupidly and without thinking. He didn't deserve a shred of my compassion or comfort; it was just my innate need kicking in. His eyes glimmered at me in the mirror. Then my resentment returned, and *Say Anything...*appeared in my head.

"However, I don't want a guy. The world is full of guys. I want a man," I recited proudly. His eyes lowered, and he looked wounded. This ride home was turning out to be slightly empowering. We rode the rest of the ride home in silence until we turned down my street. We both stared hard at the flashing ambulance lights ahead in the distance, dreading what it might be. We both gasped when it was evident the ambulance was in front of Buzz and Ava's house.

We slowly pulled up to their home and prayed it wasn't true. It was dark and dreary out now, which added to the gloom of the situation. Their cute little Cape Cod appeared lifeless and cold instead of its usual warm and inviting appearance. Buzz stood on the porch with his white tank top and suspenders, brown pants, and brown dress shoes, with a plaid shirt pressed and buttons open as if he'd just thrown it on loosely in haste. The EMTs were wheeling Ava out of their home with care; she looked tiny and frail under the tight, stiff sheets. Her hair loosely in a bun, she still looked beautiful with the oxygen mask over her mouth and her eyes closed angelically. Buzz looked like a wreck behind her, his fists clenching, eyes welling with tears, and eyebrows furrowing in uneasiness. I glimpsed Gerry in the driver's seat—since I was in the back, I couldn't get a full view of his face, but his shoulders tensed in the back toward his ears, and I could see his jaw clench. He pulled to the curb and glanced back at me. I could see the anguish in his face.

Although we probably looked ridiculous with me in the back seat and Gerry in the front, I doubt anyone noticed because of the melancholy situation. Gerry and I got out of the car at the same time, and Gerry walked briskly to his grandfather. They embraced each other with intensity and fear. Buzz began to talk softly to Gerry in his ear, his face becoming increasingly terrified. My heart broke for Buzz; his vulnerability was evident and was exploding all over the front yard. Buzz walked to me and hugged me quickly, and, looking down, he walked to the back of the ambulance and climbed in. The doors shut, and they were off. Gerry appeared lost for a second as the ambulance pulled away. He walked slowly toward me, looking forlorn and solemn.

"Mary Kate. I know we aren't together anymore and that you don't owe me anything, but I ask you as my friend, would you come with me to the hospital? I really need you right now." I could see the pain in his eyes. It didn't even occur to me to not go with him to the hospital. I cared deeply about his grandparents, and whatever was going on with our stupid teenage drama was nothing compared to Buzz and Ava's petrifying state of affairs.

"Of course I will. Can I stop home or call my mom from their house?" I asked, concerned. Of course my sick brain had to go somewhere for comic relief; the last time I'd called my mom from Buzz and Ava's house had been about a month ago. I'd gone to church with Buzz, Ava, Gerry, and his parents; we'd all piled into their huge Suburban. Immediately following Mass, his parents said they were going to stop at "Colonel Sanders's place" and asked if I'd like to come. I replied, "Sure, can I just call my mom from his house?" Everyone laughed hysterically, even Buzz and Ava. Gerry had looked at me with an endearing expression and slid my hair behind my ear and responded, "Sweetie, 'Colonel Sanders' is Kentucky Fried Chicken. You know, the guy with the white beard and mustache? That's Colonel Sanders." My cheeks burned with humiliation.

A smirk emerged on my face as the familiar sweet scent of Buzz and Ava's home filled my nose. "I know this isn't appropriate, and I apologize," I said with a cautious smile, "but I just remembered the last time I called my mom from your grandparents' place."

Gerry smirked back. "You know, I thought of the same thing. That's why I need you here, baby." He looked at me lovingly, his eyes warm with endearment. Relief washed over me, along with slight anger at the term "baby" that had escaped his mouth, but I let it slide because of the circumstances. I didn't get the impression that Gerry was going to take advantage of the situation and use this as a ploy for us getting back together, although I was still guarded and deeply wounded. I did feel empathy for him, though, and I knew how much he cared for his grandparents. He'd spent the summer we first met living with Ava while his grandfather was in "subacute rehabilitation," as they called it. That was an immense sacrifice for a guy his age to do, which was partially why I'd fallen for him so hard and fast.

I called my mom, who was luckily off that day and didn't need me to watch Maeve. I was glad I hadn't stopped home, because Maeve would have wanted to come with. Since my mom didn't drive, Maeve was always desperate for any kind of ride in a car, even if it was just to a hospital.

Gerry slowly locked his grandparents' home with a key on his key ring, still with the worry written all over his face. I swallowed my pride and resentment and sat in the front seat. He slid in the driver's seat and grabbed my hand immediately. My first reaction was to wince, but I knew inside that he needed me in a friend kind of way, not necessarily in a romantic kind of way—which wouldn't be happening between us again.

We arrived at the hospital and found his parents already there. His father had the same worrisome, vulnerable, and pained look in his eyes and in his posture as Gerry did. His mom appeared strong and emotionless, as usual, which was her understandable nursing demeanor. She saw this every day, so I knew it wasn't as traumatizing for her as it was for the rest of us. Buzz was fighting back the tears as he began to tell us the series of events that had transpired; we found out that Ava had had a stroke and that the doctor wasn't yet sure of the prognosis. Buzz had been helping Ava on the toilet when she suddenly went limp, the side of her face drooped, and she became like dead weight. Buzz could lift her, because she was light, but he was afraid to move her, so he called 911. Apparently, in the minutes before the ambulance arrived, Buzz was holding Ava while she was on the toilet, laid her head on his shoulder, and caressed her hair. Tears streamed down my face. This was unavoidable as I watched the misery Buzz was in. Watching a grown man choking up and trying not to cry is the most heartbreaking display of emotion in the world.

"I just stroked her hair and told her I loved her over and over again." Tears shot out of his eyes when he said these words, and he buried his face in his hands. He was wracked with long sobs, and Mr. McGrath ecame tearful as well and put his arm around his father. Gerry lost it soon after his dad and grandfather had. Then, one look at Gerry sobbing, and Mrs. McGrath began to weep as well. My hand went to her back as an instant reflex, and she turned to me and hugged me hard. Gerry got up and put his arms around both of us.

Of course, in this moment of utmost pain and sadness, I suddenly felt the unavoidable urge to laugh. My inability to handle negative emotion has always been both uncanny and annoying—especially right at that moment. I bit my lip to hold back the laughter. It was an involuntary reaction to the situation of each of us crying and then trying to comfort one another. My thoughts flipped to *Stand by Me* and the pie-eating contest where everyone begins to vomit on one another as a result of Lard Ass and his "barf-o-rama" plan. My tears stopped, and I felt able and willing to comfort Gerry and Mrs. McGrath as they both vomited emotions back and forth on each other. She comforted him, she lost it, he comforted her, he lost it, and she comforted him, and so on.

*What the fuck is wrong with me?* I thought. I think of a fucking barf-o-rama when they're all sitting in complete anguish about their wife, mother, grandmother having a stroke. I. Am. A. Freak!

I may be a freak, but I stopped feeling sadness and was able to comfort others, and thank the Lord, I didn't laugh. I believed it was good that I was there. We all exchanged hugs. I felt solid and secure again; my emotions had shut off, and I had the ability to console others. I cared deeply about Ava, but she wasn't my grandmother, she wasn't my family, so I believe it was good that I was there to be the resilient one to console everyone. I wasn't struggling to cope with my own pain. I wondered how hard it must have been for Mr. McGrath, a tough and robust male coping with his own agony of the possibility of losing his mother and then having to be strong for his dad, who was overwhelmed with losing his wife of fifty-plus years. How hard life is sometimes.

I looked at each of them grieving and embracing one another, and my mind veered to the movie *Parenthood*. Gil is complaining about his complicated life, and the grandmother wanders into the room talking about riding on a roller coaster. "You know, it was so interesting to me that a ride could make me so frightened, so scared, so sick, so excited, and so thrilled all together. Some didn't like it. They went on the merry-go-round. That just goes around. Nothing. I like the roller coaster. You get more out of it." I smiled again in comfort. Brilliant.

I was sitting alone in the waiting room so that I could give the McGrath family some space. I was content with my thoughts and comforted in knowing that I was here for this family I adored if they needed me. I was also selfishly grateful that it wasn't my grandmother in there. Gerry hesitantly moved toward me and kneeled down. His sooty lashes were wet from the tears, his eyes were red, and his eyelids were swollen. Witnessing him in this vulnerable and helpless state caused my heart to ache. He enfolded his arms around me, and I hugged him back hard and sincerely allowed myself to feel empathy for him—as a friend. My life could have been easier and more painless if I'd never met Gerry, never allowed myself to love him, never had to let my guard down. I liked the roller coaster...

# 24

Ava was suffering from bleeding of the brain and had to undergo immediate surgery. The emotional barf-o-rama had ceased, and everyone sat in the waiting room looking solemn and quiet. Everyone deserves someone to fall apart with.

The doctor came out, and Buzz sprinted to him so fast I thought he was going to knock him over. The surgery went as well as it could have, but she would be in recovery for some time, and it could take four or five days for her to wake up. The fact that she had Alzheimer's as well would also affect her level of recovery. The doctor allowed the family to come in the room briefly and then advised everyone to go home and get some rest. Buzz wanted to look presentable for his wife, so he pulled a comb from his pocket and ran it through his thin hair and buttoned his shirt. Mr. and Mrs. McGrath held each of Buzz's hands, and they walked heads down toward the room.

"Please, Mary Kate, I need you to come with me. I can't do this alone. I really can't." Gerry looked tormented. I felt uncomfortable and confused. I struggled to stand my ground when he looked like that. I looked at his parents and realized I needed to put my anger aside for them, they have given me so much. I surrendered and let him hold my hand and walk into Ava's room.

The bed swallowed Ava up, she was so tiny. She had a bandage across her forehead, and her eyes were closed. She looked peaceful.

Unexpectedly, Ava opened her eyes wide at Buzz and stared at him as she was speaking with her eyes. Buzz touched her hair and responded with his eyes in a powerful connection that was extremely touching and beautiful to watch. Buzz began to hum a song, and it was at that moment that Ava's breathing ceased, as if Buzz's song had given her the permission she needed to leave this world. Buzz emitted a sound so painful that any feeling person would have broken into tears at the sound. It was a mixture of heartbreak, relief, and loss.

"When I said, 'Till death do us part,' all those years ago, I assumed I would go first. How am I supposed to live without her?" Buzz said with a sob. He kissed her mouth and hugged her again and said, "I'll see you again, my love."

I stood back behind everyone, trying to respect their boundaries and to be present for his parents. Buzz sobbed silently as he sat in the chair next to his beloved wife, holding and kissing her hand. It was almost too much to take, even for an outsider, to watch this man at the mercy of life and groveling to keep her alive. Mr. McGrath stood behind his father with his hand on his shoulder, weeping gently. Gerry had tears streaming down his cheeks; he quickly wiped them away and kissed Ava on the forehead.

He briskly walked toward me and grabbed my hand, and we quickly exited the room. We walked to the car in silence. I had no words of comfort to give him; my mind was empty now with the bleakness of the situation. I attempted to stay focused on my own sad emotion and to allow myself to feel that instead of distracting it away, like I usually did.

He unlocked my door with the key and opened the door for me. I slid in quickly and then reached over and unlocked his door from the inside. He climbed in quickly, and then I was jerked back rapidly by his lips on mine. Our lips were swollen from crying. My inner thighs throbbed at the intensity and passion of his kiss. His hand grasped the back of my neck and was intertwined in my hair. He kissed my cheeks, eyelids, and neck, which I allowed him to do without thinking; I was taken off guard. He kissed the tip of my nose and then put his nose to mine. He smiled at me fondly.

"Thank you for being here. You have no idea what it means to me that you'd do this for me. You're a good friend, and I love you." He said this abruptly, pecked me on the lips, and sat up to start the car.

My head spun with confusion. I found myself thinking, *Then why did you cheat on me, bastard?* I had to hold onto my anger, since it was my only protection. I slowly felt my heart caving and wanted to cease what we were doing immediately. We drove home in silence, with him occasionally grabbing my hand and kissing the top. I wanted to yell, "Stop!" I thought of *When Harry Met Sally*: "You see, Harry, when you say things like that, it makes it impossible for me to hate you!" I wanted to hate him. I wanted to stay mad. I didn't want to forgive him. But watching him being in pain was causing my empathy to take precedence.

There was an unspoken understanding at this point between Gerry and me. I had accompanied him to the hospital as a friend and as a friend to his family. He would call and say he was going to the hospital and I would say "Ok". Then he would pick me up, it wasn't even a question. All our relationship drama seemed so petty with what was happening with his family loss. It was the same with the wake and funeral. I was by his side at all times, and he held my hand the majority of the time, as if I was his crutch. I could no longer find it in my heart to be angry, hurt, or resentful during this time. Watching him and his family endure this process was heartbreaking; all I could feel was sympathy. Part of me was also grateful to have had this experience with them. Death leaves everyone raw and vulnerable, and sometimes it is a good thing, I suppose, to let those emotions in—to make life seem so important.

As I said, my anger had disappeared—that is, until Michelle showed up at the wake. I felt Gerry's hand tighten around my waist and his body stiffen as I noticed her presence. Selfishly, the anger, hurt, and resentment came flooding back, and I was a deer in the headlights again. I wanted to leave but didn't want to give her the satisfaction. After all, Gerry needed me throughout this painful life circumstance, not her.

My jealousy fumed inside me as I saw her flaunting her tan legs and perfect body in a tight-fitting black dress and high pointy black heels. Her blond hair, which resembled a Prell or Pantene commercial, had a striking appearance next to her black dress. I was wearing a black blazer, tweed skirt, and white blouse that my grandmother had probably found at a secondhand store. Suddenly I went from feeling important and attractive to nerdy and invisible. I started to walk away, unable to handle the inadequacy I felt in that moment, but Gerry's arm tightened around me. I was experiencing a million emotions I was no longer protected from, and I prayed for my wall. Crying would actually be appropriate in the situation, because we were, in fact, at a wake, but I didn't want that conniving skank to see me cry.

I looked up at him pleadingly as I sensed my body begin to tremble. He held my hand tightly at his side, and we walked away together from the bereavement line. We stepped outside and were met by a cloud of delicious-smelling cigarette smoke from guests outside. Gerry steered me to the side of the building and turned me toward him. He wore a black suit and crisp white shirt, and I couldn't help but admire his physique and sexiness in that moment. I realized this was probably an inappropriate thought, given the circumstances, but my body and hormones apparently had their own brain. We were technically legal adults yet still teenagers emotionally, and we didn't dress to the nines very often. Gerry placed his hands on the sides of my face and stared in my eyes intently. When his eyes pierced me in the darkness under the streetlight, I was immediately defenseless.

"Listen, I love you," Gerry said, sounding sincere. "She's nothing to me. What you have done for me in the last few weeks has made me love you more, and I think you're more beautiful than ever. Your heart is what makes you stunningly gorgeous. She would be a hideous witch if we could see what she looked like on the inside. I don't know why she's here—maybe she feels obligated because most of my friends came to show their respect—but she knows how I feel about you. To be honest, I told her everything," Gerry said hesitantly.

My body flinched and stiffened as I wondered when he'd told her this...shortly after he hooked up with her, or what?

"Told her? When?" I asked, feeling sheepish and shaking with anger at the same time.

Gerry took a deep breath, closed his eyes, and then looked at me again. "She called me a couple of days ago. I told her that it was a mistake and that I'd been drunk. I told her how much I loved you and that I'm in love with you, and I asked her to please stop calling me."

I was again ambivalent with emotions; part of me wanted to insert my heel up his ass, and part of me wanted to jump him right there. I supposed there wasn't a better moment for him to have told me this, since all our time together had been spent watching his grandmother die. We really hadn't talked on our way to and from the hospital. We just held hands, and I did my best to remain his friend during this time.

"Baby, I thought about telling you, but I've just been so grateful that you've supported me through all this, and I assumed you wanted nothing to do with me, other than being a friend, so I figured, why even tell you? Even if you never kiss me or touch me again willingly, I won't be with her, and I really can't be with anyone, because I'm in love with you. I was drunk and lonely that night, and it wasn't your fault. I was being a stupid asshole guy. Like you said, the world is full of guys. I want to be a man. I want to be a man for you. You make me want to be a better man." Gerry said all this while gazing intensely at me.

His eyes had this dreamy, glossy appearance, as if I could see his love for me inside them. I heard in the distance from someone's car radio in the parking lot this hair-band song called "Love Hurts," and I felt a wave of affection and love wash over me as well. I believed him, I loved him, and I wanted to forgive him. He smirked at me.

"Well," I said with a smirk, "I can't take credit for that line. I stole it from *Say Anything*...but it's true. I don't want a *guy*; I want a *man*."

"You're crazy about me, too, aren't you? You love me, don't you? I can see it in your eyes," Gerry said, looking hopeful as he placed his hands around my waist. I nodded slowly, unable to speak and feeling completely vulnerable. He kissed me slowly, and I let him, unable to resist. My body charged against his, and I was left feeling sexy and beautiful again within his arms. Our kiss deepened briefly, and then we stopped as we both realized we were in the parking lot of a funeral home at his grandmother's wake.

"Please forgive me. Please don't leave me again. Please trust me."

I wanted to say yes wholeheartedly, yet something inside me was still was hesitant. "I'll try," I said sincerely.

He smiled. "I don't blame you. Trying is better than nothing," Gerry said, sounding relieved. He put his arm around my shoulders tightly, and we walked back into the funeral home. I felt whole and solid again—invincible.

Michelle, sitting in the assembly of chairs surrounded by Gerry's friends, was utilizing this opportunity to flirt and play, as if it was a social setting. I spotted Buzz sitting alone, so I dismissed myself from his friends and made my way over to him. I sat down next to him and held his hand. His solemn, vacant eyes met mine, and he managed an almost unnoticeable upturn of his lips. He slowly lowered his head, with his eyes looking down at my hand in his. He wore a black suit as well as a black shirt and tie. His thin hair was still slicked neatly toward the back. His olive skin looked sallow and almost jaundiced; the texture of his skin was weathered but supple.

"Ah, Mary Kate; You're good for my grandson. Looking at your hand in mine reminds me of my Ava when we were young. You guys better hold onto each other. It goes by fast, believe it or not." Buzz emitted a small smile that didn't match his sorrowful eyes. His eyes were black and appeared lifeless and lost. He was staring longingly at the casket holding his beautiful bride, so tiny and eternally beautiful. He choked back a sob.

"Pretty soon they're going to close that thing up, and I'm not going to be able to see her anymore." Buzz let go of my hand and pulled out a black cloth handkerchief that he held to his eyes. My eyes welled up again in response. I put my arm on his shoulder. He patted my hand, stood up, and walked to the casket and knelt down before his wife. I looked down at my hands now, thinking about what he had said and thinking about true love and how they had found it at such a young age; their love seemed to have withstood the tests of time. Shelley, still a sad, blubbering mess, then came and sat next to me. We embraced, and she grasped my hand. I sat with her in silence, both of us staring sadly at the casket.

I looked over at Gerry, who was still standing among his friends with his hands in his pockets. His friends still surrounded Michelle like a pack of wolves surrounding their meal. She stood up and moved toward Gerry. I could see his body stiffen and his jaw clench. She whispered something to him, he nodded, and she hugged him. He seemed to pat her back abruptly, as if to quickly dismiss her. It looked like he said, "Thank you for coming," and then abruptly headed toward me. He sat down next to me and clutched my hand with his right hand and placed his left arm around me. I peeked over to where Michelle was, and my eyes met hers. She sneered and turned away toward her other suitors. She could have anyone she wanted, but of course she wanted the guy who was a challenge and was taken. Well, I hoped he was and that he was telling me the truth. Only time would tell.

The funeral went as expected: depressing, sad, and heartbreaking. Attending the funeral luncheon was like watching an old movie with a cast from all over Europe: Italian, Irish, Polish, Austrian, and German. Some were from Ava's Irish and German side, some were from Buzz's side. I loved listening to the different accents and old stories that were being told throughout the room. I learned that Buzz was adopted, which explained a lot because his last name was

McGrath but he appeared Italian and Polish; hence the schnoz as he would say. Many of the attendees still dressed in the same style of the forties and fifties. Buzz was laughing with some of his brothers and sisters. It was good to see him laugh. Everyone seemed to have a drink in hand. The choices were either a dirty martini or a Manhattan, in honor of Ava's favorite drinks. I had to admit that I was impressed by Ava's choices in booze—that was strong stuff.

I took a sip of Gerry's Manhattan, and my eyes bulged out of my head. I thought I'd have a dirty martini instead, since vodka and olive juice seemed like they'd be less potent.

"My poison is vodka."

He laughed and kissed me on the cheek.

Gerry didn't seem to leave my side at all and proudly introduced me with, "This is my girl, Mary Kate." I liked the sound of "my girl." He was touching me at all times, either stroking my hair, having his hand on my back, holding my hand, or drawing circles on my shoulder with his thumb. Every few minutes he would give me a kiss on the cheek or peck on the mouth, and I have to admit, physical touch is when I feel most loved, so I enjoyed every second of it. Occasionally I'd have a flash of anger or hurt or fear, but it would subside quickly, because when he was like this, I couldn't imagine us any other way. He could be so sweet, affectionate, thoughtful, flirtatious, and sexy that it was impossible to remember how much I'd hated him and how angry I'd been.

Gerry finished his Manhattan, which I was impressed about—I was still sipping my dirty martini and was unsure if I could finish it. I decided to make a meal of it and continually refilled my martini glass with blue cheese–filled olives. My grandmother had also found me a black wrap dress that was a little too small for me in the chest, but I wore it anyway, thinking about how hot Michelle had looked the day before. I'd thrown some hot rollers in my hair quickly in the morning. I hypothesized that if I put more effort into my appearance, I wouldn't feel so inadequate, especially if that skank decided to make another unwanted appearance.

"I know this is probably not appropriate again, but you look exceptionally pretty today, sweetie." His eyes traveled from my face to my neck, chest, and cleavage. I was wearing the claddagh ring charm on a silver necklace he'd bought me that went down my chest in a *V.* The *V* of the dress went a little farther down. His eyes danced around my necklace and cleavage, and he smiled. "I really like your...uh... necklace."

I laughed, knowing what he was referring to. I smacked his leg. "You bought me the necklace, weirdo, so I know you like it," I said with a giggle. He laughed, too, and kissed my cheek and slid his hand on my knee.

"I'm sure it's because you look extremely hot today, or maybe grief is an aphrodisiac, but I want you so fucking bad right now." Gerry's eyes had that wicked sexy look, and his lips pouted out in a crooked smile. I laughed and tried to take a decent sip of my dirty martini. We were totally underage, and I didn't have much experience with booze, so the alcohol was surging through my veins in no time. Of course, I was throbbing between my legs as well from the booze and the way he was looking at me. He scooted his chair farther under the table and guided my hand between his legs, toward his massive bulge.

"See what you're doing to me right now, Mary Kate?" he asked me desperately. Unfortunately he hadn't driven there separately, and we were stuck at the restaurant. Gerry buttoned his coat and smiled at me as he stood up. "I have to step away from you for a moment and calm down in the men's room," he said teasingly. I continued to work on my dirty martini, which I was able to tolerate now that it was halfway finished. That little Ava drinking Manhattans and dirty martinis seemed comedic to me, but with the way I was feeling, I could understand why she and Buzz had had so many kids.

Shelley suddenly appeared next to me, giddy and looking intoxicated. "Hey, MK Hey, that rhymes! Ha ha. Hey, MK, ha ha." *Oh Lord, she's bombed,* I thought. "What's up?" she said. "Gerry told me what happened with you two, and I'm really sorry. My brother's such a dickhead sometimes. Guys are such asthholes," she said, slurring some more. I wasn't sure I wanted to continue this conversation. "Listen, MK, he loves you. He's been an absolute wreck without you. He wouldn't come out of his room, and he could barely eat or drink anything, my mom said. It's really nith of you to be here. We all love you." She gave me a sloppy hug. I did love his family, and I think I'd been partially grieving the loss of his family when Gerry and I had broken up.

Gerry reappeared and sat next to Shelley. He whispered something in her ear, and then she took her car keys from her purse and handed them to him. Butterflies jumped in my stomach with excitement. Gerry winked at me and took my hand. We made our rounds saying good-bye to everyone. Buzz kissed Gerry and me three times; he held my face and kissed me on the left cheek, then the right cheek, and then the left again. I giggled. "Please, Gerry, bring your girl over more often now—I'll need the company," Buzz said, kissing us again.

"Mom, Dad, I'm going to take Mary Kate home in Shelley's car and hang out with her for a little while," Gerry said to his parents when we were leaving. His parents thanked me for being there and hugged me tightly. It seemed like an eternity saying good-bye to the endless stream of men at the bar who resembled the cast of *Goodfellas*. My cheeks burned as I felt my breasts spilling from the dress as I leaned over to kiss some of the men sitting down. I'm sure they enjoyed my company now after witnessing the cheap thrill I was providing them. My rack was out of control in that dress. It was really annoying. I know most girls would love to have this problem, since most girls complain about being flat chested, but I just felt too young for these things. Quite frankly, I was not mature enough to handle them. I did not know what clothes to wear. I do not think any eighteen-year-old should have DDs; it's a lot of responsibility. It was a lot of pressure. It also hurt my back and shoulders lugging those things around.

We made a fast exit to Shelley's car. I felt like a dog in heat, consumed with desire. His eyes were darting into my body as if he was peeling my dress off me with his eyes. I wanted to pounce on top of him as soon as we got into the car, but I figured we'd better leave the parking lot first. He drove down the street with his hand on my leg and flicked the top wrap of the dress to the side, exposing my entire leg. A whimper and a sigh escaped his lips. My eyes bored into his hand, as if they were madly willing it to move up my thigh. His hand seemed to obey my command. His hand traveled slowly up my thigh as my clit throbbed and swelled with desire. I threw my head back on the headrest and glanced at him. His eyes were wild and feral, as if he could wolf me down in one bite. The electric silence was buzzing with our breath and chemistry. The inability to take each other immediately because he was driving was maddening.

We approached a stoplight, and he abruptly threw the car into park. He removed his suit coat and tossed it in the back seat, and within seconds he was devouring my mouth and tongue. My nipples were thumping with vibration, and my breasts felt heavy and full as they pressed against his hard chest. My entire body surged with need, and my hand mindlessly traveled to his swollen and stiff bulge in his pants. An anguished moan emerged from his lips into my mouth, and he pulled me tightly toward him. My legs spread and opened, one over his legs and one behind his back. I was completely lost in the moment of intense craving when a car horn rudely interrupted our session and startled us back into reality. We were both dizzy and panting wildly. He made a sharp right turn, and I was going to mention us finding a hotel, but at that point I knew I wouldn't be able to wait. My legs were still spread open and painfully throbbing, and I was becoming untamed and savage, like I was ready to attack. My own hands began to massage my breasts as if I was possessed by my own desire. He growled as he beheld me doing this and slid his right hand up my inner thigh. When he reached my swollen clit, my body jerked with relief and madness. He groaned, and with his teeth clenched he mouthed, "Fuck!"

The car swerved into a dim parking lot near a forest preserve. It was dusk, and it appeared deserted. He quickly parked the car, took the keys out of the ignition, and threw them onto the dashboard. He grabbed my right knee and yanked me toward him. His left hand brushed my dress to the side, and he slid his hands up the sides of my thighs and hips, gliding my wet thong panties down my legs. My heart raced, and my clit tingled. Within seconds, his mouth was on my clit, and I shuddered and screamed with delight. His mouth was causing my body to stiffen and thrash around. Foreign sounds were escaping from my lips. His hands were spreading my legs apart and sliding up the sides of my body to my breasts, which were now exposed completely, as the dress was now fully untied and at my sides. Waves of pleasure and tingling took hold of my body and my mind, and my hips thrust madly against his mouth and tongue. Intense throbbing radiated inside me, and tender aching consumed my body until I exploded into his mouth.

He reclined and moved the seat back, and I immediately straddled him, unbuttoned his shirt rapidly, and kissed his neck and chest. He groaned, and I could feel him about to burst out of his pants. I unbuttoned and unzipped his pants. He kissed my mouth and lifted his ass and me off the seat so he could slide his pants down. His hands were cupping my ass on top of him, and his dick was hard and pulsing against me. I reached into my purse and handed him a condom. Gerry looked in my eyes intensely and he grabbed my neck and pulled my mouth to his. "I want you so bad Mary Kate. I have wanted you since the day I met you. I love you so much." My heart was racing and my body was trembling, there was no time to think. He moaned into my throat as he penetrated inside me. I had a slight wince of pain, but thankfully he had made me come with his mouth so I was wet, open and ready for this. He slowly moved my hips up and down around him. His hand was around my neck and fingers intertwined in my hair as he pulled my mouth to his roughly. His body stiffened, and I moaned "I love you" into his mouth as we both detonated around each other. I collapsed on top of his chest and listened to our breathing and heartbeats, rapid and in sync with each other.

"Wow," he murmured after a few minutes, once our breathing had slowed and our hearts had calmed.

I agreed and smiled. "Wow."

"God, I missed you," he said as he inhaled and kissed the top of my head.

I turned my head to face his; his eyes were dancing toward mine, his face aglow with happiness. My heart leaped at the sight of him. "I missed you, too," I said sincerely and with a slight crack in my voice.

We gave each other silly grins as we adjusted our attire; Gerry winked at me and started the car. He drove slowly to my house, avoiding Buzz and Ava's route, and turned down my block from the opposite end of the block. When he arrived at my house, I could see my grandmother's small red car parked in front. My cheeks flushed; I was concerned about facing my grandmother. *Gawd, I'm a tramp,* I thought. Then Judd Nelson's voice kicked in my mind: "Being bad feels pretty good." I smiled to myself, and the guilt subsided.

I gave Gerry a quick peck on the lips and told him my grandmother was over, so I had to go. I didn't want to have another full-blown make-out session in front of my house.

He nodded and appeared to understand. "I love you, sweetie," he said with his eyes piercing my soul, and I shuddered.

"I love you, too," I said, and my heart leaped. His cheeks flushed, and he ended up getting out of the car and walking me to the door. I was embarrassed, because it seemed that we both looked slightly disheveled. To prevent any lingering good-byes on the front porch, I kissed him quickly and slipped into the house quietly, without looking back, and shut the front door.

# 25

My grandmother and mom were sitting in the living room, or the "parlor," as my grandmother referred to it. They both had mugs of coffee. My mom was speaking quite loudly, because my grandmother was going deaf yet refused to get a hearing aid for fear that she would "look old," as she said. We found this comical, because yelling to someone in public usually indicates that someone is elderly and hard of hearing. My grandmother looked smashing, as usual, wearing a frilly plaid blouse, a camel blazer, stylish brown pants that flared at the bottoms, and purple pumps; her beehive was exceptionally high today. The room smelled of Charlie perfume, coffee, and Doublemint gum. The scent immediately relaxed me; I always felt safe and comforted around my grandmother.

"Oh, hello, dear!" my grandmother said loudly. I walked to her and kissed her on the cheek and gave her a quick hug, wondering if she could smell the sex on me. I prayed she couldn't.

"Well, look at you, sexy," she then said to me. My face burned. *She knows*, I thought.

"Get out of here, Gram," I replied, dumbing it down.

"That dress looks great on you! Can you believe it was only five dollars? Unbelievable what people give away these days. That wrap dress is a classic. Trust me, darling, you'll be able to wear that dress twenty years from now." I laughed and shook my head at her, hoping I could afford to buy my own clothes twenty years from now.

"I found some cute jeans for you and a few other things in that bag on the stairs, honey," my grandmother said excitedly. She did have a gift for finding some decent clothes that I didn't feel were completely obvious they'd come from a thrift store. My grandmother would refer to this as more of an "upscale secondhand store," although the bottom line was that it was a thrift store. I grabbed the bag enthusiastically, because I desperately needed some new duds and I knew she liked to watch my reaction when I was pleased with her finds. I gasped when I pulled out a pair of slightly worn Guess jeans, Guess overalls, a yellow tank top with the tags still on, and a cream-colored peasant-style blouse that went well with the faded pale-blue jeans. The famous triangle on the back pocket was an essential stamp of coolness. I embraced them to my chest excitedly and hugged her. She laughed and then straightened her blazer when I let her go.

"I'm glad you like them, dear." My grandmother was beaming.

I ran to the basement to wash the clothes so I could try them on, since I was kind of grossed out when I thought of who'd worn the clothes before me. I removed the stapled price tags and washed the clothes in hot water. They were button-fly jeans, which I wasn't crazy about, and they had zippers on the bottoms. Wasn't sure what those were for or what they were all about in general, but I wasn't picky. All I had were dirty-ass Chic or Sassoon jeans or jeans from companies that weren't even in business anymore. I remembered when Gerry first set eyes on my Chic jeans, he shook his head. "Baby, I'm going to hook you up." He winked and smacked my ass. The next time I saw him, he presented me with a square box with adorably cool jeans from The Gap. My first not previously owned jeans felt like a milestone in my life.

I was smiling to myself when I was interrupted by Maeve, who was an expert at silently sneaking up on people. She startled me, and she giggled. My chest ached when I noticed that my little sister had grown some and had lost a little of her baby fat in her cheeks. Her eyes appeared exceptionally striking, and her two differently colored eyes were much more noticeable today in the light coming from the window in the basement. I couldn't decide which eye I liked better— one was hazel, and the other was slate blue—but both were equally cool. Her strawberry-blond hair appeared redder and more vibrant than usual. She was starting to look more grown up, which made me proud and scared at the same time.

"Get over here, you little rascal," I growled to her, and she laughed. I grabbed her arm and pulled her to me and tickled her. She laughed again, and I gave her a hug.

"I missed you," Maeve said, her voice muffled from her face being in my stomach.

I smiled. "I missed you, too, little one," I replied fondly.

"Who are you calling 'little one'? I'm almost as tall as you! See?" She sternly held the side of her hand on the top of her head, which was equivalent with my breasts. This made me feel uncomfortable, considering I was still wearing this skanky wrap dress with my cleavage hanging out.

"OK, OK, you're getting tall. Now let's go upstairs; I need to put some comfy clothes on." I put my arm around her shoulder and guided her toward the stairs.

"You look pretty in that dress, Mary Kate. You look so…old," she said softly.

I laughed. "I was thinking you look older, too. You have gotten taller."

Maeve looked up at me and smiled proudly. "I figure I'm probably going to need a bra soon, and maybe some deodorant," she said with a smile.

"Get out of here—you're not *that* old yet!" I said, sounding extremely freaked out, and I tickled her again. "Actually you are kind of stinky."

"Hey!" Maeve yelled as she attempted to tackle me.

She giggled. "Guess what? A boy in my class said I have hairier legs than him!" Maeve said this proudly, obviously not realizing that this could be a negative comment.

"I'm sorry, did that bother you?" I replied empathetically.

"No, of course not! He sounded impressed. Why would that bother me?" she said matter-of-factly.

Maeve did have some hairy legs, and she probably should have shaved them soon, although she hadn't asked, and I didn't think our mom could handle it right then. She'd been really overwhelmed, I'd noticed. Her brow had been almost permanently furrowed for the past week. I wasn't sure what was going on. I knew that with each of us getting older, the less child support she would receive. She was already working like a dog. A strange emotion emerged inside my stomach as I thought about what I'd just done and how my mom and dad had probably been the same way with each other when they were eighteen. But life happened. I wasn't sure if the emotion was guilt or shame, but it was uncomfortable.

I was interrupted by the phone, startling me out of my thoughts. "Hello?"

"Hey," Gerry said sweetly, breathing heavily over the phone.

A shit-eating grin emerged on my face in spite of myself. "Hey," I replied, beaming.

"I can't stop thinking about you," Gerry whispered intensely.

I throbbed. "Really?" I replied stupidly.

"Yes! You're the hottest chick on the planet!"

"Get out of town. Now you're getting a little crazy," I said with a laugh.

"Can I take you on a date tonight? I'm a wreck. I need to see you!"

"You just dropped me off fifteen minutes ago, silly!"

"So? I can't get enough of you."

"OK," I whispered with a grin.

"Yay! I'll pick you up in an hour." He hung up.

Part of me squealed and throbbed; another part of me had that surreal guilt or shame emotion. Somehow in my gut, I felt like this was a mistake, but then why did it feel so good? A part of me felt as if I was going backward and regressing, like when you're potty-trained but you realize as a toddler that it's too much work to wipe your own ass, so you go back to diapers. Was I making a mistake by letting him in again after he'd hurt me so badly? What if he cheated again? What if he broke my heart again? Well, I supposed it was too late now. I'd already let him in, and my hormones had gotten the best of me.

I removed my previously owned and broken-in Guess jeans, Guess overalls, and tops from the dryer. I slipped the jeans on, and I had to admit, I looked smashing. The jeans fit in all the right places, although a wince of guilt pinched me suddenly when I remembered about the Gap jeans Gerry had bought me and how he always enjoyed it when I wore them. But my grandmother was still there and was anxiously awaiting my trying on the treasure she'd scored at the thrift store. I decided on the overalls instead and the yellow tank top so my grandmother would be pleased. I thought about Ava and how she was gone and how my grandmother wouldn't be around forever, either, so I decided that she took precedence. I did my hair half up and half down, put on pale-pink lip gloss and blush and mascara, and was pleased with my appearance. When I strolled down the stairs, my grandmother was sitting on the love seat right next to the stairs, and she gasped with pleasure.

"Oh my! Darling! You look ravishing! The whole ensemble complements your raven hair and pale skin so exquisitely," my grandmother said, gushing.

*Who talks like that?* I thought. I'd feel ridiculous speaking in such a manner around my friends, but that was how people spoke back in the day. My mind flashed to the photos of Buzz and Ava, and I wished I could have lived in that time. The nineties weren't exactly my cup of tea.

I walked out the front door when Gerry arrived; he was two hours late, which surprised me. He did not get out of the car. He didn't smile at me when I got into the car, looked me up and down, and he turned toward the road. I heard him breathe heavily from his nose.

I immediately felt that familiar clench in my stomach. That feeling like I was walking on eggshells and that anything could set him off. It was interesting how I could see this so much more clearly now that we hadn't been together for a while. My initial response was to ask him what was wrong, but I stopped.

He pulled into the Burger King parking lot, which made me glad, because of course I was starving. He looked at me and asked me what I wanted. I noticed he looked down at my breasts under the overalls and his nose flared. Then he turned away without waiting for me to say what I wanted, and he just ordered the same for both of us—which was fine, because I eat anything.

Whatever was wrong was his problem, not mine. I wanted to ask what we were doing, but instead I started flipping through the stations. I settled on the Led Zeppelin song "Black Dog."

The song kind of reminded me of my dad. My mind flashed to a memory of him barbecuing on the grill while playing music and telling me the different band names and singers as each new song came on. I remembered wrinkling my nose and shaking my head no when he asked me if I liked each song. He laughed and said, "You will later." I remembered smiling, too. My dad and I had a moment that day, and I had to admit: he did introduce me to this kind of music, for which I was grateful. I remembered I was sitting on the sidewalk, just watching him sing and thinking he was the cat's ass. He was smoking and playing the air guitar with a cigarette in his mouth; when he bobbed his head up and down, it made me giggle.

I was smiling and lost in the memory when suddenly the Led Zeppelin song switched to some cheesy Air Supply song. "Hey!" I yelled reactively to the sudden song change. "I was listening to that!"

"Jesus, Mary Kate! What decade do you live in? You keep listening to all this old-ass shit. Get with the nineties." Pfft. He blew air out of his mouth and shook his head.

I felt a little fire inside me start to ignite, like when Ralphie is about to kick Scut Farkus's ass in *A Christmas Story*. I gritted my teeth as if he'd just insulted my mom. "Oh, and this shit is better? Air

Supply? Are you serious?" I smirked, knowing that if I told any of his friends that he'd just turned off Led Zeppelin in favor of Air Supply, he would be teased mercilessly.

"Oh, sorry, you don't like Air Supply? What? You don't have the record, so it's not cool?" Gerry retorted, and I rolled my eyes and looked out the window.

*What does that even mean?* I thought. I crossed my arms.

"Hey, I'm asking you something, I ignored him. "Hey, I'm speaking to you. Look at me when I'm talking to you," Gerry said in a demanding tone.

"You know what? I don't have to respond to you. We're talking about a song. This is so stupid."

"So, someone like you shouldn't be fighting with me," Gerry said, still holding me and driving.

"What does that mean? Someone like me?" I was really confused now; he'd never said anything like that before. It sounded like he was heading for below the belt. The shame started to kick in. He was smiling that evil, conniving smile he had when he knew he was getting to me; that hateful smile reminded me of a bully getting the best of his prey. I started to feel nauseated when I thought about how stupid I'd been earlier. Where the hell did this come from?

"What the hell is wrong with you? How could you say these things to me?" I screamed, fighting back the tears.

Just then, the drive-through woman was handing us our food. I'm sure most people would wonder how I could eat at time like this, but my stomach doesn't care how I feel most of the time. I moved over closer to the door to eat my delicious burger in peace.

"I'm not done with you yet. Where do you think you are going?" As he said this he grabbed my shirt and the waist of my overalls and pulled me toward him.

"Hey, man! Get your hands off my new shirt!" I said, now becoming really annoyed.

"It's not new—your grandma got it for you at the thrift store," Gerry said mockingly

"So? What's the difference? It's new to me. Sorry I'm not rich like you," I said, and I didn't want to eat anymore. This was serious now.

"People like you always give people like me what they want," he said. "You really think you'll be getting out of here, Mary Kate? You really believe you're going to be a college graduate, don't you? You'll probably be working at the Greasy Spoon when I graduate," he said with a smirk. He released my clothes as if he was now disgusted with them or me. *What the fuck?* I was so furious I could spit. That blind rage was building inside me again. I was so shocked and confused.

"I cannot believe you are treating me like this and especially everything that just happened. What the hell is this about?" I screamed.

"OK, I'll show you." Gerry pulled over, put the car in park abruptly and grabbed something out of his glove compartment. He tossed an envelope at me. A bunch of pictures fell out all over the floor of the car. They were all flipped over and upside down. He sat there with his arms crossed, looking at me with a pompous look on his face.

As I began to gather the pictures together, a flood of clarity washed over me as I saw the pictures were of homecoming weekend. I bit my bottom lip as I flipped through picture after picture of me laughing hard or smiling with my arms around different guys or their arms around me. I laughed at some of the pictures of Mairead and me looking sloppy drunk and laughing hysterically. The bruise on my face combined with the dingy yellowish tank top almost resembled a Halloween costume of me dressing up as white trash. I guess that explained where the anger was coming from, yet I could not wipe the smirk off my face. I had so much fun that weekend. The pictures made me laugh—I could not help it

"What the fuck are you laughing about? You look like a whore." Gerry said this with a flat expression and those vacant black eyes.

"Whatever, I was having fun. I didn't do anything wrong," I said, still smiling because the pictures were so funny.

"Michelle stopped over a little bit ago with these pictures. She thought I would want to see these. I bet you didn't know that Michelle's sister is Sandy, the one that dated your brother." *The fucking South Side of Chicago—the connections never end* I thought.

"Like I said, I didn't do anything wrong. I was talking to other guys, so what? You hooked up with someone else; I only thought about it." I was an eerily calm angry then. Just waiting for my moment to get the hell out of that car forever.

"Wait, what do you mean you *thought* about it?"

"It doesn't matter Gerry. I can't believe I trusted you. I can't believe I felt bad for you. You have problems. You need help." I was crying now tears of anger and shame. I was not hungry anymore.

"You. Are. A. Cunt."

# 26

Now I have returned to the present, grimacing at the playback of our relationship and could not believe after all that, it's over. I have to stop getting sucked back in. I also laughed that I pulled a Rizzo and whipped my drink at him and my burgers too! Rizzo would be proud. I was also proud of myself that I kept my phone disconnected all night—that was what my gut or instinct told me to do. I woke up at 5:00 a.m. with my head spinning about the cemetery with Marty and yesterday's events with Gerry. Part of me wanted to connect my phone and listen to the messages that I am sure Gerry left. However, I could never again be sucked into this crazy psycho lifestyle. I could not help but think, if I am going through this now, what would our future be like? But how would I have the strength? It was a cycle.

I decided to walk and clear my head. I began replaying things Gerry had said from yesterday, and the tears were streaming down my face. I was so angry with myself. I was disappointed with myself. I despised that I felt so worthless. I hated that everything had to be so hard for me. I resented it whenever things seemed to be so easy for everyone else.

I imagined the end of *Some Kind of Wonderful*, where Amanda Jones says, "I hate feeling ashamed. I hate where I'm from. I hate watching my friends get everything their hearts desire. I gave into that hatred, and I turned on what I believed in." It's funny how I had seen these movies so many times, but so many parts I never paid attention to as much were now popping in my head. I guess that was because I never allowed myself to really feel pain or be vulnerable. The emptiness and "lost" sensation I felt inside right then was awful and scary; but so many of the good feelings I'd had over the last year were also scary. It's better to live and feel, I suppose.

While I was walking, I had this instinct to enter a church. . I did what my instinct told me to do and went inside despite not knowing the religious denomination of the church. I genuflected out of habit and sat next to an African-American woman with a warm, welcoming face and shining brown eyes. She smiled at me, and I smiled back. I was sitting there trying to remember the last time I'd been to church. When my Dad left and I watched the pain my mother was in, I stopped going. I was angry with God for allowing that to happen.

The preacher discussed the topic of free will. He said that "God gave us the freedom to make our own choices. That is free will. It's unfortunate when some people's choices hurt others, but that's all part of your journey. Your life isn't a destination; it's a constant flow of change and growth to prepare you for eternal life. Embrace every day: the good and the bad ones."

It was almost as if I was meant to hear this. It was as if the preacher was speaking to me. I suddenly felt love and peace. It seemed like my guardian angel had guided me there. When Mass was over, I felt like a weight had been lifted from my soul, and I felt whole, as if my wall was up again but in a healthy way. As if that wall was on my terms. As I was walking down the aisle, the woman sitting next to me handed me a slip of paper. Her eyes were so bright, it was as if she could see inside my soul. She smiled at me, and I took the slip of paper. I was confused. When I got to the vestibule, I read the piece of paper. It was from a verse from Psalm 68:5: "A Father to the fatherless, a defender of widows, is God in his holy dwelling." Beneath was written, "God is the only Father you need."

I looked around to see if I could find this woman after I read the paper she handed me, but she was gone. Why had she given this to me? How did she know I was fatherless, in both senses of the word?

This was so surreal that it felt angelic in a way. It was extremely random. I walked home, and I found myself smiling and at peace, knowing that "God is the only Father" I needed. When I considered God as my father, the resentment and anger toward my dad seemed less intense, because he was only human. Suddenly I recognized that both of my parents were just doing the best they could. Perhaps I should not be so judgmental, considering I got sucked into a similar situation that I could not truly handle. Maybe that is also why I got so attached to Gerry—for his family, his parents whom I respected. Those are not the right reasons to date someone.

I thought of Amanda Jones again, who says at the end of the movie, "I used to think I would rather be with someone for the wrong reasons than alone for the right ones. I'd rather be *right*."

Then I went downstairs to look for my mom to tell her this crazy story about Gerry, church, and the African-American woman. I knew she would believe it. She always said we had a guardian angel. Somehow my mother had never lost her faith, no matter what happened to her. My mother was the strongest, bravest, and the most courageous woman I knew.

Since this divine intervention that seemed to be meant to happen for me, I found myself praying again, and I joined a Chirp group with my mom the next week. Chirp stood for CRHP—Christ Renews His Parish—and luckily there was a weekend retreat coming up in a few days. The weekend retreat was designed to bring parish members together and emphasized continued growth in community and in Christian life. It was designed to provide a renewed sense of belonging to the parish. Basically it was a weekend away, and that was what I needed. I am sure every religious denomination has something similar. After our first meeting, I laughed at myself and teased my mom that we were both turning into a couple of nuns. Of course my uncomfortable mind found comic relief again in thinking about the

Blues Brothers saying they need to go visit "the Penguin," also known as the head nun at their orphanage, who beat them and appeared to float and open doors with the power of God. Since I felt awkward at church, I entertained myself by imagining Joliet Jake at church saying, "I have seen the light!" about getting the band back together.

My grandmother graciously offered to spend the weekend at our home so my mom and I could both attend the retreat. Then my mom would not have to worry about Michael having a party or Maeve roaming the streets unaccounted for.

The retreat began with a lot of ice-breaking activities with introductions. We laughed a lot, and we became a quickly cohesive group.

Basically the retreat was free, and you could donate what you could afford—even ten dollars was acceptable. You were to bring your own toiletries, pillow, blanket, etc. I had no idea what to expect, and I was the youngest person there. It seemed like a big, grown-up sleepover. Everyone was in comfy clothes, and the environment was laid back.

Some parishioners prepared a presentation about their story. We cried together and then laughed together, and I related to many of the brave parishioners who stood up to tell their story. Some of these women experienced physical abuse, poverty, being homeless, or losing a child to suicide or cancer, which truly helped put things in perspective. Everyone has problems and we all have our journey, which seemed to be the ongoing theme of the presenters—that a higher power is preparing you and teaching you.

Finding my faith again truly provided me with this belief that I did not have to figure this all out on my own and that I should trust myself again. I acquired a sense of empowerment within myself, which was a quite amazing feeling. Throughout the retreat, I learned a lot about myself and my mother. My mother was not ready to present her story; however, seeing my mother in that setting shed some insight into what she'd had to go through. I recognized that she and I were very similar at the age of eighteen. The only difference was that my mother was already married with a child, Mairead, on the way—a reality that I could fully grasp after what I had just gone through. How lucky was I to have a second chance?

# 27

The last three weeks of May were fairly easy at school, and I kept myself busy with my Chirp group, work, and school. I had no idea what I was doing in the fall yet; my grades were not good enough for me to go away to college yet. I decided I needed to take it day by day. I couldn't believe I was actually graduating—there was a time when I first began high school that I pretty much didn't give a fuck at all about anything and almost let myself flunk out. That would have been disastrous. I could not have three Fs in a semester; I already had two. My biology teacher gave me a D minus, which was literally what prevented me from getting kicked out. I owe that woman big time. My guidance counselor truly helped me as well. I didn't see her that often, but when I did, she really made me think. If I failed, I would only be hurting myself, and it would not be revenge to anyone. She said succeeding is winning. Succeeding is the best revenge. I was so thankful that I attended an all-girls high school after all. It really helped me embrace being a woman and an independent woman some-day. Despite my resentment toward my mother, I didn't realize that I was slowly on the path of being just like her without any future goals or plans for my education and career. If I didn't want to be dependent on a man, I would need to get my shit together and find a career.

I only had four tickets for my ceremony, and my grandmother drove my mom, Maeve, and me. We were all wearing outfits picked out by my grandmother from her secondhand store. I had to admit, she was correct. People do give away some very nice threads. I thought we all looked smashing. Joy went to a different school than me, and she came outside when she witnessed us all heading to the car.

"Whoa!" Joy exclaimed like Joey from *Blossom*. I laughed. "You guys all look so nice!" Joy said, sounding shocked.

"Thanks. I suppose we do clean up well."

"You want to come to my graduation tomorrow?" Joy asked. My eyes widened, surprised that she asked me.

"Whoa!" I replied back, attempting to sound like Joey, too, but not as well as Joy's impression. I never considered asking Joy because I only had four tickets. "I would love to. I would be honored. You have enough tickets?"

"Yes. My parents are both coming, but that is it. I need you there," Joy said, looking down. She reached in her pocket and lit a cigarette. I felt stupid now, not asking Joy to attend my graduation. It was as if Joy read my mind. She blew out the smoke and smirked. "I know you had to ask your grandmother so she could drive you." We both laughed, both of us still amazed that in 1992 my mom still didn't have her driver's license. "Maeve needs to see you graduate, and of course your mom needs to be there."

I smiled, relieved.

"The cemetery was so fun. We need to do more things like that this summer!" Joy beamed.

"It really was. Definitely!" I replied genuinely. I felt this urge to apologize to her for not being around, becoming obsessed with Gerry, and letting our friendship take the back burner. I wanted to vow to her I would never do this again and that no matter how happy I was with a guy, I would always make time for us, no matter what. I stammered, attempting to find a way to say this. I had never seen a movie that addressed this topic. I stood there with my stupid wide-eyed face, thinking. Joy smirked again when she saw my eyes. She took a long drag of her cigarette, blew out the smoke, put out her cigarette with her flip-flops, picked it up, and handed it to me. (Her parents flipped when they saw cigarettes.)

"I've been thinking, let's not think about the fall and enjoy every day we can together this summer. We won't let guys come between us again. Tommy and Gerry are history. Now it's time for us. It's kinda crazy that we are *women!*" Joy said, and I beamed at her. My brain kicked on.

"I guess it's better to swallow pride than blood," I replied, quoting Watts from *Some Kind of Wonderful.*

"What does that even mean?" Joy laughed. I laughed too, not completely sure.

"I think I would rather swallow my pride and admit that I was wrong instead of having you kick my ass and me swallow blood?" I replied, questioning my translation.

"I get it, I think, you freak. I love you," Joy said and hugged me. I hugged her back.

"See you tomorrow for your big day."

As always, my grandmother looked fabulous and classy; however, her driving was another side to her. She was extremely cautious, and I was laughing to myself thinking of *Ferris Bueller* when his father is stuck behind the elderly woman with the beehive. That is probably how people felt behind my grandmother. As we were about to approach the busy street, my grandmother slammed on the brakes, and we all jerked.

"*God damn* squirrel!" my grandmother exclaimed in almost a southern accent. My mom opened her eyes wide and looked at Maeve and me in the backseat. Maeve and I looked at each other. We all began to laugh. We had never heard her swear, yell, or display a southern accent. My grandmother did not laugh, and we all did our best to not laugh anymore. She drove about twenty miles per hour to my school, and we all felt like we couldn't talk because we did not want to distract her. She did not have the radio on, and it was slow and painful. I was grateful when we finally arrived at my school.

My graduation was more emotional than expected. People were hugging me good-bye and getting emotional. I guess I just assumed I would see all these people every day. When this hit me, I began to become emotional too. It is a terrifying feeling in a way, like, "Now what do I do with the rest of my life?"

# 28

After Joy's graduation, we went out to lunch at this bar and grill. Joy saw a sign about a summer Sunday softball league. "We are doing this! Let's round up people we know," Joy said adamantly.

It sounded crazy to me to be underage but sponsored by a bar. I started to come up with reasons why we shouldn't, and Joy said, "Don't start. We are doing it. Don't think about it." I nodded yes. Of course, Joy had been playing baseball since she was a kid and was also on varsity in high school. She was the pitcher and, of course, amazing. I had only played kitten ball in little league. I was sure I sucked. However, it seemed like Joy wasn't having it.

Throughout the next week Joy began working on rounding up friends to play. I called Sam and asked her to play, and she was all about it. This surprised me, because she seemed too pretty or like she wouldn't want to get dirty or break a nail. Sam was the youngest in her family, and all of her sisters apparently played in this league, so this seemed to be no big deal to her.

The first game was the following week. Since we were new to the league and we'd joined a week ago, we got the shittiest color T-shirts, literally. We got shit-brown T-shirts that said "Dirty Nelly's Softball League." This bar was a legend in the neighborhood. They had an outdoor beer garden, lemonade and vodka stands, and bands that played every Sunday. It did always look like fun whenever I walked past the beer garden. I was nervous about it but also very excited.

I put on my shit-colored T-shirt, and all I had to wear that was clean were jean cutoffs.. I made a note to myself to buy some athletic mesh shorts when I got my next paycheck because I threw the maroon ones that Gerry gave me away. I felt ridiculous wearing jean shorts to a softball game, but I didn't have any choice. I forgot all about it in no time. I slathered sunscreen all over me, put my hair in a ponytail, and put on my baseball hat. It was just a softball game.

Joy was out in front at exactly 11:00 a.m. She'd never been punctual before, but for softball games and drinks, she was, apparently. Joy had sunglasses on, a ponytail, spikes, low-cut socks showing off her perfect tan legs, black mesh shorts, and a white tank top.

"You ready for this?" she said excitedly. "I'm pumped!"

"Where's your shit-brown T-shirt?" I asked, suddenly freaking out when I compared how good she looked to how dorky I looked.

"It's on the porch. No worries. Uh, what are you wearing?" Joy asked with a smirk on her face.

"Shut it. I don't have any athletic shorts; I promise I'll buy some next week when I get my paycheck."

"I have some shorts you can borrow; I'll go grab them for you." Joy was about to leave when Sam pulled up in her cute powder-blue Jetta.

"Wassssuuuupppp!" Sam yelled. She looked cute and dressed appropriately, unlike me.

"I was going to go grab MK some shorts," Joy said hurriedly. "I'll be right back."

"No way," Sam said. "We don't have time. You look cute, MK Who cares?"

Joy shrugged her shoulders and grabbed her T-shirt, and we hopped in. Sam put the top down, and immediately I was also excited. It was a beautiful seventy-five-degree day, with not a cloud in the sky and no humidity. As we pulled up to the fields, we saw people in T-shirts in all the colors of the rainbow huddled in different groups, waiting for assigned fields. All the other softball T-shirts were fun, bright summer colors. Lime green, baby pink, daffodil yellow, powder blue, kelly green, lilac purple, and then there was us: shit brown.

"My sister said since it's our first year, we got to pick the T-shirts last. She said everyone has been brown—it's kind of like a rite of passage or being a freshman. But who cares—it's going to be a blast!" Sam said excitedly. Her body rocked from years of tennis: blond hair pulled into a low ponytail, long tan legs, and sexy cut arms. She put on sunglasses and a New York Yankees baseball hat. I felt inadequate immediately but tried to shake it out of my mind. I remembered what my mother always said: don't compare yourself to others, or you'll never be happy. My mom would always focus on my positive aspects; I just couldn't remember them right at the moment.

All the girls on our team were friendly and excited, just like us. I felt like a dork as I noticed everyone else dressed in athletic gear. I untucked my T-shirt to cover my shorts and felt a little better—not as obvious that way. Joy, the natural-born leader, took to making the batting lineup. I went up to her and strongly advised putting me as last at bat.

"Would you relax, Mary Kate?" Joy said, clearly irritated with my lack of confidence. "It's softball; it's supposed to be fun. No one's going to judge you or expect you to be good. I strongly suggest you have a couple of beers after we get to the bar."

"We're going to the bar after this? How?" I asked, both shocked and impressed.

"I'll show you later—I got the IDs for us," she said with mischief in her eye.

"No way. You're something else!" I said proudly.

The game started, and we played against the kelly-green team. I took notice of the players and saw that everyone was playing pretty average: they were all dropping pop-ups and laughing. I began to relax a little; maybe this wouldn't be so bad. Maybe I could focus on being the worst player, and then I might surprise myself. I was all about lowering my expectations of myself so that I could be pleasantly surprised.

Joy hit a line drive right to the pitcher, who caught it and then laughed; she seemed surprised at herself. Sam was up next and struck out. Phew. This really was no pressure. The next three batters did pretty well and got on base. So, the bases were loaded, there were two outs, and then it was my turn. Great. I took a deep breath and did my best to focus on doing "as bad as I could." I thought it would be best if I just didn't swing; I hoped I could get walked to first and then bring a score home.

I went up to bat, took a deep breath, and stood there waiting for the bad pitches to come so I could get four balls and get a walk. The pitcher, who'd been laughing at herself earlier, now appeared to be confident and intense. I began to sweat. The pitcher did an under-hand toss that landed right behind the base. "Strike one!" the umpire yelled in an annoying voice that sounded way too serious for a casual girls' Sunday softball league.

*What a dick*, I thought.

The next pitch, again, was a slow toss that landed perfectly right behind home plate. *St-rike two!* Man, this umpire was ridiculous with taking his job so seriously. My mind began racing as I thought about Cameron Frye and Ferris Bueller at the baseball game: "Hey, batta batta batta, sa-*wing* batta!" I smiled and wiped my sweat mustache off with my T-shirt. I didn't want to strike out not even swinging.

Joy called a timeout and came running to me, smiling. "No worries. It's zero to zero," she said calmly.

Of course I flashed to Cameron and Ferris again. "Who's winning?" I said with a smirk.

She smiled back. "The Bears," she said without skipping a beat.

Not to be too dramatic, but the next events almost occurred in slow motion, with the theme from *The Natural* playing. I wiped my face again with my T-shirt, trying to look serious. The pitcher kept turning around to make sure no one was stealing bases, a couple of times even trying to psyche them out by flinching the ball, like she was going to throw it and get them out. *Come on*, I thought, *enough with this.* She sneered at me and tossed the ball in her signature underhand pitch. My grandfather had taught me when I was in little league to watch the bat hitting the ball. The advice to "keep your eye on the ball, even when you swing" was drilled into my brain, and I did watch the ball. With all my might, I swung the bat while keeping my eye on the softball, and I saw the bat hit the ball. I nearly pissed myself.

It was a line drive between right and center field and bounced on the ground and over their heads before the outfielders could catch it. I started hauling ass. Joy, who was coaching first, laughed hysterically and waved me to second. The center-field and right-field players both ran to the ball at the same time and collided with each other. I passed second base, and the third base coach was waving me to home, jumping up and down. I touched third base and looked to my left to see the left-field player run to right field, get the ball, and throw it to the pitcher. On the sidelines, imagine ten girls in shit-brown T-shirts jumping slowly up and down screaming "slide!" The pitcher was running toward me with a determined look; she was totally going to tag me, but what the hell? I decided to slide and make a show of it. So I went for it, with the take-the-job-too-seriously umpire watching home plate like a hawk and leaning over the catcher. The catcher was a small, sweet girl, who looked petrified that I was going to slide into her. I was going to dive forward and decided against it, so I threw my left leg forward and slid into home. The pitcher had already reached me, and with both hands holding the ball, she jabbed the softball into my gut one inch before home plate.

"*Yyyyeeeerrrr out!*" the umpire screamed too loudly. My teammates were still screaming, cheering, and jumping up and down. My upper thigh stung, but I was laughing insanely. Fucking women's softball—it was hilarious. I suddenly felt a surge of confidence and a little wiser. All the girls from the team were smiling and patting me on the back; my face blushed, and I felt a little shy. I looked at Joy, who was smiling at me and shaking her head.

"You never cease to amaze me," she said and put her arm around me.

"You always get me to do crazy things," I said to her.

"Let's see that thigh and sweet ass of yours," Joy said playfully. My leg was covered in shit-brown baseball-field dust to match my shirt. I had a couple of scrapes, but it made me look kind of tough. Of course I thought this would distract attention from my jean shorts; now at least I looked somewhat athletic.

"Cool. I can't wait to get to that bar and celebrate," Joy said, clearly impressed.

We ended up losing the game; the kelly greens scored four runs, but no one seemed to care. We scored three runs because of my RBI and errors on the other team, but at least it was a close game and not a slaughter.

After the game, Joy put her arm around me and held up a fake ID for me. When I looked at it, I burst out laughing. I was looking at a real driver's license of someone named Amneh Shalibeh who appeared to be of Arabic descent. Joy's ID was apparently my sister, Aya Shalibeh. How the hell was this going to work? Sam, with her tan skin, brown hair, and brown eyes maybe could have passed for many ethnicities. I, on the other hand, am clearly of Irish, possibly English, descent. There was no way I'd be able to pull this off.

Joy seemed to be able to sense that I was totally skeptical. "Hey, it's worth a try," she said. "I heard it's a blast."

I didn't respond. What was the worst that could happen? I could be turned down. We drove to the bar in Sam's car in silence. Of course everyone was checking us out, because we were in this kick-ass car with the top down. Nothing like drawing attention to us, but I guess it was a good thing for the bouncers to see us; most under-age kids don't own a car—or at least don't have a car like that. Sam's parents had bought that car for Sam and her sister to share. Other people didn't know that.

"Just act confident," Joy said assuredly.

Sam and I were not as sure of ourselves. Sam's ID was pretty good, since she had her older sister's. I made a note to myself to ask Mairead to get me another one of her IDs right away. I could hear a band playing "Hey Jealousy," and it looked like probably a thousand people were in the beer garden. Everyone looked dirty, grungy, and sweaty. I'd fit in perfectly. As we walked up to the bouncers, they watched us intently with smartass expressions on their faces. They probably knew we were full of shit; I was sure we screamed "underage." Joy went first, cool as a cucumber, and handed them her ID. They looked at it, smirked, and handed it back to her. She paid her three-dollar cover charge and walked into the bar. My eyes bulged out of my head. Holy smokes! She'd just gotten into a bar at eighteen years old! Sam went next, not as confidently, but her face was serious as a heart attack. She looked down and handed the bouncer her ID; he handed it back to her, stamped her hand, and took her three-dollar cover. She speed-walked into the bar and went straight to the bathroom.

My hand trembled as I handed him my ID, not at all as calm or cool as my counterparts. I kept my eyes down at first, but I couldn't help looking up at the bouncer. I got goose bumps on my arms when I met his gaze. He was totally hot: brown eyes, black hair, and completely built. He winked at me, stamped my hand, and said, "That'll be three dollars, miss." I had to contain myself from jumping up and down like a complete nerd. Of course I fumbled around with all my singles rolled up in my pocket. I dropped a couple of singles and was totally considering leaving them until the hottie bouncer guy bent over and began to pick them up for me. I then felt like I should pick them up, too, so I began to bend over as he was lifting his head up, and the back of his head banged into my lip and my nose. My eyes began to water.

"Oh my gosh, miss! I'm so sorry," the bouncer yelled. What the hell was he sorry about? He'd been picking up my money for me that I'd dropped, and I was a complete klutz! He handed me my money and put his hands on the sides of my face to look at my face. Damn it all to hell, he was going to get a closer look at me and see I was definitely not of any kind of Arabic descent!

"I didn't want to mess up a beautiful face like yours! It doesn't look like any damage was done," he said. "Let me make it up to you. My name's Jimmy. You let me know if you need anything in the future here, and I'll hook you up. Hey, you know what? We're having a little contest later, so I'll definitely find you when it starts."

What kind of contest? What the hell? I couldn't have this dude yelling out my Arabic name across the bar. I'd be the laughing stock of the South Side! I nodded and got the hell away from him as quickly as I could. I went straight for the bathroom, where I'd last seen my friends going. I mean really, what an outfit we were! I couldn't believe it had worked.

Joy and Sam were standing at the bar, as if they did this every weekend, but it seemed like they were hitting it off. They were drinking a pitcher of lemonade and totally smiling at me. Joy was leaning on the bar, holding a cigarette in one hand and her drink in the other, suddenly looking much older. Sam was grinning ear to ear, probably buzzed already. I walked over to them, smiling as well, and they handed me a cup of lemonade. I could smell the alcohol immediately, but it was cold, and I was dying of thirst. I sucked the cup dry in one continuous sip. Their eyes were open wide, staring at me in shock. Sam's mouth dropped opened a little bit. I felt immediate tingles, and relaxation hit me.

"Sam, don't you go doing that. Mary Kate has alcoholism raging through her veins—she can handle her drink," Joy said deadpan to Sam. "I'm not sure about you, though, so take it easy today." Sam nodded and seemed to take Joy completely seriously. Sam was so sweet and innocent that I felt like she was too vulnerable to even be in this situation we'd found ourselves in. I laughed and looked at Joy with grateful eyes; I appreciated her sense of humor, especially right now. I'd never do something like this, but it was so fun to experience it. Joy was usually right about this stuff; I made a note to myself to listen to her more often.

"Yeah, Sam, I'm sure I need to take it easy, too. I needed to do something! Did you see what happened when I dropped my money at the door?" I said with my cheeks flushed from embarrassment and booze.

"Uh yeah, real smooth. I thought you'd blown the whole operation!" Joy said sarcastically. We all laughed. The band was playing

"Give It Away Now," and we stood back and listened for a while. Between the game, the sun, the music, the drinks, and the total excitement of the situation, I felt euphoric. Joy looked completely satisfied and happy. Sam looked giddy and dorky in a cute kind of way. When the song ended, I had started to tell Joy and Sam about the contest the bouncer had mentioned when I felt a tap on my shoulder.

"Hey! Are ya ready for the contest?" Jimmy asked a little too overzealously, I thought.

"Uh sure. What do I have to do?" I said nervously.

"You'll see," he said, and he winked at me again. He put his arm around me and walked me over to the beer garden. They had an inflated Slip 'N Slide rolled out from the entrance that stretched about thirty feet to where we were standing and a couple of inflatable pool rafts tied around the two poles, I assume so we wouldn't slide right into the bar stools. I began to put two and two together, and my palms began to sweat. Jimmy grabbed the microphone and yelled for everyone's attention. The band must have been on break, and the crowd quickly silenced as a response to his yelling into the microphone. I got the feeling this was a regular occurrence at the bar, because everyone clapped and cheered. Jimmy talked in a fake Irish brogue that was actually pretty good.

"Welcome to another fabulous Sunday at Dirty Nelly's, everyone! We have here our female volunteer today for the Slip 'N Slide contest. Now we need a male volunteer. The winner will receive free pitchers all day of our famous dirty lemonade!" Jimmy yelled.

In about two seconds, approximately twenty-seven guys had lined up on the Slip 'N Slide. Jimmy had his arm around me with the microphone in the other hand, and we walked down the lineup. He looked each guy up and down, smiling. The crowd was yelling and screaming, and finally he selected a guy with a very young face who looked underage as well. He had a little beer gut, enormous calves, a black softball T-shirt from the bar's men's league, and silky mesh shorts; he looked more like a soccer player than a softball player. Jimmy took his arm off me and raised my arm up. Oh, for fuck's sake.

"OK, here we have our female contestant, Freckles," Jimmy said. The crowd cheered, and then I heard some guys yelling, "You're goin' down!" I assumed this was my opposing teammate's friends. Jimmy took his hand off me and then lifted the other guy's arm up.

"OK, now we have contestant number two—let's call him Baby Face!" Jimmy yelled. The crowd cheered, and I looked over at Joy and Sam, who were laughing like crazy until they caught my gaze, then they immediately yelled, "Boo!" I laughed; my only two fans. I was so uncomfortable with all the attention. I just wanted to fly under the radar and be at the bar with my friends, not standing in front of all these people. I leaned over to Jimmy and whispered in his ear if Baby Face could go first. I wanted to see how he did it. He smiled and shook his head. I glanced at Baby Face, who was rolling his neck around and jogging in place like we were about to enter a boxing match together. I was confused at first, but then I began to laugh. He looked ridiculous.

"OK, Apollo Creed, you can go first," I said to Baby Face sarcastically. He looked at me like I'd just spit in his face. Man, was he serious. The other bartenders were wetting down the Slip 'N Slide with a hose that they probably used to hose down the puke and cigarette butts from the beer garden. I motioned to Joy and Sam to come over to me. They strolled over giggling, and I guessed they were already drunk. I needed a cigarette before I did this.

"As usual, you've outdone yourself, MK Just use the same determination you did at the game today." Joy laughed hysterically at her own joke, confirming my suspicions that she was already hammered. Sam was laughing, too, but she looked a little confused. She probably didn't know what the hell Joy was talking about; the softball game memories were so far away.

"Shut it! Can I have some of your smoke?" I said, annoyed. I wanted to be where they were, in drunkie land, not here, doing this. My buzz was fading fast, so I gulped down the rest of Sam's drink. She looked at me thankfully, probably knowing she had already been overserved. I took a couple of puffs of Joy's cigarette and watched

QUILLAN KELLY-DUNN

as Apollo "Baby Face" Creed took off running from outside the bar, went through the entrance, and flew down the Slip 'N Slide at lightning speed, slamming into the pool raft. Damn, he had on those slippery shorts. He grimaced and held his shoulder, and the crowd erupted in cheers. He smiled as a result. Jimmy ran over to him and held up his arm.

"Let's hear it for Baby Face!" Jimmy said, smiling like game-show host. I was clapping and smiling until I realized I had to go next. A cloud of fear hung over me. I had to get this over with. The bartender hosed the Slip 'N Slide again. I walked to outside the entrance, just like Baby Face had. I looked at Joy and Sam, who were still in their perpetual-laughing state. The crowd was silent again and staring at me, which was annoying. I couldn't wait to get the hell outta there!

"Herrreess Freckles!" Jimmy said, sounding like Ed McMahon introducing Johnny Carson.

I took off running and then dove onto the Slip 'N Slide, my stomach still hitting the concrete underneath despite the inflated Slip 'N Slide; the wind was knocked out of me.

I slid about one foot and stopped abruptly. The crowd was silent.

Damn jean shorts! Denim wasn't a slippery material, and it acted as a paste on the Slip 'N Slide.

I was mortified. I was trying to catch my breath and could hear the crowd laughing around me. I looked over at Joy and Sam, who both had their hands over their mouths, probably covering their laughter. Assholes. Jimmy came running over to me with a worried look on his face.

"Oh my gosh! Are you OK?" he asked, looking and sounding sincere. He put his arm around me and helped me up. Luckily, the band began playing, and soon the crowd began to disperse toward the stage. I nodded, and he walked me over to the nearest bar stool. I pointed to the ladies' room instead, and I quickly ran to the privacy of the stall. I sat down and put my head on my knees. I took a couple of deep breaths. I wished I was invisible. How humiliating. I went to the washroom, and as I was washing my hands, I noticed a pair of abandoned sunglasses sitting on the edge of the sink. My wish had come true: oh, thank you, my drunk fairy godmother! It was the next best thing to being invisible; I could at least *feel* invisible.

I walked out of the ladies' room wearing the sunglasses, immediately feeling more confident and ready to face the world again. Jimmy was standing behind the bar and smiling. He came over to me.

"I like the glasses. If you ever need anything, you let me know. We're having two winners today. You get pitchers of lemonade on the house every time you come here, got it? So what's your name again?"

I grimaced, knowing he probably knew that my ID was fake and that my real name couldn't possibly be Amneh. My mind raced to come up with an acceptable reply.

He smiled. "Never mind, Freckles," he said. He put his arm around me and walked me toward the bar. He handed me a pitcher of lemonade and vodka and some cups. He patted me on the shoulder and then walked behind the bar. I beamed at him. I turned around to find my two friends standing right behind me.

"Savages," I said to them. They both laughed. We walked to the bar, and I poured them each a fresh drink, free thanks to my humiliation. We didn't talk about the incident, and I soon became grateful for my lifetime supply of Dirty Nelly's lemonade and forgot about how I'd acquired it.

We all took notice of the band, which was playing a different kind of music now—older stuff. *My kind of tunes*, I thought. I looked at the singer and realized that he looked familiar. He was hitting a tambourine on his leg and singing "What's Going On" by Marvin Gaye; it was so perfect that it gave me goose bumps on my arms. I closed my eyes and totally let the music fill my soul. When he finished, I jumped off my stool and clapped like a maniac. I looked at Joy and Sam, who were laughing at me again. No one else seemed to share the intense passion I had for this song. I slowly sat back down and sipped my drink sheepishly. The two of them continued their Lemovox-infused conversation, which I was having a hard time following—it was all gibberish. Vodka is key for making friends fast, it seems.

It was now approaching dusk, and I didn't want to take my sunglasses off, even though it had become difficult to see with them. I loved how I felt like I was invisible and ten times more confident with them on. The band launched into "Break on Through" by the Doors, and the three of us could no longer contain ourselves. We all danced and jumped up and down like fools. Everyone else seemed to be doing the same thing until it seemed like a full-blown mosh pit. Suddenly my sunglasses became appropriate, and I noticed a few other people putting their sunglasses on as well. Soon everyone was screaming, "Everybody loves my baby!" over and over. We were all like a cult, mesmerized by the song and chanting the same verse over and over. Some guys from the crowd picked up the singer, who was soon being carried over the crowd as he continued to sing, "Eve-rie-body loves my bay-bay!" It was the coolest thing I'd seen so far in my eighteen years.

Joy, Sam, and I were now on the same wavelength as far as drinks go and were totally entranced with the atmosphere, dancing, and drinking. We had the momentum going, and without skipping a beat, the band continued on a Doors montage by playing "Roadhouse Blues." We continued to dance until they played a song I'd never heard, but it was like the sound triggered something inside me that had unleashed my true animal instincts. I went berserk, dancing wildly and letting guys rub up against me. I was grinding with different guys and suddenly felt like a sexual being instead of a girl; I couldn't believe myself. I'd never heard this on the radio and wasn't that familiar with the song. It was like this song had triggered a reaction in me like Pavlov's dog. I didn't care who saw me, and I wasn't self-conscious at all. It must have been the alcohol goggles, but all I knew was I was having a blast.

When the song ended, this animal triggered by Jim Morrison was tamed and gone. It was as if I'd been temporarily possessed. I shook my head for a second and went to the ladies' room again to compose myself. I was soaked with sweat, especially under my sunglasses. I wiped my face with a wet paper towel. *What the hell was that?* I thought to myself. I thought I'd better quit while I was ahead; I was having a blast, but I was sure that had been the climax of the evening, and it would be all downhill from there.

I came out of the ladies' room and saw that the band was taking a break. Sam and Joy were nowhere to be seen, and then my eyes were suddenly magnetically drawn toward the bar when I saw the singer of the band standing at the bar and getting a drink. I immediately forgot everything I'd just been thinking in the bathroom and walked over to him as if I was possessed again. My confidence was brimming at this point with alcohol and euphoria from the dancing.

"Hey. You guys are amazing!" I said to the mystery singer, who was even cuter up close; he also appeared much younger now.

"Thanks, Mary Kate," he said to me with a smile. "That means a lot, coming from you," he said, appearing sincere, but he was still looking at the bar and not at me. I frantically flipped through the files in my brain for his name and searched his face for something familiar about him. His sandy-brown hair was messy and sticking up; he was extremely good looking. Nothing—no recollection right now. My brain was currently in an alcohol fog as it went slowly through the files. I needed to stall until I could place him.

"What was the last song you played? I'd never heard it before. It was the best song I've ever heard!" I said passionately. He blushed, smiled, and looked at me. When his oceanic eyes met mine—Marty! Oh...my...gawd! I recognized him at last.

"That song's called 'Peace Frog,' by the Doors," he said. He smirked at me, and his expression changed. The bartender gave him a drink, and he nodded to him and took a giant sip.

"What are you drinking there?" I asked flirtatiously. He seemed to smile at the fact that I'd recognized him finally.

"Jack and Coke, Mary Kate," he said with a wink. His drink looked delicious. I was starting to get an acidy feeling in my throat from the dirty lemonade. I waved to the bartender to give me a Coke but hold the Jack. I'd had enough booze for one day..

"I thought I was going to faint when you guys played 'What's Going On' earlier," I said, which was true.

"I appreciated your applause; tonight's my first time singing with these guys. This is my brother's band. I was regretting choosing that song until I heard a faint 'woo hoo!' and clapping from all the way over there. That's when I realized it was you. I was laughing when I saw your sunglasses. As usual, you were cracking me up without meaning to." Marty said this all intensely, with a sincere smile on his face. I felt all warm and tingly inside.

"Thanks," I said nervously. "Well, I had no idea it was you. I was truly pumped about the music. I don't hear that song often, and you did a kick-ass job."

"Thanks," he said nervously. His eyes looked at the stage; he nodded and then looked back at me. "We're going to be playing again in a few minutes. You have any requests?"

"You could play that song again! I loved it," I said, a little too excited. He looked a little hesitant.

"Uh, I'll let you borrow the CD. I don't think I can play the same song again," he said, looking distracted; he drank his drink quickly until it was empty.

"Oh yeah, whatever, everything you've been playing rocks, so...I doubt you know 'Livin' on a Prayer'?" I said, my voice raspy from yelling over the noise. That song didn't seem to go with his genre so far. I'd begun to like Bon Jovi recently because their first album was already like ten years old at that point. I slurped my Coke, feeling foolish for asking.

"I have to go now," he said, looking at the stage. "I heard you and McGrath broke up. Is this for good?"

"YES!" I replied without hesitation. He released a big smile and a sigh.

"Glad to hear it. Is it safe to ask for your number now?" Marty asked.

"I thought you'd never ask," I said, and then I cringed at how stupid I sounded.

"I'll try and find a pen," he said. "And don't leave. I want to talk to you more after we're done," he added.

I was beaming, with a big, stupid drunk grin on my face. He smiled and laughed, probably at me again.

I put my sunglasses on again, this time watching the stage and knowing I could stare at Marty now and wouldn't look like a total creep. I ordered water and another Coke so I could sober up a little. I was fading fast and he was telling me I couldn't leave—that was a lot of pressure. I had no idea where my friends had gone, and I was torn if I should look for them or continue to watch the greatest cover band of all time. I giggled to myself.

I decided I needed to make sure my friends were OK. I walked around the bar, and both of them were nowhere to be found. I checked the bathrooms; no one was retching or passed out on the toilet, so that was a good sign. But then, where the hell were they? Eventually I found Joy between a wall and the jukebox, with a guy in front of her. It was *Rich*! She had her flirty smile going, so I settled on not interrupting her. Still no sign of Sam, but I was not worried about her, since she knew a lot of people at the bar from her sister's softball team. It was completely dark outside by now, and I couldn't believe I was still standing; this had been the longest day ever. I heard the drums and guitar going and ran back to the stage. I found a table and a stool open right next to a speaker, so I sat there, staring at Marty intently like I was with the band.

The band started with the Rolling Stones song "Sympathy for the Devil." I knew every word and jumped up, both arms above my head and singing like I was at a Stones concert. Everyone in the audience started chanting "hoo hoo," and I felt that trancelike state kicking in again. This continued throughout every song, and I decided that I was now Marty's band's biggest groupie. I didn't even know the band's name, but I'd find out for sure. I stared at Marty, and waves of attraction came over me: he was incredibly cute, but there was more to him now. We'd always clicked, our conversations had always flowed, and he was funny. Now, to find out he was in a band! And the fact that he was in a band that played all my favorite music bumped him up to being twenty shades hotter in my book. I lifted my sunglasses to get a better look at him. His eyes met mine, he gave me a crooked smile, and I smiled back. I was grimy, sweaty, dirty, and buzzed, and when he looked at me, I felt beautiful. It was intoxicating, and I felt dizzy. I was sobering up, but he was getting me drunk again just by looking at me. The sounds around me faded into silence, and I couldn't hear anything, as if someone had put headphones on my ears. I just stood there, frozen, staring at him as he stared at me.

Then I heard, "Womp...*womp*...womp." I jumped up and screamed!

Marty sang, "Tommy used to work on the dock." I nearly shit myself and jumped up and down again. It wasn't really a dancing song, but something about "Livin' on a Prayer" made me want to go berserk. It seemed to have the same effect on the rest of the crowd. We all pounded our fists in the air while Marty and his bandmates all screamed, "Whoa oh! Livin' on a prayer! Take my hand, and we'll make it, I swear!" and the crowd screamed back, "Whoa oh!" It was fucking kick ass. I was pouring with sweat. Out of nowhere, Joy and Sam appeared, jumping up and down and pumping their fists in the air with me. When the song ended, the whole place was screaming, hooting, whistling. Marty smiled and looked down sheepishly. His T-shirt was completely soaked, and so was his hair. Of course he was growing better looking by the minute, and it wasn't beer goggles because I was sobering up.

Joy, Sam, and I went to the ladies' room to regroup, wipe our sweaty faces, and use the facilities.

All at the same time, we all said to one another, "Where have you been?" We all laughed. The place was big, but not that big to completely lose one another, which we had. There were a lot of little crevices in the beer garden and corners in the bar that could disguise you and keep you out of view without even trying.

When I looked in the mirror, I looked like a wet dog. This further deflated me. I wanted to go home because I was tired and I looked horrifying, but he'd asked me not to leave. I didn't want to blow my chances *and* be rude. I wasn't going to let my vanity stand in the way of watching him perform. The band was amazing, and even if I did have competition with other chicks who were probably drooling over him, he had asked for my number and had specifically asked me not to leave. Maybe he liked his women sweaty and disgusting, I figured. He must have been a fan of the wet look.

I walked with them out of the bathroom. I looked back at the stage and saw Marty and another guy in the band singing "The Boxer." It was spectacular—I wished I had a tape recorder! A few stragglers hung by the stage, slow dancing with each other. A few drunken girls were dipping and spinning each other. I didn't move for the entire song, and when it ended, I saw I was alone and had lost Sam and Joy again.

When I heard chords from the guitar, I gasped! I knew I was in immediate danger once Van Morrison's "Into the Mystic" began to play. A surge of lust went through me, and I wanted to run to the stage and attack Marty. I was able to control myself, but my lust for him was taking over my body. I closed my eyes and danced, feeling like an animal again. The music possessed me, and I felt nothing except the rhythm. I knew every word, and I sang along to the passionate lyrics. I opened my eyes, and our eyes locked as he sang the words of the song:

> We were born before the wind
> Oh so younger than the sun
> Erse the bonnie boat was won as we sailed into the
>     mystic
> Hark now hear the sailors cry
> Smell the sea and feel the sky
> Let your soul and spirit fly into the mystic
> And when that foghorn blows I will be coming home
> When that foghorn blows I want to hear it
> I don't have to fear it
> I wanna rock your gypsy soul
> Just like way back in the days of old
> Then magnificently we will float
> Into the mystic.

During the melody he continued to look at me and put the micro-phone in the stand. The other singer began singing the second cho-rus. I thought I was going to die at the intensity of passion going through me. Marty stepped off the stage and was walking toward me, the expression on his face so determined. My heart leapt as he came closer to me. He grabbed the sides of my face, and his mouth was on mine. I kissed him back, it seemed with every ounce of passion I had, but without effort. My emotions were focused and clear, yet I was completely lost in the moment. We were swaying to the music and kissing like we were alone in the middle of nowhere. I had no concept of time or place. It was as if time paused.

The song eventually ended, and we both slowly opened our eyes. He put his forehead to mine and smiled at me. I smiled back, sud-denly feeling foolish and vulnerable.

He lifted his head straight, looked to the band, nodded, and then turned to me. "You have no idea how long I've wanted to do that," he said, breathing heavily.

"I really do have no idea," I replied shyly. My breathing was heavy, my chest throbbing and my legs wobbly.

"Let's get outta here," he said, and just like that, we were walking outside. He stopped at a car and turned me toward the car so my backside was against the car door and my head was leaning back onto the hood of the car. He was the perfect height for me where he could spread his legs and lean toward me. His hands moved to the small of my back and then under the back of my shirt and onto my skin. His fingertips ran over the indention of my spine, and the feeling of his hand on my bare skin intensified our making out and breathing. A few minutes ago I wanted to go home and go to bed, and now I was magnetized next to him. Faint sounds of people exiting the bar in-terrupted our make-out session. We looked at each other and smiled fondly.

"I've waited for this since that night we met out at the cemetery. Well, even homecoming weekend. Actually, when we worked to-gether," Marty said persuasively and smiled. I was intrigued by his mysterious entries and exits in my life. I gasped and gazed up at him, my head and body trembling. He placed his warm palm on my neck and rested it on my collarbone, and he kissed me softly, which caused me to exhale involuntarily as he knocked the wind out of me. My heart seemed like it was in my throat. We seemed to be kissing for hours when something caught my attention.

I heard a car idling next to us; we pulled away from each other simultaneously. I pulled away sheepishly, assuming it was the cops. But it wasn't the cops: it was Gerry.

"Marty! Hey, Marty!" he yelled from the driver's seat of his mother's hatchback. Marty just smiled smugly at Gerry and pulled me closer to him. Gerry's eyes blazed, and his chin tightened. He screamed, "How does my dick taste?"

It was closing time. Of course, the entire population of Dirty Nelly's consumers were exiting the bar into the parking lot as the asshole screamed this. My mouth dropped open. My cheeks burned. I knew I shouldn't say anything, because that's what he wanted. Gerry laughed and gave me this look of contempt.

Reactively, I turned toward the busy street and crossed it quickly. I felt my eyes welling up with tears of embarrassment and humiliation. I didn't want him to see me cry and was certain Marty wouldn't call me after that comment. I felt like damaged goods. Gerry made me so fucking mad. Soon I was seething with anger, and I took off running to my house and didn't look back.

I thought of *Some Kind of Wonderful* again! When Harty Jenns tells Keith, "Did she do you? Well, you get her used." I felt that same disgust for Gerry as I did for Harty Jenns in that scene, except this wasn't a movie—this was real life. My life.

My house was always open, since we had nothing to steal. I walked in to my mom sleeping on the couch. She tried her best to stay up to watch her favorite show, *Scarecrow and Mrs. King*, but she always feel asleep. My grandma was next to her on the couch. They were both sitting on the couch with their arms crossed, chins to their chests. I wished I had a camera; it was so stinkin' cute. Maeve was on the floor sleeping stomach down, head turned to the side, wearing shorts and no top, the backs of her feet facing up, feet completely filthy, as usual. For a moment, I felt calm and happy. I loved my family. We were broken, but we'd mended the rip, and it seemed the bond was now stronger than ever before.

I peeled off my disgusting softball T-shirt and shorts and got in the shower. Light-brown water soon filled the tub from the dust from the softball fields. I was nasty. I washed my hair twice, brushed my teeth twice, and took some Advil. I was grateful I was off on Sundays and Mondays. I was going to sleep all day tomorrow. I went to my room excited for sleep and crashed in seconds. That had been one long-ass day.

I was sitting on my bed, Joy lying on her belly wearing a white button down top, white jean shorts, with her long golden-tan legs criss-crossed, heels near her butt, her toes in a French manicure. She was lying on the tops of her hands, facing me, looking dreamy. I was just staring at her, mesmerized by how stunning she was. I thought, *I wonder what it feels like to be that beautiful.*

"You are beautiful," I said to her.

"Me? You are! Look at yourself," she said sternly. I got up to look in the mirror; I was wearing a strapless white satin gown. I didn't recognize myself. *What? Why am I dressed this way?*

"Remember, you made that pact with yourself that you'd marry the man you made out with during 'Into the Mystic'?" Joy said with a smirk.

"Holy shit!" I screamed.

I popped up in my bed and gasped for breath. I was coated with slick moisture, with the sounds of Van Morrison in my mind. I lay back on my pillow and placed my hand on my forehead. I was panting. I turned to the side to look at the clock. I winced in pain; the sides of my ribs were killing me. I hadn't swung a baseball bat in five years. Muscles I hadn't used since fifth grade were throbbing from softball the day before. My thoughts went back to Marty and whether that had really happened or if I'd dreamed it. Was I drunk? Was it real? Then I remembered what Gerry had said to him, and I covered my eyes and lay back on the pillow.

Was Gerry going to continue to sabotage my future with anyone else? I knew I'd made the right decision in not going back out with him; our tumultuous relationship had seen better days. He was convinced I was "the one," but how do we really know? We were almost nineteen years old. I mean, I'd love to believe that you could find true love like the young Buzz and Ava, but times had changed. I didn't want to turn out like my mom, marrying the first guy she was ever with. Then she was stuck with a bunch of kids, and he left her to fend for herself. How is that healthy? I wanted to explore, travel, go to college, hang out with my friends, and generally enjoy life. At one point, I'd been ready to spend the rest of my life with Gerry, but luckily our spell got broken, and I woke up. I'd been blinded with love and infatuation. I'd been insecure with myself, and he "completed me," in an unhealthy way. I shouldn't need a guy to survive or feel good about myself. I knew I should be happy with myself before I could hope to be happy with someone else. I had a long way to go. It was amazing how I hadn't seen Gerry in weeks, and I saw him for one minute the night before, and somehow he consumed my thoughts again.

I went downstairs to make something to eat, and I decided I would go walking again to stop the flood of Gerry thoughts. The guy was a mind fuck. Then my mom's phone rang. I answered reactively.

"Hello, may I please speak to Mary Kate?" It was a female voice. "This is," I replied, sounding like my mother.

"Hey, Mary Kate, it's Shelley McGrath." Her voice was shaking. "Hi. Um, I just wanted to let you know, we're all really sorry that you and Gerry broke up. We all miss you. We love you. But we understand you have to do what you need to do. Gerry came home last night in a rage and wanted to go to your house. My mom and dad talked to him last night and this morning. We're all here right now, and we wondered if you would speak to him." Shelley sounded really nervous. What was I going to say? No? With his parents right there?

"OK," I replied, wincing and gritting my teeth. I heard some muffled voices, and he got on the phone. I immediately put my hands on my hips and stuck my nose in the air to feel proud.

"Hi," Gerry said very softly. "Listen, I know you must hate me, and I'm really sorry. I know I've said sorry to you a million times, and I know you could never forgive me, but my...uh...parents want me to—or they want you to—call the police on me if I ever act like that again. I know I need to leave you alone, and you deserve to be happy. I blew my chance many times." His voice was cracking, and he sounded choked up, but then he continued. "I realize I need help, and I'm going to counseling and anger-management classes next week. I hope someday you can, uh, forgive me, and, uh, be my friend...I mean, forgive me." Gerry was breathing heavily through his mouth, as if his nose was stuffy, and it sounded like he was crying. Of course I somehow felt bad again. I wanted to unleash on him for embarrassing me the night before, but he sounded pretty humiliated, too.

Gerry sounded sincere—maybe because his parents were sitting there, or maybe he really meant it—but I couldn't stay mad after this. "Thank you," I replied, unsure what else to say. "I know that was hard for you to say. I want you to be happy, too, and we're very young. I do forgive you." I meant it.

"OK, thanks," Gerry said, "Oh! My parents said that the car is yours so don't feel like you have to return it because we aren't ... together anymore." He said with a quiver and crack in his voice. He hung up abruptly before I could reply. I was shocked his parents had suggested I call the police on their son, but they were pretty tough people, so I knew they meant it. His family had gotten me through some tough times. I would always love them.

The phone rang again, which I knew was going to happen because he'd hung up too quickly. I sighed and answered.

"Hello, may I please speak to Mary Kate?" It was a guy's voice.

"This is she," I replied quickly and formally, again sounding like my mother.

"Oh, hey, Mary Kate, this is Marty. I got your number from Rich." I could tell he was smiling, and I smiled, too.

I loved his voice already. I laughed nervously. "I guess Richard isn't a dick." I laughed and slapped my forehead. Was that really the first thing I said to him? I was so nervous, my hand was shaking. Marty laughed.

"Well, I was calling because I wanted to see if you wanted to do something today," Marty inquired, his voice sounding a little scratchy and hoarse. My mind went to him singing the previous night, and I felt a throb and butterflies in my stomach.

"I'd love to," I replied genuinely. My heart was pounding. I didn't even care what we did; the answer was *yes*.

"I know you like old music, so there's this Van Morrison cover acoustic singer playing at this bar where my brother works up north. I was thinking we could go, say at like four or so. Also, if you would do me a favor?"

*Anything.* "Sure," I replied, holding my breath, grateful I hadn't said "anything" out loud.

"I also know you're off today, but I'd like to go to the Greasy Spoon for lunch, well actually soon. I've been craving their food lately. Would you mind going there on your day off?" He asked this in his hoarse, sexy voice.

Even though I worked there, I could always eat their food. It was awesome, plus it sounded amazing right then, since I was kind of hungover and hungry. "Yes, I'm actually starving right now," I said a little too quickly.

"Great—me, too. I'll meet you there in like an hour?"

"Yes!" I replied, again too excitedly.

"Oh, and Mary Kate, just to let you know: all those old guys who sit at the counter all day have an ongoing bet with me that I'll never go out with you. Apparently, everyone except you knew I was crushin' bad." He laughed.

My smile beamed and my cheeks burned at the thought of everyone knowing this at work except me. Again, I had no clue. "I'm such a dipshit," I replied without thinking. I felt really comfortable, like I'd known Marty my whole life. I was completely myself but excited, too. I couldn't stop smiling, and my cheeks hurt.

Marty laughed. "Shut up, you are not. It's just part of your charm. Anyway, I'll see you in an hour," Marty said, and he hung up.

I did a little dance like George Jefferson while I sang the theme song and background singing to *The Jeffersons* *"Movin on up"*…and jumped in the shower. On to the next chapter in my life.